Large Print Tro
Trocheck, Kathy Hogan, 1954-
Irish eyes

Irish Eyes

Also by Kathy Hogan Trocheck
in Large Print:

Homemade Sin

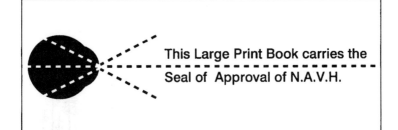

This Large Print Book carries the
Seal of Approval of N.A.V.H.

IRISH EYES

A Callahan Garrity Mystery

Kathy Hogan Trocheck

Thorndike Press • Thorndike, Maine

Published in 2000 by arrangement with HarperCollins Publishers Inc.

Thorndike Press Large Print Mystery Series.

The tree indicium is a trademark of Thorndike Press.

The text of this Large Print edition is unabridged. Other aspects of the book may vary from the original edition.

Set in 16 pt. Plantin by Rick Gundberg.

Printed in the United States on permanent paper.

Library of Congress Cataloging-in-Publication Data

Trocheck, Kathy Hogan, 1954–
    Irish eyes : a Callahan Garrity mystery / Kathy Hogan Trocheck.
    p. cm.
    ISBN 0-7862-2837-7 (lg. print : hc : alk. paper)
    1. Garrity, Callahan (Fictitious character) — Fiction.
2. Women detectives — Georgia — Atlanta — Fiction.
3. Cleaning personnel — Fiction. 4. Police corruption — Fiction. 5. Irish Americans — Fiction. 6. Atlanta (Ga.) — Fiction. 7. Large type books. I. Title.
PS3570.R587 I75   2000b
813'.54—dc21   00-056815

For
Dorothy K. Trocheck
1926–1999
and Julia Hogan Tobin

Acknowledgments

The author gratefully thanks those who doled out advice, comfort, or sustenance during the hatching of this book, including Major M. G. Lloyd of the Atlanta Police Department, W. Albert Oetgen, Moira Eileen Drennan, Eamon Dolan, and Eileen Dreyer. In addition, thanks are due the Mahaffey family of Avondale Estates, Georgia, who provided me with the perfect writer's retreat. Lastly, thanks are due the 170 American police officers who in 1998 lost their lives in the line of duty. Their bravery and sacrifices are not forgotten.

1

One of my clients, who has superb taste in these things (he's gay), gives me a bottle of Bushmills for Christmas every year, and every year I hoard it until the afternoon of St. Patrick's Day.

At six o'clock on the afternoon of the appointed day, I took the bottle down from its hiding place in the cupboard over the refrigerator. I set two Waterford tumblers square in the middle of the scarred oak kitchen table. I poured a fingerful of whiskey for Edna, my mother, who drinks hers neat, and one for myself, on the rocks with a little water. Solemnly, we clinked glasses.

"Selah!" said Edna.

"Back at ya," I said.

She dealt herself a hand of solitaire. I went to the kitchen counter and fiddled with the radio until I found WABE, the local National Public Radio affiliate. Usually, we listen to the news this time of day, but today I was hunting for the station's annual all-Irish program.

As soon as I sat down I had to jump back up and turn off the radio. They were playing "Danny Boy."

Edna gave me a quizzical look.

"Not that one," I said. "It's too early in the day. It always makes you cry."

She nodded thoughtfully. "You could be right. It's better to work up to all these things." She slapped a row of cards facedown on the table. "Although," she added, "all those lousy songs get to me."

"They remind you of Daddy?"

She sighed. "He sure loved St. Patrick's Day. Remember?"

"How could I forget? He used to make us dress all in green, head to toe. Then drag us over to Christ the King for Mass with the archbishop."

"You kids marched in that parade every year from the time you were babies," Edna said. "One year one of the Meehans brought a goat cart into town. You remember that? We piled all you kids in a damn goat cart and your daddy walked on one side of you and Billy Meehan walked on the other side, both of them grinning like idiots, and that goat prancing down Pharr Road like some kind of fine Arabian stallion."

"I remember being in a cart," I said. "The goat had a little straw hat with an Irish flag sticking out of the top. And Daddy bought us hot chocolate because it was so cold that day. And Maureen threw up all over my green plaid skirt, the little snot."

"She always did have a weak stomach," Edna said, smiling. "Go ahead and turn the radio back on. Maybe they'll play 'McNamara's Band.' "

But they were playing "Rose of Tralee," and Edna's eyes got suspiciously moist, so that she had to duck into the bathroom because, she claimed, she'd dribbled something down the front of her blouse. But she didn't come back for another five minutes, and when she did, she hadn't bothered to change her blouse, so I knew it was a ruse.

It started raining around six-thirty, softly at first. But soon rain started coming down in slashing gusts. I was standing at the back door, looking out at the lightning flashing and dancing on the horizon, when somebody banged at the front door.

Edna looked up from her cards. "Get that, would you?"

I almost didn't recognize our visitor, he was so changed from the last time I'd seen him.

Six-four, with dark hair slicked back from his forehead and a pair of stylish horned-rim glasses, he looked like a mutual-fund banker, not the slapdash cop I'd known for fifteen years or more.

"Bucky?"

Bucky Deavers pushed past me into the hallway. "Christ! It's coming down in buckets out there."

He stood there, dripping rain onto the floor, until I came to my senses and took his coat. Under the raincoat he wore a forest green blazer, pleated khaki slacks, a crisp white shirt, and a shamrock-print necktie. He had a sprig of heather pinned to his jacket lapel.

"Very nice," I said, motioning for him to turn around, which he did, ending with a little mock curtsy. "Is this another of your phases?"

"We're going to a party," he said, grinning.

"We? Who we?"

"We, as in you and me," he said.

The last party we'd been to together was a Halloween frolic at the Euclid Avenue Yacht Club, where he'd gone as Jackie Kennedy in drag.

"Where's your pink pillbox hat?" I asked.

"At the dry cleaner's," he said. "Blood spatters are hell to get out of pink. Come on, Garrity. Get going. We're late already."

"What kind of party?" I wanted to know.

"Whaddya mean, what kind of party? Did you just resign from the Irish race, Garrity?

It's St. Patrick's Day."

"I know what day it is," I said. "And that's why I'm staying home, where it's safe. You know my policy about this, Bucky."

"Yeah, yeah," he said, waving his hand dismissively. "St. Patrick's Day is amateur night. You wouldn't be caught dead in Buckhead, yada, yada, yada. But that's okay. We're not going anywhere near Buckhead. So get dressed, would you?"

I looked down at my blue jeans and my blue work shirt. "Supposing I were to go to this party with you. What's wrong with what I've got on?"

He shook his head sadly. "It's a party, for Christ's sake. You look like a refugee from a hippie commune. Come on, Garrity. You've got a pair of world-class gams under those jeans. Throw on a dress or skirt or something, would you? Something green, preferably."

I narrowed my eyes. "What's the deal here, Bucky? Since when do you care how I dress?"

He pushed me down the hall toward the kitchen, where he couldn't miss the aroma of the lamb stew that had been simmering on the back burner all day.

"Edna," he called. "You here? Talk some sense into this pigheaded daughter of yours, would you?"

Edna broke into an ear-to-ear smile when

11

she saw Deavers. She's always had a soft spot for the big goofy lug. "Sense?" she said, getting up and giving him a hug. "I gave up on that long ago."

"Tell her she needs to get gussied up for this party we're going to," he said, slipping an arm around her waist. "Hey. You come, too. It'll be fun."

"Not for me," Edna said. "You couldn't get me out on a night like this for love or money. But you go, Jules," she said. "You could wear that green dress. The one I got you last Christmas."

"You mean the sister dress? The same one you bought Maureen? No thanks," I said, making a face.

"Well, anything then," Bucky said. "Come on, would you?"

"Something's up with him," I told my mother.

Bucky propped a foot on one of the kitchen chairs, took a handkerchief out of his pocket, and dusted off an already spotless oxblood loafer.

"There's somebody I want you to meet, that's all."

"What kind of somebody? Not one of your little Pop-Tart girlfriends, I hope. Jeez, Bucky. That last one — what was her name? Muffy? Fluffy?"

12

"Buffy," he said. "Her name happened to be Buffy. Short for Elizabeth."

"Yeah," I said. "Her. You should have seen this poor girl, Ma. She was so young he had to order her a Happy Meal at McDonald's. She was so young she couldn't remember the first season of *Friends*."

"She was twenty," Bucky said. "And Buffy happened to be very smart. A straight-A student."

"Where? KinderCare?"

He looked at his watch. "All right. You can cut the comedy now. You've made your point. The person I want you to meet is somebody very different. She reminds me of you, a little bit, God help me. Now, could we get the lead out and get going?"

"Okay," I relented. "But I'm not cutting her meat for her."

2

All things considered, we'd had the usual lousy winter in Atlanta. Of course, February is my least favorite month of all. In a good year it's twenty-eight or twenty-nine days of damp and cold, punctuated by brief late-winter snowstorms that always manage to foul up traffic and life in general. This year was no exception to the rule. We'd had snow the last week in February, a tornado the first week in March, and yet another snowstorm the second week of March.

Edna and I live in a wood-frame Craftsman bungalow in an eccentric in-town Atlanta neighborhood named Candler Park. The house is as old as my mother, meaning it's seventy-six, and it's just as cranky and creaky as Edna. The basement had been flooded three times already in March, and every time I had to wade through knee-high water to pump the water out and relight the furnace pilot light, I cursed the day I'd bought the old house.

Bucky pointed at our roof, which sported a

neon blue vinyl tarp tacked down over the front porch.

"You bought your house a shower cap?"

"Essentially," I said. "We're gonna have to get the porch roof patched. It's leaking like a sieve, but I can't afford to fix it right now. Not with tax time right around the corner."

Bucky nodded sagely. He's heard all my rants about the evils of self-employment, especially in March. Edna and I run a house-cleaning service named the House Mouse. It's a nice little business and a nice change from my previous career, which was as a detective in the Atlanta Police Department. I'd quit the force and bought the business in a snit ten years ago, after the bosses had refused to transfer me to the all-male homicide squad.

Still, police work, like venereal disease, gets in your system and is hard to shake. I'd gotten a private investigator's license right after quitting the force, and while I don't take cases very often, I'd made up my mind the previous year to keep the license renewed just in case.

Bucky opened the passenger-side door of his little red Miata with a flourish. Was this the same guy who'd spent years inventing new and various ways to gross me out?

He started the car and zipped out of my driveway, heading north toward Ponce de Leon Avenue.

"Looking good, Callahan," he said, glancing over at me. "Really. I mean it."

"Thanks," I said, tugging at the hem of the loden green skirt. I'd put a black turtleneck sweater over the short green skirt and under it I wore black ribbed tights and black leather boots.

"I don't look too dominatrix?"

"Not for me," he said, waggling his eyebrows.

So it was the same old Bucky. Bucky Deavers had been my partner on the robbery squad, and we'd stayed best friends ever since, although, given our often hectic lives, we sometimes go for months without seeing each other. My girlfriends don't understand our relationship. I tell them Bucky's the brother I never had — and I have two. It was just like Bucky to drop back into my life on a night like this, expecting me to pick up and follow along after him. And it was just like me to agree to do so.

"Where's the party?" I wanted to know.

"I'll only tell you if you promise not to back out."

"I'm already dressed up now," I said. "You know I don't waste makeup and pantyhose on just anybody."

"It's at the K of C," he said.

"Shit."

16

I'd spent far too many Friday nights of my youth at the Knights of Columbus hall on Buford Highway. Lenten fish fries, summer barbecues, rowdy, beer-soaked Christmas parties; my daddy had hauled all the Garritys to the K of C on every possible occasion over the years. It was his duty as a Catholic and a father, Daddy said, to keep his children in touch with Catholic fraternalism. And to drink as much fifty-cent beer as my mother would allow.

"Can't we just go to some bar in Buck-head?" I asked plaintively.

"What's with you?" Bucky said. "This is your heritage, Garrity."

"Not mine," I said through clenched teeth. "My daddy's maybe, but not mine."

"Whatever," Bucky said.

We drove in silence then, and after a while the steady slap of the windshield wipers reminded me of some old tribal drum cadence. When it had played a dozen times I realized I was hearing an old fiddle tune in my head.

"Whose party is it?" I asked, wanting to be rid of the skull symphony.

"The Shamrock Society of Greater Atlanta," Bucky said proudly. "Our first annual St. Patrick's Day party."

It took me a minute to make the connection. "The Shamrocks? Not those Irish assholes?"

He raised an eyebrow. "Irish assholes? I'm one of them, you know. And so are you — whether you want to admit it or not."

"Irish, yes. But I'm not one of their kind of Irish. Anyway, since when is there a Shamrock Society in Atlanta? I thought those were only active in the big-city police departments in Boston and Chicago and New York."

He smiled smugly. "Atlanta's a big city now, Garrity, in case you hadn't noticed. You know Boylan, right? He put everything together, got the charter and all that stuff."

"Not John Boylan?" I asked.

"Sure. You know any others?"

John Boylan was one of those professional good old boys who'd been around the APD for years. He'd made a name for himself by clearing a string of serial murders in the late eighties, but since that time, he'd been resting on his laurels.

"Boylan," I said, my voice dripping acid. "What's his title, Exalted Shillelagh?"

"Boylan's the president," Bucky said, failing to find humor in my little joke. "You think this is all cornball stuff — huh?"

"You gotta admit, it's kind of hokey, Bucky."

He frowned. "The Shamrock Society happens to have a pretty damn noble history, Garrity. Founded fifty years ago by a bunch of cops in New York as an Irish-American police fraternal organization. It's the real deal. We've got forty members in Atlanta. More than five thousand nationwide. You oughtta see these guys march. We're getting a bagpipe unit going here. It's gonna be awesome."

For the first time I realized that his enthusiasm was genuine, and I felt bad for raining on Bucky's parade.

"I'd like to see them march," I said, trying for sincerity. "I'm a sucker for bagpipes and men in skirts."

Which was true. One note of "Amazing Grace" usually reduces me to a puddle of tears.

The parking lot at the K of C hall was crammed full of the most testosterone-charged vehicles Detroit could muster: pickup trucks, Explorers, Expeditions, Jeeps, Blazers. It was a cop crowd, all right. I spotted a bumper sticker on the back of a mud-encrusted Dodge Jimmy that seemed to sum up nicely the group's collective thinking. "Kill 'em all," it said. "Let God sort out the rest."

"I feel naked," I said, huddling inside my down-filled jacket. "I left my assault rifle in my other purse."

"Be nice," Bucky warned as we pushed

the front door open.

"Jeez," I said, reeling backward. The Knights of Columbus hall was a swirl of noise, color, heat, and motion. A three-piece band was playing country music on the small elevated wooden bandstand at the back of the room, and the dance floor was packed. Green and orange crepe-paper streamers and balloons fluttered from the low ceiling, and the smell of boiled corned beef and cabbage was strong enough to peel paint.

"Rockin'!" Bucky said approvingly.

He took me by the hand and bulldozed us through the crowd toward the bar, where the partyers were lined up four deep.

"Jacky!" Bucky hollered, waving some money in the air. The bartender, a wizened old man wearing a green ball cap and green apron, looked up and waved at us. "Gimme two," Bucky shouted, handing the money over the heads of the others.

Two tall plastic cups foaming over with beer were handed back over the heads of the men in front of us.

Just as I tipped the cup to take a sip, a guy in front of me lurched backward, sending half my beer down the front of my sweater.

"Hey," I said angrily.

The guy turned around. He was short and stocky with a ragged gray beard, a thatch of

20

graying reddish hair, and an impressive beer gut that jutted six inches over the belt of his sagging polyester pants.

His red-rimmed brown eyes drooped at the corners, their melancholy no match for his wide smile.

"Callahan Garrity? What's a nice little girl like you doing in a den of iniquity like this?" He crushed me to him in a hug that spilled the rest of what little beer had remained in my cup.

"Corky," I yelped, "you're wasting good beer."

He let me go with a final wet kiss to the lips. "Better on ya than in ya," he said. "Let's run away and get married and have babies, shall we?"

Corky Hanlon was seventy, if he was a day, and the last I'd heard, he'd been married for fifty years.

"What about Marie?" I asked teasingly.

"She won't mind at all," Corky assured me. "Just as long as I'm around to sign over the Social Security check on the first of the month."

I'd known Corky and Marie Hanlon all my life. They'd lived on our block in Sandy Springs; Corky had been my brother's Little League coach; their daughter Betsy was our favorite baby-sitter. Their son Chuckie had been the recipient of my first preteen crush.

"What are you doing here?" Corky asked, raising his voice to be heard over the din from the band, which was playing a Patsy Cline tune. "I thought you'd left the job."

"I did," I said, turning to introduce him to Bucky. "My friend dragged me here tonight."

Bucky and Corky shook hands. "Friend?" Corky said, raising an eyebrow.

"Not that kind of friend," I said quickly. "Bucky was my partner. He's a detective on the homicide squad. And he's a member of the Shamrocks."

Corky gave Bucky an approving slap on the back. "Corky Hanlon," he said. "Fulton County Sheriff's Office. Or I was until I retired five years ago. Now I just hang around here with all the other old farts and talk about Viagra and Preparation H."

"The Preparation H part I believe," I told Corky. "The Viagra? Never."

We stood and chatted for a while like that, Corky and I catching each other up on the families, Bucky sipping his beer and surveying the room, looking but not finding.

Bucky drifted away once for twenty minutes or so, came back and ordered another round of beers for the three of us.

The band segued into a medley of Irish

songs. Bucky tugged at my hand. "Come on, Garrity, let's dance."

We didn't dance as much as we bumped butts with the drunken cops on the dance floor. Bucky was in a high old mood. He gripped me close to him and hauled me around in a whipsaw series of dips and swirls.

"Peg o' my heart," he warbled in my ear. "I love you. Peg o' my heart, I need you. Since first I heard your lilting laughter, it's your Irish ass I'm after . . ."

I laughed and gave him an affectionate thump on the back. "What's your girlfriend going to say if she walks in on you carrying on like this with me?"

"She'll probably beat the crap out of you," Bucky said. "Lisa's little, but she's mean as cat dirt. It's what I love best about her."

"High praise," I said.

"Shut up and dance," Bucky said.

"Peg o' my heart. I love you. We'll never part. I love you. Dear little girl, sweet little girl . . ." His voice was loud and wondrously off-key.

But the giddiness was infectious. I chimed in on the last verse. "Sweeter than the rose of Erin, are your winning smiles endearin' . . ."

Before the song was over, Corky Hanlon was tapping Bucky on the shoulder. "The next one's mine," he informed us.

He was shorter than I by an inch but a practiced ballroom dancer. Now the band was playing "When Irish Eyes Are Smiling." They ran through the first verse and Corky joined in on the second.

His voice wasn't bad.

"I've never heard that second verse before," I told him.

"There's a lot you don't know yet, Julia Callahan Garrity," Corky said as he smoothed our way around the floor.

"Tell me something," Corky said. "If this Bucky fella isn't your boyfriend, does that mean you're still unattached?"

I laughed at his lack of subtlety. "I'm attached," I assured him. "But he's out of town tonight."

I told Corky all about Mac. "His name's Andrew MacAuliffe. He's a planner with the Atlanta Regional Commission. We've been together about eight years now."

"MacAuliffe," Corky said, letting the sound of it roll around on his tongue. "Irish or Scottish?"

I winced, knowing what came next. "He's Scots-Irish."

"Meaning he's not one or the other," Corky remarked. "And certainly not Catholic, I'm sure."

It wouldn't do to get started down this

road, so I tried changing the subject. "How are the kids?"

But he would have none of it. "And why not married?" Corky demanded. "You're not getting any younger, you know."

He sounded like Edna. "Mac was married once. He's got a grown daughter. But we like things just the way they are. He's got his house and dogs, and I've got my house and the cleaning business, and I do a little private-investigative work every now and again. Why should we get married?"

Corky tsk-tsked, and we finished out our dance in the same spot we'd started, near the bar. Corky looked at his watch and raised his eyebrows.

"Better get going," he announced. "Before Marie locks me out."

We said our goodbyes and promised to keep in touch.

Bucky stood watching the dancers, sipping another beer.

"She's still not here?" I asked.

He shrugged. "She got called out on a case around three this afternoon. A couple crackheads found a woman's body in the backseat of an abandoned car over on Glenwood Avenue. Maybe she's still tied up with that."

"You're dating a cop?" As far as I knew,

this was a first for Bucky. His usual variety of cupcake was young, blond, and clueless. They tended to be waitresses, aerobics instructors, or dancers.

"Wait until you meet her," he said. "She's nothing like the others. She's not like anybody, Callahan." He took a gulp of beer, tugged at the collar of his shirt. "No kiddin'. If I believed in soulmates, she'd be mine. She's that perfect."

I'd heard it all before, but the thing about Bucky was, he always meant it. He fell in love hard and fast and often. From my perspective, he was a thoughtful and tender suitor — with the attention span of a two-year-old. Once, a few years ago, a group of us had been at dinner in a fancy downtown restaurant when Bucky's squeeze du jour got up to go to the ladies' room. When she got back, Bucky was standing at the bar, asking one of the waitresses for her phone number.

"You want to try to call her?" I asked.

"I already paged her twice," Bucky said. "Come on, let's eat."

We sat at a tiny table at the edge of the dance floor and Bucky shoveled in the corned beef and cabbage, greasy fried chicken, and potato salad. I picked at a pile of potato chips and dip. It was one of those parties with a lot of noise and a lot of people, but nobody you really cared to talk to.

Bucky didn't seem to notice. He table-hopped around the room, slapping backs, shaking hands, always watching the door for the arrival of his soulmate.

Bored, I drank three more beers and found myself glancing at my watch in between sips.

"Having fun?"

I looked up. John Boylan placed a casual hand on my shoulder. I forced a smile.

"Just grand," I said.

"A pretty lady like you all alone without a date?" Boylan asked, sitting down without waiting for an invitation. "That's what I call a shame."

"I had a date," I said pointedly. "He went to get us a beer."

"Who, Deavers? Thought he was all tied up with Lisa Dugan."

I looked around the room now, hoping Bucky would come back and rescue me. But all I saw were swirls of various shades of green. A dull throbbing was starting in my temples.

"Bucky and I are old friends," I told Boylan. As if he didn't know.

"And what about us?" he asked, leaning closer. "Aren't we old friends?"

27

3

Back in the late seventies and early eighties, or P.M. — pre-Mac — I'd had what could euphemistically be described as a "free-spirited love life." I never thought of myself as someone who slept around; rather, I preferred to think of myself as serially monogamous. There were maybe half a dozen serious relationships back then. It was in the days before I instituted my policy of never dating anybody I worked with. So I "went with" a couple of cops, along with a lawyer and a salesman and a professional grad student and a guy who never really had a job but always seemed to have plenty of money.

In between those "serious" relationships, I partied with the guys in the office, meaning cops. It was fun and carefree back then. We were all young and ambitious, intense in our belief that we'd make the world a better, safer place to live.

Looking back on it now, those singles summers have a dreamlike quality, like one long coed softball game at Piedmont Park, followed by endless smoky afternoons hunched over cold beers at Manuel's Tavern.

I was a cute young thing at the time, and pretty damn vain about how I looked in my PAL baseball jersey and tight cutoffs. It was after one of those games — we were all sitting around Manuel's, watching the Braves on TV — that John Boylan sat down next to me and whispered in my ear that he'd been watching me all afternoon.

It was heady stuff for me. Boylan was a big deal, in his thirties, a star in the homicide unit, the man who cracked the Bathtub Murders.

Those murders — five young women brutally raped and slashed to death, all found in bathtubs full of water — were the talk of the town that spring. The murders happened within a ten-day span in early April. Women who lived alone were buying Rottweilers and shotguns and security systems. Until John Boylan noticed. He noticed the victims' cars. All shiny clean, with little pine-tree deodorizers hanging from the dashboard. It was Boylan who'd traced the deodorizers back to a car wash on Roswell Road, Boylan who interviewed a nervous attendant who couldn't account for his whereabouts on the nights of the murders, Boylan who'd found the murder weapon — a box-cutter, hidden behind a false panel in the attendant's black Camaro.

John Boylan in those days was quite the stud. He had the early Burt Reynolds look down pat — big dark handlebar mustache, hair that tickled his open shirt collar, skin-tight blue jeans, high-heeled cowboy boots, and an ever-present cigarette.

Boylan bought me a beer, then another beer. He suggested we go somewhere for a quiet dinner. I was thrilled, of course. I needed a shower first, so we went back to my apartment, which was in one of those singles complexes that had sprung up all over Atlanta in the seventies and eighties. The only thing that makes me proud about that evening was that I didn't sleep with the guy. Oh sure, there was a lot of heavy necking and heavy breathing, but Boylan's beeper went off before we got around to actually doing the deed.

It wasn't until the next day, when my girlfriend Paula asked me where I'd gone after Manuel's, that I discovered my new boyfriend was married with three little kids.

Later that day, when Boylan got into his unmarked city unit, he was displeased to find a steaming-ripe dog turd carefully placed on the driver's seat, alongside a note from me. Funny — he never called again.

Funny, too, how Boylan's star status had dimmed over the years. He'd had two divorces that I knew of, and no particular success since the Bathtub Murders. The blue jeans had been replaced with one-size-fits-all sweat pants and the handlebar mustache was gone, as was most of the rest of the hair on his head.

"We had some good times back in the old days, didn't we?" he said now, winking broadly.

"Did we?" I said. "I honestly don't remember."

"Sure you do," he said, stroking my shoulder.

Bucky walked up then, holding a beer in each hand. "Boylan!" he said, his face lighting up. "Great party, man."

"Thanks, buddy. Where's your lady?"

"Working a case," Bucky said. "A Jane Doe in an abandoned car. She said she'd meet me here, but it's getting kind of late."

"Really late," I said, standing up, as though he'd given me my cue. "And I've got a long day tomorrow. Bucky, you think you could give me a ride home?"

Bucky frowned. "Right now? Everything's just getting hopping. The band'll be back from their break any minute now. And Lisa still might make it."

"I could give you a ride," Boylan offered. "I was just saying my good-byes to everybody."

31

I gave Bucky the signal, tugging on my left earlobe. After all the years, he knew it well. He shrugged, took a long swig of his beer, put them both down on the table.

"Nah," he said. "It's late. I'll take her home."

I was fuming by the time we got to the car.

"Thanks a lot for making me beg," I told him.

"What? What'd I do?" Bucky said.

"Boylan. You know I can't stand the guy. You saw him standing there, his hands all over me. And yet you did nothing. Jeez."

He started the car, muttering under his breath.

"What?" I said sharply.

Bucky shook his head. "What'd you want me to do? Draw down on him? Challenge him to a duel? He was just being friendly. Boylan's not a bad guy. Loosen up, for Christ's sake."

He revved the Miata's engine and spun out of the parking lot doing at least forty miles per hour. When he ran the red light at the next intersection it dawned on me that I'd seen Bucky down at least five beers within the past hour.

I glanced over at him. "Are you sober enough to drive?"

"I'm fine," he said. "You wanna nag me

about that, too? Christ. No wonder you're still single."

"Just let me off at the corner," I said, doing a slow burn. "If you want to get stopped for DUI, maybe hit and kill somebody, be my guest. Only let me out of the car first."

"Christ," he said again, taking the next corner at an even higher speed. "I told you, I'm fine. I didn't even finish most of those beers. Kept setting them down, and when I went to pick 'em back up, they were empty."

"Yeah, that happens when you suck it down like water," I said. "Slow down, Bucky. I mean it."

"Fuck you very much," Bucky said, again under his breath.

I made a show of checking my seat belt to make sure it was buckled tightly, but there was nothing else to do. I sat very straight and quiet, and when I looked down at my lap, I noticed my hands were clasped so tightly both knuckles were white.

A mile from home Bucky took a sharp left into a small strip shopping center on Ponce de Leon. He parked in front of a liquor store. The neon sign in the window said it was the Budget Bottle Shop. The windows were covered with beer and liquor signs. He cut the engine. "Be right back," he said.

"What the hell?" I asked. "The last thing

you need is more booze. Take me home, dammit. Right now."

"Just hold your water," Bucky said. "Gotta pick something up in here. Be right back. Swear to God."

He slammed the door and I reached over and pushed the power lock button. The parking lot was dimly lit, and the only business that looked open was the liquor store.

I sat and fumed. Should have stayed home, I told myself. By now, Mac would have called from Nashville. He'd gone up there at the first of the week for a job interview. I was both dreading and anticipating hearing from him. He'd been dissatisfied with his job for more than a year, and I hated it that he was hating his work, but on the other hand, I couldn't contemplate his moving to Nashville. Us moving to Nashville. He wanted me to go too.

I leaned my head back and closed my eyes. My temples were throbbing. I wanted a hot bath and some aspirin and my bed and my house. My house. Not some fancy new house in a subdivision in Nashville, Tennessee. My wood-frame Craftsman bungalow on Oakdale suited me just fine. My life suited me too. Why couldn't it suit Mac?

And where the hell was Bucky? I sat up and peered at the front of the liquor store. It was impossible to see inside with all the posters and beer signs in the store's window. Damn him. I wondered what his new girlfriend would think about his coming home with a snootful of beer. Things had changed in Atlanta. In the old days, a cop wouldn't ticket another cop. If you got stopped for running a red light or weaving from lane to lane, all you had to do was flash your badge, and all was forgiven. But not anymore. The new chief of police was a woman full of reformist's zeal — a real ball-buster. If Bucky — or any other cop — got stopped for DUI, he could be in deep shit with the bosses.

I thought about tapping on the car horn. Piss him off royally. Like I was pissed off. Thought better of it. My head hurt. I leaned back and closed my eyes again. Come on, dammit.

The Miata's clock ticked off a couple minutes. I opened my eyes when I heard the pops. They were faint. Two of them. Pop. Pop. I sat up, blinked, looked around the parking lot. There was one other car in the lot, a rusty white Buick LeSabre. Traffic on Ponce was what you'd expect for that time of night — busy. The pops could have been a car backfiring, maybe.

Just then the front door of the liquor store was flung open. A woman — young, thin, black — ran onto the sidewalk. She had pink sponge rollers in her hair, and her mouth was twisted wide open. She was screaming. "Jesus! They done shot him. Jesus, Jesus. Somebody help." And then the screaming turned into sirens, sirens from every direction, shrieking through the cold, thin night air.

4

She was crouched down, screaming her lungs out, clutching her head as though it might break apart. I raced past her into the liquor store.

Bucky was on the floor, facedown, facing the door. A cardboard six-pack carrier lay on the floor beside him. Harp. Three of the bottles were smashed. Bits of glass were splattered all over the floor. A foaming yellow puddle spread around Bucky's outstretched hand. Blood trickled from a damp place on the side of his head.

I knelt down beside him. My ears were buzzing. Screams. The woman wouldn't quit screaming. I put my fingers below Bucky's carotid artery, felt a thin, thready beat.

"Call nine-one-one," I yelled, turning around to look at her. "Tell them it's a code three. Signal sixty-three, you hear? Officer down. Tell them it's an officer down. We need an ambulance."

The crying was high-pitched, not real. The girl squatted down behind the counter, stood up. Now she was holding a largish bundle, wrapped in a blue-and-yellow-striped blanket. The child kicked a bare foot, screamed louder. He had a thick halo of dark fuzzy hair, and angry tears streamed down the fat little face. How old? Maybe nine months?

"He coulda killed my baby," she cried, rocking the child to and fro. "I was holding my baby and he looked at me, pointed the gun, then run out."

"Call nine-one-one, damn you," I screamed. "Right now."

I rolled Bucky over as gently as I could. A thin stream of blood trickled down his neck. His eyelids were barely open. I pried one open, bent close to see. "Bucky?"

He blinked, coughed a little. I put my head to his chest. He was breathing, but the breaths were uneven, fluttery.

Christ. What to do? It had been fifteen years since I learned CPR at the academy. Where to start? Hurry, dammit. He was dying. Dying on a dirty linoleum floor in a pool of blood and beer.

I closed my eyes, tried to find a pocket of calm.

ABC. I could hear the instructor, hear the cadets parroting her. ABC. Airway, breathing, circulation.

Assess first. Okay. He was breathing on his

own, but that could stop at any time, I knew. His heart was beating. What about his airway? I wiped my hands on my shirt, inserted two fingers in his mouth. He gagged, weakly. His throat was clear.

Behind me, the girl was still babbling. "I done hit the panic button. Like Pete said. I hit it soon as he run in. Jesus. We wasn't doin' nothin'. He just shot him. Put the gun up to his head. Click. Pow. Click. Pow."

I got up and ran over to the counter, but it was surrounded with a yellowed Plexiglas shield.

"Give me the phone," I ordered her.

She pushed the receiver through a slot in the shield. "Now dial nine-one-one."

I took a deep breath, started talking as soon as the dispatcher acknowledged me. "This is Callahan Garrity. We have a signal sixty-three at the Budget Bottle Shop on Ponce de Leon." I looked over at the clerk, who was jiggling the crying baby on her hip. "What's the street number here?"

"Huh?"

"Address, dammit. What's the address?"

"Sixty-seven eleven."

I repeated it to the operator. "Gunshot wounds to the head," I said. "We need an ambulance right now."

I hung up the phone. The police station was

only a few blocks away; Grady Memorial Hospital with the biggest trauma center in the South was less than three miles. Hurry, I prayed. Dear God, hurry.

The sirens were getting closer. Police cruisers. Four or five, impossible to tell how many.

"They just shot him," the clerk whimpered, starting to cry again.

I whipped off my parka, balled it up, and knelt down on the floor, pressing the fabric to the side of Bucky's head to stop the flow of blood. Something in my mind registered how small the bullet hole was. With the fingers of my left hand, I pinched his nostrils closed. Put my mouth over his and exhaled hard. And again, and again. I sat back on my knees. Still breathing.

"Bucky? Can you hear me?"

His eyelids fluttered. He seemed to look right at me. "W'as up?" His voice was weak but, by God, he was alive.

The sirens were right outside. The door flew open and a wave of cops rolled through. Eight of them. Outside, more sirens.

"He's a cop," I shouted as they moved toward us. "He's been shot in the head at least twice. Right side, behind his ear. He's breathing on his own. We've called for an ambulance."

"What happened here?" The cop was thin,

with acne-scarred mocha-colored skin and a penciled-looking mustache. The nameplate under the badge said Durrence. He knelt down on the floor beside me, put his hands on Bucky's chest, and started to push. "Who shot him?"

"Some dude," the cashier volunteered. "The dude just walked in out of the stockroom and shot Bucky in the head. Shot him twice and run out through the door he come in through."

Durrence leaned down and looked in Bucky's eyes. "Christ! I know this guy. It's Deavers. Parini — get on the radio. Tell 'em we need the route to Grady cleared. Then call Grady and tell 'em we got GSW to the head. Have 'em page Doc Solomon.

"Who are you?" Durrence asked.

"Callahan Garrity. I'm a friend of Bucky's. I used to be on the force."

"You know what you're doing here?"

"Not really," I said.

"Let me."

I scooted over to give him better access to Bucky.

Parini took his radio off his belt and started speaking into it. More cops crowded into the store. The two cops who'd followed the first one in moved toward the door. "What's back there?"

"Storeroom," the clerk said. "Pete's office. The dude must have gone out the alley."

The cops drew their 9-mm service weapons and inched through the doorway. "Police!" one of them called, but the voice echoed against the concrete walls.

"The dude that shot him. What did he look like?" Parini asked.

"He had on a mask," the girl reported. "Like one of those ski masks with the holes for eyes and mouth. I ain't seen nothin' else but that mask."

"What about you?" Parini said, looking at me.

"I don't know," I said, biting my lip to keep from crying. My legs and hands were twitching uncontrollably. I clutched Bucky's hand in mine. It seemed cool. I needed to do something, cover him with something, do something besides hold my jacket to the hole in his skull.

"I was outside in the car. We were here maybe five minutes. I heard the gunshots, and she came running out saying he'd been shot. God. What's taking so long for that ambulance?"

"He coulda killed Faheem," the clerk cried. "I was holding him up, showing him to Bucky, when the dude ran in. But he acted like we wasn't even here. Didn't say nothin'.

Just put this little bitty gun up beside Bucky's ear and shot. Bam. Bucky fell down and Faheem, he started screaming. I was screaming too. And the dude leaned over, bam, shot Bucky again. And then he ran out. I hit the panic button like Pete said."

Outside, over the din of the other sirens and Faheem's angry wails, I heard the deep *whoop-whoop* of an approaching ambulance.

The first paramedic in the door was a woman with frizzy red hair. She pushed a stretcher loaded with what looked like red plastic toolboxes. Right behind her came her partner, a lanky young white kid in his early twenties, yelling into a radio.

"What's the deal?" the woman demanded, lifting the tool kit off the stretcher. She snapped rubber gloves onto both hands. The kid did the same.

"White male, late thirties, two apparent gunshot wounds anterior to left ear," Durrence said. "We started CPR."

"He was talking," I said eagerly. "Right before the officers got here. I called his name and he looked up at me. He said, 'What's up?' "

"Okay, ma'am, you did good," the woman said gently. "We'll take over now."

More cops flooded into the room. There must have been a dozen, then twenty. The paramedics worked over Bucky. The kid inserted a breathing tube in his throat, then attached an ambu-bag to it, pumping it rhythmically. Another mask went over Bucky's face, which had grown still and pale, and tubes connected him to a portable oxygen tank. His snowy white shirt and shamrock tie were covered with blood. His face was streaked with more blood.

I stood up and walked away, dizzy and nauseous. I huddled in a corner, afraid to watch, unable to look away. Hurry, I whispered. For God's sake, hurry.

The clerk leaned over the counter in order to get a better view. "Oh no. Oh man. No. Bucky. Ooh. He gonna die?"

I walked over and stood in front of her, blocking her view. My legs were shaking. It was so cold in here. I rubbed my hands over my forearms, trying to get my circulation going. "What's your name?"

"Deecie," she whispered. "This is some shit. You know? I ain't believin' this shit."

"Deecie, I'm Callahan. How do you know Bucky?" I asked.

"Why you think he come in here? He works here. Security guard. Me and him is tight. Bucky's my homey."

I pointed toward the door. "What was Bucky doing when the shooter came in here?"

"I already tol' you. He was standin' there. He wasn't doing nothin'."

"Where does the outside door lead?"

"Alley," she said. "Runs back of the shopping center. And there's a driveway, goes down to that road behind here. But I don't be goin' out there. It's nasty. Pete, he told me to park my car there, but I told him I ain't parking in that shit. Be rats and roaches and all kind of scary shit out there. Winos hanging around, wanting money or beer."

"After the guy ran out, did you hear a car, anything like that?"

She shook her head. "I wasn't studyin' no car. Faheem was crying and I was crying and I wanted to get out of here, 'case the dude came back."

I heard cases snapping shut behind me. "All right," the woman said. "Let's roll. Call the hospital."

The kid got on the radio again. "This is unit two-six. We're en route with a victim, late thirties, possible gunshot wound to the head. Victim is unresponsive. He has a spontaneous heartbeat of one hundred, blood pressure is one hundred over seventy. He's been intubated and bagged. We'll try to get an I.V. line started en route. Our ETA is five minutes."

I turned around. They had Bucky on the

stretcher, a mask strapped over his face, a brace wrapped around his neck.

"Either of you know his name?"

"Bucky," I said. "Bucky Deavers. He's a homicide detective."

She nodded soberly. "Thought I recognized him."

"How is he? Will he make it?"

She didn't answer my question. She bent over, put her lips close to his ear. "Hey there, Bucky. Hang on now. Let's get you to Grady."

They wheeled the stretcher toward the door.

"I want to go with you," I said.

"Not right now," Durrence said. "We need to get a statement from you."

"I told you what I saw," I said, my voice shrill. "Nothing. I heard just two pops. That was it."

"All right," Durrence said. He flashed a quick smile showing small, even white teeth. "Come on now. Calm down. You can go see your friend later. The detectives are on their way. They'll want to talk to you, then you can go to the hospital."

"Look," I said. "I'm a P.I. An ex-cop. I used to work with Detective Deavers on the robbery squad. Let me just go to the hospital. We can talk there. All right?"

It would not be all right and I knew that. The two cops who'd gone into the stockroom came back into the store. One was talking quietly on his radio. There were more sirens. Cops kept coming into the store. It was the signal sixty-three. Officer down. The one radio call no cop ever wanted to hear. It would bring every cop in a twenty-mile radius converging on the Budget Bottle Shop in a few short minutes.

The bell on the front door jingled. Two more men walked in. One white, one black. The black one wore starched blue jeans, a sport shirt, and a blue windbreaker with the letters "APD" stenciled on the front in eighteen-inch yellow letters. The white one wore a conservative business suit and a dark green ankle-length raincoat. He had a snap-brim fedora with a little feather in the hatband. The hat man frowned when he saw me.

"Who let her in here?" he barked.

Durrence looked surprised. "She's a witness, Major."

Lloyd Mackey pushed the fedora to the back of his head. He had mild blue eyes and a blond walrus mustache starting to go gray. "Aw, gawddamn, Garrity. What the hell happened? Who shot Deavers?"

Before I could answer, the Hispanic cop ran from the stockroom, visibly excited. "De-

47

tective Washington," he called to the black cop. "We got a weapon back here. A twenty-two. Saturday night special. We found it beside a pile of empty beer cartons in the alley. You wanna take a look?"

Mackey nodded and the two men went with him into the back room.

The clerk, Deecie, was still trying to shush little Faheem. "Look here," she called out. "Is it all right if I take him in the back, fix him some formula?"

"Come on," Washington said. "You can show us where everything's at back here."

"Shit."

I turned around. Mackey was kneeling down, looking at the broken beer bottles and the puddle of blood. The place was a mess, discarded rubber gloves, bloody gauze pads, bits of plastic and paper packaging from the supplies the paramedics had used. He looked up at me. "How bad?"

Major Lloyd Mackey was Bucky's boss, commander of the crimes against persons division. I'd never worked under him, but his men liked him. We'd tangled a few times in the past, but I'd always taken his animosity toward me as a professional necessity. I was a P.I.; he was a cop. If I got in his way, he'd give me a kick in the ass. It was understood. It was his job.

"Two bullets, right above the ear," I said. "Not so much blood, really. He was still breathing when they took him to Grady. He talked to me. Knew who I was. That's good, right?"

"Yeah, good." Mackey stood up, took a handkerchief, and wiped off his hands. He walked around the store. It was small, cluttered. Shelves lined the walls, each with hand-lettered signs for the major liquor food groups: scotch, whiskey, vodka, gin, wine, and beer. A large cooler for beer and wine stood to the right of the cashier's cage.

"What were you doing here?" Mackey asked.

"Bucky's idea," I said. "We'd been to the Shamrock Society's St. Patrick's Day party, over at the Knights of Columbus hall on Buford Highway. I made him leave early, to take me home. He wanted me to meet his new girlfriend."

"Dugan? She was there?"

"She never showed up. Guess she was still on a case. I got bored. We got kind of pissy with each other after that. On the way home, he just pulled in here, said he'd be right out. I stayed in the car, locked the doors. I was halfway asleep when I heard the shots."

"You didn't see anybody go in or out?"

"No, but like I said, I was leaning back with

my eyes closed. There was only one other car in the lot, an old white LeSabre."

Mackey walked to the door and looked out. Blue and red lights twinkled atop the sea of emergency vehicles in the parking lot. "The LeSabre's still out there. Probably the girl's. How about that other car? That yours?"

"No. It's Bucky's."

He shook his head. "Hell. I forgot. The little red sports car. Deavers's wet dream."

He stood in front of the counter, looking up at the Plexiglas shield. "Deavers didn't say why he wanted to stop? Did he mention that he wanted beer or cigarettes or anything?"

I hesitated for a moment. I didn't want to get Deavers nailed for drunk driving, but on the other hand, the hospital would take blood samples, and the blood samples would turn up alcohol. Besides, what was a DUI charge to a guy with two bullets in his brain?

"No. He just said he'd be right out. I assumed he wanted beer or something. I was ragging him about how he'd already had enough beer at the party. I was afraid he'd get stopped for DUI."

I was standing beside Mackey, looking at all the hand-lettered signs on the wall. "No Credit." "No Two-Party Checks." "Absolutely No Sales to Minors." "Do Not Remove

50

Single Beers from Six-Packs." The house had a lot of rules.

A camera was mounted high on the wall, directly behind the cash register. A little red light flashed below it.

"I hope to God that thing was working," I said.

"It better be," Mackey said.

5

Traffic on Ponce de Leon Avenue had come to a standstill. Police cruisers blocked all four lanes of the road in front of the shopping center and uniformed officers directed traffic onto side streets. A fire truck rolled up as I walked out of the store with Mackey. More police cruisers were jammed into the parking lot, units from every jurisdiction within a thirty-mile radius of the city. Three Georgia Highway Patrol cruisers were parked on the sidewalk. Uniformed officers stood around, talking on radios, pacing back and forth in front of the closed stores. Yellow crime scene tape was looped all the way around the entire shopping center. A dull thudding noise overhead made me look up. A yellow helicopter hovered over the roof of the liquor store, a searchlight pointed toward the ground.

"Washington's gonna take you to the office, get a statement from you," Mackey said. "He'll give you a ride home if you want."

I sighed. "I've already told you everything I know. As soon as you get what you need, I'm going to the hospital. I want to see how Bucky's doing."

He nodded.

Washington plunked a magnetic blue bubble light on the top of his detective's sedan as we snaked our way around parked cars all the way down Ponce deLeon to City Hall East, just two miles down the street in a huge red-brick building that once housed a regional Sears-Roebuck distribution center.

He was chewing gum, his jaws working like a jackhammer. "You say Deavers was talkin'? Even after he was shot?" He was trying to sound casual. "Maybe it won't be so bad."

"I'm hoping," I said. "He looked up at me. 'What's happening?' That's what he asked me. Like we'd just run into each other in a bar or something 'What's happening?' Doesn't that sound just like Bucky?"

"That's Deavers," Washington said, chewing vigorously. "Shot twice in the head, he wants to know what's happening. Surprised he didn't crack a joke, maybe take a peek up your skirt."

He blushed slightly, realizing who he was talking to. "Sorry."

"It's okay. He was like a little brother to me, you know? We were partners back when I was on the job. Used to run around together."

Washington pulled the sedan into a fenced-off area in the basement garage of City Hall East and directed me toward a door marked "Police Personnel Only."

"You ever been in here before?" he asked as we waited for an elevator.

"No. Last time I came to see Bucky, you guys were still over in that crappy task force office off North Avenue."

"It's not too bad here," Washington said. The elevator stopped on the fourth floor and we got off. He gestured down a hallway toward where a Mexican-looking woman ran a vacuum cleaner over an acre of blue industrial carpet.

"We got more room, got a couple of interrogation rooms, a conference room, our own coffee lounge. You notice downstairs, we got Gold's Gym. That's cool. You work out?"

I had to laugh. "Do I look like I work out?"

He shrugged. "You look all right to me."

He was being polite. I'd been skinny as a kid, but since I hit thirty, I'd been waging war against the same twenty-five pounds I'd gained and lost over the past decade.

Washington showed me into a small office that had the sharp chemical smell of new paint and new carpet. I sat in a wooden chair opposite the battered metal desk. Not everything in the office was new.

"You want a Coke or something? Coffee?"

54

"Nothing," I said. "Let's just do this, so I can get over to the hospital."

He brought a small tape recorder out of a drawer of the desk, along with a yellow legal pad. "Okay. This is Wednesday, March seventeenth, eleven-thirty P.M.," he started. "I'm interviewing, uh." He shut the recorder off. "Say your full name for me."

"Julia Callahan Garrity," I said, spelling the last name. "I use Callahan professionally."

He turned the recorder on again and we went over the same list of questions. I gave him the short version of the St. Patrick's Day party, what Bucky and I talked about, and how he had stopped at the Budget Bottle Shop, saying he was just going to run in for a minute.

"He didn't mention that he worked there?" Washington asked.

"No," I said.

"Didn't say he was picking up a paycheck, or wanted some beer, or to talk to somebody?"

"He just said he had to get something and would be gone a minute." I gave a protracted sigh to let Washington know my answer wasn't going to change.

"And you saw no cars coming or going from the parking lot. Saw nobody, is that your statement?"

"It was late, I was tired and mad at Bucky for making me wait," I said. "I closed my eyes. I was halfway asleep when I heard the shots."

"Tell me about the shots."

"Two. Pop. Pop. The sound was very faint. It didn't even register with me that they might be gunshots. I thought firecrackers. Then the girl came running out of the store, screaming that they'd shot Bucky."

" 'They?' "

"I think that's what she said. 'They.' I went in there, found Bucky lying facedown on the floor. The smashed six-pack of beer was on the floor beside him. I turned him over and started CPR. The girl was still screaming. She said she'd hit the panic button. Is that what I think it is?"

"Yeah." Washington chewed some. "Silent alarm, wired direct to police dispatch. The button's mounted under the counter. Lot of liquor stores and check-cashing outfits got 'em."

"The girl was so whacked out, I had to go over to the counter, get her to dial nine-one-one so I could tell them to send an ambulance," I said.

"And you didn't see anybody inside the store."

"Just the girl. Deecie, she said her name

was. And the baby. Faheem. He was scream-ing like a stuck pig."

"Was the door to the back room open at that point?"

I had to think about that. "I don't know," I said. "I didn't notice it, so maybe it was closed."

"What did the girl say happened?"

"She said Bucky was talking to her. She was holding the baby up for him to see and the dude ran in from the back room. She said he didn't say anything to them, just put the gun to Bucky's head and fired. Then he ran out the way he came. She said he was wearing a ski mask, with holes for the eyes and mouth. And she said she didn't know if he was black or white."

"Detective Washington?"

We both looked up. Mackey was standing in the doorway, grim-faced, his hat pushed to the back of his head. "Could I speak to you for a moment?"

Washington turned the tape recorder off and went out into the hallway. I sat with my hands folded, waiting.

Five minutes later, Washington came in again. He leaned back in his chair, looked up at the ceiling, shaking his head, muttering.

"Something wrong?" I asked.

He kept staring at the ceiling.

"Was it about Bucky? Did the hospital call? How is he?"

Washington sat back up. "It wasn't the hospital. It was about the girl."

Now I was confused. "What girl?"

"The cashier from the liquor store. Deecie Styles."

"What about her?"

Washington opened a desk drawer, got out a piece of paper, took the gum out of his mouth, folded the paper around it, and placed it on the top of his desk.

"She's gone."

"Gone where?"

"We don't know. Parini thought she was in the back room, changing the baby or something. The crime scene was a zoo. You saw how many people were there. Sixty or seventy, probably. Parini got ready to transport her back here for questioning, but she was gone. Vamoose. Adios, amigo. Her and the baby."

"Where could she go? She had that baby. How about her car? The white Buick parked out front?"

"The car's still there," Washington said. "But Deecie Styles booked it out of there. We called the store owner, got her address, sent a unit over there. She lives with her aunt in some apartments over on Memorial Drive.

The aunt says she hasn't seen her."

"Where could she go?" It was unbelievable. A hundred cops on the scene, and the only witness to Bucky Deavers's shooting had disappeared. "She couldn't have gotten very far," I said. "She was carrying her baby. Faheem."

"That's not the only thing she was carrying," Washington said. He reached in the desk drawer, got a pack of Juicy Fruit gum, took out a piece, held it up to me, an offering.

"No thanks," I said. "What else did she have?"

"The videotape. From the security camera. And all the money from the store safe."

6

Washington pulled the sedan over to the curb at the corner of Decatur and Butler streets, right in front of the hospital.

He took a business card from his shirt pocket, wrote a number on it. "That's my beeper," he said. "The major wants me back over at the Bottle Shop. I'd appreciate it if you'd call, give me a heads-up on Deavers . . . if, you know . . . either way."

His deep brown eyes were already weary. He'd have a long night ahead of him.

"I'll call," I promised. "Either way." I hesitated before getting out of the car. "Detective? That girl — Deecie Styles. How do you know she took the money from the store? Isn't it possible the shooter took it?"

"She took it," Washington said. "The owner says he was at the store around eight P.M. He cleaned all the big bills out of the register. Put it in the safe in his office. The shooter couldn't have known about that. Only the girl knew. And that's why she ran."

Why not run as soon as the shooter left? I

wondered. Why hit the panic button and wait around for the cops if you're going to steal from your employer? But I didn't ask those questions. I thanked him for the ride and got out.

The rain was little more than a soft mist now, but it had left deep puddles on the sidewalk as I splashed my way toward the emergency room entrance.

In the past four years, the hospital authority that runs Grady Memorial has spent hundreds of millions of dollars expanding and remodeling the old yellow brick complex that has for decades cared for the city's desperately ill and hopelessly indigent.

Now Grady has a new façade of taupe and green marble, with soaring cast-iron arches and two-story windows along the Butler and Gilmer Street entrances. At first glance, it looks more like a luxury hotel than a hospital.

But if you looked closer, it was the same old Grady. Winos were scrunched up on the cast-iron benches where they'd always slept, covered with newspapers or sleeping bags. It was a tighter fit now that the city had installed armrests at three-foot intervals on the benches, but I suppose alcohol dims the idea of discomfort.

More homeless people huddled together under the parapet jutting out in front of the hospital entry. Young girls barely in their teens paraded by with babies in strollers, tugging wailing toddlers by the hand, and at least a dozen hospital workers in pink and green scrubs stood in a knot, puffing furtively at the cigarettes they were no longer allowed to smoke inside the hospital, pointedly ignoring signs that politely requested "Please Refrain from Smoking in the Plaza."

I pushed the big double doors open and walked into the lobby, and followed the red "Emergency Clinic" signs and arrows. I walked hurriedly past an elevator lobby with signs directing patients to Tower A and Tower B, briefly amused at their designations. In the bad old days of segregation and Jim Crow, Atlanta locals called their hospital The Gradys, because at one time the hospital was an H-shape, with one half dedicated to white patients, the other dedicated to "coloreds."

The green marble corridor wound through the heart of the hospital until it dumped me out into a sour-smelling area designated as the "Emergency Room Reception Area."

Semantics aside, it was a waiting room, and it smelled and looked only slightly better than the familiar old one.

It was packed, stuffy, and overheated, with people lolling on the vinyl benches and leaning against walls, waiting their turn for treatment. The bad weather had flushed out an unusually large and motley contingent of street people, gnomes, so-called because they lived under the overpasses along the nearby Downtown Connector, whores, and GOMERs, whose name was an acronym for Get Out of My Emergency Room. But the gnomes and GOMERs were vastly outnumbered by the cops.

They were from everywhere, transit cops who worked for the Metropolitan Atlanta Rapid Transit Authority, Fulton County Sheriff, City of Atlanta, DeKalb County, Georgia State Patrol. At least fifty uniforms were packed into the room.

Over near the triage area, the city's police brass had staked out their turf. The police chief was there, standing in back of a podium decorated with the APD insignia. She was speaking into a bank of microphones, her smooth mocha face calm and implacable, her hair braided into her usual tight coronet, her elaborate uniform resembling that of a generalissimo of a small banana republic. I recognized three deputy police chiefs standing around her and, off to the side, looking disturbed, was the mayor, with three uniformed police bodyguards at his side.

A dozen reporters, mostly from the local

television and radio stations, stood around the chief, shouting questions at her.

Most of the chief's answers seemed to consist of stock phrases such as "That's under investigation" or "The department's full cooperation."

Lloyd Mackey stood at the chief's side. I edged around the group and caught his eye. He stepped toward me and touched my elbow, guiding me into a corner where we could talk without being overheard.

"How is he?" I asked.

"He's upstairs in surgery," Mackey said. "The docs haven't told us anything yet. We're still trying to reach his family."

I pushed a strand of wet hair out of my eyes. "His parents are dead. His mother died several years ago. Anyway, the cops were pretty much his family."

"Personnel is going through his records to be sure," Mackey said. "We don't want any relatives finding out about this when they turn on the news tomorrow morning."

"I can't believe any of this is happening. Detective Washington told me the clerk took off with the videotape from the security camera. And the money from the safe. I don't get it. I really don't. I was there. The girl was scared witless. She couldn't even dial nine-one-one. I don't see how she had the presence of mind to go in that back office, take the tape, and empty out the safe — with all those dozens of cops milling around, and then take off carrying a screaming baby. On foot."

Mackey frowned. "Washington should have kept his mouth shut. That stuff about the clerk isn't for public consumption. You got me?"

I looked around at the rows of cameras that were setting up for the chief's press conference. "Fine. I'm not the one who alerted the media about all this."

"The clerk's name isn't going to be released," Mackey said. "Not yet anyway."

"I understand." A thought occurred to me. "You don't suspect the girl had something to do with shooting Bucky, do you?"

Mackey was watching the chief conferring with her assistants. "Our investigation is in the preliminary stage. That's all I can tell you. You know the rules, Garrity."

"I know Deavers is in this hospital with a bullet in his head," I said fiercely. "What I want to know is how it got there, that's all. You seem to forget, Major, that I was there, too. The shooter could have taken me out, too. I need to understand what happened. I'm not some lowlife ambulance-chasing reporter, you know. You asked about Deavers's family. I'm his family. He was closer to me than my own brothers. And I have a right to know what's going on with your investigation."

Mackey was stone-faced. "You'll be informed as we see fit. That's the best I can do. Tomorrow, you can call Captain Dugan. I'll authorize her to release any information that's pertinent to you."

"Dugan," I said. "Bucky's new girlfriend?"

"Captain Dugan," Mackey repeated. "She's at the scene right now."

A tall, white-haired man pushed his way through the cops and the reporters. The chief frowned when she saw him, but reached out and shook the hand he offered anyway. A wave of reporters pressed forward when they saw the newcomer.

"Pete," one of them called out. "Can you tell us what happened tonight?"

"Christ," Mackey muttered.

"Who's that?" I asked.

"Pete Viatkos. Owns the Budget Bottle Shop. I thought everybody knew Viatkos."

"Not me," I said. "He some kind of celebrity?"

"He's a legend in his own mind," Mackey said. "Kind of a cop groupie, I guess you'd say. He sponsors a golf tournament in May, as a benefit for the Police Benevolent Association. Hires a lot of our guys to work security, sponsors a couple of APD softball teams."

Viatkos stepped up to the bank of microphones, glanced at the chief for permission to speak. She nodded.

He cleared his throat. "Uh, I'd just like to say that me and my family are praying for the recovery of the officer who was shot in our store tonight. As a lot of you know, we at the Budget Bottle Shop regard this city's police officers as the finest in the country." His speech had a formal tone to it, and a slight accent. "Our officers are heroes, all of them. And I want to put the scum who shot this officer on notice: 'Whoever you are, don't think you can get away with this cowardly act. You can run, but you can't hide.' "

The chief nodded her agreement. "Thank you, Mr. Viatkos. I'd like to announce at this time that Mr. Viatkos just informed me that he is offering a ten-thousand-dollar reward for the arrest and conviction of the person or persons responsible for this shooting."

Now it was the mayor's turn to get into the act. Not surprising, since he rarely misses a photo opportunity.

"And Chief," the mayor said, gliding toward the microphones, turning his chosen profile toward the camera, "the city will add ten thousand dollars to that reward money. Our office also just contacted the governor's office, and Governor Barnes has said that the state will match our reward money, bringing the total reward for this cowardly dog who attacks our law enforcement officers to thirty thousand dollars."

The cops in the room started clapping their hands and stomping their feet in approval.

"About damn time," someone called from the back of the room.

"Any other questions?" the chief asked crisply, retaking command of the podium.

"I got one." A uniformed officer, short and balding with a craggy face and beaky nose, stepped out of the circle of reporters.

The assistant chiefs looked startled. The chief looked pissed. "Yes, Officer?"

"Officer Rakoczy," the questioner said. "Ignatius R. Rakoczy. Chief, since you seem to be so concerned about this officer who was shot at his off-duty security job, I wondered if you could tell us why the city doesn't pay our officers enough of a living wage that they wouldn't have to work two and three other jobs just to make ends meet."

The chief's jaw dropped. Her eyes narrowed.

"Yeah," somebody from the back called. "Ask her why we ain't getting a raise again this year."

"Ask her how many jobs most of our guys work," somebody else called. "Ask her how

68

many jobs she has to work."

I looked over at Mackey, thought I saw a ghost of a smile flit across his lips.

One of the assistant chiefs stepped forward then, stooped over to speak. "It is our understanding that Detective Deavers was not working at the Budget Bottle Shop when he visited there as a customer this evening. That'll be all now."

More questions were shouted, but the brass were leaving, ignoring the ugly little scene that was threatening to develop.

I turned around to say something to Mackey, but he was gone. I spotted him pushing through the swinging doors to the treatment area and I hurried to catch up.

"Major," I called.

He turned around. "Garrity, go home."

"Where are you going?" I asked. "Has there been a change in Bucky's condition? Is there any news?"

"He just came out of surgery," Mackey said. "Go home. Call Captain Dugan tomorrow."

7

I wandered out to the ambulance ramp. It was clogged with police cruisers and ambulances. Uniformed cops stood around talking and smoking. I recognized one of the EMS drivers as a guy I'd known years ago when I was still on the force. His name was McNabb.

I went back inside the ER and fed three bucks' worth of quarters into a vending machine for a pack of Marlboros. In a convenience store cigarettes cost about two fifty, but at Grady, I guess, they wanted to hammer in the message that smoking was bad for your health. Bad for your wealth, too.

McNabb watched me approach, his eyes narrowed. He looked me up and down. Not in a sexual way. Anyway, the last thing I looked that night was sexy. I'm nearly forty, and on good days, when I've paid a little attention to my appearance, like, say, applying lipstick, mascara, and a little mousse to tame my unruly mop of nearly black hair, I've been told the effect is rather pleasing.

Tonight, though, my hair was a mass of frizz from the rain and humidity, my makeup was smeared, my black stockings riddled with runs, and my skirt spattered with Bucky's blood.

"Garrity." It was McNabb's version of a hug and a slap on the back. Mr. Congeniality, that was McNabb.

I struggled to remember McNabb's first name, but I came up empty. McNabb was the only name I knew him by.

"McNabb. How's it hanging?"

"Not too bad," McNabb said. "At least I don't got two bullets in my head."

I winced, but knew McNabb didn't mean anything by the remark.

I opened the pack of Marlboros, fished one out for myself, and offered the pack to McNabb. He took two. Good old McNabb. He lit up, offered me his match, but I shook my head and put the cigarette in the pocket of my shirt. Can't stand cigarettes, but they're useful in breaking the ice.

I thrust my hands into my jacket pocket. "Some bad shit tonight," I said.

He nodded. "Real bad. You worked with Deavers, didn't you?"

"Yeah. We're pretty tight."

He cocked his head and let twin plumes of smoke drift out of his nostrils. "Thought I heard you'd quit the force. Heard you'd moved out of town."

"No. I quit, but I got a P.I. license, and I'm running my own business." He didn't need to know it was a cleaning business.

"How'd you come to be down here to-night?"

It was a fair question, and I couldn't expect to get information if I didn't give it freely. "Deavers and I went to a St. Patrick's Day party together. He was taking me home, but he wanted to stop at the liquor store first."

"You hear anything in there?" He nodded toward the swinging doors that led into the ER.

"The docs are still working on him," I said.

"Gonna need a lot of work, from what I could see," McNabb said, getting a pinched look.

"He's pretty tough," I said. "I'm praying he makes it."

McNabb took another drag on the Marl-boro. "If you're his friend, you better be praying he kicks tonight. 'Cause if he does live through the night, a gunshot wound like that, that's a shitload of brain damage. If he lives, he'll be a vegetable."

"God." I couldn't let McNabb see me cry. I swallowed hard and blinked back the tears.

"I liked Deavers," McNabb said. "He was a

decent guy. Not a jerk like a lot of those detectives, think they're God or something, 'cause they got a gold shield. Hell, we marched in the parade together this morning. That's why this doesn't seem real. I saw him when they brought him in. He was still wearing his tie. I saw that, I felt sick, really sick."

"You marched together? Where was that?"

McNabb looked at me like I was stupid.

"The parade. You know, St. Patrick's Day? We marched with the Shamrocks. Must have been two dozen guys. Not bad for an outfit that only got started up last year."

"You're a Shamrock too?"

"Sure," McNabb said. "I joined last year. Spent a hundred bucks on the green jacket to wear in the parade. We had a breakfast this morning too. You know, green grits, green beer, like that.

"McNabb's as Irish as pigs and potatoes. Deavers too. Hey, Garrity. You're Irish, aren't you? Only you're not a cop no more, so I guess you wouldn't be eligible to join."

I didn't know Deavers was particularly Irish. I always just thought of him as an All-American boy. The part that was so surprising was that Deavers had joined this Shamrock outfit. Bucky was a dedicated nonconformist and nonjoiner. He'd been the first grown man I knew to have his ear pierced. He was always proud of the fact that he didn't vote because he didn't believe in declaring a party affiliation. He used to bitch and moan about the fact that, as a member of the APD, he automatically had Police Benevolent Association dues deducted from his paycheck, even though he didn't care to belong to the PBA.

"So Bucky marched in the St. Patrick's Day parade today?"

"We all did," McNabb said. "Boylan made a big deal about how we needed to make a good showing. For recruitment purposes. We looked pretty sharp too. Kehoe tears it up on that bagpipe of his. You know the guy. He musta played 'Amazing Grace' half a dozen times, though. I think it's the only song he knows. And the marching was kinda raggedy, on account of all the green beer we put away right before the parade. But the green jackets looked sharp. And you shoulda seen Captain Dugan in that sweet little kilt of hers. Swear to God! All of us were praying for a gust of wind."

"Captain Dugan? She's in the Shamrocks?"

"Oh, hell, yeah," McNabb drawled. "That's probably the only reason Deavers joined. If she had wanted him to join NOW, he woulda had a sex change and done it. Lisa Dugan says jump, Deavers, he says, 'How high, hon?' "

"Hey, McNabb!"

We both turned around. The stout woman who'd been cleaning up the ambulance stood stooped in the doorway of it, looking pissed. "You wanna get your ass over here and help get this unit cleaned up? I'm not your mother, you know."

McNabb sighed, threw his cigarette butt into a rain puddle, and ground it out with the toe of his shoe. "Duty calls," he said.

Some time after two — it was way after the mayor left, and only shortly before the chief's bodyguards persuaded her to leave, I went home, for lack of anything else to do.

The house was quiet when I let myself in the back door. I locked up and headed for my bedroom, stopping at Edna's door to listen in. Inside, I could hear Edna's whistling snore and a second set of deep breaths. I knew without looking that we had company; my four-year-old niece Maura, who slept with Edna whenever she came for a spend-the-night.

"Sleep tight," I said, passing by to my own room.

I was sure I wouldn't sleep. I left my soiled clothes in a heap on the floor and I climbed in bed wearing only my panties and one of Mac's old football jerseys. I pulled the quilt over my head and exhaled a long, deep breath. The sob took me by surprise. I curled up in a tight ball, a defense mechanism to keep my terror and grief at bay, but the insistent daggers jabbed away at me until I sat up in the bed and stuffed the corner of the quilt in my mouth to muffle the sobs that would surely wake all of Candler Park.

At some point, I went into the kitchen and got the bottle of Bushmills and a glass and took it back to bed with me. I choked on the first sip of whiskey, but forced it down, hiccuping loudly. When the bottle was half gone, I drifted off to an uneasy sleep.

Whiskey dreams. I was dressed in something floaty, gauzy, whirling over a cloudlike dance floor to the music of a bagpipe. I could hear the music, but I couldn't see the piper, whose form and face were obscured by billowing puffs of clouds. I kept dancing closer, to see who the piper was, but every time I got near, the clouds shifted and the piper drifted away.

It seemed as if I danced for a long time. Finally, the piper disappeared completely, and I lay down on the clouds and drifted off to sleep. But someone was touching me, pulling at me, calling my name.

"Ca'han? Wake up, Ca'han. Want some pannycakes?"

I opened my eyes. Maura was sitting on the bed, patting my face with sticky hands that smelled of maple syrup.

She smiled and I could see that she'd lost another baby tooth since the last time I'd seen her a week ago.

"Gramma says get your lazy bee-hind up!" Maura giggled, pulling at the covers.

I washed my face and hands, pulled on some sweats, and followed my niece into the kitchen, where bacon was frying in a cast-iron skillet and Edna had the radio tuned to a black gospel station.

"Coffee?" I asked hopefully.

She poured some into one of my jadeite coffee mugs and put it before me. "I saw the paper. About Bucky. I'm so sorry, hon. Is that where you were so late last night?"

"Yeah," I said, stifling a yawn.

"It's in the paper," she said, sliding the *Atlanta Constitution*'s front section in front of me. "Says he's in critical condition. And you were right there! It's a wonder you didn't get killed!"

The *Constitution*'s front page was mostly devoted to a coup in some little Eastern European country. But at the bottom of the front page they had managed a five-inch box and a headline announcing POLICE DETECTIVE CRITICAL AFTER LIQUOR STORE SHOOTING. They'd run a fifteen-year-old mug shot that must have been Bucky's graduation photo from the police academy. His hair brushed the collar of his white shirt in the photo, and you could just barely see the gleam of the diamond stud in his right ear. HOMICIDE DET. CHARLES BUCHANAN "BUCKY" DEAVERS.

Edna was reading over my shoulder. "I never knew his middle name was Buchanan."

"Me neither," I said, skimming over the story and feeling a twinge of irrational jealousy that the reporter knew something about Bucky that I didn't.

"There's another story on the local page," Edna said, turning back to the bacon. "Says the department's internal affairs is investigating the shooting."

"Say what?" I pawed through the paper, discarding all the sale circulars and classified sections until I came to the metro section. "Why would internal affairs be investigating? Bucky's the one that got shot. It was a holdup. The shooter was wearing a mask."

Edna stabbed at the sizzling bacon with a long-handled fork. "They don't really say why it's under investigation. Just that it is."

I picked up the phone and dialed Grady's emergency room. I didn't have to look up the number. My sister Maureen had worked at Grady for years before she'd adopted Maura, whose murdered mother had been married to my prodigal brother Brian.

"Patient information, please," I said. The

78

patient information person put me on hold before I could say a word. "Hold, please." I didn't have much choice.

I read the article about the shooting while I was on hold. Edna was right; it didn't say much, just a statement from the chief that it was a new department policy involving any shooting of any Atlanta officer. The article also noted that the chief was "reviewing" the fact that her office hadn't been notified that Bucky was working any part-time job, which was against department policy.

"Christ," I said angrily. Deavers was in the hospital, a bullet in his brain, and the chief was pissed that he hadn't gotten a hall pass before taking on a second job.

"Excuse me?" a voice on the other end of the line said.

"Oh, uh, nothing. Could you tell me the condition of one of your patients? Charles Deavers? He was brought into the emergency room late last night."

She came back on the line a moment later. "I'm sorry, that information isn't being released to the public."

I could have argued with her, but I knew it was useless. "Can you just tell me if he's still alive?" I asked pleasantly.

"His name is in the computer," she said. "That's all I know."

Edna slid a plate in front of me. "Any word?"

"He's apparently still alive," I said, pushing the plate away. "Sorry. I just can't."

She put the plate in front of Maura, who happily dived into the pancakes with both hands. Maura loves pancakes.

I drank my coffee and reread the story in the paper. When I'd finished, I took the cup to the sink and rinsed it out.

"Can you handle things this morning?" I asked Edna. "I've got to go check on Bucky. There's nothing I can do, I know, but I can't stand this feeling of helplessness."

Edna went over to the desk and picked up our daybook. She slid her bifocals down on the end of her nose and glanced over the day's schedule.

She pursed her lips and shook her head.

"What?"

"I promised the Easterbrookses you'd pick them up this morning, and take them over to Bettye Bond's house. They haven't worked in three weeks, and I hate to disappoint them. And after all, Bettye is their client."

"Can't you go?" I asked.

Edna nodded at Maura. "I would, but I don't have her car seat. Please? It won't take more than an hour. They've been up and dressed since six A.M. They called before you got up, just letting me know they were ready."

"I'll go," I said. "But the two of them can't clean Bettye Bond's house by themselves."

"Neva Jean's meeting them over there," Edna said. "And Ruby's coming too, after she gets done with her Thursday morning standing."

Baby and Sister were waiting at the curb in front of the senior-citizen high-rise when I pulled up beside them. They weren't hard to spot. Baby was decked out in a tomato-red Atlanta Falcons sweatsuit and a Dirty Birds baseball cap sporting black feathers winging off the front bill. Sister was dressed in a shapeless cotton housedress worn over what looked like black tights. She wore a pair of brand-new black Converse sneakers, their laces flopping untied, and she had a large plastic shopping bag dangling from her right hand.

"Woo-ooh," Baby called out. "Look who come to pick us up in a fancy new truck." She guided Sister by the elbow, gently inching her toward the door. I hopped out and ran around to open the back door of the van for them. "Hey, Miss Baby. Hey, Miss Sister."

Sister grabbed me and hugged me around the neck. She smelled like lily of the valley and mentholatum cough drops. Her filmy brown eyes twinkled behind the Coke-bottle glasses, and she ran her fingers through my untidy curls in a vain attempt to straighten them. "How come we got the boss lady pickin' us up today? Edna got too fancy for herself?"

"No. We had a big fight over who got to pick you up, and I won 'cause I'm bigger and meaner," I said.

Sister grinned. "I know that's a lie. You might be younger and stronger, but ain't nobody meaner than Edna Mae Garrity."

When I had them safely buckled into the backseat of the van, I headed back toward Druid Hills and Bettye Bond's house.

The girls were, as Edna had predicted, raring to go. They've been working for us ever since we bought the House Mouse, and the two of them, well into their eighties, we guessed, had been cleaning houses in and around Atlanta so long they still remembered streetcars, nickel Cokes, and the bad old days of Jim Crow.

Sister was the older of the two. She'd been legally blind for as long as I'd known her. Baby, the younger, was nearly stone-deaf. When they'd first come to work for us, Baby was still driving, counting on Sister to let her know if there was an ambulance or police car sneaking up on them, or if somebody was honking their horn if Baby lingered too long at a green light. We'd persuaded them to stop driving a couple years earlier, after Baby developed diabetes. Living in a church-run high-rise, and savers their whole lives, neither of them really needed to work, but the Easterbrooks sisters had worked their whole lives, and they weren't about to stop just because they'd already outlived most of their old clients.

Nowadays, we try to give them a job every week or two, and always send along somebody else to help out. Sister likes to polish silver, and Baby can still push a dust mop around, and the two of them are plainly everybody's pets, and they know it.

Sister dug around in the plastic grocery sack. "Know what I got right here? Something special for Miss Bettye's party."

"What's that?" Baby said. "You bring a sack lunch for us?"

"It's something special for the party," Sister said loudly.

"Hope it's some Thunderbird wine," Baby said, chortling and reaching for the bag. "Miss Bettye, she knows how to throw a wingding."

Sister slapped Baby's hand away.

"Thunderbird? Nasty wine for a fine lady's party? You hear that, Callahan? Hear what Miss Baby Easterbrooks be thinkin' about and it ain't even noon? Call herself a Christian and she be wantin' to drink liquor on the job?"

"You never drank no liquor on the job? What you call that little bitty bottle I seen in the bottom of your pocketbook there, Miss Thing?" Baby retorted.

"That's my nerve medicine," Sister said serenely.

"You got a nerve callin' it medicine, and that's a fact," Baby said, getting huffy. She leaned forward in her seat and tapped me on the shoulder. "Callahan, sugar, ask Miss Thing how come her nerve medicine looks and tastes just like King Cotton Peach Brandy?"

"No, Callahan," Sister said softly, whispering. "Ask Miss Baby Easterbrooks how come a girl got saved when she twelve years old knows so much about liquor and such like that. While you at it, why don't you ask Miss High and Mighty what Mama saw that time she come home early from Wednesday night Junior Ambassadors meeting and caught Miss Baby in the parlor sittin' in the pastor's son's lap, and I'm not talking like it was Santy Claus's lap she was a-sittin' on."

"What you say?" Baby hollered. "What she say, Callahan?"

"Girls," I said, stifling a laugh. "Come on, now. Be sweet. What's in the bag, Miss Sister?"

Sister brought out a large doughnut-shaped item wrapped tightly in foil and topped with a red satin bow.

"This here is one of my coconut pound cakes. Miss Bettye, she's a fool for pound cake. When me and Baby worked for her by ourselves, I used to bake her a pound cake every month. Got paid five dollars cash money for it, too. One time, Miss Bettye, she told me, she served that cake at bridge club, told them ladies she made it herself. That's why she had me keep on makin' 'em, 'cause them ladies loved that cake so good. When Edna called and said we was helpin' Miss Bettye get ready for a big do, I got out my pan, and I said, 'Sister, let's bake a cake.' "

"How nice," I said. "Bettye Bond will be thrilled. You two are her favorites."

As promised, Bettye Bond made a big fuss over the Easterbrookses. "Thank God," she said when Sister handed her the cake. "I could eat this whole thing all by myself, Sister. But I won't, 'cause I want to save it for my guests."

"Huh!" Baby said, glowering. "You wanna eat a cake cooked by an old blind lady? How you know she didn't put soap powder 'stead of flour in that cake, like she did last week when she thought she was cookin' grits and instead fixed up a big ol' pan of Comet

Cleanser for breakfast?"

Sister ignored Baby. "You got plenty of silver polish for me, Miss Bettye? I hope so, 'cause Baby over there, all she good for is runnin' her mouth."

I left them with Bettye, promising her reinforcements would be along soon.

It pissed me off, having to go through a metal detector before I could enter the new police headquarters at City Hall East. It pissed me off even more when the uniformed officer searched my purse for hidden knives, guns, or pipe bombs.

We're bomb crazy in Atlanta now. All over the South too, I guess. Ever since some right-wing losers started blowing up abortion clinics and gay nightclubs and even Olympic Centennial Park, there's not a government office in town you can enter without being searched. I knew the reason behind it, but it still pissed me off.

I took the elevator up to the criminal investigation offices. A civilian secretary frowned when I told her, no, I didn't have an appointment to see Major Mackey, and, no, he wasn't expecting me. She smiled smugly when she looked up from the phone. "He can't see you right now. He's with the chief."

There were two ugly orange plastic chairs

pushed against the far wall of the office. I sat down on one of them. "Fine," I said. "Could you call the major and tell him I said I'll wait?"

She didn't like it, but she did it. I'd brought some paperwork along, so I pulled it out of my purse, and started reading the computer printouts. Edna keeps the House Mouse books, and she'd been working on our taxes for the past several weeks. I winced when I saw the numbers. In my old liberal college days, I'd railed against capitalist pigs. Now I was one, although only a very small-potatoes capitalist pig. Still, I hated paying taxes as much as old John D. Rockefeller himself.

A door opened and a woman with blond upswept hair poked her head out. "Miss Garrity. Could you come back now?"

I stood up and followed her down the hall past a warren of small offices and smaller cubicles. She was in her early to mid-thirties, trim, with heavily muscled calves, like a runner or a career tennis player maybe. She wore a conservative navy suit that looked on the expensive side for somebody making a secretary's salary at city hall. The skirt was a hair on the short side, but not aggressively so. She stopped at a door at the end of the hallway and gestured me to go inside. But nobody was behind the desk.

She stepped in behind me, closed the door, and sat down at the desk. That was when I noticed the nameplate on the battered city-issue metal desk.

"Capt. L. E. Dugan," it said. Bucky's new girl.

8

Lisa Dugan was not the kind of cupcake Bucky Deavers usually went in for. I'd never known Bucky to date a woman born in the same decade he was born. Hell, come to think of it, he'd never dated a woman before, just a series of girls. Cute, fun-loving, air-headed girls were the Deavers type.

Captain Dugan was beautiful, but she was no girl. There were fine worry lines at the corners of her hazel eyes, dark circles under those same eyes, and just a hint of sag to her chin. I couldn't help it. What did he see in this chick? I wondered.

She sat back in her chair and watched me watching her. The office was nothing special, just a desk, two chairs, a computer, and a phone. There was a bank of file cabinets behind her desk. A green plant, maybe a philodendron, draped limp leaves over the edge of the cabinet. There were some framed photos, snapshots of Lisa Dugan holding a puppy, Lisa Dugan and a little boy, and another picture of just a little boy. No photos of Deavers.

I felt glad about that. Finally the phone rang. She picked it up, listened, said, "Thanks," and disconnected.

"That was the hospital," she said. "There's been no change." She bit her lip. "Last night I talked to one of the doctors. I guess he figured, since I'm a cop, I could take bad news. He said there isn't going to be a change. Not unless Bucky gets an infection, or pneumonia, something like that."

"Bullshit," I said hotly. "He has no right to say something like that. There are other doctors in this town. This guy doesn't know everything. Bucky talked to me last night, did you know that? He opened his eyes and looked at me and talked. So don't tell me he's brain dead. 'Cause I was there. And I know Bucky. I know how goddamn stubborn he is."

"Stubborn." She said it with a sigh. Then she stuck out her hand and I shook it. "I'm Lisa," she said. "Bucky told me all about you. He kept saying we had to get you over for dinner. Only I suck as a cook. And I felt sort of, I don't know, funny, about meeting you."

"He took me to that party last night so that we could meet," I said. "He talked about you all night long. To tell you the truth, I was getting a little jealous."

She raised an eyebrow.

"We were buddies. Pals. It's just that I

hadn't seen much of him in the past few months. I had no idea he was seriously involved with somebody. But it's not like I was his girlfriend or anything. I never slept with him. He told you that, didn't he?"

"We didn't talk a lot about who he had or hadn't slept with in the past," Lisa said. "We're both adults. I knew he'd had a life before me, and I certainly had one before I met him. We didn't talk about the past at all. But I figured you were special in a different way."

She was trying to butter me up. Why?

"You said the doctor said there wasn't going to be a change," I said. "What's the situation right now?"

She paused.

"Major Mackey said you'd talk to me," I said. "I'm family, you know."

"The bullet was a twenty-two, we think. At least, the entry wound is small, and the gunman left a twenty-two at the scene, so that's what we're assuming. It's still in there, lodged in his brain. The doctor said it did a hell of a lot of damage. He's breathing on a respirator. And they've got him heavily sedated."

I felt numb, thinking about Bucky, in a hospital bed, tethered to a lot of machines.

"What about the girl at the liquor store? I know she's missing. Have they found her yet?"

The friendly look on Lisa Dugan's face vanished as quickly as it had appeared.

"You know I can't talk about that."

"Why not?" I asked. "Who am I going to tell? Come on, Lisa. You say you know how Bucky felt about me. I've got a right to know what's going on with the investigation."

"You were a cop," she said, emphasizing the past tense. "Now you're a civilian. A civilian with a habit of butting her nose into police investigations. But that's not going to happen this time. Major Mackey was very clear about that. And I'm very clear about it." She gave me a level look. The hazel eyes could get very frosty. "Don't fuck this up, Callahan. It's too important. We're gonna find the guy who shot Bucky, and when we do, we want everything right. You know the law. You know if the chain of evidence in this case gets messed with, it's history. So be the friend you claim you are. Go home. Say a prayer for Bucky. Say one for me, too, if you would. And leave it alone."

"I'm not fucking anything up, Lisa. But I'm watching. And I'm listening. I was there when it happened, so it happened to me, too. And I want to know why. Why'd this guy just walk in and put a couple bullets in Bucky's head? He didn't take anything, didn't shoot the clerk, didn't look around to see if there were any other witnesses. He just shoots Bucky and leaves? And half an hour later, the only witness to the shooting also disappears? I got questions, you better believe. Like right now, I'm wondering, why is the chief already calling in internal affairs on this? And what's this bullshit about saying Bucky broke department policy working an unauthorized job?"

Dugan got out of her chair. "No comment," she said.

"Since when do cops have to get the chief's permission to make a living?" I asked. "Cops have always worked second and third jobs."

"No comment," she said again. She opened the door and waited by it. I got up and stalked out of there, no wiser than I'd been when I went in.

9

At the hospital, they'd moved Bucky to the neuro ward. They wouldn't let me see him, but a nurse there who recognized my name said she'd gone to school with my sister Maureen and worked with her in the ER.

"He's stable," said the nurse, whose name was Veneta. "There's a waiting room over there," she added, pointing down the hall. "His doctor makes rounds after lunch, maybe you could catch him then."

I got a Diet Coke from a vending machine and went looking for the waiting room.

The room was small and nearly full. I almost turned around and left when I saw who was sitting in the middle of a green vinyl sofa. John Boylan. He looked up when I came in, gave me a weak wave. Sitting on one side of Boylan was a white guy I didn't recognize, but he had that unmistakable cop look about him: the polished shoes, the erect posture and short hair. On the left of Boylan was C. W. Hunsecker.

He got up when he saw me, we hugged, sat back down.

"You hear anything?" C.W. asked, his voice low.

"He's stable," I said.

C.W. frowned. His blue-green eyes were red-rimmed, and his face was much thinner than the last time I'd seen him. "What's the matter," I said teasingly, "Nickells got you on a diet?"

Linda Nickells was C.W.'s wife and one of my best friends. They were both cops, that is, former cops. C.W. had been captain of the robbery squad when both Bucky and I worked there; Linda, his second wife, was a homicide detective whom I met when I was working for an antiques-dealer client accused of killing a teenage girl.

We had a lot of history, me, C.W., Bucky, and Linda.

C.W. struggled to his feet, reached for his canes. "Let's take a walk," he said, looking around.

It was painful, watching him walk like that. Linda assures me that he isn't in pain, doesn't mind the canes, but it hurts me just the same. The sight of him always reminds me that he needs those canes because of me, because a homicide suspect had shot him when I'd been too slow-moving. After the accident, they'd given C.W. a desk job. Not long after that, he took a disability pension and bought a security business. And not long after that, Linda, worn out from trying to be a good cop and a good mother to their two-year-old son, Wash, had quit too, to work in the security business with C.W.

I followed C.W. out to the vending area. He got a pack of gum, offered me a stick. "Sorry. I didn't feel like talking about Bucky in front of those Irish assholes back there."

"Boylan," I said. "He's not one of my favorites either. The other guy, I don't know."

"You don't know Michael Kehoe?"

I thought about it. "I've heard his name recently, but I don't know the guy."

"You wouldn't," C.W. said. "Kehoe is with the DeKalb S.O."

"Since when did these guys get so tight with Bucky?" I asked. "I never heard him mention them before. And what's with the Irish assholes bit?" I asked. "Remember who you're talking to here, laddie."

"You may be Irish, but you're not one of them," C.W. said. "Sorry. I just can't take their racist bullshit, you know?"

It dawned on me then. "Kehoe. He's the one who's president of the Shamrock Society. With Boylan. Bucky's new best buddies."

Now it was C.W.'s turn to be surprised. "Since when did Deavers get buddy-buddy with those guys?"

"Recently, I guess. Bucky came over last night, wanted me to go to this St. Patrick's Day party they were throwing. He wanted me to meet his new girlfriend. She never showed, but I did have an unhappy reunion with Johnny Boylan."

"Your old boyfriend," C.W. said.

"We went out once. I didn't know he was married. The guy makes my skin crawl. I can't understand how Bucky got mixed up with a loser like Boylan."

"You don't know the half of it," C.W. said.

"What's that supposed to mean?" I wanted to know.

C.W. gestured toward the waiting room. "Those guys — those assholes. Supposed to be some damn Irish-American police fraternal organization — right?"

"I guess. That's how McNabb described it. They march in parades and drink green beer. Harmless fun."

"That's a load of crap," C.W. said vehemently. "Boylan. You know what he's famous for?"

"Besides chasing anything in a skirt? What?"

"Bashing in heads down in the projects. Loves to beat up the brothers, then come back to the squad room, trade nigger jokes with his buddies. He worked for me once, back in the early nineties. I had him transferred down to the airport precinct, get him out of my sight. How he's stayed in the department this long — and the chief's black and knows the score — I don't get it."

"So he's a bigot," I said. "The world's full of bigots, C.W. We Irish do not have the exclusive franchise on hatred."

"Those guys do," C.W. insisted. "They might as well be the Klan. You take a look at their membership roster. All white, all good old boy. All asshole."

C.W. was a third-generation Atlanta police officer. His grandfather was one of the first black officers sworn into service with the city, back in the days when black cops weren't allowed to arrest white citizens or even shower in the same precinct with white officers. But three generations of Hunseckers had made a career of policing, and C.W.'s own career had been pretty impressive until the shooting.

"Hey," I said. "Look at the African American Patrolmen's Association. I don't see any white names on their roster. Does that mean they're racist? Come on, C.W., I can't believe there's anything sinister about a bunch of dumb micks who wanna dress up in kilts and pretend to be leprechauns every March seventeenth. What's the harm?"

C.W. chewed his gum agitatedly. "I hear things, okay?"

"What kind of things?" I asked, wanting to defuse his anger. "Boylan's the one who put the overalls in Mrs. Murphy's chowder?"

"Funny," he said. "But I can't believe you didn't recognize Kehoe's name. Think — you don't remember hearing about a Michael Kehoe a few years back? When the issue was discrimination? Only he charged that it was reverse discrimination?"

I glanced back at the waiting room. One of the men was standing up, reading notices on a bulletin board. He was tall, with thinning blond hair and a high forehead and pants that rode low on bony hips. That Michael Kehoe?

"Okay, I remember," I said. "Didn't he used to be a priest before he went into law enforcement?"

"Not quite a priest," Hunsecker said. "What do you call them before they graduate from priest school?"

"A seminarian."

"Yeah. A seminarian. His summer assignment was to assist as a chaplain in the DeKalb Sheriff's Office. But he liked cop work so much he quit the priesthood and went to the academy instead," Hunsecker said. "He was supposedly in line to be assistant chief deputy, but then he got passed over for the job — by a black guy."

"And Kehoe sued for reverse discrimination and won."

"Won big," Hunsecker said bitterly. "The court ordered the sheriff to make him assistant chief deputy. The other guy, Oscar Braymore, got shoved into some nothing job in warrants. He quit the department; last I heard, he's selling used cars. But Kehoe? He got his back pay plus damages of, what I heard, nearly a million dollars."

"He's a rich man, then," I said, not taking my eyes off Kehoe. "What's he want with some dipshit sheriff's job?"

"Revenge," Hunsecker said. "Wants to stick it in everybody's face. He was a white man and he was wronged and he made 'em pay. Besides, he claims the lawyers got most of the money."

"He must be real popular over at the S.O.," I speculated.

"They made him assistant chief deputy of nothing," Hunsecker said with some satisfaction. "He pushes paper, punches the clock, spends most of his time organizing these Shamrock clowns."

"So Kehoe's a jerk and Boylan's a bigot," I said. "I'll give you that. What kinds of things are you hearing? You never heard anything bad about Bucky, right? You know he wasn't like them."

Hunsecker's face softened. "Deavers. Damn. I don't want to believe anything bad about him. I saw that thing in the *Constitution* this morning. About internal affairs investigating. Then I see Boylan and Kehoe in there, weeping and wailing, it makes me wonder, that's all."

"Wonder what?"

"Nothing," C.W. said. "Let's get out of here. The doctors won't tell us nothing, anyhow, and I'm thinking a chili dog might taste good about now."

I knew what he was thinking about. "Nickells lets you eat that stuff?"

"How's she gonna know unless you rat me out?"

"Okay," I said. "My van's in the garage. I'll fly if you'll buy."

"Deal," he said.

The Varsity sits high atop North Avenue overlooking Interstate 75 and the nearby Georgia Tech campus like an aging fifties battleship. It's probably the last place left in Atlanta with curb service.

I pulled into a slot on the top deck, gave the carhop our order: three chili dogs, an order of rings, a fried apple pie, and a Coke for C.W., and a plain hamburger and Diet Coke for me.

"You getting prissy on me, Garrity?" C.W.

101

asked. "Was a time, you could outeat any-body, anytime."

"Ten years ago," I said. "Right now, my idea of middle-aged crazy is having half-and-half in my decaf espresso."

He shifted his weight in the front seat of the van. I knew he was trying to get comfortable.

"What's so bad you couldn't talk about it in the hospital?" I asked. "You're giving me bad vibes, Hunsecker."

"It's not me putting out the vibes," he replied. "It's those Shamrocks."

"You're getting me mad with all these Irish put-downs," I warned. "If you know something, tell me."

He chewed his chili dog, took a sip of Coke. "I don't know anything. I'm not on the force, and I mind my own business. Don't have many connections anymore. But Linda and her girlfriends, well, you know how gals like to gossip."

I narrowed my eyes. "You're treading on thin ice here, bub."

He sighed. "I'm just trying to tell you how it is. Gossip, or at least that's what we thought. It was just something Linda overheard. The women detectives, they all get together once a month, it's a girls' night out kind of thing. Linda goes, 'cause she misses seeing her girlfriends. Misses the action."

"Don't we all?"

"They were at some Mexican restaurant they always go to. Place has dollar margaritas. It was late, the tequila was flowing pretty good. There were maybe a dozen gals there, all cops or cops' wives. Linda went in the ladies' room, and as she's fixing her makeup, she hears these two women talking, stall to stall. 'Where's Kirstee tonight?' one of the women asks. Kirstee, that's Kirstee Boylan, she's a detective in auto burglary, married to your old boyfriend. She's what? Wife number three or four?"

"Who's counting?" I said.

"Anyway, the other one says, 'She's working security at a bank in Buckhead, at least that's the story she gave me.' And the other gal, she kinda laughs. 'You see that brand-new BMW she's driving? I need me a job like that.' And the other woman says, 'Don't joke. Okay? It's not funny. Somebody's gonna get hurt. I told her she's crazy messing with that shit.'

"Linda tiptoed out, waited around outside to see who the women were. It was two gals who work in vice. Gals Linda's known for years."

"Did she find out what they were talking about?"

"Not that night. She felt funny about asking. Next day, she made some phone calls. Nothing. But you know how Linda gets. She's like a terrier, once she's on something. So she had me make some calls. About Kirstee Boylan. What kind of security work she does."

"And what did you find out?"

C.W. dipped an onion ring in a paper cup of ketchup, then covered it with a frosting of salt. "Nothing. I've got a buddy in records. I had him check. You know, there's a new policy, cops have to have written approval to work off-duty."

"That's what I heard last night. And that's why internal affairs is so interested in Bucky."

"That's just it," C.W. said. "Kirstee Boylan isn't approved to work any off-duty security jobs."

"So she forgot to get her permission slip signed," I said.

"Lots of people forgot a lot of stuff," Hunsecker said. "After I read that story in today's paper, I got curious. Called my buddy back. All of a sudden, Kirstee Boylan's been approved to work two nights a week at the SouthBank branch on Roswell Road. And according to the records, the approval was signed two months ago."

"You're not the only one with friends in the

right places," I observed. "She covered her ass. Got the permission postdated. I still fail to see anything sinister in any of this."

"I run a security business, provide guards to places like banks," Hunsecker reminded me. "We pay our guys ten thirty-five an hour. None of them is driving new cars. And there's no scary stuff involved. It's boring as hell. The worst thing you get is a bunion. So what were those two women talking about?"

"I give up," I said, reaching my hands in the air.

"You're being deliberately dense," C.W. said.

"So educate me."

He leaned forward. "Look. Security guards are my bread and butter. I got twenty, thirty cops working for me. Most of it's nuts-and-bolts stuff. Nightclub bouncers, guys directing traffic during lunch hour in front of the Burger King, guys riding around in little funny cars outside the mall, maybe work Wrestlemania over at the Georgia Dome. My guys don't get rich. They use the money to supplement their incomes. Buy a secondhand car for their kid, pay orthodontists' bills, alimony, child support, take the family to Disney World on vacation."

"Yeah?" I was trying, but I still wasn't making the connection.

"I'm black, right?"

"So you say. Although the green eyes always make me wonder."

"Honky in the woodpile," C.W. said. "Anyway, just because it's the way these things work out, most of the guys who work for me are also black. We got a few white dudes, but mostly my contracts are on the South Side, and my guys live on the South Side, and they're black."

"Racist pig."

"Probably," C.W. said mildly. "Lately, my guys are hearing things. Like, the white guys, they're pulling down some heavy change working security. Banks, stores, restaurants, clubs. Mostly on the North Side."

"Maybe some security company on the North Side is paying more."

"Uh-uh," C.W. said, shaking his head. "I checked. These guys work directly for the owners, not for a security company. At least that's the story they tell anybody who asks. See, I had one of my guys ask a white buddy of his how could he get a good security job like he had. The white guy got all jumpy about it. Said he didn't know about any security jobs."

"So?"

"The white guy's name was Hurley. He's one of those Shamrocks. They got a gig,

Callahan. I don't know what it is, but it's some kind of gig, and it's something smells bad to me."

"And you think Bucky was in on something bad, too? Because he worked an off-duty security job, and he's white, and happened to join some fraternal organization because his new girlfriend wanted him to? Please."

"All right," C.W. said. "Don't believe me."

He ate another onion ring, took a bite of chili dog, wiped his mouth with his paper napkin.

He gave me a sidelong glance. "What's this about Bucky joining because of his new girlfriend?"

"See?" I said. "Now will you listen to me? I talked to one of the paramedics at Grady last night. He's in the Shamrocks. He marched in the parade with Bucky yesterday. His name's McNabb."

"Jimmy McNabb," C.W. said. "I know him."

"McNabb said Bucky only joined because Lisa Dugan is in it. You know how Bucky is. He never joins anything. He just did it because she wanted him to. What you boys call pussy-whipped, I guess."

He let that slide. "You ever meet this girlfriend?"

"Met her for the first time this morning. I

don't think we're going to be best friends."

"I've heard about her. What's she like?" C.W. asked. "Never known Deavers to date a cop before."

"She's nothing like any of his other girls," I said. "Older. Smarter. I gather she has a kid. Very professional-acting. A career gal, I'd say. She has an accent, not Southern. And definitely not from around here."

"Yet she made captain. And in homicide," C.W. mused. "She went very far, very fast."

"That occurred to me too," I said. "Does Linda know her?"

"Not really," he said. "Linda told me about Lisa Dugan when she got the promotion. She says this woman doesn't hang with the other gals. Keeps herself to herself."

"But she joined the Shamrock Society. Doesn't seem to fit."

"Maybe she likes green," C.W. said.

We went back to the hospital after lunch. Maureen's buddy Veneta was on the phone when we walked up. She put her hand over the receiver.

"Your friend's been moved upstairs," she said. "That's the only news I have. His pulse and heart rate are steady. He's still on the respirator."

She saw the look of disappointment on my face, and gave me a sad smile.

"You know the story, don't you?"

"Story?"

"He's not going to wake up," Veneta said gently. "It's sad, but it's true. We try to tell families that, but nobody wants to believe it. They always want to believe in miracles."

I bit my lip. "A miracle wouldn't hurt, would it?"

When I left the hospital, I ran to the parking lot, dodging greasy rain puddles. I started the van, couldn't think what to do next. The Varsity hamburger sat like a rock on my gut. The burger wasn't the only thing upsetting me. C.W. had me all confused, and now they were saying Bucky wouldn't make it, no matter what.

It occurred to me that maybe some good hard physical labor would be in order.

I called Edna from my cell phone. "Everything cool at your end?"

"Everything's a disaster at my end," Edna said. "You won't believe where Neva Jean is."

"Not at Bettye Bond's?"

"I wish," Edna said fervently.

"How about Betty Ford's?"

"They don't put people in rehab for drinking Mountain Dew," Edna said tartly. "But you were close. She's in jail."

"What jail? What did she do? What did Swannelle do?"

Swannelle is Neva Jean's husband. Where goest Neva Jean, goest Swannelle, and unfortunately for us, where goest Swannelle goest a shitload of trouble.

"They're down in Hapeville," Edna said. "I didn't get all the particulars. But it was Swannelle that called, and he wasn't in jail, so I guess it was just Neva Jean that got arrested. There was some trouble at a bar they were at. Mulroney's, or something like that. Anyway, he wanted me to go to the bank and get some money to bail Neva Jean out, but I can't go, because I've still got Maura."

"I see. Does that mean I need to get down to Hapeville?"

"I believe I would," Edna said. "Let me know what happens."

10

Swannelle McCoomb is a scrawny guy, 120 pounds of grease and grit. Neva Jean calls him "a lover, not a fighter." But you don't want to get him riled up. He was riled up now.

His face kept getting redder and his high-pitched voice kept getting louder as he leaned farther across the desk to make his point to the clerk sitting behind it. His thinning brown hair was sprinkled with green glitter and brushed back from his forehead in his trade-mark Conway Twitty pompadour with the Elvis Presley ducktail in the back. He wore a kelly-green sweatshirt that said "I'm Irish — Kiss My Grits." His pants bagged in the seat and were cut off at the knees, where they were met by bright orange wool socks. He wore green shoes that turned up at the toes with lit-tle bells that jingled when he stomped his foot, which he was doing right now. He was the man of every woman's dreams — at least in his own mind.

"I done tol' you," he hollered, "my wife is

111

gonna lose her job if you don't let her out of there right this minute. Now, lemme see the police chief or somebody can tell me something right."

"Swannelle?" I put my hand on his shoulder. He wheeled around and had his fist cocked, ready to take a swing at me. Instead, he grinned broadly when he saw who it was.

"Hey, Callahan," he said, grabbing my arm. "You wanna tell this heifer 'bout the mistake they made arresting my wife?" He jerked his thumb in my direction. "This here's a private investigator we've put on retainer until we get this mess straightened out."

I felt my face burning. "Uh, Swannelle, why don't we just get Neva Jean's fine paid and then we can discuss this later?"

"Fine?" he squawked. "Why are we gonna pay these Mickey Mouse Keystone Kops a fine for false arrest of my innocent wife?"

The clerk, a sixtyish white woman with dyed black Mamie Eisenhower bangs, sat back in her chair and gave Swannelle a deadpan look that said she'd seen and heard it all, and none of it made the slightest bit of difference to her.

"How much is the fine?" I asked, unzipping my pocketbook.

She looked down at the sheet of paper in

front of her. "Let's see, public indecency, that's two hundred dollars. Destruction of property comes to another two hundred thirty dollars, according to the complainant."

"Two hunnerd and thirty dollars?" Swannelle hollered. "For what? A couple of cheap pictures and a lamp the Salvation Army wouldn't take?"

The clerk didn't blink. "They got it all wrote down right here. Tiffany lamp, seventy-five dollars; glassware, fifty dollars; commode, seventy-five dollars; mirror, thirty dollars."

"That commode wasn't worth no seventy-five dollars," Swannelle said, slapping his hand on the counter. "It didn't even flush. And it was not my wife's fault that lamp got broke. She wasn't even aimin' for the lamp."

I counted out the bills, put them on the counter, pushed them across to the clerk, who didn't bat an eye. She re-counted the money, wrote out a receipt, and handed it back across to me. She turned around, opened a drawer in a cabinet behind me, and handed across a manila envelope.

"That's the suspect's personal belongings," the clerk said. "Inventory is on the front of the envelope. Wedding ring, keys, Swiss Army knife, mace, tear gas spray, and a wallet containing eleven dollars and forty-two cents.

The officer confiscated the brass knuckles and the numchucks. They're illegal in this county."

Swannelle grabbed the envelope and tore it open. "I wanna see that ring. Make sure they didn't swap Neva Jean's diamond for some hunk of glass." He looked up, gave the clerk the fish-eye. "That's a flawless eighth of a karat pink diamond in that ring. Nobody better have tried the old swap-arooney."

He held the ring up to the light, examined it, gave the clerk another fish-eye, then put it in his pocket.

The clerk picked up the phone, punched an extension, told somebody, "Mrs. McCoomb can be released now."

He started to say something, but just then the door opened and a uniformed police officer brought Neva Jean into the lobby.

"Swannelle?" Neva Jean fell into his arms, covering him with kisses. He wrapped his arms around her, or as much of her as his arms could get around, and patted her hair, which had streaks of green and orange in it and stood out like some sort of oversized bird's nest.

She was dressed in a faded blue jumpsuit that had "Hapeville City Jail" stenciled across the back and she was sobbing and had thick black streaks of mascara running down her face. It was a deeply touching moment.

"Are you okay, muffin?" Swannelle asked tenderly. "They didn't work you over with no hoses or nothin', did they?"

"It w-a-as aw-haw-ful," Neva Jean wailed, hiccuping between syllables. "They didn't have no cable or nothin'."

Swannelle's face got hard. He stomped over to the counter. "My attorney will be in touch with you people. In the meantime, you people better be thinking about a little matter we call false arrest."

Edna poured a can of Mountain Dew over a glass of ice and handed it to Neva Jean.

"Nice and slow now, Neva Jean," she instructed. "Tell us what happened last night."

Neva Jean took a long slurp of Mountain Dew. We'd gotten her cleaned up a little, and most of the green hair dye was gone, but she still didn't look like anything you'd want to meet in a back alley.

Neva Jean might look like a two-dollar trailer tramp, but, as Edna often reminded me, she has a heart of gold. Or maybe it was brass. She was our first employee, had actually come with the House Mouse, like the original pink Chevy van and our first client list. She was unpredictable, unreliable, and unbeatable when you finally got her down to cleaning houses.

"We heard on the radio, Y106 — y'all ever listen to Rhubarb Jones? — that they was having a contest down at Mulroney's in Hapeville, for St. Patrick's Day. The person who pulled the craziest stunt to get Rhubarb's attention would win a thousand bucks, plus two front-row tickets to see Hank Williams, Jr. And you know how Swannelle is about Hank Williams, Jr."

Edna rolled her eyes. We knew.

"So Swannelle had one of his most fabulous ideas ever. He says, 'Hon? We gonna get me up like a leprechaun, and you gonna be my little pot o' gold?' Get it? pot o' gold? You would not believe how hard that man worked on those costumes. I had no idea he was that good with a glue gun and a can of spray paint. We took pictures, too." She reached for her suitcase-sized pocketbook. "Y'all wanna see?"

"Maybe later," I said. "I for one would like to hear how a leprechaun and his pot o' gold manage to get themselves arrested for public indecency and destruction of property."

Neva Jean sniffed. "I didn't want to hurt Swannelle's feelings, after he worked so hard on the costumes and all, but after he got done with my pot o' gold costume, and we got me into it, I realized he'd forgotten something important. Being a man, it wasn't something he'd take into consideration."

"A trap door?" Edna is wise in many ways of the world.

She nodded. "It wouldn't have been so bad, but we got to the bar, and I was feeling funny, wearing that big old nail keg sprayed gold and it was kinda short — me being a full-figured gal and all. So I was drinking that green beer pretty good to get over my shyness. And they was lining up all the contestants, so Rhubarb could get a good look at us all, just as soon as he got there. And that's when the trouble started."

"What happened?" I asked.

"There was this woman — I don't know what she was supposed to be, unless maybe it was a green Marilyn Monroe. I mean, she was all green — green hair, green face, green legs, and big old green titties spillin' out of that slutty dress of hers. And she kept rubbin' up against Swannelle, putting her hands on him, askin' him did he wanna kiss her Blarney stone. The way women always want to do."

"It's a terrible problem for Swannelle, all that animal magnetism," Edna said.

"And I was getting pretty mad about it," said Neva Jean. "I mean, I'm standing right there. And then this drunk at the bar, he kept picking my gold coins and eatin' 'em."

"Some guy was eating your gold coins?" I asked. I had no idea the bar scene by the

117

airport was so kinky.

"They were foil-wrapped chocolates," Neva Jean explained. "The kind Jewish kids get for Hanukkah. It was the only kind Swannelle could find at the Buy-Rite on such short notice. Anyway, this fella was ruinin' my costume, so I asked him real nice to stop, only he wouldn't. And you know me, I don't like to make a scene, so I told Swannelle, 'Watch my beer. I'm going to the bathroom.' "

"This is gonna be the part where we get to the public indecency, I bet," I told Edna.

She looked at her watch. "I hope so. It's almost two o'clock. My stories are fixin' to come on TV pretty soon."

"I had to pee real bad," Neva Jean explained. "But there was a long line outside the ladies' room. And even though I explained real nice about how I was in a hurry and I didn't wanna miss Rhubarb Jones's judging, none of them bitches would let me cut in line. And by now, my eyeballs are floating in green beer. So I hollered over to Swannelle, come help me."

"And did he?" Edna asked.

Neva Jean sighed. "There wasn't nobody in line for the men's room. He pointed that out right away. So he says, 'Hon, you go on in there and go. Nobody cares.' But the lock was broke. So he goes, 'Hon, I'll stand out here and guard the door, and you go on in there and get out of that nail keg.'

"So I did," Neva Jean said. "But I was having a heck of a time gettin' out of it. Me bein' so full-figured and all. Finally I got it off, and I'm standing in that men's room, trying to figure out what to do about the urinal, and then I hear a lot of yellin' and hollerin' outside the door. And Swannelle, he's yellin', 'Come on, Neva Jean, Rhubarb's here and we're gonna miss the judging.' And the next thing the door opens, and some big old guy is staring at me — me standing there in my green panties and not much else."

"I thought Swannelle was guarding the door," Edna said.

"He was, but this guy was bigger then he was, and I guess he really had to go. He got me by the hand and pushed me right out of that bathroom, me in my panties and green hair."

"Into the bar?" Edna asked.

"I told you this was where the public indecency part came in," I said.

"It coulda been worse," Neva Jean said, "but hardly anybody was paying attention to me by then, because Rhubarb Jones was there, and he was beginning to judge the contest. Only my pot o' gold was in the men's room. And Swannelle was so set on winning that contest . . ."

Edna looked at her watch again and sighed. "I'm missing *As the World Churns.*"

"Cut to the chase, Neva Jean," I urged.

She took another long swig of Mountain Dew. "Anyway, I banged on the door, asked the guy real nice to give me back my nail keg, and he wouldn't answer, so I pulled the door open, and he threw the nail keg at me, and I got mad, and tried to bonk him over the head with it, but he ducked and I missed, and I kinda broke the toilet in two with the nail keg."

"Must have been a pretty big nail keg, bust a toilet," Edna said.

"She's pretty full-figured, Ma," I said.

"I screamed for Swannelle, but he didn't hear me 'cause of all the ruckus, and because he had his face pushed into that Marilyn Monroe's green titties, and that made me mad, so I kinda threw the nail keg at him — just to get his attention, mind you, and it missed, and I hit this lamp and knocked over some glasses behind the bar, and the next thing I know, cops were streaming into the place, and they grabbed me and threw me in the car and told me I was under arrest for public indecency."

"And destruction of property," I added.

11

Neva Jean swore she was too frazzled from spending a night in the slammer to even consider helping Baby and Sister to clean Bettye Bond's house. Edna gave me that look. It's a real time-saver, that look of hers. Without it, we might spend forty-five minutes to an hour bickering over a particularly sticky issue. But when Edna gives me the look, I go.

So I went. And it was a good thing. When I got there, Bettye Bond was cutting the crusts off a plate of cheese sandwiches and Baby and Sister were ensconced in easy chairs in the den, sipping Cokes and watching *As the World Churns*.

"The poor dears are just worn out from all that silver polishing," Bettye said apologetically. "I was just fixing them a little something."

I let the girls have their tea party while I attacked the house. I started with the bathroom on the top floor, and by five-thirty I'd worked all the way down to the ground floor, mopping, scrubbing, dusting, and polishing as I went.

Bettye stood in the foyer and sniffed appreciatively. "Heaven," she said. "Callahan, there's just no better smell than a clean house. I think I love this fragrance better than any perfume in all of Paris."

I modestly agreed. The late-afternoon sun was filtering in the big Palladian window in the foyer and the newly cleaned glass sparkled like diamonds. The mahogany handrail of the staircase gleamed under a light coat of lemon wax, and the deep red Oriental rug under our feet had been shaken and vacuumed and replaced on the oak floor, which I'd just finished damp mopping.

Bettye paid me and tipped the girls so royally they gasped at the wad of bills she pressed into their hands. Really, it was too bad I had to take her money. Women like Bettye Bond are becoming increasingly rare around Atlanta. She's the kind of customer I love, the kind who really understands and appreciates the fine art of domesticity. Bettye had inherited beautiful silver, crystal, and furniture from her mother-in-law and her own mother, and she took good care of her things.

Later, say around May, I knew the girls and I would be back for a two-day spring cleaning. Bettye would work right along beside us, and we would get the handsome old house ready for summer, taking down the heavy damask draperies in the downstairs rooms, rolling up the Orientals and storing them in lavender-scented trunks in the attic. We would clear the tabletops of Bettye's collections of majolica, porcelain snuffboxes, and silver-framed family photographs. In their place we would hang simple linen drapes, arrange sisal rugs, and scatter sun-bleached seashells.

"Ooh-wee," Sister exclaimed once she was strapped into the backseat of the van. "You see how much Miss Bettye done give me?"

"How much?" I asked.

"Fifty dollars, cash money," Sister said.

"What's that?" Baby screeched. "You sayin' she done paid you as much as me and all you done all day is set in that chair and complain about your so-called nerves?"

"At least I was polishing silver while I was a-settin'," Baby retorted. "I didn't see you do a lick of work, and that's a fact."

"Pull over right there, Callahan, darlin', would you?" Sister asked. We were stopped at a light in Midtown.

"What for?" I asked. The girls' high-rise was still several blocks away.

"Just wanna do a little grocery shoppin' before we go home, since I got all this cash money," Sister said.

I looked, but all I saw in the direction she was pointing was a liquor store.

"See that," Baby said, shaking her finger in Sister's face. "All she think about is that likker, likker, likker."

Sister shook a finger right back at her. "Likker don't got nothin' to do with it. I need to go in that store there and get my Lotto ticket. That's my lucky store. You just jealous 'cause you know I hit the lotto last week and won me eighty-eight dollars."

It had gotten dark and the only person in sight was a homeless man who was slumped against the wall outside the store. And I didn't care if I never saw the inside of another liquor store. I clicked the power lock button. "Sorry, girls," I said. "No time tonight. But you call Edna tomorrow, and she'll take you to the Kroger and you can buy all the Lotto tickets you want."

Once I had the girls safely off-loaded at the senior citizen high-rise, I headed for my own house.

I called the hospital from my cell phone. This time the patient information person couldn't have been nicer. "Mr. Deavers is in serious condition," she said.

The house was empty except for the smell of chocolate chip cookies. Edna always baked when Maura was over. There was a Tupperware container of Toll House cookies on the counter and a note on the kitchen table. "Gone to bingo. Leftovers in fridge."

Leftovers, hah. I poured myself a tall glass of milk and took the cookie jar into the den. I found the remote control and began surfing channels in between dunking the cookies in the milk and enjoying my favorite subversive activity.

I watched one of those entertainment news shows for a while. They were full of speculation about who would win in the upcoming Academy Awards. Since I hadn't seen a single nominated movie I got bored after a while and started surfing again.

One of the talking heads on Channel 2 was droning on about a property-tax rollback in DeKalb County. On Channel 11, they were droning about some bill the General Assembly was trying to pass. Channel 5 was just droning, period. It struck me how similar all the talking heads were. It's some kind of law in Atlanta television; all the anchor teams are black/white combinations: older, fatherly white guy paired with younger, attractive, but professional black chick. Every single news channel in Atlanta had identical, interchangeable anchor teams. Some of the teams had, in fact, switched team members more than once.

Maybe I was dozing when I heard Bucky's name mentioned. I sat up, nearly spilled my milk.

It was Channel 2's investigative reporter, a serious-faced Geraldo Rivera clone.

"Channel 2's news has learned exclusively that Atlanta Police now believes that the police detective wounded in an apparent liquor store holdup last night may have had some involvement in the robbery itself."

"What?" I screamed, sending the Tupperware and cookies flying.

"In a startling new development in the case, sources close to the police told Channel Two tonight that investigators with the APD's internal affairs division have new information that seems to implicate homicide detective Charles 'Bucky' Deavers in a crime spree that may have involved at least half a dozen robberies at automated teller machines in and around the city," the reporter said.

"Channel 2's will keep viewers posted on the case as new leads develop," the reporter said.

The phone started ringing as soon as I switched channels.

It was Hunsecker. "You see what Dave Kaycrest was saying on Channel Two just now?"

"I saw it, but I don't believe it," I said. "It's bullshit, C.W. Bucky never robbed anybody. Who the hell is behind this? Do you hear anything?"

Silence. "You don't want to know what I'm hearing," C.W. said.

"Tell me," I demanded. "I want to know what kind of shit the cops are trying to hang on him."

He sighed. "You're not gonna like it. Hell, I don't like it. Bucky worked under me. I trained the guy. It hurts me as much as it hurts you."

"Just tell me."

"What I'm hearing, it's just bits and pieces. See, they been having these robberies at ATM machines. But not your typical kind, where the bad guys stake out a machine and stick up the first person walks up to get some money out. This is different. All the robberies have been of businesspeople going to the machines to make their night deposit. Big money. Cash, like six, seven thousand. These guys, that's all they hit. They wait till the manager of a bar or a restaurant or a store goes to the ATM to make the deposit, bang — they jump out, wearing masks, pointing guns, they take the money away. No shooting, no alarms, nothing. What I hear, there have been eight or nine robberies like that. All around the city."

"Bank robberies? How come this is the first we're hearing about it?"

"It ain't technically a bank robbery," C.W.

pointed out. "That's the beauty of it. See, the bad guys hit before the money ever gets inside the bank. No bank robbery, no FBI. That's why the cops been keeping it so quiet. Three or four of these hits happen, it's interesting. This many hits, of this much money — the cops start wondering how come the bad guys are so smart."

"How does Bucky tie into any of this?" I asked. "He was shot at a liquor store. And I was right outside, waiting in the car. Even if he was up to something fishy, why would he do it with me around? Why him?"

"I don't know," C.W. said. "Maybe because he was working that security job at the liquor store. That guy who owns the store, the Greek. I forget his name. He got hit three or four months ago, trying to make a deposit at an ATM in Little Five Points."

"This is all wrong, C.W.," I insisted. "I'm telling you, Bucky wouldn't anymore pull a robbery than I would. He was a cop, C.W. One of the good guys. There's something else behind this."

"Like what?" C.W. asked.

"I don't know. Listen, there's something I forgot to tell you, something they haven't mentioned in the news. There was a witness in the store that night."

"Who?"

"The clerk. A young girl named Deecie. Deecie Styles. She was working the counter when the shooter ran into the store. She saw the guy."

"So what's the problem?"

"The problem is she's gone. She ran off right after the cops got there. She's got a baby. A little boy, not even a year old. One minute she was there, the next minute, in all the confusion, the store swarming with cops, she'd vanished. And C.W., that's not all. There was a surveillance camera mounted above the cash register. She took the videotape with her. And about twelve hundred dollars in cash, from the store's safe."

"I'll be damned," C.W. said. "I got some good sources, but nobody said a word to me about a girl."

"You know Ellis Washington?"

"I know him," C.W. said. "Worked with him for a couple years before I quit. He's a good man."

"He's the one who told me Deecie Styles was missing," I said. "Mackey was furious when he found out Washington told me about it. He made me promise to keep my mouth shut about her."

"Some chance of that," Hunsecker said.

"Washington made it sound like the girl planned the whole thing," I said. "But I don't buy it. I was there, C.W. She was completely unhinged. And she had a baby with her. None of this makes any sense to me."

C.W. laughed. "What's wrong with you, Garrity? You were a cop once. Since when does robbery or homicide make sense? It never makes sense. All this talk about master criminals, evil genius. That's a bunch of crap and you know it. Most of these bad guys, they're just lazy, stupid fuck-ups. Shit happens, that's all. This time, the shit happened to somebody we care about."

"Bucky wasn't stupid. He wasn't lazy and he wasn't a fuck-up," I said. "And he wasn't a criminal, either. This afternoon, you said something. You said the white cops had something going, some kind of scam with security jobs. You still think that's true?"

"Maybe," he said cautiously. "So what if it is?"

"What if Bucky somehow got mixed up in the scam? What if he knew something he wasn't supposed to know? And that's what got him shot?"

C.W. snorted. "You got an overactive imagination, Garrity. It's a scam, that's all. These assholes got a little gig that's against department policy. But it ain't nothing that big. Ain't nothing could get Bucky shot. It's just business as usual."

"I don't think so," I insisted. "That girl, Deecie. She didn't run because she'd stolen the money. She ran because she was scared. Scared of what she'd seen."

"A safe full of twenties is what the girl saw," Hunsecker said. "What you call your crime of opportunity."

"No. There's something else. That girl saw something she shouldn't have."

"What if she did? You gonna track her down and ask her about it? That's why we got a police department, Garrity. You take my advice, you mind your own damn business. Stay out of it, you hear?"

"I hear," I said. But my mind was already racing.

"C.W.," I said, "you being in the security business, do you do pre-employment screening for your clients?"

"Sure," he said. "Drug testing, credit history, lie detector tests, all like that. That's Linda's specialty. You oughtta see her on the computer. You give her a modem and a data base, there ain't nothin' she can't find. Why do you ask? You fixin' to start doin' urine testing on all those ladies working for your cleaning business?"

"I might," I said.

12

I sat and brooded about Bucky for a long time. Finally, I got out a yellow legal pad and started to doodle, a habit I have when I'm trying to bring order to a world of chaos.

The facts were few — but brutal. Bucky had been shot twice in the head. A cheap .22 had been found at the crime scene. The only real witness to the shooting was a hysterical teenager named Deecie Styles. Her account of the shooting had been brief — a lone, masked gunman who said nothing and took no notice of the terrified clerk. And now Deecie Styles had vanished.

What else did I have? Questions. A long list of questions and doubts and damn few answers. Looking down at my notes, I was forced to admit maybe the police brass were justified for having their own doubts about Bucky.

What really had happened at the Budget Bottle Shop last night? Only twenty-four hours had passed, but the details didn't seem to hang together. I tried to make a sketch of the store layout, but the only thing I drew was a blank. Every time I tried to summon up a vision of the store, it came out in fragments, the green linoleum floor, the smashed beer bottles, the Plexiglas-enclosed cashier cage, the glimpse of winking red and blue lights outside in the parking lot.

I had to go back. I had to see the store again and make it real.

I was in the bedroom getting dressed when I heard the back door open.

I stiffened, looking around for some kind of weapon. My 9-mm Smith & Wesson was in the pantry, of course, locked away in a box on a high shelf where Maura's prying fingers couldn't reach it.

"Callahan? You home?" I relaxed. It was all right. The intruder was Mac. Only Mac.

"Be out in a minute," I called, pulling a heavy cable-knit sweater over my head.

I met him in the living room, put my arms around his waist, tilted my head back, and took a good long look.

"What?" He was amused. Gave me a nice long kiss. "Have I got spinach in my teeth? Spaghetti sauce in my beard?"

"Nope," I said. "I missed you. That's all. Just want to make sure you're still the same."

He was. I've always been glad Andrew MacAuliffe came into my life when he was already in his mid-forties, ten years older than I. I'd grown tired of men who were fixer-uppers, or worse, merely boys — big immature babies wearing grown-up clothes.

Mac was no handyman's special. I liked him the minute we met. I liked his bushy silver beard and wavy gray hair, the blue-gray eyes with deep laugh crinkles at the corners. I liked his chapped, weather-beaten hands and the way he looked in a good dark business suit, and the way he looked, even better, bare-chested, wrapped in a towel just coming out of the shower.

"I missed you too," he said, kissing me again, as if to prove it. "Didn't Edna tell you I called last night? I waited up till midnight, thinking you might call back."

"Last night? Oh, God. You didn't hear about Bucky?"

"I saw it this morning in the *Constitution*. I picked up the paper at the airport when I got in. I'm so sorry, babe. It's bad, isn't it?"

My eyes brimmed with tears. I nodded. "The doctor, this one know-it-all, he says it's really bad. That Bucky won't make it. There's a lot of brain damage, they say. But Mac, last night, right after it happened, Bucky opened his eyes. He looked right at me. And he talked. He knew it was me. He asked me, 'What's happening?' So it can't be as bad as they say, can it?"

Mac knew what I wanted to hear, but unlike me, he's a terrible liar.

"I don't know, Callahan," he said slowly. "Two bullets lodged in the brain? And I heard somewhere that the smaller bullets do more damage than bigger ones. But maybe you're right. Weirder things have happened."

For the first time he noticed the heavy sweater. "You going out?"

"Back to the liquor store," I said. "The Budget Bottle Shop. Last night, everything was a blur. It all happened so fast. I can't make sense of anything. So I need to go back, try to process it all."

He frowned. "Why? It's a police investigation, Callahan. Let them work it. They've got the equipment, the manpower, everything. You told me before, if a cop gets hurt or killed in the line of duty, nobody rests until the perp is brought in."

"You don't understand," I said. "The cops are already trying to say Bucky was involved in something that got him shot. Some sort of bogus robbery spree. I was there, Mac. It's a crock of shit. Bucky would never have gotten mixed up in something like that. And even if he had, he wouldn't have brought me along for the ride. He knows me better than that."

Mac shook his head, put his jacket on again.

"You going home?" I asked.

"I'm going to the liquor store. With you."

"You haven't asked me how it went in Nashville."

I looked at him sideways. We were stopped at a light. "I'm not sure I want to know."

Mac and I have had our ups and downs over the years. We'd split up once, for a year, after he'd admitted having a one-night fling with his ex-wife. But the past few years things had smoothed out. We live in separate houses in separate parts of Atlanta, coming together when we want to, staying apart when we need to. We'd gotten mellow and really good together.

The previous Friday, while we were having dinner in his cabin in the woods north of town, I'd gotten blindsided.

"Got a call today," he said slowly. He sat back in his chair and his blue eyes were watching me closely.

"Yeah?"

"You ever been to Nashville?"

"I went to Opryland once. Drove past Johnny Cash's house. Saw Tanya Tucker buying a cherry Slurpee at a convenience store off the Briley Parkway."

"I'm going to Nashville on Monday," he told me. "Thought maybe you could ride up there with me."

"Didn't they close Opryland?"

"Just the theme park. Actually, I wasn't thinking about that. I was thinking about interviewing for a job."

"In Nashville?"

He ran his fingers through his hair. He needed a haircut. "In Nashville. They've just created a new position, metro planning and zoning manager. A guy called me about it this morning. They've been quietly checking me out. Want me to come up and talk to the commissioners who do the hiring."

"You've already got a job," I pointed out, feeling dread, panic, alarm.

"I'm a political football in Atlanta," Mac said. "We're strictly an advisory board at the Atlanta Regional Commission. Developers and politicians are gonna pave this town over, and I'm starting to think there's nothing anybody can do to stop it."

"You can. You do," I said. "You stopped that mega-mall from coming in down in Henry County."

"They're going to move it to Cherokee County," Mac pointed out. "The county commission chairman's got four hundred acres for sale just outside Canton. It's the same old thing. Nashville's different. They've rewritten the county charter, given some real teeth to zoning and land-planning ordinances."

I poured myself another glass of wine. I was drinking Chardonnay. The red stuff gives me a rash.

"What do you say?" he asked, leaning forward.

"I think I'm never setting foot in that mall in Cherokee County," I said, feeling my cheeks get hot.

"About Nashville. About me moving there. About you going with me."

I swallowed. "You want me to leave Atlanta." It was a fact, not a question.

"I want you to go with me. Just think about it, will you? If you go up there with me Monday, you could drive around, look at some neighborhoods, kind of get the feel of the place."

I drank my Chardonnay and a whole glass of water, then I helped myself to his red wine. Rash be damned.

"I've lived in Atlanta my whole life," I said feebly.

"Me, too," Mac said. He reached over and took my hand. "It's not Katmandu, you know. Nashville's what? Five, six hours up the road?"

"That's a long way," I said. "What about the dogs?"

"Rufus and Maybelline aren't particular about where they live, as long as there's trees to pee on and a bone to chew."

"What about Edna? I can't just move off and leave her."

"She'd come with us," Mac said, like he'd planned out the whole thing. "We'll get a place with a mother-in-law's suite. Like an apartment. She'd love it. You know she's crazy about country music. Every time I come in the house she's watching TNN."

"She's crazy about the cable network, not the town," I said. "You'll never get Edna to move. Not again. I don't believe dynamite could get her out of this house."

"Why don't we ask her?" Mac said. He got up and came around the table and started kissing my neck. He can be very persuasive that way. We never did finish dinner. Just before I fell asleep, he snuggled up to me again and whispered in my ear. "Just think about it. Okay?"

Come Monday, I begged off the trip to Nashville. Too much stuff going on with the House Mouse was the reason I gave. I'd thrown some things in a suitcase, made some halfhearted notes to Edna about what needed doing, but when Mac pulled into the driveway in his Blazer, my stomach knotted up and I thought I'd puke.

I met him at the door, shaking my head. I think he halfway expected me to wimp out.

"What now?" He was matter of fact, not angry.

"Big charity fund-raiser at Bettye Bond's house this Saturday. She wants the place hosed down, attic to cellar. The place is nine thousand square feet. There's no way the girls can handle it without me."

He kissed the tip of my nose. "But you're still thinking about it — right?"

"I'm thinking."

"Did you mention it to Edna?"

"Not yet."

"Coward. I'll be back Thursday," he promised. "Talk to Edna, will you?"

"They offered me the job," Mac said quietly.

"Why wouldn't they? You're the best there is."

"Did you talk to Edna about it?"

I bit my lip. "There wasn't time. We've been so busy, and then with what's happened to Bucky . . ."

I looked over at him pleadingly. "You didn't say yes, did you?"

"Not yet," Mac said. "They have to take a

formal vote at their public hearing next month. But as far as they're concerned, the job's mine if I want it."

"I guess the question is, do you want it?"

He kept his eyes on the road. "I want the job. But I don't want to go to Nashville alone. I want you and Edna to go with me."

"Your job," I said, feeling my throat tighten. "We keep talking about your job. You seem to forget I have a business here. Remember? The House Mouse? And what about the girls? And my clients? I can't just walk away from all that, Mac."

"You could sell the House Mouse. It's a going concern. You could start a new business in Nashville. Anything you want. Or just stay home for a while. You wouldn't have to work. I'll be making enough money."

"Forget it," I said quickly. "I don't need a meal ticket."

He gripped the steering wheel so tightly his knuckles turned white. "Is that all I am to you? A meal ticket? I thought this was the year we were going to seriously consider the future."

The future. Here it was again. We kept bumping into it. For years, Mac and I have danced around the issue of marriage, wanting to be together, yet each of us stubbornly insisting on maintaining our own homes. We'd

141

never been able to come up with a suitable compromise, other than living apart most of the time. But now he was trying to weight our seesaw existence in his favor — all the way to Nashville, Tennessee.

"This is the year we consider the future," I said. "But it's only March. Don't rush me — okay? Anyway, is Nashville our only option? Couldn't you find something better right here in Atlanta? I mean, for God's sake, the paper is full of jobs. All the time. We're the friggin' capital of the New South, Mac. There must be something right here that's at least as good as Nashville."

"Not so far," Mac said. He pointed off to his right at the strip shopping center. Two cop cruisers were parked in front of the Budget Bottle Shop.

"Is this the place?"

"This is it," I said.

We sat in the parked car for five minutes while I got busy with my pencil and legal pad, sketching the layout of the shopping center.

"That's the worst drawing I've ever seen," Mac said, leaning over my shoulder. "Rufus could draw better than that."

I gave him the pad. "Here, Mr. Engineer, you do it."

He started sketching. His lines were straight,

142

and as far as I could tell, they were even to scale.

I got my purse and opened the car door. "You going in?" he asked. He didn't look happy about it.

I pointed at the police cars. "Couldn't be safer. Now. Relax. I'm just going to look around, pick up a few things we need."

Mac handed me a twenty-dollar bill. "As long as you're shopping, I'm out of Jack Daniels. Black label, of course."

"Of course."

The bell jangled as I pushed open the heavy plate-glass door. Two uniformed cops leaned against the front counter, chatting with a man behind the Plexiglas cage. They gave me a careful look, then, apparently deciding I was harmless, they went back to their discussion, which seemed to revolve around a basketball game in progress on a small portable TV perched on the counter.

I stood in the middle of the store, looking down at the linoleum. No trace of the blood or broken beer bottles that had littered it the night before. I stood in front of the whiskey section, looking for Jack Daniels. Rather, I looked like I was looking for Jack Daniels. Instead, I was trying to memorize the store. How the rows of dusty bottles were arranged, where the doors were, how high the front window reached to the ceiling.

The stockroom door was located right next to the gin department. I ran a finger over the bottles of Beefeaters and Tanqueray.

"Excuse me," I said, stepping in front of the counter. The cops looked up, surprised. So did the man behind the Plexiglas shield. It was the owner, Pete Viatkos, the guy I'd seen at the emergency room the night before. He wore a loose black sport shirt and wrinkled khaki slacks and was smoking a cigarillo.

"Is there a bathroom I could use?"

Viatkos frowned. "No public bathroom. Sorry."

I did a desperate little dance. "Please," I whispered, "just for a minute."

Viatkos shook his head again. "My insurance," he said. "Not allowed."

One of the cops took pity on me. "What about if I stand outside?" he asked. "That'd be okay, wouldn't it, Pete?" He gave me a sympathetic smile.

"Just like my wife. She can't go nowhere she doesn't have to use the john."

Viatkos shrugged. He put one hand under the counter and I heard a buzzer sound.

The cop opened the stockroom door and stepped aside to let me pass.

The back room was unheated and dimly lit. The walls were of unpainted concrete block.

Stacks of liquor crates lined the walls. A small forklift was parked in the far corner near a heavy metal door. The door to the alley? The cop pointed to an open door.

"In there, through the office. Don't know how clean it is. You know these Greeks."

"Thank you so much," I said, heaping on the gratitude. The funny thing was, I was so nervous, I really did have to go.

He reached around the doorway into the office area and flipped on a light. A bare bulb hung over a cheap wooden desk wedged in the corner of the tiny airless room. Two banks of file cabinets and metal utility shelving took up the rest of the room, which was decorated with dusty beer posters and broken neon signs.

I pushed open the hollow core door to the bathroom and locked it behind me. The cop hadn't been lying about the state of the bathroom. It was filthy. Suddenly I didn't have to go anymore. I stood in the middle of the room and looked around. It was so small I could touch each wall standing in one place. A commode, a sink with a leaky faucet, and a metal shelf holding rolls of toilet tissue and paper towels were the only furnishings. The floor was concrete with a drain in the middle. In the wall, high above the commode, was a narrow window made of frosted glass. I'm terrible about measurements. I took my hands, measured my shoulders, held them up toward the window. Yes, I thought. The window was big enough to crawl in or out of. But the glass was puttied in, and there didn't appear to be any hinges.

I sighed and flushed the commode, turned the water on high, reminding myself to disinfect my hands once I got home to my own, clean bathroom.

The cop sat at the desk in the office, leafing through a magazine.

"Okay?"

"Much better," I assured him.

13

Pete Viatkos and the other cop were intent on their basketball game. I wandered around the store picking up bottles and putting them into the rusty A&P shopping cart I found near the doorway. Most of the wine in the store was of the screwtop variety, but I found a dusty bottle of Kendall-Jackson Chardonnay, an interesting Chilean red, and the Jack Daniels for Mac.

I moved over toward the cooler, which stood next to the counter. The shelves were stacked with singles and ponies of beer and malt liquor. Most of it was the usual stuff, Bud, Miller, Coors. There were only a few imports. I saw Killian's Red, Heineken, Amstel, and Guinness. But no Harp.

"Excuse me," I said.

Viatkos's eyes were glued to the television set. UNLV was behind by five but pouring it to U. Conn. He didn't bother to look up. "What?"

"Do you carry Harp?"

"No."

Funny, Bucky had a six-pack of the stuff last night.

"My boyfriend really likes Harp, but it's hard to find in this part of town," I said, trying another tack. "Do you ever carry it?"

"Sometimes," Viatkos said. "Check tomorrow. The truck comes on Friday."

I unloaded my purchases onto the counter. Cop number one, the one who was watching the game, lifted the hinged trap door and moved around behind the counter and started totaling me up on the cash register.

"Sixty-six even," he said, his eyes wandering back to the set.

I counted out the cash. He took the bills and put them in the register. The drawer was stacked high with twenties and tens. It was nearly ten o'clock and Viatkos hadn't bothered to empty the cash out of the register tonight. But then, his store had already been robbed recently. Why lock the barn after the cow's gone?

"Where's Deecie tonight?" I asked, trying to sound lighthearted. "Couldn't get a sitter?"

That got Viatkos's attention. "You know Deecie?"

"Sure," I said. "I just work down the street. I stop in here at night sometimes. Is she all right?"

"She quit," Viatkos said, glowering.

"Oh." As long as I was pushing it, I decided to push a little more. "I'm sorry to hear that. She was a nice girl."

"A thief," Viatkos said, spitting the words. "The girl was a goddamn thief. You see her around town, you call me here at the store. I catch up with her, you'll get a reward."

"Hey, hey," number one cop said, laughing uneasily. "Go easy, Pete." He gave me the big smile. "Pete's worked up. We had a little incident in here last night. Maybe you heard about it on the news."

I let my eyes go big and naïve. "That's right! That officer got shot. Oh, I'm so sorry. I didn't mean anything." I backed away toward the door, rolling the cart with me.

I tapped on the passenger-side window and Mac unlocked the door. "What took so long?" he demanded. "I was getting kind of worried."

"Sorry," I said, stowing the liquor on the backseat. "I was taking the fifty-cent tour."

"Find anything interesting?"

"Maybe. Drive around back, would you?"

He started the Blazer's engine. "Whatever you say."

We circled to the end of the shopping center. It wasn't much of a center. There was a discount video rental store that seemed to specialize in Spanish-language movies, a closed-up Chinese restaurant called the Jade Dragon, and another closed-up storefront that had a For Lease sign in the window. "Call Parthenon Properties," the sign urged, and a phone number was listed.

"Parthenon," I said. "Wonder if that's Pete Viatkos's company? It would be interesting if he owned the whole shopping center."

"Viatkos?"

"Yeah. He owns the liquor store. Why, you know him?"

"Of him," Mac said. "He owns a parcel of land out in Rockdale County. It's zoned agricultural, but he wants to put some kind of industrial park out there. The county commission is falling all over themselves to make it happen."

"That's bad?"

"It fronts on a two-lane county road. No way it could handle the kind of heavy traffic a park like that would create. We're studying the proposal, but I can tell you right now we'd recommend the zoning request be turned down."

Mac turned the Blazer around on the backside of the shopping center. It was dark back there, and the asphalt was full of potholes. Abandoned grocery carts lay on their sides, and Dumpsters spewed trash.

"Not exactly a garden spot," Mac said as

the Blazer crept forward.

I pointed at a wall of cardboard beer crates that leaned against the back of one building. "That's the liquor store," I said. "Pull up."

He nosed the Blazer within five feet of the back of the store, his headlights shining on the heavy metal door. Something small and furry scurried by the door.

"No wonder Deecie didn't want to park back here," I muttered. "It's like something out of Stephen King."

"Seen enough?" Mac asked, yawning.

"Almost," I said. "Deecie said there was a road back here. I want to see where it goes."

At the far end of the strip the asphalt curved away, into a narrow driveway that dipped sharply below grade. Mac put his brights on and inched forward. Sure enough, at the bottom of the drive, a two-lane road passed by.

"What street is this?" I asked. Even under good conditions I am what some would call directionally challenged. But it was late and dark, and I couldn't picture exactly where we were.

"Don't know," Mac said. "I don't see any signs." He turned to the right, and after a block, the road dead-ended into a trash dump. More shopping carts, burned-out mattresses, and junk cars spilled out of a thinly wooded area.

He turned around and we passed the back of the shopping center again. This time, the road intersected with a real road. "Woodbridge Way," I said, reading a street sign. "I never knew this was back here."

The houses on the street were modest one-story wood-frame cottages, mostly of World War II vintage. Large expanses of weed-covered empty lots were sprinkled all down the street.

"All these houses were condemned by the state when they were trying to put the Presidential Parkway through," Mac said. "But the neighborhood associations fought the state tooth and nail, sued them in federal court, and eventually won. But it was too late for a lot of people. As soon as they started condemning, the state bulldozed a lot of the houses. That's why all the vacant lots."

"I knew a lot of stuff was condemned over in Inman Park," I said, looking around. "But I had no idea the property extended over this far. I wonder why nobody ever built on those lots?"

Mac laughed. "The state still holds title. If you think it doesn't pay to fight city hall, try fighting the State of Georgia."

"Let's see where Woodbridge takes us," I said.

He turned right. "I can tell you where it

takes us," he said. "North Avenue. We're not even two blocks from Manuel's."

Manuel's Tavern is an Atlanta landmark in a city whose idea of a landmark is anything built before the Gulf War. It's a big dark barn of a place that sits at the corner of North Avenue and Highland, and it's the closest thing the city has to a real old-fashioned beer joint.

"You get any dinner?" I asked.

"A package of mixed nuts on the plane. I came directly to your place from the airport. You want to get some dinner?"

I was still full of cookies and milk, but a cold beer sounded good. Besides, Manuel's is a cop hangout. It was a good bet there would be at least half a dozen cops inside, holding forth. I wanted to hear what the scuttlebutt was over at City Hall East.

14

We found a booth in the front room, ordered a J.J. Special for Mac and a cold draft for me. By now, I really, really needed a bathroom.

"Be back in a minute," I told Mac. He was watching the basketball game. Everybody in Manuel's was watching the game.

Everybody except me. I washed my hands twice in the ladies' room. Instead of going back to the booth, I decided to make a loop through the back room. Every table was full. I saw a couple of people I knew — you never go to Manuel's without seeing somebody. Tonight, there were a couple lawyers I knew from college days, a nurse who once worked at Grady with my sister, and a woman who works the checkout at the neighborhood video store.

The cops were seated in the back corner of the room, eight of them, at two round tables they'd pushed together. They were all in street clothes, but there were three radios heaped in the middle of the table alongside two full pitchers of beer.

I knew some of the guys. Ellis Washington and the other homicide detective named Parini were there.

I stopped at the lawyers' table, waved to my sister's friend. When I got to the back of the room I tapped Ellis Washington on the shoulder and pointed at a vacant chair. "This seat taken?"

Washington looked surprised to see me. "Uh, yeah. I mean, no. Go ahead. Sit down, if you want."

I sat. Washington found a clean glass and poured me a beer.

"You guys," he said. The others turned away from the game. "This is Callahan Garrity. A friend of Deavers. Used to be his partner. She was there last night — at the liquor store."

Parini gave me an acknowledging nod. "How's it going?"

"Okay," I said. "Anybody call the hospital tonight? Last I heard, this afternoon, Bucky was listed in serious condition."

One of the uniform cops chimed in. "I called around six. No change."

"How's Lisa Dugan holding up?" I asked.

Parini and Washington exchanged looks.

"Did I say something wrong?" I asked.

"Captain Dugan doesn't talk about her personal life," Washington said. "We're not supposed to know she's been shacking up with Deavers."

"Oh."

"She's still back at the office," Parini said. "She hasn't gone home since it happened. The only reason we're here is to take a dinner break. She wouldn't come. Said she wanted to be by the phone in case something breaks."

"How about that girl — Deecie Styles?" I asked. "Anybody get a line on her whereabouts yet?"

Washington gave me a look. It said I should shut up.

"I saw the news tonight," I said, plunging ahead. "Channel 2 is saying the chief asked internal affairs to investigate the shooting. They hinted that the chief suspects Bucky had something to do with what happened last night."

I looked around the table. Each of the men wore identical deadpan expressions.

"Well?"

Nothing.

"Dammit," I exclaimed. "I'm not a reporter. So don't give me that no-comment shit. I'm Bucky's friend. Can't any of you guys give me an idea what they're talking about?"

Parini twirled his beer mug around. "Ask the chief."

"I'm asking you guys," I said plaintively. "You were all at the hospital last night. So I'm assuming you're his friends. I'm assuming you really did know Bucky."

"We know him," Parini said. He glanced over at Washington, who gave an almost imperceptible nod of his head.

"That job Deavers was working at the liquor store — he was working two other jobs too. The guy was killing himself working all this overtime. We all work second and third jobs. We got families. We got to if we want to make a living. This friggin' city don't pay jack shit for wages. But you heard what the chief said when somebody asked her about a raise — right?"

"She didn't say anything," I said.

"Just my point," Parini said, slapping the table with the palm of his hand.

"I'm hearing rumors," I said, looking around at the others.

"Like what?" Parini wanted to know.

"That there's some kind of ATM robbery crew working the city," I said.

"We get ATM robberies all the time," Washington said, interrupting. "Why not? A machine that spits out money on command? The things draw bandits like shit draws flies. I made my wife and daughter cut up their ATM cards. Too dangerous. But is that supposed to have something to do with Deavers?"

"Maybe," I said. "What I heard — "

A hand gripped my shoulder. I turned half-way around in my chair. Mac stood glaring down at me, his mouth pinched in fury.

"I thought you were coming right back," he said. "Your beer's warm. I already ate." He reached in his pocket, brought out a wad of bills. He took my hand and folded my fingers over the money. "When you get ready to go home, call yourself a cab. This one's going off duty." He turned and walked rapidly out of the bar.

I felt my face go hot. Shit. I'd done it again. I'd gotten carried away, trying to pry information out of these cops. But Mac had to know that was why I wanted to stop in at Manuel's. He had to know how torn up I was about Bucky. Damn him. He'd turned everything around. All because I was selfish enough to tell him I didn't want to give up my life in Atlanta to move to Nashville with him. Screw him, I thought. Screw him and the horse he rode in on.

I turned around and looked at the cops. They were busily trying to act as though they hadn't witnessed Mac's little temper tantrum.

One of the radios in the middle of the table squawked. Parini reached gratefully for it, held it up to his ear, gestured at Washington.

"That's it. Boss lady calls."

They put their money on the table and left.

The other cops looked down at the table, embarrassed at being left alone with me.

"It's okay," I said, managing a weak smile. "I'm out of here, too."

I made as graceful an exit as I could, went to the bar, and asked Bishop, one of the waiters, to call me a cab.

He raised an eyebrow but did as I asked.

15

Edna was in the kitchen playing solitaire when I came in the back door.

She looked pointedly at the clock. It was past midnight. "Who was that let you off at the curb?"

I should have known she'd been peeking out the window at me. The woman was a mastermind at surveillance. Keeping a secret from her is a hellish experience.

"It was a cab. I took a cab home from Manuel's."

She laid a row of cards on the table. "Did I tell you Mac called last night?"

"No, you didn't mention it," I said.

"Well, he did. And he said he had some big news for us. What kind of big news?"

I slammed my purse down on the table. "He's moving to Nashville." Then I got the Bushmills bottle, some ice, and a glass, and stalked off to bed.

It was the same dream I'd had the night before. The music was faint, and I was dancing, and each time I'd come close to the ghostly piper, the clouds would swirl around, obscuring his face.

The song the piper was playing was sad. I was dancing and crying at the same time, the teardrops falling on the clouds and sending up shafts of mist. If I tried hard, I could hear the words. Something about the flowers dying, and someone saying a prayer near a grave. At some point I realized the song was "Danny Boy."

All night long I did the cloud dance and sang that song, the same lyrics over and over; familiar yet strange. And when I woke up in the morning, my pillow was soaked from all the unknowing tears.

16

"What's this about Mac moving to Nashville?" Edna demanded.

The phone had been ringing off the hook. A typical Friday at House Mouse headquarters. It was ten A.M., the first lull we'd had all morning.

"He's been offered a job there. Director of regional planning and zoning," I said, spreading jelly on my biscuit.

"Why would Mac want to move to Nashville? He's got a job here. A home, the dogs. You." She gave me a sharp look. "You two haven't been fussin' again, have you?"

You'd think my own mother would be partisan. But no, Edna is ardently pro-Mac.

"He walked off and left me at Manuel's Tavern last night," I told her. "That's why I had to catch a cab home."

"Well, if Mac left you, it was probably because you provoked him."

"Whatever." I didn't feel up to debating Edna. I'd already called the hospital. Bucky's condition hadn't changed. I'd talked to my sister Maureen, too, and that had gotten me in an even darker mood.

I had my yellow legal pad out, writing up my notes of the previous evening's research. Something was way out of kilter with this shooting. That much I knew.

I reached for the phone, but Edna pushed it away from me.

"Before you go off on this wild goose chase of yours, I want some answers to my questions," Edna said. "Now. Tell me straight. What's going on between you and Mac?"

"Nothing," I snapped. "He wants me to sell my house, sell the business, and uproot both of us and move us off to some damn subdivision in Nashville, Tennessee. I told him, 'I like my life in Atlanta, I like my home and my business, and I'm not moving.'"

Edna's nostrils quivered. "Who said anything about me moving?"

"Mac. He knows I wouldn't go off and leave you behind."

"So," she said, hands on her hips. "The two of you have been having a nice big fight over whether or not I'll move to Nashville — but nobody bothered to consult me on the matter."

I stared at her. "I knew you wouldn't want to move."

She stomped her foot. "What the hell

makes you so sure you know anything, little missy? What makes you so sure I wouldn't move to Nashville?"

My jaw dropped. "But . . . Maura's here. And Maureen and Steve. And Kevin and his boys, and your friends and the girls and the bingo babes. I just assumed — "

"You know what happens when you assume?" she asked.

It's one of my mother's favorite mantras. "You make an ass out of 'u' and 'me,' " I recited.

"Right," she said.

She pulled a chair up and sat down beside me. "Really, Jules," she said, pushing a strand of hair out of my eye. "I don't want you jeopardizing your relationship with Mac based on where I'll live. I'm an old lady, but not so old I can't fend for myself. Here or in Nashville. You know what I think?" she asked gently.

"You probably think I'm afraid of making a commitment to Mac," I said, echoing one of her favorite lecture themes to me. "And I think you've been watching too much *Oprah*."

I reached for the phone again. This time she gave up without a fight.

"Secure Services." Linda Nickells's voice was crisply professional. Not a hint of a Southern accent, even though she'd been born and raised in Ocilla, Georgia. She is C. W. Hunsecker's most valuable asset — personal and professional — and she never lets him forget it.

"What are you doing for lunch today?" I asked.

"Hmm. Tuna fish with low-fat mayo, carrot sticks, and for dessert, half a big old juicy apple."

"Boring. Don't tell me you're dieting again."

"Always," she said. "Little Wash is going into kindergarten next year and I'm still in a size eight."

"My heart bleeds," I said. "How about you feed the tuna to the cat and we go to Sundown for lunch instead? My treat."

The Sundown Grill on Cheshire Bridge Road is Nickells's favorite restaurant. She loves any kind of Mexican food, but I happened to know she'd kill for one of their crabmeat quesadillas.

"You're bad," Linda said. "But how come you're treating me so nice?"

"It's Bucky," I said.

"I am so, so sorry, girlfriend," Linda said softly. "C.W. stopped by the hospital last night. They wouldn't let him see him. What can I do?"

"Your husband was bragging on your skills

with that computer of yours," I said. "I know you guys do a lot of pre-employment checks and that kind of thing. I've got somebody I want to find who doesn't want to be found. I think you can help me."

"Who?" Linda asked. "Just a minute. Let me get a pencil."

"Her name is Deecie Styles," I said. "I'm not sure how it's spelled. Better check Styles with a 'y' and an 'i.' "

"Who is she?" Linda asked.

"She's the only witness to the shooting," I said. "She was working in the liquor store when the bad guy shot Bucky. Saw the whole thing."

"Where'd she go?" Linda asked.

"That's what I need to find out," I said. "She took off as soon as the police got to the scene. And if Washington is telling the truth, she took the videotape from the security camera as well as twelve hundred dollars from the safe. Just disappeared."

"Washington?" Linda said. "Ellis Washington?"

"Yeah. You know him?"

"I know him."

"What's that supposed to mean?"

"We dated a few times before I started going out with C.W.," Linda said. "Nothing wrong with that."

"Did you part on friendly terms?"

"Sure," Linda said. "I was friendly, but he was brokenhearted. Ellis is all right. A little bit stuffy, but his heart's in the right place. He's a stand-up kind of dude."

"Maybe you could call him, wangle some information out of him," I said. "He won't tell me jack."

"I don't know," Linda said reluctantly. "You know how C.W. feels about me getting mixed up in police business. We're out of that racket, Callahan. You, too. Why do you want to mess in something like that?"

"I don't want to," I said. "But the chief of police is already floating rumors that Bucky was involved in some robbery crew, and that's how he got shot. It's bullshit. And in the meantime, the guy who put two bullets in Bucky's head is wandering around free. You and C.W. were cops, Linda. C.W. still works security sometimes, doesn't he?"

"Every once in a while," Linda said.

"So it could have been your husband who got shot. It could have been you. It could have been me."

"All right," she said, sighing. "Give me whatever information you've got. I'll see what I can do. But just don't go expecting miracles. And don't mention any of this to C.W."

"My lips are sealed," I said. "See you at the Sundown at one?"

"Make it twelve-thirty," Linda said. "If you get there before I do, order me a frozen margarita. No salt."

It took every ounce of self-control I possessed to order an iced tea while Linda sipped her pale yellow margarita. I needed to keep my wits about me.

"Well?" I said expectantly.

She reached down into her purse and brought out a sheaf of computer printouts.

"Deecie Styles. Styles with a 'y,' " she said. "Her real name is DeSaundra Charmaine. D. C., get it? Last address was Memorial Oaks Apartments, unit six-J. I got the phone number for you. It's listed to a Monique Bell. That must be the aunt you said she lived with. By the way, that baby of hers? Faheem? He's sick, Callahan. He's got sickle cell anemia."

"How'd you find that out?" I asked.

"Easy. I figured if she had a baby, she probably had it at Grady, which means she's in the Grady system. One of the Secure Systems guys works part-time in medical records. He looked it up for me. And no, I'm not telling you his name. I'm not doing this again, Garrity. Sure enough, Faheem Styles turned one year old back in October. The mama's supposed to be taking him for his clinic appointments, but the nurse I spoke to said she's missed his last two appointments, including today's."

He was so little, I mused.

"How sick is he?" I asked. "Is it like diabetes, where you die if you don't get your insulin?"

"Not as bad as diabetes," Linda said. "See, with sickle cell, the blood cell is sickle-shaped, and they sort of get caught in the joints, and then you get swelling and lots of pain. It's kind of like when your kitchen drain gets clogged with grease. It can't move anywhere. And you get a lot of pain. So when somebody with sickle cell is in a crisis, that's bad. They give 'em pain medication and a lot of fluids. I got a niece, she's fifteen, with sickle cell. The kid spends a lot of time in the hospital, but then other times, it's like she's perfectly normal. If this baby, Faheem, is in a flare-up, and he doesn't have his steroids, he could be really sick, poor little guy."

"He was screaming his head off the night Bucky was shot," I said. "I thought it was because he was so scared."

"Scared and sick both, probably," Linda said.

"So," I said, taking a tortilla chip and dipping it in some salsa, "she's got to get him to a doctor sooner or later — right? That's good."

"She can't run too far with a sick baby,"

Linda agreed. "Unless she leaves him with the aunt or another relative."

I pushed the basket of chips toward Linda; she pushed it back toward me.

"What else have you got?"

"Got her DOB and SSI," Linda said. "That could help us track her if she gets another job or applies for any kind of government benefits."

"How did you get that?" I asked. "Did Washington give it to you?"

"I decided against calling him," Linda said. "C.W.'s still kind of sensitive about the fact that we dated. Anyway, I don't need Washington."

She wiggled her fingertips at me. "It's all online. Deecie was working for a liquor store, right? That means she had to have a work permit from the State Alcohol Control Board. And their database is online. While I was at it, I ran a couple other checks. But I didn't come up with anything else. Deecie doesn't have any credit cards, doesn't own any property, doesn't have a car."

"She drives one though," I said, leaning forward. "Or she did. An old white Buick LeSabre. It was parked in front of the liquor store the night of the shooting. But it was gone last night."

"Police impound lot," Linda said.

"No car. Sick kid, no job, no credit cards. I wonder where she went," I said.

Linda shook her head and laughed.

"What?"

"You just described a way of life for most poor young black girls living in the inner city," Linda said. "Come on, Garrity, you wanna find this little girl, you better lose that middle-class white mentality of yours."

The waitress brought our food just then. Linda had the crab quesadilla; I had what I always have, Eddie's Pork, which is a roast pork tenderloin served with sides of mashed potatoes and hot pepper–spiced collard greens. We ate and drank and gossiped until our plates were empty and our bellies hurt from laughing about old times.

"This was fun," Linda said, scooting her chair back from the table.

"Yeah, we need to get together more often," I agreed. "Seems like I hardly ever see you and C.W. anymore."

"Well, what's new with you and Mac?" Linda asked. "Any more talk of marriage?"

"No," I said. "That subject is currently closed."

"Oh," she said. "It's like that, is it?"

"Like that."

17

Baby and Sister were overjoyed to see me standing at the door to their neat little apartment. "Lookee here, Sister," Baby called over her shoulder. "Callahan come all the way over here to visit."

"I've come to give you a job, if you think you're up to it," I said, allowing myself to be seated in one of three flowered armchairs in the minuscule living room.

"Cleaning or detecting?" Sister asked.

"Detecting," I said.

Baby clapped her hands gleefully. "All right," she said. "What you need us to do?"

I filled them in on my need to talk to Deecie Styles. Told them about her little boy and that she was the only witness to Bucky's shooting. I also explained that Deecie lived with her aunt, a woman named Monique Bell, how the little boy was sick, and Deecie was on the run from the law.

The girls nodded understandingly as I outlined their mission. Old they might be, but the two of them had an uncanny ability to worm information out of people. They loved intrigue, loved to play-act. The black Gish sisters, Edna and I called them.

"What you think, Baby?" Sister had asked, soliciting her sister's opinion on the right approach to a fact-finding mission.

Baby gave it some thought. "Church visitation committee? I got me a new hat and pocketbook, and we got some tracts we could hand out."

Sister pursed her lips, thought about it, shook her head no.

"You right," Baby said. "How 'bout Publishers' Sweepstakes Prize Patrol? We got Callahan's van. Prize Patrol come in a van. I seen it on the TV."

"Where we gonna get a big check from?" Sister asked. "Prize Patrol got flowers and champagne and a big ol' check. Everybody knows that."

"I got it," Baby said, snapping her fingers. "Callahan said this girl got a sick baby. Nursing sisters, they take care of sick babies, ain't that right?"

I parked the van across the street from the Memorial Oaks Apartments, under a bare-branched tree that provided the only shade on the block. The late-winter sun spilled a molten golden aura over everything, but even the buttery sunlight did little to brighten the squat red-brick apartment houses.

"You sure this is the right address?" Baby asked, staring out the window. "I been living in Atlanta all my life, and I never been on a street like this here."

It was close to three o'clock, but groups of men loitered in front of every building, passing paper-sack–covered bottles. Overturned trash cans rolled in the grassless yards in front of the brick buildings, which had been spray-painted with signs and symbols I took to be gang markings. The street was lined with junked cars. A group of teenage boys were playing a pickup game of basketball in the middle of the street, using a hoop somebody had bungee-corded to a telephone pole. Three girls sat on the hood of a car in front of my van, passing a reefer and yelling obscenities at the players.

"This was a mistake," I said, pushing the power lock button. "Maybe I should take you girls home. Linda said this was a rough neighborhood, but I had no idea it was this rough."

"Don't look too bad to me," Sister objected. "Look at them little children playing ball. That's nice, isn't it? A playground right here for the children to be playing in?"

"Them ain't children, you blind old fool," Baby said. "Them's mens. Able-bodied mens hanging around on a street in the middle of the day when they oughta be working a job. And look over there at them womenfolk."

Five or six women sat on folding metal lawn chairs outside the steps to Building 6. They had a portable television hooked up to a long orange extension cord that snaked inside the building.

"Ain't nobody over here got a job?" Baby fussed. "Why they sittin' there watching that television with trash and all kinda nasty stuff layin' in their front yard? What kinda place is this, Callahan?"

"No place for you girls," I had to admit. I turned the key in the ignition.

"Now wait just a minute," Sister objected. "You tellin' me we got all dressed up in our nursing sister disguises and you ain't gonna let us do our job? That ain't right. That ain't right at all."

The two of them did look splendid in their blue uniforms with white aprons and old-fashioned white nurses' caps, with white stockings and thick-soled white shoes. I'd forgotten that the Easterbrookses were longtime nursing sisters at their A.M.E. church, charged with the serious responsibility of reviving church members who fell ill or "fell out" during services.

"This place isn't safe," I said reluctantly. "I

175

can't let you wander around here asking questions. No telling what might happen. I'm sorry, Miss Baby, Miss Sister. But I'll pay you anyway."

Baby put her hand over mine on the steering wheel. Her skin was cool and dry to the touch, like onionskin paper.

"Them women there don't look so bad," she said, nodding toward the group watching television. "Lazy as they are, they probably wouldn't let nothin' bad happen to a couple of old ladies like us."

"You sure?" I asked, torn between wanting to find Deecie and needing to keep the girls safe.

Baby patted the pocketbook she held in her lap. "Don't you be worryin' about us, Callahan. I got me something keep anybody from messin' wit' Baby Easterbrooks."

"What you got?" Sister asked, leaning over the seat back. "You got that can of spray mace? Lemme hold on to that."

"Lookee here," Baby said, sliding her hand into the oversized tote bag she held in her lap. She drew out a heavy eight-inch-long iron cylinder, and before I could object, thwapped it in the palm of my outstretched hand.

A bolt of pain shot up my arm. "What the hell is that?" I yelped, yanking my hand away.

She clacked her dentures menacingly.

"This here is my in-surance policy," Sister said.

Baby leaned over the backseat of the van and brandished a similarly sinister-looking sap. "Got mine right here!" she chimed in.

"But what are they and where'd you get them?" I asked.

Sister held her weapon up close for inspection, and for the first time I noticed a hole through a pointed end of the thing.

"Hey," I said. "It's a sash weight."

"Good old-fashioned window sash weight," Baby agreed.

"I haven't seen one of those since I was a little kid," I said. "Where did you get these?"

"Miss Bettye Bond," Sister said. "We found 'em in a box out in the storage shed."

"Did she give you permission to take them?" I asked.

Sister, who is usually scrupulously honest in most matters, does have an unfortunate tendency toward acquisitiveness, like a magpie given to picking up bits of shiny foil and string. Mostly the things she appropriates for herself are harmless and worthless, things like a box of false eyelashes, or an old raincoat, or the occasional piece of cheap tableware.

"Miss Bettye, she don't care nothin' about an old box of sash weights," Sister said. "I ast her about a shotgun I found down in the cellar, but she said Mr. Ralph still uses that every now and again. So I took the sash weights instead."

"And if any of these no-count young'uns around here tries to mess with me, I'll show 'em what a sash weight feels like upside the head," Baby announced, shaking the weapon in my face. "Come on, Callahan, unlock this car door, sugar. We got work to do."

It was pointless to argue with them once their minds were made up. Anyway, we were so close. Surely somebody would know something about Deecie Styles.

"All right," I said. "But be careful. I'll stay right here in the van, watching. If anybody says or does anything threatening, promise me you'll leave. Okay?"

"Ain't nobody gonna mess with women of God," Sister said blithely, unlocking her door.

I watched while they approached the group of television-watching women.

A huge woman in a red sweatsuit got up and towered over Baby and Sister. I had my hand on the door to go in for the rescue, but something made me wait.

A moment later, the fat woman was gesturing for Sister to take her chair. Another woman with a waterfall of lacquered lemon-colored hair stood up and offered her kitchen chair to Baby, who also sat down.

I rolled the window down, but could hear nothing over the blare of the basketball players' boom box.

The women scooted their chairs up closer to Baby and Sister, who were talking a mile a minute, gesturing and smiling. No telling what outrageous story they were concocting, but from my point of view, it looked like the women were buying it.

After five minutes, Baby approached the van, her self-satisfied smile proof that they'd struck paydirt.

"Come on out of there and meet our new friend," Baby said. "We told them you work at the Grady, and that you want to help that little baby, Faheem. Don't pay no mind to that fat woman talking trash."

The women looked up at me as I approached, their faces a mask of wariness.

Baby pointed me to an older woman who wore an apron and held a dishpan full of stringbeans on her lap.

"This here's Miss Garrity," Baby said. "Miss Garrity, I'd like you to meet Austine Rudolph. She know all about that little boy."

I held out my hand. Mrs. Rudolph wiped hers on her apron and shook it. So far, so good.

"Mrs. Rudolph," I said. "I guess my colleagues told you why I'm here. I'm an out-reach worker with the pediatric sickle cell clinic at Grady Hospital. We're concerned because Deecie Styles didn't bring her little boy in for his appointment today."

"Oh, now Grady got concerned." The fat woman laughed. "And they done sent you around to see what's the deal? Child, please."

"Faheem sick again?" Mrs. Rudolph wrinkled her brow in concern. The apron was one of the old-fashioned bib kinds, cotton with red rick-rack trim. My grandmother must have had dozens just like it.

"Have you seen Deecie in the past few days?" I asked, ignoring the fat woman as Baby had instructed me. "It's kind of important. Faheem needs his medicine, or he'll be in a lot of pain."

I winced inwardly at the lie. Austine Rudolph's wide calm face was not the kind of face you like to deceive. But I had a job to do, and anyway, it was true. Faheem was sick, and he did need his medicine.

Mrs. Rudolph shook her head from side to side. "The police come around here this morning asking about Deecie. Seem like she in some kind of trouble. Any y'all seen Deecie?"

The skinny woman looked at the ground. "Monique say Deecie moved out. That's what she told the police."

"When?" Austine Rudolph asked. "I ain't hear nothing about that. Deecie, she sometime have me baby-sit Faheem when she works. She didn't say nothin' to me about moving."

"Is Monique Bell at home?" I asked, trying to stay small and quiet and nonthreatening.

The fat woman pointed toward the door to the apartment house. "That's her crib, right in there. Go ahead on and see. I ain't seen her today. Could be she sleeping. Could be she drunk."

"Might be she sleepin' and drunk," cackled the skinny one.

"Y'all hush," Mrs. Rudolph proclaimed. She set her dishpan down on the ground, grunted, and stood up.

"Let's go see," she said, not unkindly.

The hallway smelled like bacon and ripe diapers. Mrs. Rudolph banged at the third door to the right of the entry.

"Monique?" She rang the buzzer and called again. "Monique? It's Austine, honey. You awake in there?"

She waited a moment, then pounded again. "Monique. Come on, girl. Wake up. Somebody here to see about Deecie."

A door opened across the hall and a little girl popped her head out. "Y'all looking for Deecie? Deecie ain't here. She tol' my mama —"

A hand reached out and jerked the child inside. "Shut up your mouth right this minute," a man's voice boomed. The door slammed shut. We heard a slap and then a sharp, high cry. "Did I tell you to shut up with that stuff?" the man said.

"Lord help us all," Mrs. Rudolph whispered. She looked sad. "Monique must have gone to the store or something. I don't know about Deecie. Guess she could have moved. She got a boyfriend. William. I don't know where he stays."

"William," I repeated. "Do you know his last name?"

"Just William. He drives a big white car. He's not Faheem's daddy. Faheem's daddy is in the jail."

I reached in my purse and got a business card. It was very plain. Just my name, Callahan Garrity, and my phone number. No title, no address.

"Mrs. Rudolph, it is very important that I contact Deecie Styles. I really need to find out where she's staying, and talk to her."

Austine Rudolph stared at the card and shook her head up and down that she understood. "Tanya, the little girl across the hall? I'll ask her later on, when her daddy's not around. Tanya, she loves Deecie. Bet she knows where Deecie went to."

"It would be very helpful if I knew where Deecie is staying," I repeated. "A phone number, address, anything like that would be helpful."

I hesitated, wondering if I should offer a small cash incentive. I decided against it, worrying that it might offend Austine Rudolph.

"Deecie, she's a good mama," Mrs. Rudolph assured me, walking back down the hallway with me. "If she missed the baby's appointment, must be something wrong."

I turned around. "Has she said anything was wrong?" I asked gently. "Did she seem upset or nervous the past two days?"

Mrs. Rudolph wrapped her hands in her apron. "I don't care what anybody says. She's a good girl. Works hard at that job. Minds her own business. You don't find Deecie out runnin' in the streets like some of 'em around here. She come home late night before last. Faheem was crying, and she couldn't get him to stop. Monique, she screamed at Deecie to make him shut up, so Deecie brought the baby over to my place. I rocked him until he was wore out."

"Did Deecie say where she'd been? Did she mention any trouble at work?"

Mrs. Rudolph bit her lip. "She was upset. I know that. That girl likes to talk. But that night, she wouldn't say a word. Next morning, I got up, she and the baby were gone. And there was two twenty-dollar bills on the table."

She cut me a sideways look. "Why the police looking for her? You think Deecie in some kind of trouble?"

I nodded.

"You think you could help her?"

"I'd like to," I said. "If I could find her and talk to her."

She touched my shoulder. "Go on outside and wait by your car. I'll be out in a minute."

I rounded up the girls and we sat in the van and watched the basketball game. It had gotten warm, and the kids had stripped to their waists, hanging shirts on a shaggy holly bush at the edge of the lot.

There was a slight tap on the glass. Austine Rudolph stood at the curb with her hand on the shoulder of the little girl from the apartment house.

"Tanya," she said. "Tell this lady what you told me about Deecie."

Tanya wiped her nose on the back of the sleeve of a pink-and-white-striped shirt. "William come and got Deecie in a cab yesterday morning. Me and Mama was going to the store, and Deecie was getting in the cab. And she had a suitcase and Faheem's bag. Deecie look scared. I ask her was she goin' away, and Deecie just shook her head. She look sad. Then she give me some money. Ten dollars. And she told me not to tell nobody where I got it from. Mama made me go inside and she talked to Deecie. And then William and Deecie and Faheem went away in the cab, and Mama said Deecie was going on a trip."

Mrs. Rudolph gave Tanya an approving pat on the back.

"Did Deecie tell your mama where she was going?" I asked.

Tanya shook her head no.

"Did you see what kind of a cab they went away in?" I asked.

"Yellow," Tanya said.

"Probably B&E Cab," Mrs. Rudolph said. "The man drives that cab, he stays parked up at the Eastlake MARTA Station. Lot of folks live here ride with that fella."

I hesitated. "Did you tell the police what you just told me?"

The little girl's eyes got very wide, and she put the three fingers of her left hand in her mouth and sucked hard. "My daddy told me to keep my mouth shut. He told the police we don't even know Deecie. My daddy told a lie, didn't he?"

Mrs. Rudolph patted her shoulder. "Grown-ups got different ways of saying things, Tanya.

Your daddy probably forgot about knowing Deecie."

"Thank you, Tanya," I said. The little girl smiled shyly.

"I thought of something might help," Mrs. Rudolph added. "How you maybe could find William. Deecie, she used to bring me bread sometimes. Cake and rolls too. She say William work someplace where they let him take stuff that's old."

"A bakery?"

"Maybe," Mrs. Rudolph said. "Or some kinda store or something."

"Do you remember what kind of bread it was?" I asked.

"Oh yes," Mrs. Rudolph said. "That bread was good. Doubletree Farms. I like the cinnamon raisin kind."

"Thanks," I said.

"Say," she said, "my phone number is in the telephone book. Mrs. Austine Rudolph. You think you could call me if you find out where Deecie gone to? Let me know about Faheem? That baby is my little lamb."

"I promise," I said. "If I find Deecie, I'll let her know you're worried about her."

"You do that," Mrs. Rudolph said. She looked at Baby and Sister. "Y'all take care now. I'll be praying about Deecie and Faheem."

"We'll be praying too," Sister called.

We watched her take Tanya back inside the apartment house. The women we'd been talking to were standing now, and pointing toward the van.

"Did we do good?" Baby wanted to know.

"Very good," I said. "I don't know what I would have done without you two."

While we were talking to Mrs. Rudolph, the kids had moved their basketball game directly in front of the van, blocking the whole street.

I gave a tentative little toot on the horn. The teenagers studiously ignored me, running and shooting. One of them even bounced the basketball off the van's bumper, laughed, and then ran over and did a slam dunk in the hoop.

I bit my lip and glanced over at Sister, who'd insisted it was her turn to ride shotgun.

"Uh-oh," Sister said, sizing up the situation nicely.

I rolled the window down.

"Hey, fellas," I called. Very friendly. Very casual. "Could you call a time-out for a minute? Let me by?"

All but one ignored me. He was on the short side, powerfully built, wearing a sleeveless red jersey emblazoned with a cartoon Tweety Bird.

"Yo," he called, walking toward the van.

187

He had a yellow do-rag tied around his head, and baggy black shorts that hung past his knees.

He sauntered up to the van and leaned in my open window until his face was inches from mine.

"What's this fool want?" I heard Baby mutter.

"S'up?" Tweety Bird asked. His breath smelled like beer and jalapeño peppers.

"I'd like you all to move out of the street for a minute so that I can take these ladies home," I said, trying to shrink away from him.

He glanced over at Baby and Sister. "How y'all doin?" he drawled.

"We're tired," Baby said snappishly. "And you boys are in the way."

"Game ain't over," Tweety said. "Lil' Bit, he on a shootin' streak."

"If you could just take a time-out —" I started.

He reached over and grabbed at the slender gold chain around my neck, the one that held Edna's St. Christopher medal.

"Say. This is nice," he said, his fingers sliding down toward the medal.

"Hey," I said sharply, slapping his hand away.

He looked surprised. Straightened up, called

over his shoulder. "Yo, Lil' Bit. Come tell this bitch here we ain't playin'.'"

I didn't wait to hear what Lil' Bit might have to say to us.

"Hang on, girls," I said quietly. I threw the gearshift into reverse and stomped on the gas pedal, and the van jerked backward, away from the curb. Tweety, whose hand had been on the window jamb, was knocked off balance and nearly fell.

"What the fuck?" he yelled, recovering after a second.

I was trying to watch where I was going in the rearview mirror, but out of the corner of my eye, I saw the group of them, six in all, charging toward me.

Suddenly there was a sharp crack, and a small pinhole appeared in the glass of the windshield.

"They shootin' at us?" Baby asked.

I didn't intend to stick around to find out. I stomped the accelerator and, barely missing the parked cars lining both sides of the curb, managed to back all the way to the corner, making a sharp left before I threw it into drive and got the hell out of Dodge.

"Have mercy!" Baby yelled. "Wish we'd had Bettye Bond's shotgun back there."

My hands didn't stop shaking until we were a mile away. I pulled into the first convenience store we came to.

"Are you girls okay?" I asked.

"We're all right," Sister said.

"Callahan?" Baby said, her voice trembling a little. "You got any cash money? I believe I'd like to get me a cold beer, settle my nerves."

We settled on a four-pack of kiwi wine coolers.

18

After I dropped the girls back at the senior citizen high-rise, I drove over to the Eastlake Park MARTA Station and parked by the cab stand. Yellow cabs came and went, but I didn't see a cab that matched the description Mrs. Rudolph had given me. At four-thirty, the trains started disgorging people headed home from downtown. Two cabs pulled up in front of me at the stand.

A battered green-and-white minivan with a sign mounted on the roof that proclaimed it "Mexitaxi" parked behind me. He tooted his horn. I ignored him, and he tooted again. Finally, he got out, walked up to the side of the van. I locked the door and rolled the window down an inch.

"Hey!" he said angrily. "You can't be parking here, lady. This for cabs."

"I'm looking for somebody," I said. "The man who drives for B&E cabs?"

"You gotta look someplace else," the Mexican insisted, pounding the roof of my van. "This is for the cabs, not people looking for other people."

"Do you know that driver?" I asked.

The Mexican looked around. "I'm gonna call a MARTA cop, tell them you breaking the law, lady."

I'd had enough confrontations for one day. "Never mind." I started the van and pulled away from the curb.

The shopping center parking lot was full, which puzzled me until I remembered that it was Friday night.

The Budget Bottle Shop was packed. Customers lined up with carts full of merchandise, their breath leaving the store windows damp with condensation. Two clerks stood behind the Plexiglas cage surrounding the front counter, ringing up cases of beer, bottles of malt liquor, cartons of cigarettes. I stood by the beer cooler, trying to act interested in its offerings.

" 'Scuse me." A runty little white woman pulled the cooler door open and reached inside. I stepped away, watched her load two six-packs of wine coolers into her shopping cart. For the first time, I noticed a flyer taped to the wall beside the front door.

It was on cheap blue paper, and had a headline lettered with Old West type. "WANTED DEAD OR ALIVE," it said. "$10,000 Reward for information leading to capture and arrest of party responsible for the March 17 shooting of POLICE DETECTIVE BUCKY DEAVERS."

There was a grainy photograph of Bucky, the same old one the newspaper had used, of him in his dress uniform. "Contact Pete Viatkos, Budget Bottle Shop," the poster urged. "Confidentiality Respected."

A hand clamped over my shoulder. Startled, I whirled around.

"You turning into a bounty hunter?" It was John Boylan. He wore a dark blue sweatshirt with "Security" lettered across the front.

I flushed, feeling unaccountably found out, unable to frame a sensible retort.

"I was here," I said finally, wishing instantly that I had said the first thing that had come to my mind, which was Fuck you, asshole.

"So I heard," Boylan said. He hitched at the waistband of his blue slacks. "Must have been tough."

"It was."

He jerked his head toward the poster. "Pete had me run off five hundred of those babies. Posted 'em in every shitbag bar, restaurant, and gas station in Midtown. That oughtta flush out somebody."

"You work for Pete Viatkos?"

"How do you think Bucky got this job?"

"I don't know," I said innocently. "I didn't even know he was working here until after the shooting."

"Deavers was a hustler," Boylan said. "He was always looking for a little extra income. So I introduced him to Pete. They liked each other fine. Now I'm feelin' kind of bad, you know? On account of me being the one got Bucky the job."

"I'm sure nobody thinks it's your fault Bucky got shot." Personally, I was convinced it was his fault. It needed to be somebody's fault.

"Tell that to Lisa Dugan, the bitch," Boylan said sourly.

"I heard internal affairs is getting involved in the investigation," I said. "Something about unauthorized after-hours jobs."

"That's a bunch of crap," Boylan said. "This is a free country, last I heard. The APD gets my full attention forty-plus hours a week. What I do on my own time is my own god-damn business."

"Unless there's a policy against it," I pointed out.

"Fuck policy," Boylan said.

"Whatever," I said, not agreeing or disagreeing. "Hey, uh, has anybody gotten a line on Deecie Styles?"

"Who?"

I jerked my thumb in the direction of the

wanted poster. "The clerk, the only witness to the shooting," I said patiently. "Somebody told me the girl disappeared. With the video-tape and all the money from the safe. I know the cops are looking for her."

"Who woulda told you something like that?"

"Somebody who knew that Bucky was my best friend," I said. "So what about it? Does Viatkos have any idea where she might have gone?"

"I just work here. Pete doesn't tell me his private business."

"Is he here now?"

"He's busy," Boylan said. He turned around and went over to the cashier's cage, standing to the right of it, arms crossed over his chest, his holstered revolver plainly visible in the clip at his waist. Wyatt Twerp, I thought.

I went out to the van and got in, locking the door. I got the number for the Budget Bottle Shop from directory information, then I called the number on the cell phone.

"Bottle Shop." It was a man's voice.

"Pete Viatkos, please," I said.

"Speaking."

"Mr. Viatkos, this is Callahan Garrity. Does that name mean anything to you?"

"Garrity?" He ran it around a little. "You a member of the Shamrocks?"

"Uh, not at this time," I said. "Actually, I'm a former APD detective. I was the one who was in your store Wednesday night when Bucky Deavers was shot."

"Oh yeah," he said slowly. "The detectives told me there was a friend with him."

"Actually, I was waiting outside in the car," I explained. "But I was the one who called nine-one-one. Or rather, I had your employee, Deecie Styles, call them."

"What's this about?"

"I'd like to find Miss Styles, to talk to her about the robbery."

"I'd like to find her to wring her neck," Viatkos said. "But she's gone. We got cops looking everywhere for her. Anyhow, no disrespect, but what's this to you?"

"Look," I said patiently. "I'm outside your store right now, in my car. Could I just come in and talk to you?"

"I'm pretty busy," he said.

"It won't take long."

Boylan glowered as I walked past him into the stockroom. Viatkos stood at the door to the office and motioned me inside.

His office was an oversized cubicle, partitioned off from the cavernous stockroom area by walls of cheap particle-board paneling that didn't quite reach all the way to the ceiling.

A small space heater stood in the middle of the floor, making more noise than heat. He sat behind a huge metal desk and gestured for me to sit in a metal folding chair opposite it.

"You were in the store last night," he said. "Snooping around. What's your business in all this?"

"Bucky is my best friend," I said. "I want to know who shot him and why."

Viatkos took a bite of a slice of pizza sitting on a greasy cardboard box. "Want some?" he offered, pointing to the pie in between chews. "It's my busy night, so this is dinner."

"No thanks," I said. "I'm really wondering what you can tell me about Deecie Styles."

"Goddamn little thief," Viatkos sputtered. "I gave the cops her address and phone number, everything I had in my files. I'm tellin' you, you give these people a break, give 'em a decent job, some training, they turn right around and steal you blind."

"How did you happen to hire her?" I asked, ignoring his references to "these people."

"I had a sign in the window. Help Wanted. She came in one night, asked about the job, said she'd worked a cash register before. At the Kroger down the street. She looked all right. Reasonably neat. Polite. And she was willing to work the night shift and weekends."

"How long had she worked here?"

He nibbled at the curved end of the pizza crust. "Three, four months."

"On her employment application, did she list any relatives other than this woman, Monique Bell, she was living with?"

Viatkos laughed. "Application? Lady, this ain't the post office. She give me her phone number and address and her Social Security number, and that was it."

"What about friends? I understand she had a boyfriend whose name was William. Did you ever meet him? Or catch his last name?"

Viatkos picked up a paper towel and blotted his lips. "She worked for me. I didn't ask her about her social life, she didn't volunteer. I know she had a kid because a couple times she had to get off work to take him to the doctor."

The phone rang then, and he picked it up. "Yeah?"

He covered the receiver with his hand. "This is business. I gotta deal with it. You can find your way out, right?" He stood up, opened the door, and after I stepped out, closed it firmly behind me.

"Right," I said.

I could hear him talking in a low voice through the door. The stockroom lights were on and the door into the store was closed. I did a quick stroll around the area. In the corner opposite Viatkos's office was a huge stainless steel door, sort of like a safe. I looked around, walked over, and took a closer look. It was a walk-in cooler.

I glanced back at Viatkos's office door. I could still hear him talking on the phone. I yanked at the door of the cooler, looked inside. The walls were lined with cartons of wine and cases of beer, as I had expected. I scanned the boxes. Bud, Busch, Miller, Pabst, Heineken, Molson. And Harp. So the truck had come in.

I closed the cooler door and walked briskly to the door leading into the store.

Boylan was behind the counter now, sitting on a barstool, talking to the clerk, a powerfully built bald guy who also wore a shirt marked "Security."

I gave them both a little finger wave. Boylan nodded. "Come again soon."

19

Edna was waiting for me when I walked in the kitchen door, hands clinched on her hips.

"Are you out of your ever-loving mind?" she roared. "For the love of God, Callahan, what were you thinking of, taking Baby and Sister over to that hellhole?"

I tried to get around her, but she stood her ground.

"Answer me, young lady."

Cripes. It was like the time I was sixteen and she found out my girlfriend Paula and I had stolen a bottle of Boone's Farm strawberry wine and got drunk at the StarLite Drive-In Theatre.

"Well?"

"It was a stupid thing to do," I admitted, sinking down into a kitchen chair. "But the girls are all right. They were shook up, but nobody got hurt."

"No thanks to you," Edna pointed out. "My God. You could have gotten all three of you killed. Do you realize that? I've read about that Memorial Oaks place. It's a war zone. People get shot, stabbed, raped, robbed."

She was standing over me, looking down. She touched my neck, the spot where the punk had tried to wrench the gold chain away. Her fingertips felt cool against the burning abrasion.

"You could have been killed," she repeated, her voice barely a whisper. I closed my hand over hers.

"I know it. And I'm sorry. It's just . . . Bucky." Dammit, I was starting to cry now, sniffling like a stupid sixteen-year-old.

"If you'd seen Bucky, Ma, seen him lying there, with that blood, and the smashed beer bottles. There was nothing I could do for him, except try to stop the blood. I couldn't even do that."

But she didn't intend to let me off that easy. Tears and apologies be damned. Edna Mae Garrity was in the right and she knew it.

"How does it help Bucky if you take stupid risks and get yourself and Baby and Sister killed? Just what does that accomplish?"

"I was looking for Deecie Styles," I explained. "The girl who worked in the liquor store. She was there that night. She saw what happened. She's the key. I know she is."

Edna sat down at the table beside me. Her hands fumbled around on the table for a moment before they closed on the deck of playing cards sitting there. What she was instinctively reaching for, of course, was a pack of cigarettes. She'd ended a fifty-year, three-pack-a-day habit only a few years ago, after a life-threatening heart attack. The cards were her substitute.

"The key to what?" Edna asked, slapping down the first row of cards. "Bucky was shot in a liquor store holdup. Some thug. Let the police do their job. And you do yours. Which is running The House Mouse. And keep the girls out of it. You hear me?"

"I hear."

"So you say," she said, her arthritic fingers surprisingly nimble as they flipped the cards over on the scarred oak tabletop. "But I know you. When you get an idea in your head, you're like a bulldog, refusing to let go. Like your father. He was the same way."

I went to the refrigerator and scanned the shelves looking for something good. Chocolate maybe. I settled on a cold pork chop. Sat down at the table and started nibbling at it.

"Why is it that all my good qualities remind you of your side of the family and all the bad ones remind you of Daddy?" I asked.

"It's the Irish in you," Edna said. "Can't be helped."

"Don't say that."

"What?" She looked up, surprised.

"The Irish. I'm not like them."

"That's a bad thing? Since when?"

"You know what I mean," I said. "The drinking. The sloppy sentiment. Pigheadedness. The other night, at that St. Patrick's Day party, all those bleary-eyed red-faced drunks, singing and boozing and dancing — it was disgusting. I should never have gone in the first place. It reminded me of all those damn fish fries Daddy used to drag us to over there."

"Disgusting?" Her voice was mild. "You kids used to beg to go to those things."

"Not me," I said.

"Right. I'd forgotten. Miss Priss would prefer to go to the country club with one of her rich friends. Keep away from all those tacky hooligans at the K of C."

"You know what I mean," I said. "When Daddy got around all those old farts, he was different. He talked too loud, drank too much . . ."

"He worked hard all week. Supported a wife and four kids on a salesman's salary. So on Friday nights sometimes he laughed and sang and danced. That's bad?" Edna asked. "That's embarrassing?"

I shook my head in exasperation.

"You used to love to dance with your daddy," Edna said. "He was so proud of you.

203

All you kids. He took you to those fish fries so he could show you off to all his friends. Which reminds me. You'll never guess who I ran into this morning."

"Who?" I asked, happy to have the subject changed. I tapped my index finger on the ten of hearts, to indicate that it should be placed beneath the jack of spades.

"Corky Hanlon. I was at Sam's Club, picking up supplies, and he and Marie were buying a new VCR. We sat in the snack bar and had a cup of coffee together. Talked about old times in the old neighborhood. I didn't realize Corky had retired. He told me he saw you the other night, at the K of C."

"Yeah," I said. "We danced together. He was heartbroken to learn that Bucky wasn't my boyfriend. He seems to think it's time I settled down and got married."

"Well?" One eyebrow shot up.

"Well nothing."

I'd had enough lectures for one night.

I took the Bushmills bottle, a glass of ice, and my half-eaten pork chop and did a good job of flouncing my way into the den.

I got the phone and called the hospital to check on Bucky's progress.

"No change," the nurse said.

I hung up and sat and tapped my fingers on the coffee table. I'd had a day full of dead ends. Pete Viatkos had refused to give me any information about Deecie Styles. I'd run into a bunch of nothing at Deecie's last address.

She was gone. She'd taken Faheem and gone off in a cab with William. William who? I didn't have a last name, didn't have an address. All I knew about him was that he sometimes gave Deecie day-old Doubletree Farms baked goods. And what did I know about Deecie? That she'd worked at a Kroger on Ponce de Leon before taking the job at the liquor store.

Food, I thought. And not just my own current lack of it. Deecie had worked at a supermarket, William had some connection to a bakery. Maybe somebody at that Kroger could help me put them together.

The sign at the front of the Kroger on Ponce showed a photo of a dark-skinned black man named Quartez Keys was the manager. I found him in the produce department, studying a shipment of limp-looking pole beans with the produce manager.

"Call the broker and tell him to come get 'em," he told the produce man. He turned to me and smiled. "Now, how can I help you, ma'am?"

"Could we go to your office?" I asked. "It's about one of your former employees."

The office was located on a skywalk high above the store's selling floor.

"Deecie Styles?" he said, reaching for a thick notebook full of computer printouts. "That name sounds sort of familiar. Do you know when she worked here?"

"More than four months ago, I think," I said.

He wet a finger and leafed through the printouts until he came to the page he was looking for.

He ran his forefinger down the columns of print and looked down through the bifocals perched at the end of his nose. "Yes, she worked here," Mr. Keys said. "Termination date was December first. Does that help?"

"Some," I said. "But I was hoping to get some information from her personnel file. Things like most recent address, next of kin, that kind of thing."

"Oh, no," Mr. Keys said, looking shocked. "Personnel records are totally confidential. I can confirm that she worked here, but that's all I can do." He put his hands palm-down on the desktop. "So sorry."

He didn't know how sorry I was.

"I understand," I said. "But maybe I could talk to somebody who worked with her? Another of the cashiers maybe? Just informally, of course."

He pursed his lips. "This isn't about a legal matter, is it?"

"Not at all," I lied. "I'm trying to find her because she worked for my cleaning business a few months ago, but I don't have a current address to send her W-2 form. She's moved away from the address I had."

He nodded agreement. "That's a problem for us, too. Our store associates tend to be somewhat transient. The nature of the business, you see."

"Of course."

He tapped a pencil on the book of printouts, then looked down at his watch. "I could let you talk to Mary Robin Hughes. She's our head cashier. She might remember something about the young lady. Mary Robin tends to mother all these kids."

He picked up the phone on his desk, punched a button, and I heard his voice on the store's loudspeaker system, asking Mary Robin Hughes to report to the manager's office.

A moment later, she stepped into the office. She was younger than I expected, mid-forties, probably, with short gleaming dark hair and pale blue eyes. "Mr. Keys?" she said, stopping to catch her breath.

He gestured toward me. "This lady wants to know anything you can tell her about one of our former associates. A young woman named . . ." He looked down at the printout on his desk.

"Deecie Styles," I said.

"Oh, yes, Ms. Styles. I'll let you two talk now." He sat back in his chair.

Mary Robin blinked. "Deecie? What did you want to know about her? She didn't work here very long."

"Anything you can remember," I said.

"Well," she said, hesitating, "she had an adorable little boy. Faheem. He had some medical problems, and that's why she left us. Deecie was bright and capable. What else can I tell you?"

"Did you know any of her friends or family? I'm particularly interested in her boyfriend, a man named William."

"She lived with her aunt, I know that," Mary Robin said. "That was sort of a problem. The aunt worked night shifts and got pretty irritable about the baby's crying. Deecie said she wanted to move out, as soon as she'd saved enough money."

"And the boyfriend?"

"I know she had a boyfriend, because he sometimes picked her up after work," Mary Robin said. "I can't remember his name, though."

"Somebody told me he sometimes brought

Deecie day-old baked goods from Doubletree Farms. Is that a brand you sell here?"

"Absolutely," Mr. Keys put in. "We carry their full line. Breads, rolls, coffee cakes. They're very popular. Especially the multi-grain breads."

"Are they local?" I asked.

"Not really," he said. "The bakery itself is up in Gainesville, Georgia. But they do have an Atlanta distributor, and that's who makes our deliveries."

"Can you tell me the name of the distributor?"

"Sure," Mr. Keys said. "Cronk and Associates."

I looked at Mary Robin. "Do you happen to know the driver for Cronk?"

"Drivers. Plural," she said. "They switch the route drivers all the time on us. As soon as we get a guy trained to do things the way we like, they change them around on us."

"Could one of their drivers be Deecie's boyfriend William?"

She thought about that. "Let's see. Russ is our driver right now. Tall skinny white kid. But sometimes he switches around with Dave, who's middle-aged, got a potbelly that'll kill him one of these days. And before that, we had KiKi, but she quit. And there was Lawrence . . ." She smiled brightly. "And William.

I'd almost forgotten about him. And come to think of it, I think maybe the other girls used to tease Deecie about him making eyes at her."

"So William works for Cronk?" I asked hopefully.

"He used to," Mary Robin said. "But we haven't seen him around here for two or three months."

"Thanks," I said, shaking her hand vigorously. "Thanks so much."

I shook Quartez Keys's hand too, I was so happy. "Thank you so much, Mr. Keys. My mother and I just love your store."

He beamed. "Come again. Any time."

20

I always grit my teeth when I call Maureen.
It's not that I don't love her. I do, I suppose.
It's just that I find my younger sister the most
annoying person on the face of the planet.
She's been a nurse for twenty years, and
somewhere along the line somebody gave
her the idea that R.N. stands for Really
(k)Nowledgeable about almost everything.
Still, she'd worked at Grady's emergency
room for a dozen years, and she did know a
lot more about the place than I did.

Her voice was groggy when she answered
the phone. "Sis?" I said hopefully.

"Who is this?" she demanded.

"How many sisters do you have?"

She yawned audibly, and I did the same.
"God, what time is it?"

"It's only nine," I said. "I was sure you'd
still be up."

"I'm working a double shift at Piedmont
Hospital tomorrow," she said. "I took a sleeping pill an hour ago. I was in twilight time until
you called. What's wrong? It's not Mom, is it?"

"Ma's fine," I assured her. "She thinks I should get married and move to Nashville."

"That's nice," Maureen said.

"I could use some help," I said hesitantly. "It's about Bucky Deavers. You remember him? My old partner?"

"The detective who got shot in the head?" Maureen said. "I heard about that on the news. I'd completely forgotten you knew him. How's he doing?"

"Not so good," I said. "He's at Grady. I can't get any real information about him. And when I call, they say he's not allowed any visitors."

"He probably isn't allowed any visitors except family. He's probably in the SICU up on the seventh floor. Anyway, if he's in as bad a shape as I think he is, he wouldn't know whether you were there or not. So just forget about seeing him."

"I'm not forgetting about it," I said. "Bucky's like my own brother. I can't sleep at night, thinking about him. I really need to see him. I just need you to tell me how I can sneak up there."

"Forget about it," she said. "There's a dedicated elevator serving that floor. And a security guard at the desk opposite the elevator doors. I'm telling you, Jules, they won't let you in. Nobody gets past that guard unless they're accompanied by somebody from social services. And social services won't take anybody up unless they can prove they're family."

"That's what I'm trying to tell you," I said. "I'm the only family he's got."

"That won't get it," Maureen said. "Unless you can prove you're his wife or something."

"He hasn't got a wife." I was nearly shouting. God, my sister is irritating.

"I'm telling you, Jules. Forget it. Oh, shit. The phone woke Maura up. Bye."

I pushed the end button on my cell phone. Another dead end. I couldn't get in the hospital to see Bucky, because I wasn't really family. And he didn't really have any family, other than me. Except, I thought, Lisa Dugan.

Directory assistance had an L. E. Dugan in Kennesaw, which was nearly an hour north of downtown, and another in Garden Hills, which I thought was a fairly pricey neighborhood for a cop. Still, I dialed the number and crossed my fingers.

A child answered the phone. "Dugan residence. Kyle speaking." So grown up, I marveled.

"Hello," I said just as politely. "May I please speak to Ms. Dugan?"

"M-O-M-M!" he bellowed, forgetting to

cover the receiver. I had to hold the phone away from my ear.

"Find out who it is," I heard a woman's voice call back.

"Who is this, please?" the little boy asked.

"It's the office," I fibbed.

That got her attention. "Yes," she said, all business. "This is Captain Dugan."

"Lisa? It's Callahan Garrity. I'm sorry to call you at home."

"What do you want?" Lisa Dugan wasn't nearly as polite as her son.

"I want to see Bucky."

"You can't. They're only allowing family. I had to get a notarized letter from Major Mackey stating we were engaged before they'd let me go up there."

I swallowed my pride for the second time that night. It was getting to be a nasty habit.

"Please." I was wearing down my bicuspids, doing all this teeth-gritting.

"It's not up to me," she said. I thought maybe she was wavering.

"Look," I said. "Could we meet somewhere? Talk about this whole thing? I know internal affairs has some crackpot idea that Bucky could have been involved in some robbery ring. I want to help."

She was silent.

"There are rumors floating around," I said

finally. "The kind of rumors that could end a lot of people's careers, ruin their lives." I felt guilty hooking her that way, but it was the only leverage I had.

"Rumors," she said, her voice cracking. "God. I can only imagine what the departmental grapevine has to say about all this. When did you want to meet?"

"Tonight?" I asked, crossing my fingers. "You're in Garden Hills, right? I'm in Midtown right now. I could meet wherever you say."

She was thinking about it. "I just walked in the door. We haven't even had dinner yet."

"We could meet for dinner," I said. "Was that your son who answered the phone? You could bring him. I'm used to kids."

"No," she said slowly. "I'll see about a sitter. All right. There's a Church's Fried Chicken on Piedmont. You know it?"

"Church's?"

"I haven't eaten in two days. I need a grease fix," she said. "You know the place?"

"How soon?"

"Thirty minutes," Lisa said. "But I can't stay long. I'm beat."

She was sitting at a booth near the door, reading a Dr. Seuss book to a dark-haired little boy of about five. There was a bucket of

215

chicken on the table, and she was sipping from what looked like a half-quart paper cup of iced tea.

"Lisa?"

She looked up. "Try finding a sitter at nine-thirty on a Friday night."

I leaned over and looked at the book. "*Green Eggs and Ham*," I said, giving the kid my friendliest smile. "Would you eat them in a box?"

He closed the book solemnly. "I would not eat them in a box. I would not eat them with a fox."

"Smart kid," I told him. "Stick to fried chicken."

"I wish," Lisa said, giving me a grudging smile. "Kyle's strictly a cheesehead. Grilled cheese, macaroni and cheese, cheese dip. Oh, yeah. He likes French fries, too."

"How's the chicken?" I asked, gesturing at the bucket.

"I think it's the best fast-food fried chicken you can get," Lisa said. "We like the ghetto dinner usually."

"Ghetto dinner?"

"Two drumsticks, two wings, fries, and a roll. Kyle eats the fries and the roll, I take care of the rest of it."

"Sounds good," I said.

I went to the counter and ordered, then

brought my box of chicken and large sweet tea back to the table.

"Your son has beautiful phone manners," I said, making with the first shameless suck-up move of the night.

"I try," she said, ruffling his hair. "People in Atlanta seem to put a lot of emphasis on manners. The preschool had him saying 'yes, ma'am' and 'no, ma'am' practically before he could say his own name."

"Then you're not originally from Atlanta?"

She laughed. "Nice try. You mean you all didn't notice the accent?"

"Like you say, good manners rule down here in Dixie. If I had to guess, I'd say the accent is Midwest. Chicago probably. And by the way, 'you all' is plural."

"Very good." She nodded. "Kyle and I moved here from Chicago three years ago, after my divorce. My folks up home think I talk like one of the Beverly Hillbillies. They almost died the first time Bucky answered my phone."

"Were you with the Chicago PD?" I asked.

"I was an investigator for the Cook County Sheriff's Office," she said. "But my dad was career with the CPD. Kind of runs in the family."

"Mind if I ask what brought you here to Atlanta? It's kind of a long way from home."

She picked up one of the drumsticks and worked at the thick dark brown crust with a long manicured nail, nibbling delicately at the tiny pieces she broke off. It was the way a Yankee would eat fried chicken, I thought.

"My divorce. What else? Kyle's father is chief investigator in my old office. I needed some distance. Atlanta needed an experienced investigator. It didn't hurt that I was a woman. Or that my dad had friends here."

I nodded. At least she was honest.

"You came along at the right time," I told her. "When I quit the force ten years ago, it was because they wouldn't transfer me to homicide. They told me it was because there weren't any openings, but that was bullshit. Two weeks after I quit robbery, Bucky got transferred over there. They'd never had a woman homicide detective, and the former chief didn't see any reason why that should change."

She took a sip of tea. "That would be the chief who got fired after his live-in girlfriend was busted for trying to smuggle a kilo of cocaine into the country when the two of them were coming back home from a weekend in Jamaica? The one who had the cocaine tucked down in her French-cut bikini panties?"

"You mean, alleged cocaine. And I didn't know they were French-cut."

"Bucky told me that. Maybe it was just one of his stories."

We grinned at each other. It was a sister thing. Now we could get down to issues.

"Bucky and I were partners back then," I said. "In robbery. We had a lot of good times. I know the man. He isn't a thief. And he isn't a liar. He wouldn't get mixed up in this stuff. Not under any circumstances."

She glanced over at Kyle, who'd started drawing a picture on a sheet of paper in a steno pad. I noticed Lisa kept twisting a slender gold ring on her left hand. It was a claddagh. My aunt Olive had brought me one after a trip to Ireland years ago. It was still in my jewelry box, along with my monogrammed circle pin and a charm bracelet from the New York World's Fair.

Lisa saw me staring at the ring. "He gave it to me," she said shyly. "For my birthday. I gave him a matching one for his birthday. Kind of dorky, huh?"

"Sweet," I said. "I didn't know Bucky had a sentimental side."

"There's a lot about him that a lot of people don't know," Lisa said, lifting her chin.

"All of a sudden, I'm finding that out," I said. "All this stuff about Bucky I didn't know. And I've known him for all these years."

I was watching Lisa Dugan's face. The

overhead lights cast an unearthly green light on her cheeks.

"Like all this stuff with the Shamrocks. And Bucky suddenly being interested in his Irish heritage. I always understood Bucky was just a cracker."

"His mother was a Healey," Lisa said. "Her people were from Donegal."

"Bullshit," I said. "I happen to know that Bucky's mother worked in a school lunchroom in South Georgia. The only Dublin she ever heard of was Dublin, Georgia."

"His mother's people were from Donegal," Lisa repeated. "And what about you? Garrity? Irish. You know, it really surprised me, when I first moved down here, how many Irish there are in the South."

"Not so surprising," I said. "Most of them came South in the eighteen hundreds, when the railroads were being built. Laying track was hard work. Killer work. Slaves were considered too valuable to risk. So they brought in the Irish. And they stayed. You ever been to Savannah?"

She tucked a strand of hair behind an ear. "No. Bucky wanted to take me down there later in the spring. He says the azaleas are beautiful down there."

"Savannah's eaten up with Irish," I said. "Originally, they got there because of the railroads, but a lot of them stayed and went to work as longshoremen down on the docks. That's how my father's people ended up in Georgia."

"Why does it bother you that Bucky joined the Shamrocks?" Lisa asked.

"Look at the jerks running it," I said. "John Boylan. He's a scumbag, in case you haven't noticed. And he's the guy who organized this whole security gig, too. It makes me wonder, that's all."

"It doesn't make me wonder," she said coldly. "I made some phone calls after you and I talked. Major Mackey said he'd already talked to internal affairs, and that I should be expecting a call too."

"You? Why?"

"We were living together, sort of. Bucky kept his old apartment, but most nights he stayed at my place. I guess somebody thinks I know something about these robberies. Mackey wanted to know how many different jobs Bucky was working."

"He was working more than one?"

She sighed. "He worked all the time. It was starting to cause problems for us. If he wasn't working security at the Bottle Shop, he was working Wrestlemania at the Dome, or directing traffic at the Fox on the nights they had shows."

"Why?" I asked. "He wasn't getting rich on a cop's salary, I know, but why all of a sudden was he so driven to make a lot of money?"

Lisa took a sip of iced tea. "We'd talked about buying a house together. I'm getting killed with my rent because I want to be in a good school district for Kyle. The night he was shot? It would have been his first night off in two months. That's probably why he was so pissed off that I had to work late. I know he was buying that beer for us. Harp. He used to tease me about buying imported beer. I keep thinking about that. If he'd just picked up a six-pack of Bud at a convenience store, none of this ever would have happened."

I bit my lip. I'd been wondering about the Harp ever since I'd seen it in the cooler in the back of the store. What if Bucky had gone in the storeroom to get the beer? Was it possible he'd surprised the robber back there, instead of the front of the store as Deecie Styles had claimed?

"Convenience stores get held up all the time," I pointed out. I'd decided to keep my questions about the Harp to myself. "Was Bucky carrying the night he was shot?"

"No," Lisa said. "His service revolver was under the front seat of the Miata. So he was unarmed. The bastard just shot him for the hell of it."

Kyle glanced up, wide-eyed. "You said a bad word," he said accusingly.

"I meant it, too," Lisa said, her voice cracking. "But sometimes mommies say bad words. That doesn't mean little boys can say them."

"Oh," he said. He picked up a purple crayon and went back to work. He was drawing some kind of rocketship, it looked like.

"There's something hinky about all this, you know," I said.

Her eyes narrowed. "What's that supposed to mean?"

"You've been around," I said. "In what way is this like any armed robbery you ever heard of? I mean, the bad guy took no money, not even any liquor. He shoots Bucky twice, right in the head. One bullet should have done the trick. That second shot was definitely a kill shot."

"Are you saying a cop shot Bucky? One of the Shamrocks, maybe? Is that what you're getting at with all this veiled talk about the rumor mill and the grapevine?"

"Think about it," I said, leaning closer to her. "The bad guy had to have been back in that stockroom when Bucky went into the store. I think Bucky saw him, maybe recognized him, and that's why he got shot. Then the shooter bolted out the back door. And I

223

think that clerk disappeared because she knew something about it. And she was scared. Scared shitless."

Lisa shook her head, as if it would shake the idea of a killer cop loose.

"You don't know the shooter was already in the store. You said yourself that you were almost asleep. The shooter could have gone in the store without you seeing him. And the clerk boogied because she could. She probably thought it would look like the robber had taken the money."

She tugged Kyle's arm. "Come on, sport. Time to go home."

"You know I'm right," I said as she pulled her son out of the booth and helped him put on his jacket.

"I know you're not helping Bucky with all this talk," she said, biting her lip.

"Lisa?" I tugged at her hand. "Please. Stay and talk to me. I need to understand what's going on. And I want to see Bucky."

"Go to hell," Lisa said. She grabbed her pocketbook with one hand and her son with the other and literally ran out of the restaurant.

21

I slept late that night, and badly. Blue and red lights flashed through my dreams, where I was strapped down to a table, with tubes running in and out of every orifice. And all the while, through a billowing white mist, I could hear a distant piper's mournful skirls.

In the morning I stumbled into the kitchen. Edna was gone. In the middle of the floor, though, was a towering mound of pink cotton smocks. I curled my lip. Laundry day. For years we'd gotten the House Mouse cleaning smocks through a uniform service. On Mondays the service dropped off clean smocks, and Fridays they picked up the soiled ones. Earlier in the year, though, Edna had fired the service on one of her economy kicks. She'd gone to a supply house and bought three dozen smocks and declared that we would launder them ourselves.

Today was my turn.

I scooped up an armload of smocks and marched into the laundry room, where I dumped the first load into the washer.

While the water was running into the tub I looked idly down at the wad of pink. Uniforms. Identity was just a question of the right uniform.

I snatched up the cleanest smock from the dirty pile, grabbed a caddy of cleaning supplies, and headed over to Dunwoody. Maureen lived in Dunwoody. She had uniforms. Lots of lovely uniforms. And she was already at work.

"Ca'han!" At the sight of me, Maura's face was wreathed in smiles. Also in oatmeal.

Steve Cucich, my brother-in-law, did not look nearly as excited to see me. Maureen's husband and I have an unspoken, if tacit, agreement. We pretend to tolerate each other, at least in front of civilized society. Since it was just the two of us, not counting Maura, who was busy hugging my knees, he dropped the civil act.

"What do you want?" he asked, eyeing the cleaning caddy.

"It's a peace offering," I said. "I woke Maureen up last night, and I'm feeling kind of cruddy about it."

"You should," Steve said. "She didn't get back to sleep until almost midnight. I had to drag her out of bed this morning."

"I know, and I'm really sorry," I said.

"Edna says I'm a thoughtless bitch. So I thought I'd try to make it up to her."

"How?" Steve wanted to know.

I walked past him into the kitchen. "A day of House Mouse," I said brightly. "And because you're family, I'll throw in my ultra-exclusive baby-sitting service."

"You're cleaning our house?" he asked. "That'll be a first."

I picked up the caddy I'd set down on the kitchen counter. "Okay, suit yourself. I'll leave. Make sure you mention to Maureen that you turned down an offer to have her house cleaned, laundry done, and child entertained."

"Whoa!" Steve said, holding up his hand. "Never mind. I just wanted to make sure I understood you clearly. Are you serious about watching Maura? She's a handful, you know."

A bowl of tapioca pudding would have been a handful to Steve Cucich, who, Edna likes to say, is "one ant shy of a picnic."

"No problem," I said, reaching down and picking Maura up. "We'll play house, won't we, punkin?"

"House!" Maura agreed, nodding her head vigorously.

I set her down and gave her the smallest pink smock we had. It reached to her ankles. I handed her a spray bottle with her name on it.

"Whoa!" Steve said. "Chemicals? I'm not sure this is such a good idea, Callahan."

"It's just water," I assured him. "Maura always plays house with me and Edna when she comes over, don't you, punkin? She's even got her own feather duster and her own little broom."

I produced both and handed them to Maura, who immediately began sweeping her daddy's shoetops with the broom. She spritzed his knees with the water, then pretended to wipe them off.

"Well," he said hesitantly.

"Run along," I said, making a shooing motion with my hands. "Isn't there some kind of boy thing you'd like to do today?"

"There's the auto show down at the World Congress Center," he said, his face brightening.

"Go, go, go," I said. "I'll give Maura lunch and put her down for a nap afterward."

"All righty then!" he said, punching the air with his fist. "I'm outta here."

"Thank God," I said under my breath.

Maureen, of course, is the world's most fastidious housekeeper. It was downright depressing, trying to find something to clean. In the end, I disinfected all the bathrooms, mopped and waxed the kitchen floor, vacuumed all the carpets, cleaned out the refrigerator (actually, all I did was dispose of one aging head of lettuce), and straightened the sheets and towels in her linen closet.

While Maura and I swept and mopped, I ran the laundry, which amounted to only two paltry loads. Child's play. I found Maureen's stack of hospital scrubs on a shelf in her closet. Pink ones, blue ones, green ones. The greens looked closest to what I'd seen nurses wearing at Grady. I locked myself into the bathroom and squeezed into the pants, which were so tight I could barely breathe. In addition to being hideously clean, Maureen is also much thinner and shorter than I. The pants only reached to the top of my ankles. Looking at myself in the mirror, I had to admit I looked slightly clownish. Still, they would have to do. Maybe if I skipped lunch the pants would get a little looser.

I lucked out on one account, though. In the jewelry box on top of her dresser, I found Maureen's clip-on Grady I.D. badge. Although she'd worked full-time in Grady's emergency room for at least a dozen years, after she and Steve had adopted Maura, my sister had gone to work for a nursing temp agency, which meant she subbed for staff nurses at any one of a dozen hospitals around the Atlanta area. And she had badges for all of them.

I slipped the uniform and badge into the suitcase-sized pocketbook I'd brought for just such a purpose, then helped myself to a stethoscope, which I found hanging from a hook in the closet. One of the rubber earpieces was missing, but it would do. Might as well make the disguise believable, I thought.

Maura and I had the laundry washed, folded, and put away by eleven o'clock. After that, we watched her Barney video a couple times, and then I disobeyed my sister's strictest orders by tuning in to *The Simpsons*, which made us both laugh so hard we nearly wet our pants. Actually, Maura did wet her pants.

"What shall we have for lunch?" I asked, standing in front of the open refrigerator door. Another depressing sight. Maureen is big on nutrition. Three kinds of low-fat yogurt, a carton of low-fat cottage cheese, all kinds of fruit juices, and a row of containers filled with carrot sticks, celery sticks, and broccoli flowerets.

"How about a nice broccoli sandwich?" I asked.

"Yuck!" Maura said.

"Yogurt?"

She held her nose.

"A McDonald's Happy Meal?"

Maura got my purse and car keys. "Okay," I said in my strictest tone of voice. "But it has to be the low-fat Happy Meal. And we're not super-sizing those fries, little missy."

After lunch, we romped around on the McDonaldland playscape for a while, and a couple little kids looked at me funny when I tried to go down the slide, but all in all, we had a delightful Saturday morning.

Maura fell asleep in her car seat on the way home.

Steve was waiting at the front door. "Where've you been?" he asked. "Maureen called twice. You didn't say you were going to take Maura out."

"I took her out," I said over my shoulder, carrying Maura in and placing her on the sofa in the den. "We had lunch. Spinach and tofu and apple slices."

"Right," he said suspiciously. He bent over and pried Maura's fingers apart, holding up the plastic toy that had come with the Happy Meal.

"Where'd she get this?" he asked.

"Must have been that stranger in the park who was offering her candy," I said, picking up my cleaning caddy and heading for the car.

"Steve?" I said, stopping at the front door.

"What now?"

"You're welcome!"

Shift change would be at three P.M., I knew. I went home and poured myself into

Maureen's uniform, which made me look like a Girl Scout on steroids.

I was pinning the I.D. badge on the collar of the shirt when I took a close look at the photo. Maureen and I bear only a slight family resemblance to each other. Her hair is dark like mine, but poker straight. She's thinner, of course, and has a pointy chin. And she wears wire-rimmed glasses. That, at least, I could take care of by dashing into the drugstore on the way to the hospital. As for the rest of the resemblance, if anybody stopped me, I planned to just say I'd had a permanent and put on a little weight since the photo had been taken.

My pulse quickened a little when I entered the side entrance at Grady, but people were so busy, nobody even stopped and gave me a second glance. I found the elevator to the seventh floor with little trouble, but finding Bucky wasn't so easy.

Twice I'd passed his glass cubicle before I doubled back a third time, looked at the name on the door, and tiptoed inside the room. What was left of Bucky Deavers seemed only a pale, dried-up husk. His head was enveloped in white gauze only a shade lighter than skin the color of parchment. A tangle of tubes ran from his nose and mouth and arm. I wanted to touch him, to reassure myself that this waxen figure was my friend, but I couldn't. Instead, I stared down at the monitors attached to the tubes. But there was nothing they could tell me that I would understand. I stood at the foot of the bed and wept, for the second time in two days. I even wiped my nose on the sleeve of my uniform. Maureen's uniform.

"Bucky?" It came out a whisper. But there was no reply, and I didn't expect one. I inched toward the side of the bed, put my fingertips on the back of his hand, jumped a little at the warmth there. Clinically, he was alive. All the monitors seemed to say so, anyway. Gradually, my fingers curled around his, and I gave his hand a little squeeze.

"This sucks," I said chokily.

"Nurse?" The voice was so loud, I jumped, then turned.

An older man, bald, with a blue Braves baseball cap that he kept twisting in his hands, stood in the doorway. "Nurse, my wife isn't breathing so good. Could you come see about her?"

I blinked. "Your wife isn't breathing?"

"Somebody needs to see about her," he said. "I've been pushing the call button, but nobody will come."

"Sure," I said. "Let's see if we can get somebody. What's your wife's name?"

"Naomi. Naomi Butler," he said. "Could you hurry? Please?"

My sneakers made squeaking noises on the waxed linoleum floor as I hurried toward the nurses' station I had crept past ten minutes before.

"Stay right here, Mr. Butler," I called over my shoulder. The elevator doors were just opposite the nurses' station, where a black nurse was reading a chart. I pushed the "down" button and prayed the car would come fast. Finally, the bell dinged and the doors slid open. I stepped inside, immediately pushed the "door open" button. Then I hollered. "Somebody needs to see about Mrs. Butler!" The black nurse looked up to see who was causing all the commotion.

"Go check on Mrs. Butler," I yelled again. "Stat!" I let the elevator doors close.

When the doors opened again, I hurried out of the hospital, my knees shaking. This had been a mistake. A big mistake.

22

Bucky's apartment was on North Highland Avenue, across the street from Manuel's Tavern. He always claimed it was a coincidence, but he also freely admitted he was basically on the Manuel's food plan, eating dinners there most nights he wasn't working.

The apartment building was a prewar number, sturdy gray brick, and the second- and third-floor apartments had balconies overlooking Highland, which was nice if you liked watching traffic.

The key was where he always left it for us when we cleaned the apartment for him, on the ledge above the door.

I didn't bother with caution. People move in and out of the apartments all the time, most of them young professionals or well-heeled college students. Bucky had lived there for four years and I'd never known him to mention a neighbor by name.

I unlocked the door and stepped inside, and relocked the door.

For a long minute, I stood there, just smelling and remembering.

The apartment smelled like sweat and boiled hot dogs and something else, a faint perfume. The wooden floors were coated with a fine sheen of dust. Bucky hadn't spent much time here in quite a while, from the looks of things.

It was really only two rooms, plus a kitchenette and a bath. The living room was furnished in standard-issue single-guy stuff — a black leather couch, stereo speakers the size of my van, and a large-screen TV. There was a coffee table with a stack of unopened mail atop it.

I walked into the bedroom. A lumpy-looking double bed had a dark gray spread pulled sloppily up over the pillows. The nightstand held a clock radio, a couple of paperback books, and a bottle of Di-Gel. The drawer contained a package of foil-wrapped condoms, a pack of Dentyne, and some old pay stubs. I opened a drawer in the dresser. Not much here. A few ratty T-shirts, some grayed-out socks, and a pair of pajamas still in the plastic wrapper they'd come in.

I picked up the pajamas. The wrapping had yellowed. They'd been in that drawer a long time. A present from a mother or aunt? Bucky's mother had died some years ago, maybe seven or eight years since. He'd never talked a lot about his father, so I assumed his parents had been divorced.

Halfheartedly, I opened the other drawers too. Mostly I found the kind of stuff that's too crappy to pack and too good to just throw away. I had a dresser full of the same kind of stuff at home: shorts I could no longer fit into, T-shirts with faded printing, raggedy jeans I meant to cut off someday.

He'd used the top drawer as a kind of filing cabinet. Old bills, circulars, canceled checks, and a few letters. I grabbed everything and sat down on his bed to take a closer look.

I flipped through the canceled checks. Nothing startling or out of the ordinary. He seemed to use the Quik-Mart across the street as a banking center, regularly cashing checks for fifty dollars or seventy-five dollars there. He paid his rent and his utilities, made car payments, spent money the way most adults do these days. I saw checks made out to the gym, Rich's department store, Visa, and American Express.

The rest of the mail was no more illuminating. There were memos from the city personnel department explaining changes in the city's benefits package, form letters from a timeshare sales outfit in Panama City, Florida, and, finally, a blank envelope containing half a dozen snapshots with a yellow stick-on note attached to the top picture. "Deavers — Thought you'd get a kick out of these. Hell of a time! — J."

Most of the photos were group shots. Guys standing around at a party, waving beers in the air. One was of Bucky and Lisa Dugan, standing beneath a huge neon marquee at the Caesar's Palace. In the photo, Bucky was pointing up at the marquee, which proclaimed that comedian David Brenner and the Lettermen were performing live that night. Another shot was of Bucky, painfully sunburned, lolling beside a swimming pool, Lisa at his side in a black bikini.

So they'd taken a trip to Las Vegas. I took a closer look at the other people in the group shots, recognized some faces I knew, including John Boylan. Had the Vegas trip been a Shamrock outing?

I found myself staring again at the pictures by the pool. Lisa Dugan looked so cool and carefree in her little bikini, staring adoringly up at Bucky. Here was a Bucky I didn't know, with friends I didn't like, a girlfriend I'd just met, on a trip I hadn't been invited on. My mind flashed to the more recent version of Bucky, the waxen figure on a hospital bed.

My anger built as I shuffled back through the photos. In every one, somebody held aloft a beer bottle or a highball glass. The Irish assholes, partying hearty on the road. How many gambling junkets had there been? I wondered.

Absurd. Bucky had never been much of a gambler, claiming he had no talent at bluffing or counting cards. But I kept wondering. Why was he working so many part-time jobs? Lisa claimed they'd been saving up for a house. So why hadn't he given up this apartment, which he obviously hadn't used in months?

I shoved the photos back in the envelope and slipped them into my jacket pocket. I prowled around the apartment for another fifteen minutes, getting increasingly depressed and restless.

No answers here. But where?

Deecie Styles would know.

The phone was on the wall in the tiny galley kitchen, the phone book on the kitchen counter. I flipped through it and found a number for Doubletree Farms.

"This is Doubletree Farms," a recorded voice said. "Our regular office hours are Monday through Friday, eight A.M. to five P.M."

"Shit." I hung up the phone without listening to the rest of the message. For lack of anything better to do, I opened the refrigerator door. The inventory was slim: some bottled water, a jar of pickles, half a loaf of bread that looked to have fossilized over the months.

I looked at the phone again. It was still hooked up. Bucky hadn't lived here for months, yet he'd kept the phone service. Did that say something about his relationship with Lisa Dugan? Or was it just typical fear-of-commitment stuff?

There was an answering machine on the counter, next to where I'd found the phone book. No lights were flashing, but I punched the "message" button anyway. Nothing.

Every question I had seemed to come back with more questions, no answers.

I locked the front door, started to put the key back where it had always been, then changed my mind and put it in my pocket and left.

23

A soggy banner flapped against the gray stone side wall of Manuel's Tavern. It had the Budweiser logo and said "Happy St. Patrick's Day!"

I went inside and sat at one of the booths near the bar. It was close to five o'clock and I was vaguely hungry and definitely clueless.

One of the bartenders, Bishop is his name, came over with a menu. "Hey, Callahan," he said. "What's shakin'?" I looked up, surprised. It was what Bucky always used to say, whenever I called or dropped by the cop shop to see him. "What's shakin'?" he'd always ask.

"What?" Bishop asked. "Why're you looking at me that way?"

"Nothing," I said.

Bishop stood there, his pen poised above his order pad. "You eating or just drinking today?"

"Some of both," I said. "Jack and water and a J.J. Special. Mustard, pickle, no lettuce."

He nodded, writing it down. When he bent

over like that, I could see the bald spot on the top of his head. "How's law school?" I asked.

Bishop's married, has a wife and three kids, and had just started his first year of law school at Georgia State University. Some nights when I went in, I'd see him at the end of the bar, his nose stuck in a thick textbook.

"If I get through contracts, it'll be a freakin' miracle," he said. "You want a salad with that?"

"Nah. Nothing healthy. Just the bourbon and the beef."

He brought my drink and set it down on the table, then slid into the other side of the booth.

"How's Bucky?" he asked.

I took a long swallow of bourbon.

"Not good."

He nodded, didn't know what else to say. Neither did I.

"Boylan brought a poster by. We put it up on the front door," Bishop said. "The one about the reward for information leading to the arrest of the guy who did it. It's posted in the bathrooms, too. You think they'll catch the guy?"

"No real leads. Not any that I know about, anyway." I looked at him thoughtfully. "All the cops hang out here. What are you hearing about all this?"

"The usual. Guys are worked up about it. Bucky had a lot of friends. A lot of 'em are pissed off about what they said on the news, you know, that Bucky might have been involved in something that got him killed. Some kind of bandit operation."

"I don't believe that," I said, swirling the ice around in my glass. "Does it sound like anybody else does?"

Bishop looked around the room, then down at his lap. "Whiskey talk. That's all."

"What kind of whiskey talk?" I wanted to know.

He looked uncomfortable. "Christ, I don't know. It's nothing."

"Come on, Bishop, talk to me. I'm not wearing a mike, you know."

He shook his head. "These are cops we're talking about. If you think I'm screwing with these guys, you're crazy."

"Someplace else then," I said eagerly. "What time do you get off tonight?"

"Not till eleven," he said, getting up and flicking the tabletop with his bar towel. "I don't think this is such a good idea."

"It'll be fine," I said. "I'll meet you. Anyplace you say. Okay? What about Krispy Kreme?"

"Shit, no," Bishop said, alarmed. "There's as many cops there as there are at City Hall

East. More, probably."

"Someplace else then. Name it."

"Leave me alone, Garrity. I'm not getting involved in this thing."

"Bishop." I grabbed his hand. "I saw Bucky today. He's dying. He looks like a corpse already. Somebody did that to him. Put two bullets in his brain. I want that person. So I don't give a damn how scared you are. I'm scared, too. Just tell me what you know. You hear me, Bishop?"

He yanked his hand free of mine.

"Shitfuck," he said. You pick up terrible language hanging around bars. He'd have to clean that up once he passed the bar exam. Hah.

"I gotta stop at the store on the way home. Meet me there. The new Kroger on North Decatur. Eleven-fifteen. After that, I'm done," Bishop warned.

When my food came, I looked down at it and realized I'd had a hamburger for lunch. And I wasn't really hungry.

I picked at the French fries and watched the news. The place started to fill up around six o'clock. Couples stood at the bar, hip to hip, two or three men's softball teams came in, making noise as they assembled enough tables to seat two dozen people. A bunch of women filed in, laughing and carrying prettily wrapped pink and blue gifts for what looked like an office baby shower.

And I sat in my booth by myself. Saturday night and what was I doing? Sitting in a bar, drinking and brooding. I wondered where Mac was. Maybe he'd gone back to Nashville, to start serious house-hunting. Or maybe he was out with the gang from the office tonight. I wondered if he'd given notice yet.

Stop it, I told myself. If you're isolated, it was your own choice. You had a job in an office, plenty of girlfriends to pal around with. You chose to quit the force, chose to open your own business, chose to make it clear to Mac that you wouldn't be bullied into leaving everything you've earned and built in Atlanta. And anyway, you've always despised baby showers.

"Uh, Miss Garrity?" A man's voice.

I looked up.

A tall trim man with a silver crewcut stood beside me, a beer in his hand. He looked familiar, but I couldn't say why.

"Hey, there," I said, trying to make it sound like I knew exactly who he was.

"Could I sit down?" he asked.

"Please do," I said, gesturing at the seat opposite me.

"I saw you at the press conference at the emergency room. The night Deavers was shot," he said, sensing my confusion. "I'm Ignatius Rakoczy. You might have heard me asking the chief a question or two."

I smiled. "Oh, yes. That was great. I couldn't believe anybody had the balls to ask such an impertinent question. And with the television cameras rolling."

He blushed a little. A cop who blushed. I'd never seen such a thing. "My wife was watching the news at home. She almost fainted when she heard me ask it, and then give my name and everything. She was sure I'd get fired."

"Did you?"

"Not yet. But they know the police union is watching, so I don't think they'll mess with me."

"You sounded pretty steamed about the overtime issue."

"I am," Rakoczy said. His voice was deep, with the slightest hint of an accent. Not Southern, European maybe?

"Public safety officers got a three percent raise last year," Rakoczy said. "It was a joke. The mayor keeps saying there's no money in the budget. You know how many executive assistants and press-relations fellas the mayor has? There's plenty of money for those fellas. None of them makes less than forty thousand dollars a year. And none of them has ever put

246

their life on the line for the citizens of this city. There's plenty of cops don't make that kind of money. And at the same time, the city's trying to force officers with any seniority into taking early retirement. If you're over forty-five, forget it. They don't like all the medical claims. They say it's a matter of fitness. Don't you believe it. It's age discrimination, pure and simple."

"Cops have never made any money in this town," I pointed out. "What's different now?"

"The streets are different," Rakoczy said. "You quit the force how long ago?"

"Ten years," I said, sighing.

"You ever make an arrest in a crack house?"

"No. Crack wasn't that big back then. Not here."

"Ever have a twelve-year-old child wave a semiautomatic pistol in your face and threaten to blow your white ass to hell?"

"Can't say that I did."

"Ever stand in the middle of the street staring at a drunk yuppie driving a half-ton Mercedes SUV, praying he swerves in time?"

"I get your point. It's a big bad world out there."

"Everybody going into the academy knows young officers are underpaid," Rakoczy conceded. "That's part of the life. It's understood. But it was also understood that if you did a good job, kept up your training, and advanced your rank, the pay would come along, eventually. What's different now is you have career law enforcement officers, men who should be making a decent, living wage, forced to work two and three jobs just to make ends meet. And that's bad. You can't be alert on your shift if you just came off another job. It's how people get themselves killed."

"You're saying that's what happened to Bucky Deavers?"

"The day before he got killed, he worked his usual shift. Then he worked at the Bottle Shop till four A.M. Then he went home and reported for work again at nine A.M. He had maybe four hours' sleep. His reflexes — how good could they have been under those conditions?"

"I understand his service revolver was out in his car," I said. "He was unarmed. It wouldn't have mattered how good his reflexes were or how much sleep he'd had. The bastard shot him point-blank, in the head. And I don't think it was just random violence either, since you bring it up."

He looked thoughtful. "I've been wondering about that. A buddy of mine showed me the original incident report. No money taken. And Deavers — he didn't identify himself as a police officer, right?"

"I wasn't in the store at the time, and I don't know what the clerk told the police when they interviewed her at the scene."

"And the clerk has disappeared."

"The only witness," I pointed out.

"I take it you have a theory," he said.

"Let me ask you a question," I said. "Do you have a second job?"

"Of course," Rakoczy said. "And a second mortgage too. I have two kids in a private school. And my wife is a teacher. I work security at the mall near my house. Thursday and Friday nights. And I get off at midnight, so I have plenty of sleep."

"Do you know anything about an informal arrangement with certain cops who can line people up with all the security work they want?"

"You mean John Boylan?"

"Yes. Boylan's group. What do you know about them?"

His lip curled. "Drunks. Party animals. I was surprised when I heard Deavers was hooked up with them. He was always a good cop as far as I knew."

"But these other guys weren't?"

"I never thought so. They were always planning some function, golf tournaments, fishing trips, gambling junkets to Vegas and Biloxi and Atlantic City. Like a bunch of overgrown fraternity boys, with all that Irish rigamarole of theirs. It was offensive to a lot of people, I'll tell you that."

"A guy with a name like Rakoczy probably would think that, wouldn't he?" I said gently.

"And a gal with a name like Callahan Garrity probably wants to sign right up and be Queen of the Shamrocks," he shot back. "For your information, my mother was a Danaher from County Clare and a hell of a lot more Irish than any of those billygoats parading around in their green jackets and plastic derbies. No, what's offensive about those fellas is what they stand for. Drunkenness. Bigotry. Amorality. All cloaked in the disguise of good-spirited fraternalism. Spare me, please!"

"Somebody told me the Shamrocks locked up a lot of high-paying security jobs. And unless you were one of them, you could forget about getting one of those plum jobs."

He nodded emphatically. "It was understood. The good-ol'-boy network. The hell with 'em, I say. The day I suck up to John Boylan for anything will be a cold day in hell. That's what I told my wife."

I nibbled at a French fry. "You said these guys are amoral. What did you mean by that?"

It took him a minute to gather his thoughts. "They're just . . . I don't know. Rotten.

Crooked. You know? Not all of 'em, I don't mean. But Boylan, that guy, he's married, but he's always got girlfriends. And he's always working an angle. Kehoe, I don't know as well, but I've heard stories."

He shook his head, gave a wry smile. "It's nothing I can put my finger on specifically."

I leaned forward. "Can you give me a for-instance? I'm intrigued, because I've known Boylan a long time myself. And I've had the same impression as you." I felt myself blushing, but decided to confide in him in the hopes he'd do the same for me.

"Years ago, Boylan and I, uh, dated a few times. It's embarrassing, but we got pretty intimate. Then I found out he was married, with kids. I broke it off right away, of course, but I never trusted him after that."

"That sounds like the guy," Rakoczy agreed. "One time, he was back working in uniform, over in Zone Five where I worked. It was after one of those rap concerts at the Omni. They'd sold out all the tickets, and these kids that couldn't get in went on a rampage. They ran up and down the streets, smashing windows and throwing rocks and beer bottles at passing cars. One kid got shot in the neck.

"Hell of a thing. And one of the stores that got looted was a pawnshop on Central Avenue. The captain sent Boylan and two other

251

guys over there to get things under control. There were some heads bashed. By the time the store owner got down there, the place had been emptied out. A couple weeks after that, I heard Boylan was bragging about the fancy camera he'd gotten out of there. And then I heard he was wearing a new Rolex watch too. Christ! The guy was no better than the kids whose heads he'd been bashing in."

The look on Rakoczy's face was one of pure disgust.

"Boylan helped himself to a camera and a watch when he thought nobody was looking," I said, thinking out loud. "Petty theft, really. Do you think he's capable of something bigger?"

The suggestion seemed to take him by surprise.

"Like what?"

"Armed robbery?"

Rakoczy ran his hand over his chin. "Maybe. Who knows?"

We sat and watched each other warily for a while.

"You seem to have a theory you're working on," he said finally. "Would you mind sharing it with me? Unofficially?"

I wanted to, I really did. But all I had was half-formed ideas and half-baked theories.

"Maybe later," I said.

"Fair enough," Rakoczy said. He got up from the table. "I'm still at Zone Five. Call me if you want to talk."

"I will," I promised.

24

I parked over on the side of the Kroger, near a cluster of shopping carts, turned off the motor, and rolled down the windows. It was still cold, but there was a damp green scent in the air; spring. An elderly man in a red apron came out and corralled all the carts into a row, rolling them slowly toward the front of the store.

After fifteen minutes, Bishop drove up in a burgundy-colored Dodge Aerostar minivan with a bumper sticker that read: "My Kid Can Beat Up Your Honor Student."

He parked in front, looked around, shrugged, then went inside. He came out of the store a short while later, lugging two plastic bags and a gallon of milk.

I whistled softly. He looked, nodded, unlocked the van, and put his groceries inside. Then he walked over and got in my vehicle.

"Is now good?" I asked.

He swiveled his head around, surveying the parking lot. Besides his own van, there were two or three late-model sedans, a beat-up red

Toyota, and two old clunker cars that looked as though they might have been abandoned there.

"My luck, somebody will probably come along and think this is a drug deal," Bishop said, popping a piece of gum into his mouth and handing a piece across to me.

"Give me some credit here," I said, batting my eyelashes. "Maybe they'll think I'm a hooker and you're my john."

"And then if my old lady finds out, I'll really be dead," he said.

I unwrapped the gum and folded the foil into a tiny square. "So, what have you heard?"

"It's nothing," Bishop protested. "I should have kept my big mouth shut."

"But you didn't," I pointed out.

"Christ," he muttered. "You know Amy Greene? Works the lunch shift at Manuel's on weekdays? Blond ponytail? Nice-looking?"

"No," I said. "I don't usually stop by there during the day."

Bishop waved his hand dismissively. "Anyway, she's putting her husband through Georgia Tech. He's got a night job working for Alliance Bank. He reloads ATM machines. All over the city. Drives around in a little white van with these stashes of tens and twenties and fifties that he loads into ATM machines when they're fixing to run out."

"I always wondered how they reloaded those things," I said, "especially the ones that are in those freestanding kiosks in grocery store parking lots."

"Fiske, that's the husband's name, he doesn't talk a lot about it," Bishop said. "Some big security risk, I guess. He came in the bar Thursday night to grab some dinner. We got to talking, I was asking him how it was going driving the money-mobile — that's what Amy calls the bank van, the money-mobile. And Fiske says he quit. That very morning."

"Why'd he quit?" I asked, holding my breath.

"Wednesday night, he got ambushed," Bishop said. "He was down on the Southside, around seven P.M., had six machines he was supposed to service. He pulls into this little shopping center, drives up to the kiosk, gets out, and before he knows it, there's a gun growing out of his ear."

"Jesus," I said.

"Yeah," Bishop said, chewing loudly. "Fiske said the guy wore a mask. 'Gimme the keys,' he says. And then he pats Fiske down, finds his bank beeper, pockets that too. He took Fiske behind one of the stores in the shopping center, back behind a big Dumpster. He made Fiske lie down on the concrete, still at gunpoint, and handcuffed him, with his wrists behind his back. Then the masked guy, cool as you please, got in the money-mobile and drove away."

"With how much money?" I asked.

"Fiske wouldn't say," Bishop said. "He's still scared shitless. He laid in the parking lot all night long, rats running up and down his legs, roaches and stuff. Finally, seven in the morning, a garbage crew finds him there and calls the cops."

"My God," I said. "And he wasn't hurt?"

"He looked okay to me. A little pale maybe," Bishop said.

"Wait a minute. How come there hasn't been anything about this on the news?" I asked.

"Fiske thinks the bank asked the cops to keep it quiet. They don't want the general public to know there's vans tooling around town loaded with dough — and no armed guard to protect it."

"What made you think I'd be interested in this?" I asked. "I mean, I am interested. But how does it relate to the shooting at the liquor store?"

Bishop gave me a long, intent look. "The guy wore a mask, but no gloves. I told you Fiske was scared. He thought the guy would kill him. He kept his eyes on the gun the whole time. And the hand that held the gun was wearing a ring. Sort of like a class ring, big and heavy, with engraving and a colored stone. All night long, he's lying in that parking lot, thinking about what he's gonna do if he gets out of there, and he's thinking about the gun and the hand that held it. And he knew he'd seen a ring like that before. But he couldn't think where."

"And then he remembered?" I suggested.

Bishop nodded. "When Fiske came in Thursday night, there were a bunch of cops at the big table in the back. You know how they come in at the end of their shift, to kind of blow off steam? Fiske went into the bathroom to take a leak, and when he came out, his face had a funny look. Like he might pass out. I asked him what was going on, and that's when he told me the whole story about the hijacking and the money-mobile."

"You're leaving out the best part," I accused him. "What about the ring?"

"One of the cops was at the sink in the bathroom, washing his hands. He was wearing the same kind of ring. That's what freaked Fiske out. But he couldn't tell what was on the ring. After he told me, I took a pitcher of beer and some clean glasses over to their table, and just happened to ask the guy wearing it where he got the ring. FBI Academy, he says. Real proud."

"The holdup guy was a cop," I said slowly. "And not just any cop. A detective, probably. It's a real big deal for a cop to be invited to attend the FBI's police academy up in Quantico, Virginia. They only choose so many cops a year, from all over the country. They have a graduation ceremony, and the graduates all buy class rings."

Bishop snapped his gum loudly, and I jumped.

"Did Fiske tell anybody else about the ring?"

"Hell, no," Bishop said. "He only told me because I happened to be sitting there when he came out of the bathroom. He even made me swear not to tell Amy. If he knew I was talking to you, he'd wring my neck."

"Who was the cop?" I said.

"What do you mean?" Bishop was playing dumb.

"The cop in Manuel's Thursday night, the one wearing the FBI Academy ring," I said. "Who was it, Bishop?"

"Don't know his name," Bishop said. "Thinning blond hair, eyebrows a shade lighter, like the kind of eyebrows that almost aren't there. Maybe six-one, kind of skinny. Dressed in jeans and a denim work shirt."

"Who was he with?" I asked.

"Just some of the cops from City Hall

East," Bishop said. "Half of 'em, I don't know their names. A little short guy with a clipped mustache, everybody calls him Ace. A couple of Fulton Sheriff's deputies, Whiteside and Singletary, and Darryl McKenzie. You know him? I think he used to work for Atlanta, but now he works for the DeKalb S.O."

None of the names meant much to me. I'd heard McKenzie's name, but couldn't put a face with it. A thought occurred to me.

"Were all the cops white?"

Bishop gave me a funny look. "I guess. I didn't really think about it at the time. Yeah, sure, now that you mention, it was all white guys. Have they got some kinda KKK thing going? Is that why you ask?"

I laughed. "KKK? No. Nothing like that, I don't think. If the original ring guy came in again, could you do me a favor, find out who he is?"

"I can try," Bishop said. "But remember, Fiske didn't say it was that exact guy. He just said the guy was wearing the same kind of ring."

"I understand," I said.

"Good," Bishop said. He opened the van door. "I gotta go. My Fudgesicles are melting."

"Thanks, Bishop," I said, blowing him a kiss.

He made like he'd been smacked in the face. "Ow. Cut it out, or you will get me in trouble."

I was almost home when I heard the sirens. Dozens of them. The hairs on the back of my neck stood up.

I pulled into the driveway and raced into the house. Edna was in the den, watching an old black-and-white movie on the television.

"Turn the channel to WSB," I said, out of breath.

"What? This is my favorite Lana Turner movie," Edna said, moving the remote control from her right hand to her left, and out of my reach.

"Turn the channel, please!" I said. "You hear those sirens out there? That's not just a cop chasing a speeder."

She turned the channel, but the newscaster was droning on about tomorrow's weather.

I reached for the phone, called the Hunseckers.

Linda answered. "Hey, girl," she said.

"Do you know anybody in dispatch?" I asked.

"Sure," she said, sounding puzzled. "What's this all about?"

"I just heard maybe two dozen Atlanta cruisers heading out on Ponce de Leon," I said. "Can you call and find out what's going on?"

"Call you right back," Linda said.

Edna flipped the channel back to *Madam X*, but she turned the sound down. "What's happening?" she asked. "Does Linda know anything?"

The phone rang again before I could answer her.

I picked it up.

"Officer down," Linda said, her voice cracking.

"Where?"

"A Vietnamese market on Buford Highway, just inside the city," Linda said. "That's all I know. What's happening in this town, Callahan?"

"Something bad," I said.

25

The television news stations had the sketchiest of details. The cop who'd been killed was an Atlanta officer. He and his partner were answering a suspicious-person call at a Vietnamese market Buford Highway and had apparently walked in on a burglary. The burglar shot one officer and killed him, fired at the other officer, missed, and fled the scene.

Edna turned the television off and sat there, tsk-tsking. "Maybe we should reconsider about staying here in Atlanta," she said, giving me a sidelong look.

"Because of this?" I asked.

"I'm serious, Jules," she said. "That's the second cop shot in a week. Crime's awful. Drugs everywhere. Children carrying guns and knives to school. Look at what happened to you yesterday at that Memorial Oaks. And don't even mention the traffic. Lord have mercy. I went out to your aunt Olive's house yesterday and it like to have taken me an hour just sitting there in traffic on Georgia 400."

"They have traffic in Nashville, Mama," I

said. "And crime and drugs. It's everywhere. I don't think it's something you can just run away from anymore. And what about your friends? And your family? We're all right here in Atlanta. You want to leave all that?"

"Maybe," she said, her voice sad. "It's not the Atlanta I know anymore. You see somebody on the street, they just look at you real mean like. People don't howdy like they used to. Nothing's like it used to be."

"I know," I said, patting her knee. "I miss the old ways too. But it's not just Atlanta, you know. It's the whole South. Malls and McDonald's and cable TV and Wal-Mart. You can't tell Nashville from Atlanta from Jacksonville."

"We could move out to the country, not even live inside Nashville," Edna said dreamily. "Maybe a little farm. I could have chickens. My mama used to keep chickens, so I know how to keep up with 'em. I'd have me a real vegetable garden, put in some corn and beans and okra. Mac would love it, living on a farm."

What about me? I wanted to ask. But it was too late. Edna went off to bed, to dream of guinea hens and Silver Queen corn and Kentucky Wonder pole beans.

For once, I didn't dream of anything.

In the morning, the newspaper had all the

details. The dead cop's name was Sean Ragan and he was twenty-four years old, just a baby, with pink cheeks and a flattop haircut and the "gee whiz" look you see in cops not long out of the academy.

The paper said he'd been on the force two years. He'd gone to high school in Fayetteville and married his high school sweetheart, whose name was Alexis. Beside the APD photo of Sean Ragan in his dress uniform, they had a wedding picture of the two newlyweds toasting with champagne glasses in front of a towering white wedding cake.

I had to bite my lips to keep from crying when I saw the wedding picture. I pushed the local section of the paper across the table to Edna, who'd already finished reading the front-page account of the shooting.

She looked down through the bifocals perched at the end of her nose.

"I'm dead serious about what I said last night, about moving away from Atlanta," she said, her voice low. "I can't force you to do anything you don't want to do. I know that. But I'd like for you to give it some serious thought, Jules. And even if you decide not to go with Mac, I'm thinking I'm ready to move away from here. I mean it. I want out. This city's changed. I'm afraid to unlock my door anymore. Will you think about it?"

What could I do?

"I'll think about it," I promised.

"Will you call Mac, make up with him?"

"Make up?" I said indignantly. "What have I got to make up for?"

"What do you want to break up with him for?" Edna asked. "Do you love the man or not?"

I scowled at her, but didn't answer.

I read back over the paper. The police chief had held another post-midnight press conference, decrying violence in the city, and offering a ten-thousand-dollar reward for information leading to Sean Ragan's killer. The story said Ragan's partner, a twenty-eight-year-old officer named Antjuan Wayne, had been treated and released from Grady, after spraining his ankle pursuing the fleeing killer. The paper also noted that another cop, Detective Charles Deavers, was still in critical condition in the hospital's intensive care unit.

I flipped through the rest of the local section of the paper, reading the police blotter, which listed all the shootings, knifings, beatings, and hit-and-run accidents that had occurred in the previous two days.

Maybe Edna was right. Things had gotten ugly in our old hometown. Suddenly, I couldn't really remember why I had such a hankering to stay put.

I turned to the last two pages of the paper — the obituaries, or the Irish sports section, as my father used to call it. When had I taken to reading the death listings with such morbid curiosity? I wondered. Did this fascination with the dead mean I was smack in the middle of middle age?

Depressing thought. But then, the obituaries were depressing. There was a listing for Sean Ragan's funeral. There was to be a service Tuesday at Sacred Heart Church downtown, with burial at a cemetery in Fayetteville.

Mob scene, I thought. A young white police officer killed in the line of duty. The funeral would be a mob scene.

The phone rang and I picked it up absentmindedly. "Yes?"

A voice, muffled. "I'm looking for Callahan Garrity."

I put the paper down, gripping the phone tightly in my hand. "This is Callahan Garrity."

"Are you the lady that was in the Budget Bottle Shop when that police officer got shot?" the voice asked. The caller sounded like a young black man.

"I was just outside," I said, correcting him. "What's this about?"

"This is about somebody you been looking

for. Somebody you been asking a lot of questions about."

"Deecie? Deecie Styles? I have been looking for her. Do you know where she is?"

"I know right where she's at," the man said, chuckling a little.

"Will she talk to me?"

"She's scared. She's scared to talk to anybody. Folks saying she's a thief. People are after her. Deecie didn't do nothing wrong."

"I don't believe she did anything wrong," I said quickly. "I'd just like to talk to her. About what happened in the store that night. My friend got shot, nearly killed. I want to find out what she saw that night. What really happened."

"Why should she trust you? You a cop, ain't you?"

"No," I said quickly. "I used to be. But not anymore. Can I see her? I think I can help."

"Just a minute." He put the phone down, and I could hear faint murmuring in the room.

"They say there's a reward. For whoever turns in the person who shot at that cop. Is that true?"

"Yes," I said. "There's a thirty-thousand-dollar reward for the person who gives information about the shooter. Does Deecie know who that is?"

"Never mind that," he said harshly. "What

about the money? Is that for real?"

"As far as I know, it is," I said, trying to tread cautiously.

"She have to go to court, get up on a stand and tell what she saw?"

"I don't know," I said. "The posters say the information will be confidential. So I'm assuming she wouldn't have to."

"You find out about that reward, Deecie might talk to you."

"When?" I said. "Would she talk to me today?"

"I'll call back," the man said. "You tell me what I want to hear, Deecie will see you whenever I say."

26

"This is Major Lloyd Mackey. Please leave a message, or if this is an emergency, call back and ask the operator to beep me."

I hesitated. It was Sunday, and Mackey should have been off duty. But one of his men had been gunned down, so I was certain he had been working the case nonstop since the night before. If I beeped him in the middle of his investigation, he'd be so angry he might not cooperate.

In the end, I left a message saying it was urgent, and that I needed to hear from him today, and possibly had information about the shooting at the liquor store.

Five minutes later he called back.

"This is Mackey," he said in a growl. "And this better not be bullshit, Garrity. I got a man lying up in the morgue over at Grady."

I bit my lip. "I know. And I'm truly sorry. I hope you catch the bastard who did this. But you've got another man lying up on the seventh floor, and the only thing keeping him alive is a bunch of tubes coming in and out of him. I want to find out who tried to kill Bucky Deavers."

"You think I don't? Now what do you want? What's this about information about Deavers?"

I chose my words carefully. "I had an anonymous phone call this morning. Somebody who might know something about the robbery at the Budget Bottle Shop. The caller was asking whether the cash reward is for real."

"Thirty thousand dollars? Yeah, it's real. But we ain't payin' it out for some whispered phone call."

"I'm aware of that," I said impatiently. "The caller was asking whether the person who claims the reward will have to testify against the shooters, if it ever comes to trial."

"Depends on who the caller is and what he saw," Mackey said. "Come on, Garrity, you know all this stuff already. Anyway, if the person calls back, you just tell 'em to call the police department. This isn't anything for you to get involved in."

"I intend to tell them just that," I said. "But the person who called me doesn't seem to trust the police. He wants to make sure his information will be kept confidential."

"Nobody trusts the cops," Mackey said bitterly. "That's why our guys keep getting blown away. You tell your caller if he's got questions, call Major Lloyd Mackey. Tell him you talked to me, and I'm personally in charge of this case. Tell him you know me, and you trust me. Right?"

"I know you," I said. But I wondered about the trust issue. I kept thinking about what Bishop had told me, about the ATM holdup artist who wore an FBI Academy ring.

"Major Mackey, can I ask you something?"

"I've got work to do, Garrity," he said. "Can't it wait?"

"Just one question," I promised. "How many people on your force have been through the FBI Academy?"

"The FBI Academy? How the hell should I know? Maybe six of my men, but that doesn't count everybody in the department. And it doesn't count people who joined Atlanta after they'd been sent by their previous department."

"How about you? Did you go?"

"None of your business," Mackey said. He hung up on me.

I told myself Mackey was under unbelievable stress. That he was trying to do his job. That he was true blue. And I kept wondering. Could another cop have shot Bucky? Did it have something to do with the ATM robberies? Why Bucky? Was any of this connected to the killing of Sean Ragan?

I pulled out a yellow legal pad and sat down at the table to make notes. First a list of facts, then a list of questions.

Fact: On Wednesday, Bucky Deavers had been shot twice in the head with a .22 pistol. The gun had been left at the scene.

Fact: The only witnesses, as far as I knew, were Deecie Styles and her child Faheem, both of whom had disappeared shortly after the shooting.

Fact: There had been a shattered six-pack of Harp beer on the floor beside Bucky's body. There wasn't any Harp in the cooler in the store, and Bucky certainly hadn't carried it in there with him.

Fact: The shooter had exited the store before I entered, most probably through the rear door and out the alley.

I took to doodling around on the page, sketching the interior of the Budget Bottle Shop from memory. The front door, the windows, the counter, and the door to the back room. I wished I'd had a chance to go behind the counter, to get a look at the panic button Deecie said she'd pushed as soon as the would-be robber entered the store, and to see where the video camera was actually located.

While I was bent over my sketch, Edna came bustling into the kitchen. She was dressed in her good flowered blue dress, pearls, stockings, and a pair of navy heels. My God, she was wearing lipstick.

I looked her up and down. "Is the queen in town?"

"Funny."

"You look very nice," I added. "Where are you headed?"

"It's Sunday morning. I'm going to Mass," she said, adding quickly, "It wouldn't hurt you to go with me, either."

"Mass? As in Catholic Mass?"

She took her good coat out of the closet and shrugged herself into it. "You know I've been going to Mass lately."

"Twice recently," I said. "If you include Christmas Eve."

She reached into her pocket and brought out a set of silver rosary beads, which she proceeded to shake in my face.

"You laugh all you want, Julia Callahan Garrity. Your daddy and I never raised you to be a heathen. I might not have set the best example for you since he died, but I'm trying to mend my ways. And I suggest you look to mending yours."

I blinked. She was absolutely sincere. My backslidden mother was crawling back up the slippery slope of faith. Next thing you know she'd have us all sitting around the kitchen burning incense and singing "Faith of Our Fathers." Or worse, maybe she'd find her old magnetic-mounted Jesus and reinstall him on the dashboard of her Chevy.

"Why the sudden surge of religion?" I asked. "If you don't mind my asking."

She patted her blue-tinted hair. "I don't mind sharing my faith at all. I'm going to Mass to pray for Bucky Deavers. And for the soul of that poor boy who was killed last night. And then I'm going to pray that you'll see the light about this Nashville move. Sure you don't want to come along with me?"

I gestured toward my notepad. "Sorry. I've got work to do."

"That's what I was afraid you'd say." She buttoned her coat. "I'll pray double for you."

"Better make it triple," I said.

After Edna left, I made myself a pot of coffee and a plate of scrambled eggs and bacon. I cleaned up the kitchen and wandered aimlessly around the house for a while, straightening picture frames, running a dust rag over the windowsills in the living room. I turned on the television, watched an old episode of *The Andy Griffith Show*, the one where Andy explains *Romeo and Juliet* to Opie. I laughed myself silly for half an hour, then roamed the house some more, letting my mind float, deliberately avoiding the subject of what had happened at the Budget Bottle Shop.

After a couple hours of contemplating my navel, I went back to the yellow legal pad, flipped the page, and started writing questions.

How had the shooter entered the liquor store? Had the alley door been left unlocked? If there were security guards working other nights at the store, why not the night Bucky was shot? What other security guards besides Boylan usually worked at the store? Had the robber taken money from the cash register, or had it been, as Pete Viatkos claimed, Deecie Styles?

I drew a large circle around that set of questions, then started another list at the bottom of the page.

What businesses had been victims of ATM robberies? Were they all in the City of Atlanta, or had stores in other locations also been victimized? How much money had been taken? Was anybody else harmed? And what about Boylan and his boys? Was C.W. right? Was Boylan recruiting cops from the Shamrock Society to an armed-robbery ring? Could one of the Shamrocks have been involved in the hijacking of Bishop's friend Fiske?

I flipped the page and kept writing. The whole exercise was beginning to feel futile. There were too many jurisdictions around Atlanta, and I had no authority to ask the questions I wanted answered.

The phone rang and I grabbed for it, annoyed at being disrupted. The annoyance vanished when the caller spoke.

"Did you find out about the reward?"

"It's for real," I said, forcing myself to speak slowly. "The police say they can't be certain whether or not Deecie would have to testify. They say it would depend on what she saw."

"She saw it all," the caller assured me. "But she ain't going on no witness stand. She got a kid to think about."

"Faheem? Is he all right? I understand he's been sick. If Deecie wants, I could get her help for Faheem. Take him to a doctor."

"Deecie takes care of Faheem all right. She don't need you."

"But I need her," I said, trying not to sound desperate.

"Hold on," the man said. And he put the phone down again.

"You still there?"

"I'm here."

"What kinda car you got?"

"A pink Chevy van," I said.

"Sissy-ass car."

"It runs," I said, getting defensive.

"You know how to get to Shallowford Road and I-85?"

"Yes."

"You got a cell phone?"

"Yes."

"Gimme the number."

I recited the number twice.

"Get on Shallowford and keep going on past where it crosses 85. About three miles up, there's a dry cleaner's on the left side of the road, beside a Minute Mart. You be there, one hour, exactly. Wait there. Somebody will call, tell you what to do next, unless you trying something funny."

"I'm not trying something funny," I assured him.

I heard a voice in the background.

"What?" the man said. "Hang on."

He was gone again, then he came back on the line. "Okay. You need to bring a box of Pampers, toddler size. And a gallon of whole milk, some bread, and some peanut butter. Oh, yeah. Stop by McDonald's, get four Quarter-Pounders and two large Cokes. You got any wine?"

"I've got wine," I said cautiously. This was some shopping list he was giving me.

"Bring some wine, too," he said. "You ain't there in an hour, you don't talk to Deecie. And if you bring any cops . . ."

"No cops," I said firmly.

27

An hour didn't give me much time to get where I was going. I picked up the diapers and groceries at a convenience store on Ponce. The drive-through line at McDonald's was five cars long, so I pulled up to a parking space and ran inside to order.

Of course, I got the slow-motion synchronized food servers of all times.

"No fries," I said, breathing hard. "Four Quarter-Pounders and two large Cokes to go."

The girl looked puzzled, tapping the hamburger and Coke icons on her cash register keyboard. She stopped and chewed on her thumb, staring down at the keyboard as though it was the first time she'd seen it.

"I'll give you a five-dollar tip if you get me my food in five minutes," I said.

She thought about it. "We're not allowed to take tips."

"Think of it as a bribe," I snapped.

Sunday afternoon traffic was light on Interstate 85. I got off on the Shallowford Road exit as my caller had directed. Crossing over the Interstate onto Shallowford was like crossing the border into Tijuana.

Signs on both sides of the road were written in Spanish and English. I saw groups of Hispanic men standing at bus stops or congregated around cars in shopping center and apartment complex parking lots.

Most of the men, I knew, were day laborers, drawn to the Shallowford corridor by good-paying construction jobs around Atlanta's booming perimeter. Check a construction site in Atlanta and you'll hear Spanish radio stations, see taqueria trucks parked at lunchtime. Sheetrock crews, brick masons, framers, and roofing crews — nearly all seem Mexican. The apartment complexes along the corridor had become home to the laborers, many of them living six or eight to an apartment, an economy move to allow them to send most of their wages to family back in Mexico.

With five minutes to spare, I found the shopping center with the dry cleaner's, and backed into the space, so that I faced out, looking at Shallowford.

I slid a hand under my seat, feeling my Smith & Wesson 9-mm lodged there, and patted the pocket of my blazer, where I'd slipped my cassette tape recorder. Then I put my head back and exhaled slowly.

It was just after three o'clock. Three young Mexican girls strolled past the laundry, their long dark hair whipping about in the gray afternoon breeze. I could hear their laughter through the van's rolled-up windows.

Five minutes was just long enough for a chill to settle over me. I turned up the collar of my blazer and started the van so I could run the heater. Another five minutes passed, and then another.

Was the whole thing a hoax? I craned my neck, looking up and down Shallowford, seeing nothing remarkable. The cell phone rang and I jumped.

I flipped it open.

"Get out of the van and walk toward the street." It was the same voice I'd heard before.

"What about the diapers and food and stuff?" I asked.

"Leave the keys in the van. Somebody will get the stuff."

"Leave my car unlocked in this neighborhood? I'm crazy, but I'm not stupid."

"You want to talk to Deecie or not?" he asked.

"Yes, but — "

"Walk to the road. You can carry the cell phone in your hand, so we know it's you. Get out of the van right now, or forget about it."

281

I looked around. I wanted to take my gun, but I was afraid he was watching and would see me bend down to get it.

"All right," I said. "I'm getting out."

"Good," he said. "Walk fast. Right to the curb."

I gave my van a last longing look. It was cold outside, the temperature hovering just above freezing, and I'd been in such a rush I'd forgotten to grab a heavy jacket.

I crossed a strip of brown weeds and stood at the edge of the street, feeling small and vulnerable.

"A car's gonna pull up. We'll open the door. Just get in. Don't say nothing. Don't ask nothing."

"How do I know it's you guys?" I asked. "I'm not in the habit of getting in a car with strangers."

"Just do it," he said.

Cars passed, a pickup slowed down, honked the horn, and a guy leaned out the passenger side. "Hey, bay-bee!"

I flipped him a bird, then put my hands in my pockets.

A faded yellow Cadillac with tinted windows slowed and stopped at the curb. The back door opened. I swallowed hard, and got in.

The driver kept his back turned to me. A

guy in the front seat turned around. He was young, black, with a round face shaded by a Braves baseball cap. "You're doin' good," he said, his smile revealing a chipped front tooth.

I recognized his voice. He was the caller. I held up the cell phone. "Nice talking to you."

He held up his. "Likewise."

"Are you William?" I asked.

"Could be. You leave the van unlocked?"

I nodded. "I hope your buddy picks it up soon. I need my wheels."

"He's right behind us," William said.

"How's Deecie?" I asked.

"Scared. Real scared."

He handed me a red bandana. "Tie that around your eyes. You don't wanna know where we're taking you."

"Come on," I protested. "I'm not interested in turning Deecie in. I told you that. I want to help her and Faheem."

"You wanna help, you put that on and quit asking questions," he said.

The bandana smelled like cigarette smoke. I sat very still, with my hands folded in my lap. We drove in silence for maybe ten minutes, in what direction I couldn't say.

"Turn here," William told the driver. The car swayed to the right. "Slow down. Yeah. Go all the way around the back." The car slowed, and I felt it go over what felt like a speed bump. "Keep going," William coached. "See where I'm pointing? Pull over there. Give one beep, so they'll know it's us."

The horn honked once, lightly, and the driver cut the ignition. I heard the front door open and close. Then my door opened. A hand took mine and guided me out of the car. I stood unsteadily.

"Hang on to my arm," William instructed. "Nice and slow." I linked my arm in his and we inched forward. "Three steps up," he said, pulling at my arm. "Then two steps forward. Okay, now I'm opening the door, and you're gonna step over a threshold and then stop," he said. I did as I was told, taking mincing steps. I didn't like this worth a flip.

I heard a grating metallic sound, felt warm air against my face. He propelled me forward three steps, and then stopped. The door closed behind us. He pulled me forward and I stumbled, nearly tripping, until he yanked me to an upright position. "Damn, girl," he muttered. He reached over and pulled the bandana off. It took a moment for my eyes to get adjusted to the light, not that there was much of it.

We were in some kind of storeroom, cement floored, with high ceilings. Crates were stacked against walls, the lettering was in Spanish.

"In here," William said, jerking his head to the left.

A door on the left was slightly ajar, spilling light into the stockroom. The sign on the door said "Ladies."

Deecie was seated on a cracked green plastic sofa, a red plaid sleeping bag wrapped around her shoulders. Her hair was uncombed and stood up wildly from her head. There were dark circles under her eyes, and she sipped from a large McDonald's Coke. So my van really had made the trip.

There was a portable playpen shoved in the corner of the bathroom, up against a grungy sink. Faheem lay on his stomach, head turned to the side, fast asleep.

"How ya doing?" I asked, giving her a smile.

She shrugged, held out the McDonald's bag to William. "You didn't tell her about the pickles."

He took the bag, peered inside. "Pickles ain't gonna kill nobody." He pushed the door of the toilet stall open and sat himself on the commode, gesturing for me to sit on the sofa beside Deecie.

"Bucky," she said softly. "Is he dead?"

"No. He's still alive, if you can call it that."

She lifted the edge of her Quarter-Pounder, removed the pickles, and dropped them in the paper sack beside her. She took a test nibble of the hamburger, paused, then attacked it as though she hadn't eaten in a week.

I made myself wait until she'd polished off the hamburger, wadded up the foil wrapper, and disposed of it. William sat on the commode and had his lunch, keeping his eyes on me all the while he was eating.

"Deecie," I said finally, thrusting my hands into my jacket pockets and turning on the tape recorder. "Will you tell me what happened that night? Who shot Bucky?"

Her eyes darted toward William. He nodded.

She blotted her lips with a paper napkin. "Only time that night it got quiet. Bucky came in, told me hi. Then he went over to the beer cooler. He opened the door and stood there looking. I knew what he was looking for. That beer he likes."

"Harp," I said.

"Yeah. He usually took a six-pack home with him the nights he worked," Deecie said. "But man, we were busy all night. Sold a ton of beer. 'Cause it was St. Patrick's Day. We were out of all the imported beer. Molson, Moosehead, Heineken. And I told him that. So he says, 'Never mind, I bet there's some in the walk-in cooler in the back.' So I buzzed the buzzer that unlocks the door, and he went on back there."

"Did you go with him?" I asked.

"Uh-uh," she said, shaking her head no. "I told you, we'd been busy all night. That old Greek, if he catches you leaving the register, he'll fire your ass in a New York second. Bucky went on back, and I stayed out front."

"Wait," I said. "Weren't you in the store alone?"

She rolled her eyes. "I thought I was. Pete came in about six. He took the big bills out of the register and put them in the safe in back, then he told me the security guard wasn't coming in. So I'd be working alone, and was that a problem? I'd worked by myself a couple times before, and I wasn't scared. I knew where the panic button was, and cops come in there all the time, 'cause they're all buddies with Pete. And the police department is just down the street, right?"

I nodded agreement.

"After Pete left, my aunt come in the store carrying my baby," Deecie said. "Faheem was cuttin' up bad. He was really sick. And my aunt, she said she couldn't get no sleep with him cuttin' up like that. She wanted me to come home and take care of him. But I couldn't leave the store. Pete woulda fired me for sure. So I told her leave him with me. He cried for a while, but after he had a bottle, he settled down some. He slept the rest of the night. Good as gold. He woke up right before Bucky come in."

"But other than Faheem, you were alone?"

"I'm getting to that," she said. "After Bucky went in back, a guy came in the store."

"Who?" So I had dozed off while Bucky was in the store.

"Just some old guy. He was asking me about scotch, and I don't know nothing about scotch. I sold him a bottle of Dewar's. He paid cash and left. Next thing I know, Bucky comes bustin' out of the storeroom. He's got the beer in his hand, and a funny look on his face. He walked right past me, like he didn't even see me there. So I yelled at him, 'Stop, thief,' like a joke, right? And he starts to say something, but all of a sudden, the storeroom door opens again, and this guy runs out. He's got on a stocking mask, like I told you. That part was true, swear to God. And he screams something like, 'Stupid motherfucker.' And Jesus, he's got a gun!"

Deecie's face twisted in agony. Tears ran down her cheeks. "And Bucky turns around, like he's gonna run, but the guy just shoots. He shot him right in the head," she said chokily. "I never seen nothing like that. I was screaming and screaming. And the guy walks up to Bucky, puts the gun right behind his ear and shoots again."

"What were you doing during all this?" I asked.

"Screaming!" she said. "And Faheem he was screaming, 'cause I scared him, I guess. I got down on the floor behind the register, and that's when I remembered about the panic button. I pushed it, and then I was laying there, and I looked up, and he was behind the counter with me! He pointed the gun at me, and Faheem screamed, and then, I don't know. Something happened. Like he changed his mind. He was gonna kill us, I just knew it. But he shook his head, then he pushed the button on the stockroom door and buzzed it and ran out."

"He knew where the buzzer was to unlock the door?"

"Look like it to me," she said, wiping at a tear with her little finger. "Something come over me after that. I was scared, but I wanted to see what happened, where that man went," Deecie said. "I put Faheem down in his carrier and I ran into the stockroom too. The alley door was open, and I went over there and looked out. And that's when I seen it."

"What?"

"The truck. Big old white pickup truck. Parked there in the alley. Had the lights off, but when I peeked out, it started up and went racing out of there."

"You know whose truck it was?" I asked.

"Pete's," she whispered. "It was Pete's."

28

Pete Viatkos was there when Bucky was shot? The notion didn't seem to work. Why would Viatkos stage a robbery at his own store and shoot an employee in the head, leaving another employee alive to testify against him?

"You said it was Pete's truck? Was he driving it?"

"It was dark. I couldn't see who was driving," Deecie said. "But I know it was his truck. One of those really big ones, a Ford."

"Like an F-10," William put in. "That's what that old Greek drives. A white Ford F-10. He used to park out front of the liquor store."

"Is that why you took off with the money and the videotape?" I asked. "Because of Viatkos?"

"I never took no damn money," Deecie said. "That's a damn lie, if he said it. All I did was take the videotape and put it in Faheem's diaper bag. I don't know what made me take it, guess I was thinking about what Pete would do to me if I told. Anyway, who'd believe me? It don't make sense."

"What about the shooter?" I asked. "Could he have been Viatkos?"

"I don't think so," she said reluctantly. "The voice was different. And the guy who shot Bucky, he was bigger than Pete. And he was quick. Pete's a old dude. He ain't moving that fast."

"Where's the videotape?" I asked.

Deecie looked over at William, who shook his head side to side.

"Don't even think about it. That's our insurance policy," William said craftily. "Ain't nobody getting a look at that until we start talking about reward money."

"Why'd you even call me?" I asked. "Why not call the cops and tell them your story?"

Deecie looked down at her sleeping son, her expression softening. "I heard you'd been 'round, asking about me. The police been 'round too, but they calling me a thief, tellin' my aunt they gonna arrest me. And I ain't done nothin'."

"You're going to have to trust somebody," I said. "I can't get you the reward money. You'll have to talk to the cops. Tell them what you saw that night."

"They gonna believe me and not Pete Viatkos?" she asked.

William snorted. "Yeah, and pigs can fly.

That old dude's best friends with half the cops in this town. Who's gonna believe us?"

"I believe you."

A little gurgling sound came from the playpen. We all looked. Faheem was sitting up, rubbing his eyes with balled-up fists. He yawned, then started to wail. Deecie stood and picked him up, hugging him to her, making little shushing sounds until he quieted down.

She looked over her son's head at me. "We can't be staying here much longer. My baby's sick. It's cold in here. William, he been doing the best he can, but we got to get out of here. Somebody finds out we're staying here, ain't no telling what could happen."

William put a protective arm around her shoulder. "Nothing's gonna happen to you. I ain't gonna let it. I got my crew, we take care of things."

"Your crew can't prove Deecie didn't steal that money," I pointed out. "And they can't convince the police she saw what she saw. But I think I can."

"How?" William demanded.

"I know the head of the homicide unit. Major Mackey. He was Bucky's boss. He wants to find out who shot him. He wants the truth."

"What about the money?" William asked.

"When do we get the reward money?"

"The reward money depends on the police arresting and convicting the person responsible for shooting Bucky," I said. "It's very likely Deecie will have to give the police a sworn statement and testify in court."

Deecie's eyes widened in alarm. "Against Pete Viatkos?"

"You don't know he was the shooter," I said. "You don't even know that was him driving the truck. But if you were to hand over that videotape, the police could get a better look at the shooter."

Deecie stood there, swaying back and forth, making small clucking sounds to Faheem. "William?"

For the first time, he looked uncertain.

"I wanna go home, William," Deecie said. "Let my baby sleep in his own crib. Get him his medicine." She sounded tired.

William said, "You say you know this guy, the head man? And he'd be straight with us?"

"Yes," I said, trying to sound convincing.

Deecie turned to him, her eyes pleading.

"All right," William said. "You talk to the man. I'll call you tonight, see what the deal is."

"Tonight? That's not enough time," I said. "Another cop was killed last night. Every cop in the city is working that case. I don't know if

I can get to Major Mackey tonight, William. It might take a little more time."

"Tomorrow," Deecie said, deciding the matter. "Tomorrow is good enough. But no longer, okay?"

"I'll do my best," I said. "But I'd have more leverage if you'd let me see the videotape."

"We'll call you tomorrow," William said.

He put the bandana on me and helped me into the car. Or rather, the van. I could tell from the step up that we were getting into my pink van. We drove for another ten minutes or so, me masked, with my radio blaring.

I felt the van turning once, then again. He put it in park. I heard the driver's side door open, then close. Then he was by my side, speaking into my ear.

"I'm leaving now. Five minutes, you can take that off. Don't try to come looking for us. And don't be messin' us around. Okay?"

"Okay," I said.

29

Mackey's face had aged a decade in just a few days. He was unshaven, his dress shirt rumpled, the necktie askew. Stacks of files littered his desk. He opened one and flipped through it as I played the audiotape of Deecie Styles.

He cocked his head at the mention of Pete Viatkos. "What the hell?"

"Keep listening," I said.

He closed the file, picked up a pen, and started making notes as the rest of the tape played. When it reached the end, he pushed the "rewind" button and played it again.

"What do you think?" I asked.

Mackey scratched his chin with the end of the pen, pushed his chair away from the desk. "I think you should mind your own goddamn business."

"They called me," I said. "Should I have hung up? Insisted Deecie turn herself in to you? That's a lot of crap and you know it, Major. You heard what the girl said. Pete Viatkos is a cop groupie. He's got a lot of bud-

"dies in the department."

"Not me," Mackey insisted.

"Viatkos is involved in that shooting," I said. "And he's got helpers. We know that. Now we just need to know who."

"Hell, I know what you think, Garrity. You think it was a cop shot Deavers. Lisa Dugan had a long talk with me after your little date with her. You shook her up pretty bad, you know that?"

"That wasn't my intention at all," I said. "I just want to get to the bottom of this thing."

"What's this crap about a gang of cops involved in holdups? This isn't Chicago or New York, you know."

"There are rumors," I said carefully. "A string of robberies. All of them at ATM machines in the metro area. The victims are people trying to make sizable cash deposits. The pattern's the same every time. They approach the ATM machine, usually late at night, and a masked gunman takes the cash at gunpoint. So far, no violence and no clues. You could check it out, you know."

"I have checked it out," Mackey said, grabbing a folder and opening it. "Total of seven armed robberies. Not all of them in Atlanta. East Point had one, College Park, Roswell, Smyrna."

"What about the businesses who were the

victims?" I asked. "Did you check to see if they employed off-duty cops in any capacity?"

"And why would I do that?"

"Just a theory," I said pleasantly.

"I know all about your theories, and I resent the hell out of them," Mackey said, his face flushing crimson. "Our guys are out there every day of the year, laying their lives on the line for people like you. They get dirt for pay, dick for respect, put up with crooked lawyers and judges, get jerked around by the politicians and their own department, and get shot at and shit on by the bad guys. I'll be damned if I'm gonna start pointing the finger at my guys for some penny-ante stickup jobs."

I was getting pretty worked up myself now. "People like me? What's that supposed to mean, Major? Just because I'm a civilian I can't look askance when I see police corruption? You resent it when I ask questions about 'your boys'? Well, tough shit. You forget I was a cop myself. These guys aren't all blue angels, you know. Take a look at a piece of work like John Boylan. Instead of getting pissed off at me, why don't you look at Boylan? How come he gets such plum security gigs? How much city time is he spending putting together these shindigs for this Shamrock Society of his? Ask yourself what kind of rela-

298

tionship he has with Pete Viatkos, why don't you?"

Mackey stood up stiffly. "If you talk to those people again, tell them they'll need to come in to see Captain Dugan. She's in charge of that case. And we want that video-tape. I'm giving you the benefit of the doubt and assuming you haven't seen it and don't have it. Otherwise, you could be charged with tampering with evidence. I've given you as much time as you're going to get. Now I've got to talk to the chief about a funeral, then give a press conference. One of our men died yesterday, you know."

"I told you I was sorry about that," I said.

"Everybody's sorry," he said. "What about that tape? Are you going to leave it with me?"

"Depends on what you plan to do with it."

His face darkened again. He put his hand out.

I hesitated, then popped the tape out of the player and gave it to him. I turned to leave.

"Just a minute," he said, putting his hand on my shoulder.

I stopped in my tracks, raised an eyebrow.

"There's something I want you to see," he said, gesturing toward his desk.

He rifled through a stack of manila enve-lopes on his desktop, opened one, pulled out some eight-by-ten color photos, frowned, and put them back. He did the same thing with three other envelopes until he found the one he wanted. He flipped through the photos, selected three, then placed them face up on the desk.

"You think I'm being hard on you? Take a look at that."

I looked down. The top photo showed a black leather jacket, the kind APD street officers wear. The jacket had been slit down the left side. A badge was prominent on the right side, a nightstick was lain across the jacket. An officer's holster and service weapon was displayed across the bottom of the composition. Small flecks of red dotted the jacket and badge.

"What's this?"

"Crime scene photos. That's Officer Sean Ragan's uniform, the one he was wearing Saturday night when he was shot in the head," Mackey said, his gray eyes watching mine. "They had to cut it off him in the emergency room, to see if he'd been hit anywhere else."

I swallowed hard and flipped to the next photo. Gray rain-streaked pavement, small brass casings scattered about, each one accompanied by a large numbered marker. A rain-sodden rubber-banded package of dollar bills. And a smear of red that needed no marker.

"Keep going," Mackey said.

I swallowed hard and turned to the next photo. A close-up of a man's head, the skull swathed in gauze, eyes swollen and bruised, face discolored, a plastic tube protruding from the nose.

He thumped the photo with his index finger. For the first time I noticed he wore a ring on the right hand. A class ring with a colored stone. FBI Academy.

"Officer Sean Ragan," Mackey said. "This was taken in the emergency room, right after he was pronounced. We took this just before his widow was brought into the room to say good-bye. They had to clean the body up before they let her in to see him."

If Mackey was looking to get a reaction from me, he would be disappointed. I flipped back through the photos, to the first one.

"Ragan," I said. "Is that an Irish name?"

"Get the hell out."

Edna set the kitchen table with her big Blue Willow soup bowls, blue-checked napkins, and the recycled jelly jars she likes to use for iced tea. She leaned down and opened the oven door, bringing out a black iron skillet full of cornbread.

I lifted the lid of the kettle and dipped a strainer in to lift out the ham bone she'd used to flavor her eight-bean soup.

"What time did you tell C.W. and Linda to get here?" she asked, looking down at the cornbread. "You think I oughta put this back in the oven so it doesn't get cold?"

"I told them to get here at seven-thirty, and it's just now that time," I said. "And no, the cornbread won't get cold. You know how C.W. is about your cooking. When I told him you'd made soup, he was practically jumping for joy."

The doorbell rang.

"Told you," I said.

C.W. was carrying a bottle of red wine; Linda had a box of chocolate candy, which Edna put away in the pantry for "later."

"Where's Wash?" I asked.

"At my mama's," Linda said. "The two of them have a standing Sunday night date. Besides, I had a feeling this wasn't going to be a kid's kind of night."

"Afraid not," I said, taking their coats.

"She's got a bug up her rear about Bucky Deavers," Edna volunteered. "Friday, she took two of my eighty-year-old girls over to Memorial Oaks, where they proceeded to get mugged and shot at. Then, today, she got in a car, blindfolded, and went off with a bunch of strangers to who-knows-where."

"That true?" C.W. asked.

"Not all of it," I said. "We didn't get mugged, and it wasn't a gunshot, it was a rock thrown at the windshield. I think. Anyway, let's eat first, before Edna's cornbread gets cold. I'll give you the run-down after dinner."

The four of us tucked into Edna's eight-bean soup like there was no tomorrow, with Edna beaming every time somebody dipped back into the kettle for another bowlful.

"Lord have mercy," she said. "I thought I'd made enough soup for Pharaoh's army, but y'all have about cleaned me out."

"No lunch," C.W. said, sounding apologetic.

"What?" Linda screeched. "The man ate two ham sandwiches and a quart of potato salad for lunch today. Don't let him fool you, Edna, he just loves home cooking. And he doesn't get much of it at our home, I'll admit."

"Linda knows every takeout place in town," C.W. said, patting his wife's hand.

"Takeout," Edna said, sniffing. "When I was coming up, the only takeout in our house was when my daddy took out the trash to be burned."

"Here we go," I warned our company. "She's off on the good old days."

Edna shot me a look. "Atlanta's changed," she declared. "Too much crime, too many people, too much traffic."

"I hear that!" Linda said.

"I think it's time to move," Edna went on. "Did Callahan tell you Mac's been offered a wonderful new job in Nashville? He wants us both to move there with him, but Callahan pitched a fit and they haven't spoken a word to each other since."

"Nashville?" Linda raised one elegant eyebrow. "I think you forgot to mention that, girlfriend."

"It's not really up for discussion," I said.

"She doesn't want to leave her precious business. Cleaning other people's toilets. Or this precious house. In a neighborhood where thieves steal anything that isn't nailed down," Edna said.

"Could we please change the subject?"

"Fine," Edna said, getting up. "Who wants banana pudding?"

We took coffee and dessert into the den. C.W. settled back in a wing chair, sipped his coffee, then took out a pen and pad of paper.

"I found out most of what you wanted," he said, looking down at his notes. "Although I don't know what any of it means."

"None of it means anything so far as I can tell," I admitted. "But we've got to start somewhere."

"For starters, Sean Ragan was a member of

the Shamrocks," C.W. said. "And he'd worked off-duty security too. At that Vietnamese market. The one where he was shot."

"Good God," I said.

"Not so fast," C.W. cautioned. "His partner, a dude named Antjuan Wayne, worked security there too. And he definitely wasn't a Shamrock. Not unless they've put a new definition on black Irish, with the emphasis on black."

"Huh?" Linda said, doing a double take.

"Antjuan Wayne is a brother," C.W. said. "And he was working for our old buddy John Boylan."

30

"Antjuan Wayne," Linda repeated. "Seems like I know that name. How long has he been on the force, C.W.?"

"He's no rookie," C.W. said. "My guy said he's been around for maybe seven or eight years. He used to work for the DeKalb Sheriff's Office before he went with the city."

I took a sip of coffee. "So Ragan and his partners both worked off-duty gigs through John Boylan, but only Ragan was a Shamrock. And he got killed. Bucky worked an off-duty gig through Boylan, and he was a Shamrock, and he's also got a bullet in his head. What does any of this mean?"

C.W. and Linda looked at me expectantly.

"I saw Lloyd Mackey this afternoon," I said. "And I tried to get him interested in the idea that cops were involved in this holdup gang. He went through the roof. Wouldn't even consider the idea."

"What do you expect?" C.W. said. "Even I think it's kind of far-fetched."

"There's something else," I added. And

then I told them about Bishop's friend Fiske and his ambush at the ATM machine. "The holdup man wore a mask, but he forgot his gloves," I said. "He was wearing an FBI Academy ring, C.W."

"He's sure of that?" C.W. asked.

"He saw the same ring on a cop in the men's room at Manuel's and almost passed out, it unnerved him so bad," I said.

"Can't be too many rings like that running around Atlanta," Linda pointed out. "The academy only takes maybe one or two people from the same department any given year, and they don't always take them every year."

"Mackey says there's maybe six people at the APD who are academy grads," I said. "Not counting himself."

"He went two years before me," C.W. said. "I never bought a ring, though. Didn't have the money to spare."

"What about Boylan? Did he go?"

C.W. snorted. "You kiddin'? This is an elite outfit, Garrity. I bet I could name most of the ones from the APD who are grads. Mackey, the chief, the assistant chief, Major Yates in sex crimes, and Lieutenant Tolliver in operations."

"You're not counting people like yourself, who retired, or people who went to the academy before joining the APD," I said.

"No, and that doesn't count cops from other departments who've gone, either," C.W. admitted. "There's guys from the GBI who have gone to Quantico, and Fulton County Police and DeKalb too, for that matter."

"What about women?" Linda demanded. "It's not still the good old boys, is it?"

"There were a couple women when I went, back in eighty-eight," C.W. said. "So yeah, there are probably a handful of women around Atlanta who went to the academy."

I shook my head. "This is getting us nowhere. We're grabbing at straws. Somehow we've gotta find out why. Why was Bucky shot? And how is it connected to Sean Ragan's murder?"

"That videotape from the liquor store would be a big help," C.W. said.

"It would be, if I could get Deecie's boyfriend William to trust me. But I can't get Mackey to give me any guarantees about how they'll treat Deecie. And I don't feel right lying to her about it. I mean, let's face it. We're talking about crooked cops. Guys who think nothing of sticking a loaded gun in somebody's face for a bag of money. I think I trust Mackey. I think he's one of the good guys. But what if I'm wrong?"

"Mackey?" Linda said, shaking her head. "He's a hardheaded sumbitch, Callahan, but

I just don't see him throwing in with the likes of Boylan."

"Lisa Dugan is in charge of the case," I said. "And she's one of them. She's the one who told Mackey I was trying to connect Bucky's shooting to the ATM robberies. I tried to talk to her about it the other night. She wouldn't even discuss the possibility."

"You think Bucky's girlfriend had something to do with the shooting?" Linda asked. "That is cold, girl."

"I don't know what to think," I said. "She wasn't at the St. Patrick's Day party, even though Bucky was expecting her. She was supposedly out on a call. That's something I need to check into. C.W., were you able to put together a list of guys working for Boylan's outfit?"

"Not everybody I called was home over the weekend," C.W. said, picking up his notebook. "But I got five or six names, yeah. Besides Bucky, Ragan, and Wayne, there's Kevin Phelan, works out of Southside, Tommy Bourke in communications, Dennis Farrell and Tim McMahan in Zone Four, and Dick O'Dwyer at the airport precinct. It's anybody's guess about the guys from other departments."

"How about the armed robberies? You got any information on them?"

"My sources aren't that good," C.W. said. "What did Mackey say about them?"

"Just that they were in various jurisdictions, not all City of Atlanta," I said. "East Point, Roswell, and Smyrna County have all had ATM holdups which he says fit the pattern I described. Could be more, but he just didn't know about all of them."

The three of us sat there, stumped.

"You know what I can't figure out?" Linda said, breaking the silence abruptly. "How Pete Viatkos fits in with any of this. I mean, why would he rob his own store?"

"Maybe he didn't," I said slowly. "Deecie swears she didn't take the money out of the safe. So maybe it wasn't there in the first place. Maybe this whole thing is about something else all together."

"Hey, y'all!" Edna stood in the doorway in her housecoat and slippers.

"Turn on Channel Forty-six. I was watching the news in my bedroom. They're saying something on the news about that cop shooting last night."

I grabbed the remote control and switched on the news. We were able to catch only the tail end of what the reporter was saying, something about how "Wayne has been put on administrative leave without pay, pending the outcome of the city investigation."

The reporter segued smoothly into a story about a homeless rabbit that had taken up residence in a city park.

"What was that all about?" I said.

Edna nodded knowingly. "I saw it all. They were saying that this fella Antjuan Wayne maybe didn't do all he could have to save his partner's life. Because he never fired any shots at the man who killed that boy. Not a single one. And when the police started asking him a lot of questions, he got himself a lawyer, and he says he ain't tellin' nothing to those cops, on account of the whole thing is a racist plot, since he's black and the dead fella is white."

She paused, breathless. "Did you ever?"

C.W. buried his face in his hands. Linda sighed, reached over, and started to massage his shoulders.

"You know what'll happen now?" he asked, looking up. "They'll pin that boy's killing on Antjuan Wayne."

"How?" I said. "Antjuan Wayne was his partner. Surely the department doesn't think he had something to do with Sean Ragan's killing. That's too much, C.W., even for me to believe."

"You watch," he said sadly. "The department's already suspended Wayne. He's probably got himself a union lawyer, telling him to

311

sit tight and keep his mouth shut. In the meantime, cops'll be all over that crime scene twice as hard as they already were after Ragan got shot. They might not be able to charge Wayne with homicide, but they'll sure as hell find a way to place the blame at his door one way or another. Negligence, dereliction of duty, no tellin' what they'll call it. But it'll happen. I guarantee. And his life won't ever be the same again."

"Depressing, but true," Linda agreed. "Makes me glad all over again we got out while the getting was good." She tugged at C.W.'s hand. "Come on, big man, let's get our baby and go on home."

I stood and started gathering up the coffee cups and dessert plates.

"Antjuan Wayne knows how Sean Ragan got killed," I said. "And why. And if he knows that, I'll bet he knows something about what got Bucky shot in the head."

"And he's gonna tell you?" C.W. asked, doubt in his voice.

"Why not?"

31

Once a month, we hold a staff meeting, on Monday mornings usually, to discuss business and air grievances, but mostly as an excuse to eat cake for breakfast.

Edna had gone all out this time. She'd been rattling pots and pans since at least five A.M. By the time I staggered into the kitchen at eight o'clock, the counters were lined with her creations. A towering, three-layer carrot cake with maple–cream-cheese frosting sat on my mother's good milk-glass cake stand. Next to it she'd placed an applesauce spice cake with caramel frosting. A lemon pound cake was cooling on a wire rack, and she was just finishing the icing on a red velvet cake when I walked in.

"Good Lord," I said, sticking my finger in the pan of seven-minute frosting, "I can feel my blood sugar rising just standing here."

Edna dropped the pan and her spatula in a sinkful of soapsuds. "Can you get the coffee started? The girls will be here any minute now. Cheezer was picking up Baby and Sister on his way over here."

"What about Neva Jean?" I asked, spooning coffee into a filter. "She didn't get arrested again over the weekend, did she?"

"Not as far as I know," Edna said. She put one of her flowered luncheon cloths on the kitchen table, then got her garden shears out of the junk drawer under the microwave.

"I saw the first red tulips in bloom out there by the side of the garage," she said, thrusting the shears at me. "How about clipping me a centerpiece?"

"Tulips already? Isn't it a little early?"

"It's nearly April," she reminded me. "These are an early variety I got out of a mail-order book. Come Easter, the whole yard should be in bloom."

The tulips were right where she said they'd be. And nestled in the tall pale green grass beside them I found a few tiny grape hyacinths too, which I added to the bouquet, along with a stem of peach blossoms from the tree by the back fence.

Back in the house, I put the flowers in an old blue medicine bottle and set them in the middle of the tablecloth.

Edna cocked her head and smiled approval at the effect of the red flowers; blue vase; and red, white, and yellow cloth.

"Not bad for poor white trash," she said, by

way of a compliment.

She went to the windowsill, opened the window, and leaned out.

"Gonna be spring any minute now," she said. "And a pretty one too, all this cool, rainy weather we've had. Did you see my New Dawn rose on the fence? It's covered in buds. And I swear, there must be a thousand jonquils in that bed out front."

She'd set herself up; it was too easy for me to close in for the kill. I gestured toward her garden, pregnant with bud and bloom. "And you want to leave all this? For Nashville?"

She turned and smiled serenely. "Oh, don't worry. I'm gonna dig it all up and take it with me."

Neva Jean slid a hunk of carrot cake onto a plate already piled six inches deep with spice cake, pound cake, and red velvet cake.

She took a forkful of maple–cream-cheese frosting and rolled her eyes.

"I swear, this is the first solid food I've been able to put in my mouth in four whole days," she said. "That being in jail just tore up my system somethin' awful. I think I got one of them jail bugs. Ever since I got home from there I been living on thin broth and Nabisco saltine crackers."

Ruby patted her hand. "I thought you

looked a little peaked, hon. But you're right as rain now. Eat up that carrot cake. It's full of vitamins, you know."

"That's true," Neva Jean said, shoveling in another forkful. "You can't hardly get more vitamins than what's in carrot cake."

"Or calories," I said, eyeing the slice of cake on my own plate.

Cheezer pinched off a bit of spice cake and tried it. "Great!" he enthused. "Did you use my new preservative?"

Our only male Mouse, Cheezer has a degree in chemical engineering from Georgia Tech. He's always mixing up some top secret cleaning solvent or psychedelic baking mix. I shuddered to think what ingredients he might have included in a food preservative.

"With this swarm of locusts?" Edna said. "All of this cake will be gone before lunchtime. Don't need preservatives when you've got an appreciative audience like I got."

"I know that's right," Sister said. She was wrapping a slice of the red velvet cake in a piece of aluminum foil she'd gotten out of her pocketbook.

She saw us watching her. "Oh, this is not for me," she said quickly. "Mr. Jerome, my friend over to the tower, he got a powerful sweet tooth."

"Ain't he the man been in a coma from a

stroke since last month?" Baby asked. "Our prayer circle been praying right along for him. Don't see how a man in a coma gonna be eatin' no red velvet cake."

"That's all you know," Sister sassed. "He was in a coma. But his neighbor lady up there on the eighth floor is some kind of root doctor. She come in his hospital room Friday morning and rub his face and neck all over with some kind of bad-smelling root mashed up in Mercurochrome. And do you know, Saturday morning, Mr. Jerome come out of that coma?"

"I bet he raised hell when he saw his face painted red like Injun Joe," Baby said.

"No, ma'am," Sister said. "He sat right up in that bed and said hello and asked the nurse could he please have a Coca-Cola."

"Praise the Lord!" said Ruby, the most devoutly religious of the House Mouse crew. She smiled beatifically. "That's what I call the power of prayer."

"What about the power of Coke?" I asked.

"Heathen," Edna said.

"Never mind," Ruby said soothingly. "Callahan, we all been praying at my church for the healing of your friend, Bucky. I just know there's gonna be a miracle, if it's the Lord's will."

The Lord's will must have been what kept

Ruby going all these years. In her early sixties, she's worked for us since we bought the business. Although she never married or had children of her own, she raised half a dozen "godchildren" to responsible adulthood, all on the paycheck of a cleaning woman.

"Keep praying, please, Ruby," I said. "I saw Bucky in the hospital this weekend. It looks like nothing short of a miracle is going to bring him out of this."

"All right," Edna said, slapping the table with the palm of her hand. "Now that everybody's had a bite to eat, I want to call this meeting of the House Mouse to order. We got some new business to discuss this morning, so let's get going with that."

Cheezer raised his hand, a polite boy to the end. "Edna, what about the new vacuum cleaner we're supposed to be getting? I've wired the plug back onto the cord on mine so many times it's pathetic, and you know the last time you bought bags, they didn't really fit, because that model is so old."

"I know," Edna said. "I been shopping around, comparing prices. There's a Kirby looking real good, if I can get the saleswoman to come down on price a little."

"They better come down quick before I get electrocuted," Neva Jean said. "But what I want to know is when are you gonna get that vacation schedule fixed up? Swannelle and me wanna go over to Talladega for the big race coming up. We're gonna rent us a motor home and take off on a Thursday and do the town up red."

I wondered how much time it would take to "do" Talladega, Alabama, but I quickly dispelled the thought from my mind.

"We'll have it put together by Friday," I said.

The rest of the meeting was fairly mundane. We talked about raising rates — but only for new customers. Neva Jean wanted to charge anybody with a poodle double; Ruby was fairly outraged by the fact that she'd caught her standing Tuesday morning client in bed with her regular Wednesday morning client. "And both of 'em married ladies!" she added indignantly.

Diplomat that she is, Edna managed to mollify Ruby by allowing Neva Jean to switch Tuesdays, and Wednesdays.

"I don't mind lesbians one little bit," Neva Jean said cheerfully. "At least they leave the seat down when they pee. Makes it lots easier to clean their bathrooms."

When it came around to his turn, Cheezer handed me a list. "That's all the chemicals I need to make our all-purpose kitchen spray," he said. "Ammonia, stuff like that. I can stop by the wholesale supply house this morning, if you want to give me a check or something."

"I think I've got cash," I said, reaching for my purse. I took out my billfold, but found only a couple ones.

"I forgot I had to buy diapers and milk and McDonald's hamburgers yesterday," I said, looking at Edna.

"Don't look at me," she said. "I'm tapped out."

"Never mind," I said. "When we're done here, I'll run around the corner to the ATM machine in Little Five Points. You can follow me there and get the cash for the supply house."

"Ooh, no, don't be going to those cash machines," Neva Jean said. "You're likely to get busted over the head and robbed. It ain't safe."

"It's Little Five Points, and it's the middle of the day," I said, trying to reassure her. "And Cheezer will be right behind me. It's perfectly safe."

"You don't know what you're saying," Neva Jean said. "Why, a man I met down in Hapeville the other night, owns a bar down there called Earl's Pearl. He thought he was safe Tuesday night, making a night deposit at his bank? He sure got a surprise when somebody stuck him up and nearly killed him."

"What's this?" I said. "How do you know about those ATM robberies?"

"Because I was right there in the jailhouse when they brought the man in," Neva Jean said. "That's what I'm trying to tell y'all. It's a damn crime wave, and all the police want to do is arrest innocent bystanders who just happen to be caught in the wrong place at the wrong time."

"Never mind the innocent bystander stuff, Neva Jean," I said. "Tell me what you know about an ATM robbery in Hapeville."

"That's what I'm tryin' to do," she said plaintively. "See, y'all took forever to get down there to bail me out, and I was just sittin' there in the hall, wishin' I had something else to wear besides that awful blue jail jumpsuit — can you imagine? Me with green hair and a blue jumpsuit? Anyways, this fella come in with his head all bandaged up, and he was sittin' in an office right by my holding cell, waiting to be questioned, and we struck up a conversation — even in as bad a shape as he was, he was wondering about my green hair and the gold glitter and all. And we got to talkin' and he told me about the awful experience he had at one of them ATM machines."

"You say the man owned a bar?" I said.

"Earl's Pearl," she said. " 'Cause his name is Earl. I never did catch his last name. Any-

321

way, he was tellin' me how he'd closed up Earl's Pearl the night before, well, the morning, really, and he had about eleven hundred dollars in cash money. So he went to make the night deposit like he usually did, at his bank in a shopping center around there. And he had the money in the bank bag and was fixin' to drop it in the night deposit box when a masked man came right outta nowhere. This guy stuck a gun in his face and told him to hand it over."

"Jesus, Lord," Ruby said. "I never heard such wickedness."

"It's a damn crime wave," Neva Jean repeated. "Pardon my French for saying so. Anyway this Earl, he's a real feisty little fella, but he's got big muscles from liftin' weights. He said it made him crazy mad that he'd had to work so hard and put up with drunks and cleaning bathrooms, and here this punk wanted to take his eleven hundred dollars. So Earl acted real scared, like he was gonna faint or have a fit or something, and he fell down on the parking lot and was flopping around and carryin' on, and when he thought the bad guy wasn't looking, he reached down in his boot and pulled out this little twenty-two he had stuck down in there, because he runs a bar and all. And Earl said he brought the gun out and he yelled, excuse me, Ruby, but this is a direct quote, 'I'll see you in hell before I'll give you a damn dime' and right about then somebody hit him on the back of the head and he passed out cold. When he come to, the bank bag was gone, and the back of his head was busted nearly in two."

She stopped her recitation and took a long swig of her ever-present Mountain Dew. "After all that, I figure, better safe than sorry. That's why Swannelle's gettin' me a new gun for Easter," she said. "An itty-bitty blue one. Won't that be cute?"

32

"The man's name was Earl? You're sure of that?"

"Sure as my name is Neva Jean McCoomb," she said. "And the bar was Earl's Pearl."

I looked it up in the phone book and was slightly shocked to find a listing. I called, but there was no answer, not surprising since it was only nine A.M.

Edna handed out the day's assignments and wrapped up some leftover cake for each of the girls.

Cheezer waved away the foil packet. "Not for me, thanks. I'm not really into processed flour and refined sugar."

"I thought you loved chemicals," I said.

"Just the really gnarly ones," he said.

Edna put the cake away and handed me a piece of paper and a house key. "Baby and Sister have got it in their heads to work today," she whispered. "But Cheezer's got a real busy morning, and Neva Jean and Ruby have got jobs clear up on the Northside of town. Can I trust you to keep them safe for a couple hours? This here's Ruth Matthews's house. She's neat as a pin, doesn't really need much, but she's having her bridge club ladies over tomorrow, so I promised her I'd send somebody by to fluff the place up a little bit."

"Ruth Matthews? Is she one of your LOLs?"

"Little old ladies?" Edna bristled. "She's my age."

"You know what I mean. Isn't she the one who followed me around spritzing everything I touched with room deodorizer? And didn't she call you after I left to complain that I'd forgotten to polish the silver tea service?"

"She didn't realize you were my daughter," Edna said. "And I straightened her out about silver polishing. She knows it's extra now. And that's why I thought Baby and Sister could go with you. You won't have to worry about Ruth spritzing you, because she's got a beauty parlor appointment this morning — God knows why. She's just about bald, poor old thing."

"All right," I grumbled. "But make sure you put the phone on call forward to my cell phone. I'm expecting some calls today."

"I can take a message, you know. I'm not totally senile — yet."

"I know you're not," I said. "It's just this one caller, he won't leave a message."

I shrugged myself into a pink cotton smock and loaded a cleaning cart with supplies. When I got out in the driveway, Baby and Sister were already sitting in the van.

Sister had belted herself into the front passenger seat and wore a smug expression on her face.

"Callahan," Baby said from the backseat. "Tell that old fool I'm supposed to ride up front with you."

"Are not," Sister said loudly.

"She know I always ride shotgun with you," Baby said. "She just being mean, is all. What she need to ride up there for anyway? Blind as a bat, she might as well sit in the back of the van with the groceries and the vacuum."

"Tell that hussy to sit back and shut up her mouth, lessen she wants me to turn around and box her ears for her," Sister whispered.

"What's that? What she sayin'?" Baby yelled. "I can hear what she said. And I don't have to listen to that smut-mouth talk." She unfastened her seat belt and with lightning speed was out of the van and trying to open Sister's door, brandishing her window sash weight.

Just as quickly, Sister popped the power lock button on the door, leaving Baby pounding furiously on the window.

"Go on, Callahan, drive on. We don't need that fool. Leave her right here," Sister urged.

"Now, Miss Sister, you know I can't do that. Unlock the door, please, so we can get going."

"No, ma'am," Sister said, crossing her arms over her chest.

"Please?" I wheedled.

"Tell her to put her bony old booty right in that backseat where it belongs," Sister said, loud enough for Baby to hear, which made her pound on the door even harder.

"How about this?" I said. "You ride up front this time, and on the way home, Baby gets to ride shotgun."

"All right by me," Sister said. "But you know I get carsick sometimes, riding in the back."

"I'll get you a barf bag," I promised.

When I had finally negotiated a settlement on the shotgun issue, and persuaded Baby to put her truncheon away, I thought we could ride to Ruth Matthews's house in peace.

"I ought to take the two of you back home," I said teasingly. "Which one of you tattled to Edna about what happened in Memorial Oaks?"

"Not me," Sister said loudly. "Probably that old fool in the back."

"I ain't never opened my mouth to Edna about that," Baby said.

I turned to both of them. "You swear?"

They each held up a hand in oath.

"Then how did she find out about it?" I asked. "She knew even before I got home."

"Jungle telegraph," Sister said.

"I'll ask her about it later," I said.

Ruth Matthews lived on Huron Street, a quiet street near downtown Decatur, in the Great Lakes area, a neighborhood of tidy postwar brick and frame bungalows and cottages set on neatly mowed postage-stamp–sized yards.

I recognized the house as soon as I saw it. Pink. All pink. I'd forgotten that was Ruth's house.

"Ooh-wee," Baby whistled when I pulled into the driveway. "Ain't this the prettiest color you ever seen in your life?"

I unloaded the Easterbrooks sisters, and then the cleaning cart. "If you like the outside, you'll love the inside," I promised.

I unlocked the front door and let the sisters go in before me. Ruth Matthews had a passion for pink. Or, as Edna put it, "She got hit upside the head with the pink stick."

Plush pink carpet stretched wall to wall throughout the house. The walls were painted pale pink, and the living room had a shocking-pink sofa and matching club chairs. Somebody had taken a fancy French provincial dining room suite and painted it pink with gold trim. Even the kitchen was pink — pink lino-leum, pink stove, even a pink refrigerator.

Baby loved it all. She walked from room to room, marveling at Ruth Matthews's decorating taste.

"This is the prettiest house I have ever seen," she declared, running her hand over the pink satin quilted bedspread in the master bedroom.

While Baby was declaring her love, I did a quick survey of the house. It was already spotless. There were vacuum cleaner tracks in the living room, and I detected telltale scouring powder residue in the kitchen sink.

I called Edna from the cell phone. "You sure this was the week Ruth wanted us? This place is immaculate. You could do brain surgery on her kitchen floor."

Edna sighed. "That's Ruth. Always worried somebody will have something to say about her house. I'll bet she had her cleaning lady come in before you got there."

"Her cleaning lady?" I said. "I thought we were her cleaning lady."

"Oh no," Edna said. "Ruth is kinda ticky about cleanliness. She's had a colored lady working for her for years. I just assumed Ava had retired. I guess she had Ava come over and clean before you got there, so you wouldn't think she was a big old slob."

"She has her house cleaned to impress the cleaning lady? I thought she was kinda whacked out, Ma, but that really is crazy."

"That's just Ruth," Edna said. "She does the same thing with her hairdresser's. Her older sister Inez does her hair every week, but Inez is going on ninety and can't see a thing. But Ruth doesn't want to hurt her feelings by going somewhere else. So every Monday Inez gives Ruth her regular wash, set, and comb-out, and then Ruth goes right over to the Salon de Beauté to have Frank wash it and start all over again."

"And this makes sense to you?"

"Wait until you get old," Edna said. "By the way, I forgot to put the phone on call forward. A man just called you. He wouldn't leave his name, so I gave him your cell phone number. You better hang up so he can call you."

I hung up on her and prowled around the house, phone in hand, waiting for the call to come in.

In the meantime, I got Baby and Sister set up at the kitchen table with a jar of Wright's silver polish and Ruth Matthews's already gleaming tea set.

"Just give it a light buffing," I instructed.

Ruth Matthews's house was a cleaning woman's worst nightmare; it should have had a big Sani-Strip pasted from wall to wall. I searched all the normal trouble spots: baseboards, doorjambs, the refrigerator vent, even the narrow space between the base of the commode and the bathroom wall. Each time I was stymied. No speck of grime. I didn't know who this Ava was, but I did know the woman could have won the gold medal if they ever held a housecleaning event in the Olympics.

I was peering inside the oven — lined with foil, the metal racks polished mirror bright, when the cell phone buzzed.

I caught it on the first beep.

"This Callahan Garrity?"

It was Deecie's boyfriend.

"William?"

"You find out about that reward?" he asked.

"I talked to the head man," I said. "He won't make any deals until he sees the videotape from the liquor store."

"Damn," William said. "Look here. Faheem's bad sick. Deecie's scared. She thinks he might need to go to the hospital, get an I.V. and some medicine. The thing is, I can't leave work. And she don't have a car."

"I'll take him to the hospital," I said quickly. "Tell me where she is. I'll come right now."

"We don't got any money," William said,

his voice edged in misery. "And Deecie's scared to take him to Grady, with those cops all over the place."

She was right about that. Her picture had been all over the newspapers and the television, "Woman Wanted for Questioning in Cop Shooting." She'd be picked up in a minute if she went to Grady, which was still crawling with cops keeping vigil over Bucky.

"Wait," I said. "My sister is a nurse. She works at a couple different hospitals around town. I'll call her. Maybe she could get Faheem seen at another hospital. Let me call her and see what she can do. Can you call me back in about fifteen minutes?"

"I'm out of change," William said.

"Give me the number where you're at, and I'll call you," I said.

He hesitated.

"I'm not going to turn you in," I said. "I just want to get Faheem to a doctor."

"All right," he said.

Maureen didn't sound happy to hear from me. "What did you do with my scrubs?" she shrieked. "And my Grady I.D.? I know you took them, Jules. Maura told me you were playing dress-up in Mommy's clothes."

The damn kid was too smart for her own good.

"It was just for one day," I said. "I've already washed them. I'll bring them over there today. But I really need help now, sis. There's this little boy. He's got sickle cell anemia, and he's having a, what do you call it?"

"Crisis," Maureen said. "What's that got to do with your stealing my scrubs and I.D.? If you've been parading around in that, sneaking around Grady, Jules, I'll kill you, I swear it. I could get fired if anybody found out."

"Nobody found out," I said. "What about it, could you get him seen at Egleston?"

"What's wrong with Grady?" she asked. "They've got a sickle cell clinic, she could take him there and he'd be seen immediately."

"Won't work," I said. "She's in trouble. She's afraid she'll be arrested if she goes anywhere near there."

"You want me to treat a criminal?"

"I want you to treat a sick little boy," I said. "Isn't that what doctors and nurses are supposed to do? She's a nice woman. Her kid is sick and she doesn't have any money or friends, and she's scared witless. Now. Can you help or not?"

"My friend Maeve works triage in Egleston's emergency room," she said slowly. "I could call her. See if she could get him seen. What's the little boy's name?"

"Faheem. I'm not sure about the last name.

333

I guess maybe it's Styles."

"What number are you at?" she asked. "I'll call Maeve and call you right back."

"Thanks, Maureen," I said. "Really. That's great. I mean it. I owe you big-time."

"You better get those scrubs and I.D. back to me by five o'clock today," she said. "Or I'll come over there and jerk a knot in your tail like I used to do when we were kids."

I hung up. "In your dreams," I said.

True to her word, Maureen called back ten minutes later.

"Jules? Okay, here's what you need to do. Take him right over to the emergency room at Egleston. Ask for Maeve Hewlett. She's got dark shoulder-length hair and a butterfly tattoo on the back of her right hand. She's expecting you. But you've got to get him over there now, because she goes off shift at noon."

I called William back. "Tell me where to find Deecie," I said. "I'll pick her up and take her to Henrietta Egleston Children's Hospital. My sister has a friend who works in the emergency room. She's expecting us."

"You know that dry cleaner's you met us at? It's around back of that building. There's a sign on the door says 'Groceria Mexicali.' She'll be waiting for you. You think Faheem will be all right?"

"It's supposed to be the best children's hospital in the South," I said. "They won't turn away a sick child."

33

Baby and Sister wouldn't hear of being left behind at Ruth Matthews's house, and I couldn't reach Edna to get her to come fetch them.

"Now listen, girls," I said, shaking my finger at the two of them. "We've got to go get a young girl and her little boy and take them over to Egleston. She's scared and he's sick, so no fighting, please. And I'm afraid neither of you gets to ride shotgun this time."

"What's wrong with the baby?" Sister wanted to know.

"He has sickle cell anemia."

"Ooh, my goddaughter's baby got sick as hell anemia," Baby said. "Poor little thing all the time in the hospital."

"How you come to know this girl?" Sister asked, letting Baby guide her into the backseat of the van.

I took a deep breath. "This is the girl we were looking for at Memorial Oaks the other day. She was working at the liquor store last week, when my friend Bucky was shot. She was the only witness, and she ran away because she was afraid. I'm trying to help her, but I want her to tell me the truth about what she saw that night."

"The truth shall set you free," Baby said serenely.

"I hope you're right about that," I said.

"Somebody living here?" Baby asked, incredulous at the sight of the little grocery store. "In a grocery store? With a sick baby?"

I parked in back of the dry cleaner's and left the motor running. Deecie threw the storeroom door open as soon as I knocked. She had Faheem cradled close against her chest. The lusty screams of the week before had been lulled to a pathetic whimper. He gave short little gasps in between the whimpers. His eyes were half closed, his arms and legs hung limply from the knit blanket Deecie had wrapped around him.

"He's real bad," Deecie said.

I led her over to the van, and Baby opened the back door. "Let me hold that little one," she said plaintively.

Deecie shook her head no and shied away.

"It's safer if he rides in back with them," I said gently. "I don't have a car seat for him."

Reluctantly, Deecie handed Faheem over to Baby, who cooed with delight at the touch of the child.

"A friend is expecting us at Egleston," I said as we pulled out into traffic on Shallowford Road. "They'll take good care of Faheem there."

"No cops?"

"No cops."

I pulled up to the emergency clinic entrance at the children's hospital, and let Deecie out. She took Faheem, and I gave Baby and Sister their instructions. "Sit right here. If anybody tells you to move the van, just tell them the driver is unloading a sick baby and will be right out."

"Nobody better tell us to move nothin'," Sister said belligerently. "Less they want to mess with Sister Easterbrooks."

A sweet-faced woman with dark shoulder-length hair got up from the admitting desk as soon as we walked in. "Callahan?"

I nodded yes. "This is Deecie Styles, and her son Faheem."

Maeve held out her arms for Faheem, and Deecie handed him over, relieved at the sight of Maeve's brightly flowered nurse's scrubs.

"Poor little guy," she said, stroking his chubby hand. "How long has he been breathing like this?"

"He been sick for about two or three days," Deecie said. "Last night he started breathing funny. Like he couldn't catch his breath."

Maeve handed the baby back to Deecie. "Is he running a temp?"

"He's hot," Deecie said. "But I didn't have a thermometer."

"That's all right," Maeve said, touching the baby's forehead. "We'll get his vital signs in the back, but you're right, he does feel hot to the touch. He's in crisis all right. You did good to bring him in." She got a plastic bracelet out of a drawer and slipped it around Faheem's wrist. Then she picked up a phone and spoke in a low voice. Hanging up, she reached again for the baby.

"Ms. Styles? I think Faheem's in respiratory distress. He's probably dehydrated too. Somebody's coming down from the intensive care unit, and they're going to take the baby up there, get him assessed and started on I.V. fluids and antibiotics, and something to bring down that fever and help him breathe. He's a pretty sick little guy, but we're going to get him some help."

Deecie hung her head. "He gonna die?"

Maeve winced. "No, I don't think so. But the respiratory problems are serious. You can go with him up to the ICU if you like."

"Yeah," she said, "that'd be good."

A pair of swinging doors behind the desk opened and a young blond woman in green scrubs pushed a child-sized gurney through it.

"Is this Faheem?" she asked, looking at Maeve.

"This is Faheem and his mama," Maeve said. The two of them put Faheem on the stretcher, and the other woman pushed the gurney back toward the door, with Deecie following.

"Can you wait one minute, Mama?" Maeve asked, gesturing toward the form she was filling out. "We need to get some information from you, for our records."

"I wanna go with my baby," Deecie said.

"It'll just be a minute," Maeve said soothingly. "Then you can go right up and be with him."

Deecie gave me a pleading look.

"Can't I fill them out for her?" I asked.

"Sorry," Maeve said. "It has to be the parent. She needs to sign a consent form and give us some other information." She looked over at Deecie, who had tears in her eyes. "Did you bring your Medicaid card?"

"It's at home," Deecie whispered.

"All right, we'll get that taken care of later," Maeve said, handing her a clipboard. "Just sign the consent form, and you can go on up with Faheem."

"Deecie, I'll be right back," I promised. "I'm just going to move the van into the parking lot, and I'll be right back here."

She nodded, too numb to speak. I was halfway out the door when she called me back.

"Hey, uh, Callahan?"

"I'll be right back. Really."

She dug in her pocket, came out with a key, which she held out toward me. "You been so nice to me and Faheem. And I told you lies. A lot of lies. Maybe that's why my baby sick. 'Cause I lied. This here's the key to where that videotape is at."

"Ms. Styles?" The nurse with the gurney was clearly impatient. "We need to get Faheem upstairs right away."

I took the key from Deecie. "You go on with the baby. We can talk later."

I parked the van and shepherded Baby and Sister back down to the emergency clinic. Maeve was just leaving as I walked in.

"How is he?"

"He's a very sick little guy," she said. "I didn't want to tell the mother this, but when our sickle cell kids get in respiratory trouble like he is, the prognosis isn't good. It's life-threatening, unfortunately."

"God," I said. "And there's nothing you can do?"

"We're giving him the most aggressive treatment we can," she said. She gave me a curious look. "You don't act much like your sister, do you?"

"Not much."

"Maureen told me the mother is wanted by the police," Maeve said. "Not that I care about that. I mean, my job is to take care of children. But do you mind telling me what she's done? She seems like a very loving mother."

"She was in the wrong place at the wrong time," I said.

Maeve patted my shoulder. "Well, good luck. I hope the baby will be all right."

"Thanks for everything," I said.

The girls and I sat around the waiting room well into the afternoon. They amused themselves watching cartoons and old Disney movies on the wall-mounted television. I caught up on a year's worth of *Highlights* back issues.

Around three P.M., Deecie walked into the waiting room, hollow-eyed and dejected.

"He's sleepin'," she said, sitting down beside me. "Doctor said he real sick." She paused, bit her lip. "I need another favor. I called my aunt to tell her about Faheem," she said. "And she say she'll come up here and sit with me. Till William can come. But she don't have a ride."

"I can go pick her up," I said. "And I'll drop Baby and Sister off at their apartment on the way there. Is there anything else?"

"No. Wait. Yeah. Ask my aunt, could she

bring Faheem's Boo with her."

"His Boo?"

"He got this ol' nasty teddy bear he sleep with. I forgot and left it at my aunt's place. I think he's missing his Boo."

"I'll get it."

Baby and Sister sulked all the way back to the senior citizen high-rise. "When we gonna get to do some more detectin'?" Sister asked. "You all the time runnin' around in the streets and we don't get to do nothin'."

"I know that's right," Baby chimed in. "What about that time we put that purse camera on that old doctor? Didn't we do good that time?"

She was referring to an assignment I'd given them when I was working for a client who believed her ex-husband was trying to cheat her out of marital assets. I'd rigged up a hidden video camera in the bottom of a pocketbook and sent the two of them in disguise as a pair of senile invalids. They'd performed brilliantly, of course.

"You can do some detecting," I promised. "Just as soon as I have a job for you."

"What about finding that little boy's stuffed toy?" Baby asked. "We could do that, real easy."

"Not this time," I said.

We pulled up to the curb at the high-rise, and I paid them each thirty dollars cash for their brief stint of silver polishing.

"I got a good disguise all picked out for next time," Sister told me. "Got a fancy blond wig and a sparkly dress and everything."

"She think she Dolly Parton," Baby cackled. "Old fool."

After I let the girls off at home, I floored it over to Memorial Oaks. It was too cold for television or basketball, but the cluster of men drinking from paper sacks was there on the corner, watching me with dead eyes. There were a couple girls, too, young, dressed for street success. Cars cruised to a stop beside them, transactions were made. An open-air drug and sex marketplace. The clientele was varied: blacks, whites, new cars, old cars, some with Atlanta tags, some from the far suburbs. I noticed a red pickup truck from Henry County, forty miles to the south. Even a big late-model Chrysler with an elderly ball-cap–wearing white man at the wheel cruised past. The same junk cars were parked at the curb. This time, I put my 9-mm in my jacket pocket and locked the van before I got out.

Monique Bell opened the apartment door before I could knock.

"I'm all ready," she said, fumbling for her keys.

She looked a little like her niece: light-skinned, with Eurasian eyes, a high forehead, and hair cut close to the scalp. I guessed her to be in her late thirties. She was dressed in a black Atlanta Falcons sweatshirt and blue jeans that were a size too big, a belt cinching them around her waist.

"Deecie wanted you to bring Faheem's teddy bear," I said.

She wrinkled her nose. "That stinky old thing?"

"She called it his Boo," I said. "She thinks he might feel better if he had it with him."

"All right," she said reluctantly, turning to go back inside the apartment.

I waited in the doorway while she went in search of Boo. The door across the hall opened just a crack. I felt, rather than saw, a pair of eyes looking me over.

"Tell Deecie I say hey," a small voice called. "Tell Faheem hey too."

"I will."

Monique came bustling out, a matted blue teddy bear stuffed under her arm. "Let's go," she said brusquely.

34

Monique Bell didn't utter a word all the way to the hospital, just sat bolt upright in the passenger seat, staring straight ahead, probably so she wouldn't have to look at me or talk to me.

I tried not to take it personally, but for some reason, I couldn't keep my mouth shut. I found myself chattering inanely, about the weather, about what a cute baby Faheem was, even about the farce of trying to clean Ruth Matthews's already impeccable pink house.

Monique grunted a couple times; otherwise, I would have been tempted to stop and search for a pulse.

For the second time that day I pulled up to the emergency room entrance and dropped off a passenger. "He's up in the ICU," I told her. "Maybe they'll call up there and let Deecie know you're here."

By the time I parked and got back down to the emergency room, Monique had apparently gotten over her speechlessness.

A new nurse was working the triage desk,

and she was receiving the full force of Monique's rage.

"I don't give a GODDAMN about your rules," Monique bellowed. "I got a sick baby in this hospital, and I wanna know where he's at."

"I'm sorry," the woman said, her own voice rising to the occasion. She was black and middle-aged and would have made two of Monique Bell.

She stood up and put her face right up beside Monique's. "I called upstairs and they said your niece is gone. Now that's the best I can do." She glared right back at the crimson-faced Monique.

"What's going on?" I asked.

"They trying to tell me they don't know where Deecie gone to," Monique snapped. "And I know good and well she's here somewheres, but they won't let me go up and see about Faheem."

"It's against HOSPITAL POLICY," the nurse said.

I guided Monique to a chair in the waiting area. "She's right. They only let the parent go with a sick child. And since he's in the intensive care unit, they only allow one person at a time. Probably Deecie just came downstairs to get a Coke or something. I'm sure she'll be right back."

"And then I'll go on upstairs and see about my nephew," Monique said, loud enough for the triage nurse to hear.

At four-thirty, I got restless. I volunteered to go to the hospital cafeteria to get a snack for both of us, thinking I might find Deecie there.

She wasn't in the cafeteria, where I bought Cokes and a package of cheese crackers for Monique. I went out to the main hospital lobby, but Deecie wasn't there either. Probably, I thought, she'd gone back upstairs to sit with Faheem.

But the triage nurse called the ICU nurse, who said, no, she hadn't seen Ms. Styles in more than two hours.

Monique Bell was fuming. "That damn girl. Run off and leave a sick baby. Ain't no better than her mama and all of them, runnin' around like she do."

The crankier Monique got, the more concerned I got. Deecie had been beside herself with worry over her baby. I didn't believe she would go off and leave Faheem alone.

I still had the phone number William had given me when he called early in the morning. I dialed and asked for him.

Five long minutes later, he picked up the phone, breathless. "This is William."

"William? This is Callahan Garrity. Have

you heard from Deecie?"

"When? You mean like, now?"

"I mean anytime recently. She asked me to go pick up her aunt at her apartment, and I just got back here an hour ago, but there's no sign of Deecie. I've looked everywhere, and the nurses who are taking care of Faheem say they haven't seen her in at least two hours."

"Two hours? That can't be right. She wouldn't go off and leave Faheem."

I was starting to get a bad vibe about this. "I'm going to go find her," I said.

"You think something bad happened?" he asked.

"Not at all," I lied.

"I get off at five," he said. "Then I'm coming right over to that hospital."

Monique stood in front of the triage desk, looming over the nurse, who studiously avoided looking up.

"Miss Nurse," Monique said, snapping her fingers under the woman's nose. "Hey, Miss Nurse. I'm talking to you."

"What is it now?" the older woman asked, refusing to look up.

"I want you to call back up to that intensive care place and find out how my baby is, and where my niece has gone to."

"I'll see," Miss Nurse said. She jotted down something on the chart she was working on, then picked up the phone.

"The baby's in guarded condition," she said after she'd hung up. "I talked to a nurse who said she saw Ms. Styles around three-thirty. Your niece asked her for change to get something to eat out of the vending machines in the cafeteria. Now, if you can't be quiet, I'll have to ask you to leave this area."

Monique glared at her, and Miss Nurse glared back. I went back down to the cafeteria to see if anybody'd seen Deecie.

"Skinny black girl?" the cashier asked. "She come in here, wantin' pizza. That was the lunch special. But that was all gone by one o'clock. She said she'd find something else. I told her she oughtta walk over to Jagger's, and she said maybe she would."

I went outside the emergency room entrance and looked around. I walked down the drive to Clifton Road, where the hospital entrance was. The Emory University campus sprawled over both sides of the road. Jagger's was a favorite hangout for Emory students, but it was way across campus, at least a fifteen-minute hike, and I doubted Deecie was that familiar with the neighborhood. And William had said Deecie was broke.

I hugged my arms to try to keep warm, but the chill was coming from the inside as well as the exterior. Each question I asked, every answer I got, added to my conviction. She was gone.

"What you mean — gone?" Monique Bell demanded.

William chewed a fingernail.

"I've looked around the hospital, I walked around outside, there's no sign of Deecie," I said.

William buried his face in his hands. "I kept tellin' her I'd take care of her. Sayin' I wouldn't let nobody hurt her. Somebody done got her." He looked up at me. "Ain't that right?"

"Maybe not," I said, clinging to hope. "The Emory campus is huge. Maybe she got lost and has been wandering around, trying to find her way back."

"It's getting dark out there," Monique said. "That girl never did like the dark. Used to wet the bed if I didn't leave a light on."

Monique was really working on my nerves. Slapping her face would have been highly therapeutic right now, but probably ill advised.

"We could call campus security," I said.

"Cops?" William looked dubious.

"They're employed by the university," I said. "Kinda like kiddie cops. They probably don't have any contact with the real thing."

Even as I said it I knew it wasn't true, but I couldn't think of any other way to search for Deecie.

"She dead," Monique said dully. She opened her pocketbook and pulled out a pack of cigarettes and a yellow Zippo, then got up and walked outside.

"We could just tell the campus cops Deecie brought her little boy here to the emergency room, wandered outside, and we think she got lost because she's unfamiliar with the area," I said. All of which was true.

"What if they seen her picture on the news?" William asked.

"It's a chance we'll have to take," I said. "Look. Deecie was going to have to deal with the police eventually, especially if she turned over that videotape of the robbery. If she didn't do anything wrong, she shouldn't have anything to worry about."

He studied his nails, which were pretty unremarkable. "What if she did do something wrong?" he asked.

"Like what?"

"What if she didn't say exactly how it really happened that cop got shot?"

I clutched his arm. "What are you trying to tell me?"

"Deecie knows more than what she said, that's all."

"How much more?"

"Enough to get her kilt."

I took out the key she'd given me, just before I'd left the hospital earlier in the afternoon. "Deecie said I could have the videotape," I said, turning it over and over in the palm of my hand. "She said she felt bad about lying to me, and she gave me this."

He took the key and looked at it, then handed it back. "What's it to?"

"You don't know?"

"She said she hid it. Someplace safe. That's all she told me."

Luckily for us, Miss Nurse was on her dinner hour. A young, slightly effeminate male nurse whose name tag said he was Carl was working the triage desk. He readily agreed to call campus security and let them know about Deecie.

Ten minutes later, a white sedan marked "Emory Police" glided up to the emergency room door where William and I were waiting.

Officer Cash was middle-aged, with a graying crewcut and steel-rimmed aviator glasses. He wrote everything we told him on a clipboard, and gave it all some thought.

"You don't think she might have caught a bus and gone home?"

"Her baby is in the intensive care unit," I said. "She wouldn't leave him."

"Another family member could have picked her up," he suggested.

"Her only other family is an aunt, who's here right now," I said.

"You've contacted her friends?"

William plucked the officer's shirt sleeve. "Look here. I'm her only friend. She didn't call me. Could we start looking for her? She's kinda scared of the dark."

Officer Cash finished writing up his report. "Okay, who wants to ride along with me?"

"I'll go," William volunteered.

"I'll stay here with Monique," I said. "In case she comes back."

"If she shows up, call dispatching and let them know," Cash said. "No sense beating the bushes for somebody who's already found their way back home."

35

William's face told the story before Officer Cash could.

"No sign of the girl," Cash said. He looked from me to William. "Any reason she might want to disappear? Maybe hide out?"

"Not from us," I said.

Cash looked at his wristwatch. It was past seven. "I'll ask the evening watch to keep an eye out for her," he said. "Who should we call if we should happen to see her?"

I gave him my cell phone number and thanked him. He got in his patrol car and drove away.

"Something bad's happened," William said.

But I wasn't ready to accept that. Not yet. Not when I was so close to the truth.

"She didn't have a girlfriend or somebody at the complex she might have called to ask for a ride or something?"

William shook his head no. "See, she worked nights mostly, and slept during the day when everybody else was out. Deecie was funny, she called them other women ghetto bitches. Except for that old lady used to keep Faheem sometimes."

The woman I'd met the first time I went looking for Deecie. "Mrs. Rudolph?"

"Yeah. She and Deecie got along good. But Mrs. Rudolph, she don't drive."

"It's worth checking out," I said.

"Maybe." He wasn't convinced.

We went back inside the waiting room, where Monique Bell was slumped in a chair, her head thrown back, mouth wide open, snoring to beat the band.

"Monique?"

She opened her eyes, blinked. "Where that girl go to?"

"They didn't find her," I said. "Do you think she might have called any of your neighbors?"

"Deecie? She thought she was better than all them niggers. No, she didn't give none of them the time of day."

"Not even Mrs. Rudolph?"

"Well, she liked her, 'cause the old lady thought Faheem hung the moon. But why would she call her, with me and William right here?"

"I don't know," I said.

Monique stood up and stretched. "I don't know neither. And I ain't studying staying in this here waiting room no more. I got to be at work. You giving me a ride or what?"

Since she put it so charmingly, how could I refuse?

"I'm staying here," William declared, planting himself in the chair Monique had surrendered. "In case Deecie comes back."

"She ain't coming back here no more," Monique said. "That boy nurse over there, he called up to the room they keeping the baby at. They say he in guarded condition. Whatever that means."

Monique worked as a waitress at the Holiday Inn in Midtown. She gave me the address, then promptly dozed off again.

When we got to the motel, I had to shake Monique to wake her up. She sat up, looked around, and reached for the door, without saying a word.

I had to take one last shot at finding Deecie, or at least finding that videotape.

"Monique?"

She yawned broadly. "What?"

I held up the key. "Deecie gave me this today. Right before I left to pick you up. She said she'd hidden something, something she wanted to give me. But she didn't say where it was. Do you have any idea what this key might go to?"

She gave it only a cursory glance. "Look

357

like any old kind of key. Deecie, she real closemouthed about her business. Like her mama, that way. Think she better than everybody else. She better, all right. Deecie's mama, she dead, got cut by the man she stayed with. Now Deecie, she probably dead too. Leave me with a sick young'un to raise. I ain't studyin' no key. And I ain't messin' in that girl's business. Cops come around, I'll tell 'em same as I told you. I ain't studyin' what kind of trouble Deecie Styles got into."

Monique got out of the van and slammed the door shut. After I left the motel, I decided to take another run past Memorial Oaks.

It was dark out, and the place looked more menacing than ever. I parked at the curb with my motor running and tried calling Austine Rudolph from my cell phone. No answer.

I briefly considered a door-to-door canvass, to see if anybody had heard from Deecie, or seen her. As I weighed the options in my mind, people were drifting in and out of the buildings, standing under an unlit streetlight. The two whores from earlier in the day were back, joined by two more girls who didn't even look old enough to drive, let alone turn tricks. The men stood around, drinking from paper sack–wrapped bottles, smoking what looked like hand-rolled reefers.

When I saw my old friend Tweety Bird

saunter down the sidewalk toward the van, I decided it was time to move on, before my windshield took any more abuse.

When I got home, Edna looked up from the hand of solitaire she'd dealt out on the kitchen table.

"Your sister wants to know where her uniform and Grady I.D. badge are."

"I'll get them to her," I said, sitting down at the table beside her.

"Mac called," she added. "Twice. I told him you'd call him back. Tonight."

"Maybe. Anybody else call?"

"Am I supposed to be your answering service?"

"It's been a long day, Ma," I said. "Deecie Styles has disappeared."

"You think she's dead?"

My mother has a way of cutting to the heart of a matter.

"I don't know. We looked around campus. Her aunt claims she doesn't know anything about what Deecie was mixed up in. But William, that's the boyfriend, admitted that Deecie lied about what happened in the liquor store the night Bucky got shot. And Deecie as much as told me the same thing, before she disappeared. She even gave me a key, where she said I could find the videotape of the robbery. But I didn't get a chance to ask her what the key was to."

I took the key out of my pocket and placed it on the table.

"Too big for a safe deposit box or a padlock," Edna commented. "Could be a house key."

"Could be a lot of things," I said. "But Deecie didn't have access to a car after she disappeared. I think she must have hidden the videotape somewhere around that apartment complex her aunt lives in. Either that, or near the warehouse they were hiding in over on Shallowford Road."

"That narrows it down a lot," Edna said. "She didn't give you any idea what was on the tape?"

"No. She just said things didn't happen exactly the way she told the police. And that she was sorry she lied to me."

"Lied about what?"

"The money, maybe? At first she was really insistent that she hadn't stolen any money. Pete Viatkos was just as insistent that she did steal the money. Naturally, I was inclined to believe Deecie. I mean, if she took the money, why didn't she spend some of it — for a hotel, or a doctor for Faheem? Mom, they didn't even have enough money for diapers or milk or food. I had to take groceries with me that time I met them at the warehouse."

"Maybe she didn't have the money anymore," Edna suggested. "Or maybe she was scared to spend it."

"She was scared," I agreed. "Terrified. Especially of the cops."

"That reminds me," Edna said. "C.W. wanted you to call him as soon as you got in."

I was antsy, too agitated to talk on the phone. I needed action, not words. I opened the refrigerator door, closed it just as quickly. Walked around the house trying to decide what to do. On a whim, I drove over to the grocery warehouse on Shallowford Road. It was buttoned up tight. The dry cleaner's out front was closed too. No cars in the lot. No sign that Deecie and Faheem had hidden in that back room, terrified at what the next knock on the door would bring.

I drove home. Edna had given up on the solitaire. She was working the Sunday crossword puzzle. In ink.

I called the hospital to check on Bucky's condition.

"I'm sorry," the clerk said. "The family has requested that information be kept confidential."

"Family?" I sputtered. "What family? Who made such a request?"

"That's confidential," she said smoothly.

"Bullshit." I slammed the phone down. I

361

was shaking with rage and frustration and itching for a fight. But Lisa Dugan wasn't home. Probably down at the hospital, playing the grieving fiancee.

I called C.W. "Lisa Dugan has left instructions for the hospital not to give out Bucky's condition," I said. "Can you believe the nerve of this dame?"

"Calm down," C.W. said. "They told me the same thing when I called. So I called somebody else down there. Bucky's the same. Nothing has changed. But that's not why I called you. Listen, something's going on. I've been hearing things about Antjuan Wayne."

"Like what?"

"He hired a lawyer all right, but not a union cop. No, sir, I hear he's got David Kohn on retainer."

"David Kohn? How does a street cop raise the money to hire somebody like that?"

Kohn was one of the top criminal-defense lawyers in the state. He'd recently managed to get an acquittal for a state Supreme Court judge accused of influence peddling, despite the fact that the FBI had tapes of the judge being handed a cigar box full of hundred-dollar bills by an informant over a breakfast at the airport International House of Pancakes.

"Maybe Antjuan Wayne has friends in high places," C.W. said.

"More likely friends in low places," I said. "What else are you hearing?"

"I hear the Febes are sniffing around," C.W. said. "They're very interested in what Wayne has to say."

"FBI? Since when?"

"Yesterday. Today. They're having very quiet talks with officers who worked off-duty security jobs, anybody who'd worked with Antjuan Wayne or Sean Ragan. I hear they've already talked to Pete Viatkos. And Boylan. And your friend Lisa Dugan."

"Just talks?"

"That's what I hear," C.W. said. "What about you? What's going on at your end?"

"Nothing good," I said. "Deecie Styles is gone."

"You think somebody got to her?"

"I don't think she's at Disney World," I said. "Her baby's sick, she's broke, and even her boyfriend hasn't seen her."

"Not good," C.W. said.

36

"Are you gonna call Mac now?" Edna asked, looking up from her card game.

"No," I said, reaching for my pocketbook. "I'm going out. I'll call him later."

"Save your dime," Edna said, glancing toward the driveway. "While you were on the phone I heard the Blazer pull up in the driveway."

I got up and looked out the kitchen door. Mac was striding up the walkway.

I stepped outside to meet him, away from my mother's prying eyes and ears.

"Hey there," I said weakly.

"Long time no see," Mac said. His lips brushed my forehead. A forehead kiss. Not a good sign.

"I was just leaving," I said.

"I'll go with you," he said. "Want me to drive?"

"It's all the way down in East Point."

"I've got a full tank of gas," Mac said. "And the night is young."

What could I do? How do you say no to a

guy who won't take no for an answer?

"You've been avoiding me," he said, steering the Blazer toward the Interstate.

"What's left to say? You want to move to Nashville. I want to stay here in Atlanta. You've even got Edna on your side. I think the two of you should go ahead and go. You'll be very happy together."

"You know what I want," Mac said, reaching for my hand.

I let him take it, just to see how it felt. It felt good, damn him.

"It always comes down to this," I said. "We're two different people, Mac. We want different things from life. I just don't see how we're going to make it work."

"I thought it was working pretty good up until now," he said.

"Because we had a compromise," I said. "How do we compromise on this? Move halfway between Atlanta and Nashville? Live in, what — Chattanooga?"

"Chattanooga isn't halfway," pointed out Mac, the eternal engineer. "What about if we commuted? I could spend a week down here, you could spend a week up there?"

"You'd do that?"

"If that's what it takes," he said quietly. "It'd mean spending a lot of time on the road."

"What about your new job?"

"The commissioners are all hot over the concept of flex scheduling," Mac said. "Two county executives already do telecommuting two days a week. I couldn't count on coming to Atlanta every week, but with some careful planning, I think it could work. What do you think?"

"I don't know what to say."

"Say you'll consider it," Mac said. "Tell me you'll meet me halfway on this."

"I want to," I said, squeezing his hand. "I've missed you, you know."

"Enough to marry me?"

"You're full of surprises tonight," I said. "I thought we were tabling the marriage issue for a while."

"Why?" he asked. "Marriage would simplify a lot of things."

"Which things?"

"Our lives. I'm tired of not knowing what to call you. 'Girlfriend' sounds juvenile. 'Fiancée' sounds pretentious."

"You could just call me your lady," I teased. "Or yo' bitch."

"Be serious," Mac said. "There are practical considerations too, you know. If we were married I could have you as a dependent on my health insurance plan. They've got a terrific plan up there. Dental and everything.

You'd save a bundle right there. Same thing on income tax, married filing jointly is much cheaper. Part of my benefits package would include a county car. You could drive the Blazer and we'd give Edna the van."

"You think Edna would give up her land yacht just for you?"

"Damn straight," Mac said, grinning. "She's on my side."

"I know."

"So, you'll think about it — all of it?"

"Yeah," I said. "Guess it really is too good an offer to refuse — especially since you're throwing in a car and hospitalization."

"Good," Mac said. "That's settled. Now, you want to tell me where we're going and why?"

Earl's Pearl was a classic dive. A baby-blue concrete-block box, it sat in the middle of a pothole-plagued asphalt parking lot full of pickup trucks and late-model American gas guzzlers.

Inside, the booths were all full, so Mac and I found seats at the end of the bar and asked the beefy bartender for a couple of drafts — domestic, of course.

He brought the beers and Mac paid. I could get used to this.

"Is Earl here tonight?" I asked, trying to sound offhand.

"He's out in the kitchen," the bartender said. "You need to see him?"

"Yeah, if it's not too much trouble."

He turned around, pushed open a swinging door with his foot.

"Earl," he bellowed. "Lady here needs to see you."

The door swung open again and a short bowlegged man in a pearl-buttoned shirt, blue jeans, and high-heeled cowboy boots emerged. He was in his early sixties, ruddy-faced, with bright blue eyes that took in the length of the bar.

I held my hand out to him. "Mr., uh, Earl?"

"Earl Witherspoon," he said, grasping my hand. "And I didn't catch your name."

"I'm Callahan Garrity. This is my, uh, fiancée. Mac MacAuliffe."

"Good to meet you," Witherspoon said, shaking hands with Mac. "Now what can I do you for?"

I looked around the bar. Things were pretty quiet, and the regulars were openly staring at us.

"Uh, is there somewhere private we could talk?" I asked.

Witherspoon nodded. "Yeah, I see what you mean. Bunch of damn busybodies in here. Y'all come on in the kitchen, if you don't mind the heat."

"I'll just sit here and sip my beer," Mac said.

I flashed him a grateful smile.

Earl was right about the kitchen. It was tiny and dominated by a huge griddle, where half a dozen hamburger patties sizzled.

"Now, what's this all about?" he asked.

"It's about an armed robbery," I began.

His easy smile evaporated. "What the hell are you talking about? Who are you, anyway?"

"I'm a private detective," I explained. "You met one of my, uh, associates last week, on St. Patrick's Day. At the jail. The night after you were held up at an ATM machine. You told her all about what happened that night."

The mention of Neva Jean seemed to relax him a little. "Ought to have kept my big mouth shut," Witherspoon grumbled. "Always was a sucker for a full-figured gal like that Neva Jean."

"I'm interested in what happened to you because I think it might be connected to a series of armed robberies around Atlanta," I said.

"Well, I don't know nothin' about any other robberies," Witherspoon said. "The police down here in Hapeville never mentioned nothin' about no other robberies."

"The other crimes were all in different jurisdictions; Cobb County, Fulton County, and City of Atlanta. But all of them happened at ATM machines. And all the victims were people like you, businessmen about to make large cash deposits, when they were approached by a masked gunman."

"That part sounds about right," Witherspoon allowed. "Be damned if I know where that sumbitch came from that stuck me up. All of a sudden, he was just there, cool as you please, telling me to hand over my money."

"And you decided not to make it that easy, from what I hear."

"How the hell did I know there was two of 'em? Hit me from behind, the sumbitch. Doc said I had a concussion, sure enough."

"The man who robbed you, was he masked?"

"What's your interest in all of this?" Witherspoon asked. "You say you're a lady P.I., but why do you care about some two-bit saloonkeeper way down here in the boonies losing a couple hundred bucks? The cops down here sure aren't as interested as you are."

"I used to be a cop myself," I said. "My former partner was shot in an armed robbery at a liquor store in Atlanta the night after you were robbed. The sumbitch who shot him put the gun right to his ear and pulled the trigger.

Twice. He's up in Grady Hospital, hooked up to a bunch of machines. The doctors don't expect him to live. I'm wondering if the same people might be responsible for both crimes."

"And you'd like to catch the sumbitch who did all this," Witherspoon said. "No offense, but what can a little bitty gal like you do to catch these thieves? I mean, why don't you leave it to the cops? That's their job, ain't it?"

"Because," I said, "I think it was a cop who shot my friend. And a cop who tried to split your skull in two."

"By damn," Witherspoon said. "By damn."

He fixed us both a couple of cheeseburgers and sent one out to Mac. Then he dragged a couple of barstools over to a counter at the far end of the kitchen.

"I wondered if there wasn't more to all of this than met the eye," he said, dumping ketchup on his hamburger. "I mean, I been making deposits at that machine for six or eight years. And I never made it on the same night or the same time, just in case anybody was watching. And this was the first time I made such a large deposit. The thing was, we had a pool tournament in here the weekend before that, and I was getting a little uneasy about all that cash."

"I thought you told Neva Jean it was about eleven hundred," I said.

He grinned. "I told you, I'm a careful man, Miss Garrity."

"It's Callahan. Just how much did you have on you that night — just between the two of us?"

"Four thousand, eight hundred." His expression was pained. "There mighta been a little side wagerin' going on during the tournament — just between the two of us."

"Let me ask you something, Earl. Have you ever hired off-duty cops to work security here? Like as a bouncer or something?"

"Sure," he said. "Mostly we got a bunch of peaceful drunks in here. They drink, they get drunk, I call their old lady and say, 'Come get Bubba, he's bad drunk.' But here lately, we been getting a different kind of clientele. Mexicans, Yankees, transients. I started hiring guys to stand around and look mean. Worked, too."

"Did you have a bouncer during the pool tournament?"

"Oh, yeah," Earl said. "You get some sore losers with that kind of a thing."

"Was the guy a cop?"

"Now that you mention it, he was a cop. Young fella. Seemed all right."

"Did he see how much cash you had?"

"Reckon so," Earl said. "He stayed around most nights and helped me lock up."

"What was his name?"

He went blank. "We was so busy, I can't re-call it right now. Sorry."

"How about a check stub?"

He shook his head. "I paid him in cash. That's the way it works with these jokers. They don't want to have to pay income tax. Not like us regular stiffs, anyway."

Witherspoon pushed open the kitchen door. "Hey, B.J.," he hollered. "You remember the name of that fella who worked as a bouncer for us here last weekend?"

B.J. stuck his head in the kitchen. "Christ, Earl. You don't remember? It was that guy that got shot Saturday night. Sean. Sean Ragan."

37

Witherspoon snapped his fingers. "Ragan. That's right. I ast him if he was related to old Ronnie Reagan, and he said his name was spelled different."

"You didn't know he'd been killed?"

"Hell, I don't pay no attention to what goes on up there in Atlanta," Witherspoon said. "But I hate to hear that boy was kilt. What happened?"

"He was killed in the line of duty. Shot by a burglar." I gave it some thought. "Allegedly."

"By damn," Earl said. "This is a hell of a crime streak we got going."

"Tell me what happened the night you were robbed," I said.

"Wasn't much to it," Earl said. "We're slow Mondays. That's my day off. Tuesday night was slow, too, so I decided to leave early and make the bank run."

"Was Ragan here that night?"

"He come in at eight, but since it was so slow, I told him we didn't need him. I had B.J.

to stay and finish and lock the place up."

"What time did you leave here?"

"Prob'ly before midnight."

"And you didn't notice anybody following you?"

"Hell, who thinks of a thing like that? I got to the shopping center where the bank branch is. I had the car doors locked. Nobody was around that I could see. I had the bank bag, and I had my little pistol stuck down in my boot. I got out of the car and got my ATM card out, and I was writing out my deposit slip, when this fella sticks a gun in the back of my neck and tells me to hand over the bank bag. That's when I got the idea to act like I was having a heart attack. Only I was closer to it than I like to admit. I threw myself down on the ground and started carrying on and —"

"Did you get a look at the guy's face?"

"He had on a mask," Earl said. "Like a black wool ski mask, with the eyes and the mouth cut out."

"White or black?"

"Only saw him a second. White, I'd say, now that you ask."

"Did you notice the gunman's hand? Was he wearing a ring?"

"He had a gun," Witherspoon said. "My eyeballs didn't go no further than that."

"How about the voice? Did you recognize the voice?"

"Hell, no," Earl retorted. "That mask kinda muffled his voice. I could barely make out what he was sayin'. Anyway, the gun told me all I needed to know. And like I was tellin' you, I was concentrating on getting my gun outta my boot without his noticing it. That's why I was rolling around, had my knees cinched up against my chest, so I could get my hand down into my boot. Just when I brought the gun out, don't you know, somebody tried to split my head right in two. The next thing you know, I come to and my money and my pistol was gone. Hated to lose that pistol. My ex-wife got me that for my birthday a few years ago. Fit right in my boot. I loved that little booger," Earl said mournfully.

"Did you report the gun stolen?"

"Well . . . see, I didn't actually have a carry permit for it, you see. So I didn't feel like it was all that germane to the robbery."

"What kind of gun was it?" I knew, but wanted to hear it from him.

"Just a little twenty-two. Cheap, but right handy."

"My friend was shot with a twenty-two," I said slowly. "What kind was yours?"

"Just a little Saturday-night special, really,"

he said. "Marlena got it at a flea market over there in South Carolina."

"It's the same gun," I said. "It has to be."

"By damn," Earl said.

I got up slowly, finished my beer to be polite. "Thanks a lot, Mr. Witherspoon."

"Earl," he said. "It's Earl, remember? And the beer and burgers are on the house. Say. About that associate of yours, that Neva Jean. She ain't married or nothin', is she?"

38

"Was it worth the trip?" Mac asked when we were back in the Blazer, headed toward home.

"I think I know who shot Bucky."

"Who?"

"Sean Ragan."

"The cop who was killed Saturday night? What makes you think he's connected to Bucky?"

I told him what Earl Witherspoon had said, about hiring Ragan as a bouncer, how Ragan had known that Witherspoon had an unusually large amount of cash on hand, and even where he made his bank deposits.

"There were two men involved in Witherspoon's robbery," I said. "He didn't get a look at the guy who hit him on the head. I'm betting that was Ragan. No telling who the guy in the mask was."

"Could it have been Ragan's partner?"

"Witherspoon's impression was that the gunman was white. But he wasn't positive."

"Seems pretty slim evidence," Mac said.

"Witherspoon seems like a pretty rowdy character. A lot of people in that bar could have known the stuff you say Ragan knew."

"Yeah, but listen to this. Witherspoon's pistol — a twenty-two — was taken after he was robbed. A Saturday-night special. I think it could be the same twenty-two used to shoot Bucky. It was left behind at the liquor store."

Mac nodded. He drove for a while before he had another question.

"We still don't know why. I mean, why would Ragan shoot Bucky? Did he even know Bucky? And why would a cop leave a weapon behind?"

"I don't have all the answers," I admitted. "All I have so far is some ideas. Bucky would have known Ragan, because they were both members of the Shamrock Society. And they were both part of John Boylan's ad hoc employment agency. Maybe Bucky saw something he shouldn't have seen — the night he got shot. Ragan, Boylan, Viatkos, could have been any of 'em. We know Bucky went in that back room to get that six-pack from the walk-in cooler. Maybe that's what got him killed. Maybe Ragan knew he had to keep Bucky from talking. He used the twenty-two he'd stolen the night before from Witherspoon. I doubt any of this was planned in advance. It just happened, and that's why Ragan made such a stupid blunder by leaving the gun behind."

"What makes you think Pete Viatkos was there too?" Mac asked. "Not that I think the guy's an angel or anything, but I can't see why he'd be connected with any of this."

"Deecie told me she saw Viatkos's truck, parked out there in the alley," I said. "It was gone by the time the cops arrived. And I talked to Viatkos. He's lying about something, I know it. And now Deecie's disappeared. She was the only witness, Mac. And she took the videotape of the robbery. She told me the robbery didn't go down the way she told the cops. That's why she was so scared. Because she knew she'd seen too much."

"You think Ragan wasn't killed by a burglar?"

"I'm not sure. He messed up by leaving the twenty-two behind. After all, if somebody put all the pieces together, it could connect Ragan to at least one other armed robbery. And these guys couldn't afford a blunder like that."

"I heard on the news that Ragan's partner is under investigation," Mac said. "You think he was involved in Ragan's murder?"

"No telling. He's refusing to cooperate with the internal affairs investigators, so that means something is funny. And he's hired David Kohn to represent him. Kohn doesn't come cheap. That makes me think somebody is helping Antjuan Wayne. Who? The Shamrocks? Wayne certainly wasn't a member. He's black. And according to C.W., these guys are all just one step up from the Ku Klux Klan."

Mac yawned loudly, and I did the same. Long day.

"Seems to me you're overlooking one piece of the puzzle," he said.

"Probably I'm overlooking lots of pieces. I'm on the outside looking in," I said. "Which piece are you talking about?"

"How does Bucky fit into all this? Babe, I know he's your friend, but look at what you've told me about this outfit he was in. These Shamrocks.

"You say they were involved in some kind of robbery ring, getting inside information on likely victims because they worked as security guards or bouncers. Bucky worked at that liquor store. He worked other jobs, too. How do you know he wasn't in on some of those holdups? For that matter, how do you know he wasn't the other guy who helped Ragan rob Earl Witherspoon? Maybe that's why Ragan shot Bucky. Because of something that happened the night before. Maybe Bucky was trying to screw Ragan out of the money from the robbery."

"No," I said flatly. "Bucky wouldn't have done that. You don't know him like I know him, Mac."

"People change, Callahan," Mac said quietly. "You've changed. I've changed. Bucky was an ambitious guy. For the first time in years, he had a serious girlfriend. You told me yourself he was talking about settling down. Maybe he wanted more out of life than a police pension. Maybe he got tired of having to work two and three extra jobs just to get caught up with his bills."

"No way," I said.

"Suit yourself," Mac said. "But face it, you're in over your head. Edna told me what happened when you went snooping around that housing project. You nearly got killed. And you've just told me you're on the outside looking in. Maybe it's time to share what you know with the authorities, instead of trying to make sense of it all by yourself."

"I've tried," I protested. "I told Lisa Dugan I thought a cop was involved in trying to kill Bucky. She had a fit and walked out on me. She won't even return my phone calls. And I told Major Mackey exactly what I think was going on. He's the commander of the homicide unit. He's not a stupid man. But he was enraged that I would suggest such a thing. He practically threw me out of his office, Mac. It makes me wonder now if Mackey might have been involved, too. I mean, he wears an FBI Academy ring."

"Everything makes you wonder." Mac laughed. "You're the original conspiracy nut, you know that?"

"Is that supposed to be a compliment?"

"You've taken this as far as you can. You wanted to find out who shot Bucky and why, and it looks like you've done it. If Mackey won't listen to you, tell somebody else. Tell the chief, or the GBI, or somebody like that."

"According to C.W., the FBI's involved now," I said. "I guess I could talk to one of their agents. C.W. said he heard they'd already had chats with Boylan and some others."

"Do it," Mac urged. "I'm serious. You can't take on the whole Atlanta Police Department. You've done some good work. Now it's time to step back and let the law do the rest."

"Give it to the big boys, huh? Go back to my dusting and mending?"

"You know I don't mean it like that," he said. "Are we going to have another fight?"

"Naw," I said, leaning back in my seat. "I'm tired of fighting. Make love, not war —

that's my new motto."

"That can be arranged," he said.

Mac got off the Interstate at the North Avenue exit and drove toward Candler Park. We were at the light at North Highland when I glanced over to the right, at Manuel's Tavern.

"Look at that," I said, pointing at the parking lot. It was jammed with police cruisers. And not just white APD cars. There were cruisers of every color and description. Charleston, South Carolina; Savannah, Georgia; Charlotte, North Carolina; Lexington, Kentucky; Richmond, Virginia; Detroit; Miami; New Orleans.

"Is it some kind of convention?" Mac asked, craning his neck to get a look.

"No," I said slowly. "I'd forgotten. Tomorrow is Sean Ragan's funeral. They're all in town for a cop's funeral."

"There must be a couple hundred cars in that lot," Mac said, pulling forward when the light turned green.

"The wake was tonight," I said. "This is nothing. You wait until tomorrow. There'll be hundreds more, from all over the country."

"For a cop's funeral? They don't even know Sean Ragan."

"Doesn't matter. He's a cop. A fallen comrade. When an officer's killed, especially in the line of duty, it's a mark of respect to muster as big a show of manpower as possible."

"Even if that cop is a thug? A renegade who tried to kill another officer?" Mac asked.

"They don't know that," I said. "At least, most of them don't."

I honestly tried to keep my mind off the subject of Bucky Deavers, and instead keep myself engaged on the topic of Mac and me, but the conversation petered out a few blocks from home. At least, I thought, we had agreed that a compromise might be possible. It was a start.

We kissed goodnight in the Blazer. It was a sweet, lingering, where-can-this-take-us kind of embrace.

"Come home with me tonight," Mac urged.

"Can't," I said, full of regrets. "What about Friday night at your place? I'll spend the whole weekend."

"You got a deal."

Edna was waiting by the door, her face white. "Where on earth have you been? One minute you walked outside, the next minute you were gone."

"Relax," I said, patting her arm. "I was with Mac. You'll be happy to know that we've patched things up. We might even have worked out a compromise on this Nashville thing."

"I've got bad news," Edna said. "That Major Mackey called. He said I should tell you they found Deecie Styles. Jules, she's dead."

39

I followed her blindly into the kitchen, sank down into a chair. "What happened?"

"He didn't say. Just said I should tell you her body was found this afternoon."

Deecie was dead. Faheem's mother, dead. I was dialing the police department while Edna went on fretting about that sick little baby all alone at the hospital.

There was nobody in the office. Manuel's. That's where Mackey was, of course. Where nearly every cop in town would be. Paying homage to the fallen hero. A sour taste rose up in the back of my throat.

Deecie was dead. William was right. Something bad had happened. And it was still going on. Sean Ragan might be dead, but he'd had help in those robberies. And that helper was still out there, still killing. I took the key that Deecie had given me out of my pocket and turned it over and over.

Thing had definitely gotten out of hand. First Bucky, then Ragan, now Deecie. It was time to get some help. Years ago, I'd known the FBI agents who worked in the Atlanta field office. But after the bombing at Olympic Centennial Park, when the feds had mistakenly tried to make a case against an innocent bystander, a lot of those agents had taken early retirement or accepted transfer out of the city.

The best I could do was leave a voice mail message addressed to whomever it may concern.

"This is Callahan Garrity," the message said. "I am a licensed private investigator and a former Atlanta police detective, and I have information pertaining to the shooting of Atlanta Police Detective Bucky Deavers and the murder of Atlanta Police Officer Sean Ragan. Please contact me as soon as possible."

My luck, I thought glumly, they'd probably think I was some crackpot. Oh, well. I'd tried.

I called C.W. too. "Deecie Styles was murdered today," I said.

"Shit. What do you want me to do?"

"A couple things. Your sources at the APD — have you got anybody who could check the call-out logs?"

"Maybe. What do you need?"

"Lisa Dugan," I said. "She was supposedly on a call-out Wednesday night, when she didn't show up at the St. Patrick's Day party. I want to know when she got the call, and what time she logged out on it. Also, the night before, when that robbery went down in Hapeville — find out if she was anywhere around. Hell, for that matter, find out where she was Saturday night when Ragan was killed."

"I'll try."

"One more thing. Maybe Linda could help with this. There's a young man sitting in the waiting room over at Egleston. His name is William. He's going to need a friend."

"We're friendly folks," C.W. said.

"I know. Thanks."

A rough plan had begun to form. I had to try three different spellings before directory information found him for me.

"You're sure this is a good idea?" he asked.

"I'm not sure of anything," I said tartly. "Except that these killings have to stop. You don't have to help if you don't want to."

Then I called Manuel's, asked for Bishop, and told him my plan.

He wasn't enthusiastic. "I'm supposed to get off in fifteen minutes."

"This is for Bucky," I told him. "The person who's responsible for shooting him is in the bar tonight, I guarantee it. There's been another murder, too. Just today. Come on, Bishop, I've got nobody else to turn to."

"There's a million cops in here, Garrity," he said.

"That's the point," I said. "I think it was a cop behind all this."

"Aw, all right," he said. "But if my old lady wants to know why I'm late, I'm blaming it on you."

"Fair enough."

Bishop was right. There were about a million cops in Manuel's. They were all dolled up in their dress uniforms; starched shirts, ties, jackets, all of them with gleaming badges covered in strips of black tape, mourning dress for the fallen hero. The Shamrocks were out in force, too, all of them in the same green blazer Bucky had worn on St. Patrick's Day.

Mackey was sitting at one of the big round tables in the front room. I'd never seen him in his dress uniform before, but tonight he was all starch and brass. Lisa Dugan was sitting beside him. Her face was pale against the dark green Shamrock blazer she wore. Sitting beside Lisa was a very young, very pregnant woman with soft, shoulder-length brown hair and red-rimmed eyes.

This, I realized, would be Alexis Ragan, Sean Ragan's widow. She wore an ill-fitting pink maternity dress with a big red bow at the neck, and despite the crying eyes, she looked childishly excited by all the attention being paid her by her late husband's boss and colleagues.

Mackey frowned when he saw me approaching. He stood up, put a protective hand on Alexis Ragan's arm. "This is Callahan Garrity," he said. "She used to be on the force. She's friends with Deavers."

Alexis misunderstood. She smiled up at me. "Thank you for coming tonight. I can't believe it. All these people," she said, gesturing around the room. "They're strangers. But they came here for my Sean. From all over the country. Major Mackey says it's going to be the biggest policeman's funeral this city has ever seen."

Lisa Dugan patted Alexis's hand. "They're not strangers. Fellow officers. And there are at least a hundred Shamrocks here, too. The bagpipe and drum unit is here from Chicago, you know. Ten officers."

"I'm sure it will be a very moving funeral," I said. Turning to Mackey, I said quietly, "Could I talk to you?"

He followed me to the bar, where I'd spotted Bishop as soon as I walked in.

"Jack and water," I told Bishop. "And make it a double. It's been a hell of a day."

"You got my message?" Mackey asked. "About Deecie Styles?"

"What happened? I saw her earlier today,

over at Egleston Hospital, with her little boy. She never came back."

"You saw her?" Mackey asked sharply. "When was this? Why didn't you let somebody know?"

"About three o'clock. Her baby was in serious condition. He has sickle cell anemia. I wasn't going to turn her in with a sick kid. Get real, Mackey."

"If you'd turned her in, she might still be alive," Mackey said. "We got a call about seven o'clock, from a resident at that apartment complex she lived at. The neighbor said she heard somebody in the apartment, and she knew this Monique Bell wasn't home. We sent an officer over, he found the door unlocked. The body was in the living room."

"How was she killed?" I asked dully.

Mackey tugged at the end of his mustache. "Her throat had been slit."

Bishop set my drink on the bar and I took a long gulp. "Jesus."

"There's more," he said.

"I don't want to hear any more. When is this going to end? When are you going to believe me that cops are involved in this thing? Boylan and Viatkos and the rest of their Irish asshole buddies are up to their ears in these robberies, and you know it, Mackey."

"I don't know any such thing," Mackey

said. "So just shut up and listen, would you? We found a bank bag hidden in a heat duct in the bathroom at that apartment. The deposit slip was still with it. A little over twelve hundred dollars in cash from the Budget Bottle Shop. There was no masked robber, Garrity. It was only your girlfriend, Deecie Styles. Bucky must have walked in on her while she was cleaning out the register. She panicked and shot him, then set it up to look like it was a masked gunman. That's why she stole the tape out of the video camera. And that's why she booked."

I sipped my drink. I'd been expecting something like this, ever since Edna had given me the news about Deecie's murder.

"If she shot Bucky and took the money, why'd she hang around?" I asked. "Twelve hundred dollars was probably the most money she'd ever seen in her life. Why'd she hit the panic button? She could have taken the money and run out the back door. Then, later, why'd she call me? She was ready to come in and testify about what she saw. She knew who shot Bucky. It was somebody she recognized. That's why she was so scared. And that's what got her killed."

"That money and that mouth is what got her killed," Mackey said hoarsely. "It was all over the street in that project that she was hiding money in that apartment. Some crack-head went looking for it, and when he found her instead, he cut her throat."

"Had the apartment been ransacked?" I asked.

"Who knows with these people?" Mackey snapped. "It was wrecked, yeah. That's what crackheads do."

"Have you considered that maybe it was a setup? That the killer wasn't looking for the money at all? That maybe he was looking for that missing videotape? And maybe the bank bag was planted there by the killer?"

Mackey slammed his beer down on the bar in disgust. "I'm not listening to any more of this shit."

I took the key out of my pocket and held it up for him to see. "Deecie Styles was killed by somebody who wanted to shut her up for good," I said.

"But what he didn't know was that she was so scared she called me and had me take her and the baby to the hospital. She admitted to me that she'd lied about the robbery, that it hadn't gone down quite the way she'd told it. In fact, she saw the guy's face. Recognized him. And when he ran out of the store, she saw something else. She went out in that alley and she saw a truck. Pete Viatkos's truck, parked in the alley with the lights off. A minute later, it was gone. Who was in that truck? Viatkos? The guy who tried to kill Bucky? And you wanna know who tried to kill Bucky, Major Mackey? I'll tell you who it was, but you're not gonna like it."

He leaned in close. "Who was it, Garrity? The chief? The mayor? Or maybe it was me?"

I held my empty glass up and jiggled the ice cubes. "Bishop, dammit," I hollered. "I need another Jack and water. This time, sprinkle a little bourbon over it, would you?"

Bishop brought the drink and slapped it down on the counter.

"Now make me another one," I said. "It's hot in here."

Bishop looked at Mackey, hesitated, then made another double. He put it on the bar beside the first one. "That's it now, Garrity," he said. "You're wasted. I'm not gonna be responsible for what happens when you leave here."

"You were saying?" Mackey said casually.

"I was saying your fallen hero, Sean Ragan, is a fuckin' criminal."

"You're drunk," he said.

"And you're ugly," I said loudly. "But tomorrow morning I'll be sober and you'll still look like a damn walrus. In the meantime, I've got a suggestion for you. You know that twenty-two the robber left at the liquor store?"

"What about it?"

"Whyn't you show it to a little guy down in Hapeville? His name's Earl Witherspoon. Owns a bar called Earl's Pearl. He had a big pool tournament down there last weekend, hired an off-duty Atlanta cop as a bouncer. The cop's name was Sean Ragan. Tuesday night, Witherspoon went to his ATM machine to make a big cash deposit. Only guess what? He was ambushed by a masked gunman. Witherspoon tried to get cute and draw down on the guy with a little twenty-two he had hidden in his boot. What he didn't know was that the gunman had a partner. Witherspoon got a concussion, and the bad guys got four thousand dollars and Witherspoon's little Saturday-night special.

"Sean Ragan was one of the bad guys," I said, sloshing the whiskey on the counter. "And the next night, he was in that liquor store, dividing up the take with Viatkos and maybe some others, when Bucky blundered in there and realized what was going on. Ragan shot Bucky. But he screwed up and left the gun. Saturday night, his buddies had Ragan killed. Today, when Deecie Styles resurfaced, they were waiting and watching. They killed her too."

"Fuck you," Mackey said, stalking away.

"Hey, Mackey," I called after him. "It don't matter whether or not you believe me. Hell, maybe you're in on this thing too. You're Irish, right? One of the clowns in this holdup ring wears an FBI Academy ring. I hear you're a grad yourself. Anyway, it doesn't matter. I've already talked to the FBI. And they are very, very interested in what that videotape shows."

Mackey looked over his shoulder at me. "Get your ass out of here, Garrity, before I have you arrested for drunk and disorderly."

I looked down the bar, at all the cops who'd been unabashedly listening to my conversation with Mackey.

"You believe that guy?" I asked. "Who wants to buy a girl a drink?"

Nobody spoke up. They just stared down at the bar, like I was suddenly invisible.

"Bishop, dammit, I need another Jack and water," I bawled. "I get thirsty when I'm around all these cops. Anyway, you know I'm Irish. And you know how us Irish like to drink."

A hand clapped on my shoulder. I looked up into the faintly bemused face of John Boylan.

"And what's that supposed to mean, Miss Callahan Garrity?"

"It's true, isn't it?" I waved a hand at the

people standing at the bar, waiting on their drink orders. Their green jackets were a blur. I called out the names of the ones I recognized.

"Boylan, Kehoe, Donnelly. And there's Dugan over there. Oh, yeah, Killearn, and Gallagher. And Hanlon! Hey, Corky," I called, blowing him a kiss. "How you doin' down there?"

A bleary-eyed Corky Hanlon raised his glass to me in a mock salute. "Never better, darlin', now that I've seen you. And how's that boyfriend you were tellin' me about? Is he ready to make an honest woman of you yet?"

"The hell with him," I said. "Let me buy you a drink, Corky. Hell, why don't I buy a drink for the whole house?"

Boylan's face darkened. "No, thanks," he said. "I don't want nothin' you're buying. So why don't you take your act somewhere else?"

"It's a free country," I proclaimed. "And I like it here. So I'm staying." I tossed back the rest of my drink.

Corky tugged at my arm. "Not to sound like an old maid or nothing, Julia, but don't you think maybe you've had enough now?"

I brushed his hand away. "Aw, Corky, I thought I left my mother at home tonight. Come on, be a sport and let me buy a drink for the house."

He shook his head, shrugged. "It's your money."

I slapped my American Express card down on the bar. "My plastic, you mean."

Bishop began taking orders.

When everybody had a glass in front of them, I raised mine above my head and whistled hard and shrill, the way my brothers taught me when I was a kid.

"Attention, please," I bawled. "Your attention, please."

There were catcalls and shouts of "Shut up!" and "Pipe down."

Finally the front room quieted.

"I'd like to propose a toast to the memory of two good men," I said.

"To Officer Sean Ragan, who is no longer with us, and Detective Bucky Deavers, who was gravely wounded in an armed robbery less than a week ago, not two miles from where we stand tonight."

I swallowed hard and went on. "Tonight, Officer Ragan walks a new beat. Not here in Atlanta. Not even on this earth. No, tonight, he walks a beat in heaven. A place where he'll never have to work overtime, or have drunks puke on his shoes, or have punk criminals call him a pig. So let's toast Sean Ragan in heaven — and swear that we'll all do everything we can to send his killers straight to hell when they're caught."

The room was deadly quiet for a moment, except for the silly clanging of the pinball machine in the hall by the men's room.

Finally, John Boylan, the sour smile intact, raised his glass. "To departed friends," he called.

"Hear, hear," somebody else yelled.

And everybody drank, even poor little Alexis Ragan, who took one brave gulp out of the beer mug somebody set down before her.

40

Shortly after one, I decided it was time to make my exit. Buying a round for the house had made me lots of new friends, most notably a couple of horny Broward County sheriff's deputies, who insisted I sit with them and listen to all their drug interdiction stories. Tony and Gene seemed like harmless types, and before they'd let me leave, they both made me take their business cards "in case you ever want to come visit down in Lauderdale."

Extricating myself, I walked unsteadily toward the door, and had almost made it when a skinny hairy arm snaked itself around my waist. It was Corky Hanlon.

"You can tell me to mind my own business, Julia," he said, pronouncing it like "bidness," "but your old man, if he were alive today, would thank me for telling you I'm thinkin' you're in no shape to be driving tonight. Why don't you let me give you a ride home?"

"I'm as sober as you are, old man," I said, kissing him on the cheek. "Anyway, thanks for the offer, but it's only a few blocks to the house, and I feel like walking. I'll come back for the van in the morning." I said it loudly, so that everyone at the bar could hear.

Once outside, I felt all my barroom bravado slipping away. It was officially spring, but a bitter cold wind whipped bits of paper and dead leaves around the empty street in front of Manuel's. I'd dressed for the part tonight: black jeans, black turtleneck sweater, and black commando boots. The outfit made me feel big and brash inside, but right now, after walking only a few yards, the toes of my new boots pinched and my ankles were screaming.

One foot in front of the other, I told myself, lurching along Highland Avenue toward home. Cars passed, and I flinched as the headlights of oncoming cars shone in my eyes, temporarily blinding me.

I shoved my hands in the jacket of the peacoat, glad of its bulk, gladder still for the heft of the Smith & Wesson as I curled the fingers of my right hand around its plastic grip.

After two blocks I was ready to call it quits, call a cab, anything. All those drinks Bishop had fixed me were having an unintended effect. Six eight-ounce glasses of iced tea won't get you drunk, but they will threaten to drown you. I'd been guzzling all night, and my bladder felt ready to explode.

I minced along another block and was seriously entertaining thoughts of abandoning my inhibitions and ducking behind a friendly azalea to drop trou when I heard a car behind me start to slow down.

My shoulders stiffened and my hand tightened around the 9-mm, but I didn't dare turn around. Keep walking, I told myself. Show no fear. And whatever you do, for God's sake don't wet your pants.

Now the car was pulling alongside me. I heard the hum of an electric window. "Julia Callahan," a man's voice bawled. My eyes darted to the right and I took my finger off the trigger.

Corky Hanlon leaned drunkenly out the window of a big old gray Chrysler.

"What the hell are you doin', girl? You wanna get yourself killed, walking alone in this part of town? Your mama would kick my sorry old ass if I let anything happen to you. Hop in and I'll give you a ride home."

I glanced around to see if any cars were approaching. Goddamn sweet, well-meaning old Corky Hanlon. I was less than a mile from home. He'd ruin everything if I didn't get rid of him right this minute.

"I'm all right, Corky," I said, keeping up my pace. "Really. I don't need a ride. I've got my mace. And I'm almost home, anyway."

Another car was coming up behind him now, only a few hundred yards away, slowing down. I felt my pulse racing. I had to get rid of Corky.

"Go on." I waved with my right hand. "I'm fine."

I looked over at him. He wasn't smiling. "Get in the goddamn car, Julia," he rasped. He brought a hand up from beneath the steering wheel, and I was staring into the barrel of a Smith & Wesson 9-mm, identical to the one in my pocket. Only Corky's gun was pointed right at my chest, and mine was still in my pocket.

The car behind Corky's slowly rolled forward. The headlights blinked rapidly; the driver was anxious to get around us. It was late, he wanted to get home.

"Get in," Corky repeated. "Now."

WOOOO. An ear-splitting blast of siren and a flash of blue lights. The gun in Corky's hand jerked, and in that same second I dove for the pavement, a bullet whizzing past my ear. I heard a sharp ping as the shell hit the granite curb, then I rolled over on my stomach, half on and half off the road. Another shot rang out, and I covered my head with my hands. Then I heard the Chrysler's engine roar, and as I lifted my head I saw it speed away, down Highland, its red taillights dimming in the distance.

Ignatius Rakoczy thought it was hilarious when I puked all over my combat boots.

"I thought you Irish could hold your liquor," he said, helping me up from the weedy embankment.

"We can hold our liquor," I retorted, "it's a gallon of iced tea that makes me nauseous."

He jerked his head in the direction the Chrysler had gone. "Who was that guy? Not Boylan. Not Viatkos, either. I saw them leave together. That's why I was a little late. It took me a minute to realize they weren't coming after you."

"A little late? Another second or two and I would have been a little dead." I wiped my mouth on the sleeve of my peacoat. My knees felt very unsteady, so I grabbed for Rakoczy's arm, and he steadied it around my waist.

"That was my brother's Little League coach. One of my dad's old drinking buddies. Corky Hanlon."

He shook his head. "Don't know the guy."

"Me neither, apparently," I said.

Rakoczy drove me to the Quik-Mart back at North and Highland, where I took a much-overdue pit stop in the unisex bathroom while he made the necessary phone calls.

★ ★ ★

Lloyd Mackey sat in the passenger seat of the unmarked city cruiser.

"Now do you believe me?" I asked.

He shrugged. "It wasn't a question of believing or not believing. You had no proof. It's all just guesses. The serial number on that twenty-two has been filed off. Earl Witherspoon can't really prove he ever had possession of the gun, or that it was taken from him the night he was robbed."

"Deecie Styles had her throat slit today because somebody was afraid of what she might know," I said. "And Sean Ragan's widow is going to raise her baby by herself. I didn't make any of that up. And that's a real bullet casing in the gutter over there, in case you were wondering."

The car radio crackled and Mackey picked up the mike. He put out a lookout for Hanlon's Chrysler, asked the dispatcher to send a crime scene unit to North Highland Avenue, where we were parked.

"You know where Corky Hanlon lives?" Mackey asked.

"He used to live in Sandy Springs," I said. "In a yellow brick split level with a basketball goal in the driveway and a ten-year-old sedan in the garage. His wife's name is Marie. His son's name is Chuck. He's a fireman. Corky was vice president of the Holy Name Society at our church. Last week, he danced with me and sang 'Irish Eyes' in my ear. Tonight, he tried to kill me."

"People change," Mackey said.

"So I hear."

Turned out, the Hanlons still lived in the same house in our old neighborhood. The garage door was closed. But a champagne-colored Cadillac was parked in the driveway, and there was no sign of the basketball net. Two unmarked cruisers sat at the curb, waiting.

Mackey sent the detectives around to the back of the house and posted himself in the shrubbery by the front door, just in case Corky decided to make a run for it. He agreed to let me talk to Marie Hanlon.

I rang the doorbell three or four times, and finally the porch light went on. I knew she was inside, peering through the fish-eye in the door, wondering who the hell was out there at this time of night.

"Marie?" I called. "It's me. Callahan Garrity. Can I talk to you, Marie?"

The door opened. She was shorter and wider than I remembered, but her hair was still dyed that improbable shade of strawberry blond, done up in big pink plastic rollers. She grabbed at the sash of a green terrycloth robe, bleary-eyed with sleep.

"Julia? Honey, what's wrong?"

She had me there. Everything was wrong. So where should I start?

She knew. "It's Corky, isn't it? Something's happened. Tell me."

"Did Corky come home tonight?" I asked.

"Of course he came home. Where else would he go? He lives here. He played golf with a buddy this afternoon, came home and showered, and said he had to go to a wake. For that officer who was killed. He said he'd be late. A few drinks with the boys. He'll be along home any minute now. What is this, Julia?" She peered over my shoulder, saw the cruisers at the curb.

She put a hand to her mouth. "Oh, my God. Oh, Jesus." She clutched my arm, the nails digging into my flesh. "You have to tell me, Julia. What's happened to him?"

"Corky's in trouble, Marie," I said. "We need to find him. Do you know where he might be?"

"I've got to call Chuckie," she said, turning around, forgetting I was there. "Chuckie will know."

I followed her into the kitchen. It was the kitchen I remembered from my childhood. The green linoleum was worn in places, but freshly waxed. A bowl of apples and bananas sat in the middle of the Formica dinette table.

There was a plate sitting on the counter. Sliced chicken, rice and gravy, green beans. Nicely covered with plastic wrap, so she could warm up Corky's dinner in the microwave, the way she always had when he came in late from work or a ball game or a church meeting. Tacked up above the kitchen window was a wooden crucifix. Looped around it was a bleached-out strand of palm. Palm Sunday is this Sunday, then April and Easter. She would burn the old frond, the way she always did, and replace it with a new one. That much was a constant.

Marie pulled open kitchen drawers, scrabbling for something. "My glasses," she cried. "I can't find my glasses. Chuckie and Heather just moved to Rockdale County. For the kids. The schools here are just terrible now. Coloreds, you know. Not like when you all lived here. I can't seem to remember that new number. You'd think I could remember my son's phone number, wouldn't you? But it's written down in my book. Right here in my green address book."

"Marie," I said gently. "Look at me. Don't worry about calling Chuckie right now. Think. Where would Corky go if he were in trouble? Where would he go, Marie?"

"Why, he'd come home to me," she said, smiling.

I thought about those closed garage doors.

"Marie, does Ila Jo Tice still live next door?"

"Of course," she said. "Her kids want her to move to Florida, because of her arthritis, but you know how Ila Jo is. Set in her ways."

The green address book was in the kitchen drawer with the warranties for the microwave and the dishwasher. I found Chuckie's number, called and woke him up, suggested he might want to be with his mother. Then I called Ila Jo Tice and woke her up too. It took a few minutes to find Marie's slippers. We walked next door, arm in arm, and I told Marie that Edna was fine, and that no, I wasn't married, and yes, Maureen had a big job as a nurse, and my brothers were all right and Edna had three grandchildren.

Ila Jo had shrunk, too. Or maybe I had gotten bigger.

Once we had Marie settled, Mackey and Rakoczy followed me inside the Hanlons' house, and I showed them the door from the kitchen into the garage. The Chrysler's hood was still warm. Corky was slumped over in the front seat and there was a smear of blood on the driver's side window. A blood-spattered cap was on the car seat.

That cap. I'd seen it earlier in the day. The gray Chrysler too. Corky, the cap pulled down over his eyes, cruising past Memorial Oaks. Waiting. Waiting and watching for Deecie Styles to come out of her hidey-hole.

I went back inside and closed the kitchen door. Marie wouldn't like it if we tracked mud and blood all over the place.

41

Corky hadn't had time for much of a fare-well. The note was written on the back of an old envelope.

"Marie. I'm sorry."

Mackey pulled a pair of latex gloves from his back pocket, slipped them on, picked up the gun, and looked at it.

"Ragan was killed with a bullet from a nine millimeter," he said.

"You know many cops who don't own one of these?" Rakoczy asked.

The cash, mostly twenties and fifties, was rolled up in foil-lined empty paint cans on Corky's workbench. Mackey fanned the bills out on the workbench. "Maybe ten, twelve thousand," he said. "Not so much, really," he said, looking down at the worn bills.

"Not to you," I pointed out. "But Corky was a sheriff's deputy during the sixties, seventies, and early eighties. The most money he ever made was probably twenty-five thousand a year. He bought a house in the suburbs and put a kid through college on that. I don't remember a time he didn't work an extra job."

Rakoczy jerked his head toward the driveway. "That's a brand-new Cadillac out there."

"For Marie," I said. "I bet he paid cash for it, too. First time in his life."

"Last time in his life," Mackey said dryly.

They found the knife wrapped in a towel, shoved under the front seat of the Chrysler. The crime scene technician held it out for us to see. "Blood and tissue on the blade," he said. "This is good."

I thought of Deecie Styles, and of Faheem, and I gagged.

"Some cop," Mackey said, laughing at my discomfort.

"Tonight? For once I'm proud to say I'm not a cop. Not anymore."

"What about the rest of them?" Rakoczy asked. "Boylan and those guys? And Viatkos?"

"Corky Hanlon didn't dream up this scheme all by himself," I told Mackey. "Somebody recruited him. My money is on John Boylan."

"You really hate that guy, don't you?" Mackey asked.

"You think he's not involved? You think he's an innocent bystander in this whole deal?"

"What I think doesn't matter. I've got to

413

have proof. Once I get that, I'll knock Boylan's fat mick ass in prison so fast his head will spin."

"What about Antjuan Wayne?" I asked. "Seems like he might have something interesting to say about all of this."

Mackey shrugged. "For now, it's up to the feds. Antjuan's lawyer wants to cut a deal. Wayne's saying he found out about the ATM robberies after Ragan got drunk and bragged about the new Rolex he'd bought himself. Wayne claims all he wanted out of Ragan was a chance to work some of those big-money security jobs. So he told Ragan unless the Shamrocks cut him in on the action, he'd turn them in. Ragan supposedly referred Wayne to Viatkos, and Viatkos, who didn't give a shit about ethnic Irish loyalties, suggested Wayne might be useful working at some of the black nightclubs on the Southside. Wayne swears he only did one robbery, at a strip club down there. After that, he claims, he told Viatkos he was through."

"What does he know about the Budget Bottle Shop robbery?" I asked.

"He won't talk about that," Mackey said, shaking his head. "And he's definitely not talking about Ragan's murder. Not unless the feds cut him a deal."

"What I'd like to know is, where's the

money coming from to pay David Kohn?" Rakoczy asked.

"The African American Patrolmen's Association," Mackey said. "These folks take care of their own."

It was dawn by the time Mackey and his men finished their search of Corky Hanlon's house. When I heard the thud of a newspaper hitting the driveway outside, I went out on the front porch and sat in a wooden rocking chair and watched my old neighborhood come to life.

Cars flashed by. A yellow school bus rumbled past, stopping at the same corner where my sister and brothers and I waited for the bus. Three kids clambered aboard the bus, dressed in the unisex uniform of the moment, baggy jeans that drooped around their hips, T-shirts, and ball caps turned backward. Two of the kids were black, one white.

Ours had been the house across the street, a split-level ranch much like the Hanlons', except ours was red brick, with a dark blue front door. The spindly little azaleas my mother had tended reached nearly to the porch roof now, and the new owners had converted the garage to a den with a big bay window.

I glanced over to the right and saw Marie Hanlon silhouetted in the window of Ila Jo Tice's kitchen. She was standing there, drinking coffee, watching her house, and the invaders who'd taken possession of what used to be her life. Chuckie's blue minivan was gone from her driveway.

I stood and stretched, then walked across the lawn to the Tices' house, feeling the crunch of the browned-out winter grass beneath my boots.

Ila Jo met me at the front door. She wore a print blouse and dark slacks, her hair was neatly combed, fresh lipstick in place, even though the circles under her eyes told me she had not slept the night before.

"Is it true?" she asked, her voice low. "Marie says Corky was in some kind of terrible trouble. He'd been drinking. That's why he did it."

I didn't answer at first. "Do you think she'd mind talking to me?"

"She's been talking all night," Ila Jo said. "First to the detectives, then to me. She's trying to make sense of things. Chuckie didn't want to hear a word against his daddy, of course. But Marie says she knew Corky was in trouble."

"Julia?" Marie called from the other room. "Come on in, honey."

Her hair was still wrapped up in those curlers, but she'd exchanged the green bathrobe for a fuchsia warm-up suit Heather had fetched from the house the night before.

Ila Jo poured me a cup of coffee and the three of us sat down at the kitchen table.

"He was drunk," Marie announced. "Corky never would have killed himself if he were sober. So he can still have a Catholic burial, don't you think?"

I nodded, unsure.

She went on, the words pouring out, like a spigot that had been suddenly unstoppered. "Will it be in the papers, do you think? Chuckie is so upset. He doesn't want the kids to know their Paw-Paw was in any trouble. He's going to tell them it was an accident, that Paw-Paw was cleaning his gun and it went off."

"That's probably a good idea," I said. I thought it was a terrible idea to lie to kids, but then I didn't have any of my own, so I wasn't an authority on such things.

"Corky has been so upset," Marie went on. "He didn't sleep. He'd get up in the middle of the night, and go into his office or out to the garage, and he'd stay for hours, just tinkering and piddling. He was drinking more, too, with those Shamrock fellows. Seemed like they had a meeting every night. He knew I didn't like that, but he didn't care."

"Did he talk about the other members? John Boylan? A woman named Lisa Dugan?"

Marie looked shocked. "A woman? They let a woman in? Corky told me it was just the boys. He talked about somebody named Johnny. And there was a Sean, and some other men."

"What was he tinkering with?" I asked.

"Just things. He had his gun case out in the garage, and he liked to get his guns out and clean and oil them. He'd work on that old Chrysler of his. Or he'd go in his office and lock the door. We put a desk and filing cabinet in there for an office for Corky, after Chuckie got married and moved out."

"What made you think he was upset?" I asked.

"He wasn't himself," Marie said, her eyes filling with tears. "I'd ask him a question, just a simple question, and he'd bite my head off, really cuss me out good. Then he'd turn around and cry like a baby and beg me to forgive him. 'Forgive what?' I asked him, but he wouldn't tell me."

"How long had he been like that?"

"A year, maybe? I thought it was because he was working those security jobs. He didn't really like to work nights, but he said the money was too good to turn down. And he worked Sundays. He hadn't been to Mass with me in months. You know that's not like Corky. He said it was just temporary. Easy money, he called it. We were going to take the whole family on a cruise to Alaska. That's what he was saving for."

"Where was he working?" I asked.

"Different places," Marie said. "A grocery store on Buford Highway. He didn't like that place at all. The Vietnamese man who owned it wanted him to go out in the parking lot and bring in the shopping carts. He was hateful to Corky, but Corky said that wasn't his job. Sometimes he worked at a liquor store in downtown Atlanta. He liked that better, because he mostly just sat at the counter and talked to the clerk."

"A liquor store? Was it the Budget Bottle Shop?"

"Bottle Shop?" Marie wrinkled her forehead, trying to remember. "That could be right. Near the new police station. He knew almost all the old-time officers. Not so many of the younger ones, though."

"Did he ever mention a clerk who worked there? A girl named Deecie?"

"That's the girl the detectives kept asking about," Marie said, looking up from her coffee cup. "Was she a skinny colored girl? Had a baby?"

"That's right," I said eagerly. "Did Corky work with her?"

"Sometimes," Marie said. "I told the detectives that. Later on, Corky told me she stole a lot of money from that store, and that Pete, that's the owner, wanted to find her and make her give the money back."

"Did Pete ask Corky to help find her?"

"She lived over in colored town," Marie said. "You know how those people are. Won't say a word to a white person. Terrible neighborhood. Corky said a little boy no bigger than our grandson Adam tried to sell him some of that dope."

Marie rambled on some more about Corky and his plans for their family cruise, and how she needed to talk to Father Drennen about funeral arrangements.

She stopped talking suddenly. "Was he in pain, do you think?"

"No," I said. "It was very quick."

Some solace.

I went home and took a long hot bath. My knees were scraped and my hip was bruised from the previous night's acrobatics.

Edna was talking on the phone when I came out of the bathroom into the den. She hung up, her face stricken. "That was Ila Jo Tice," she said. "She told me about Corky Hanlon."

"I'm sorry," I told her.

"Poor Marie. Ila Jo says the police asked Marie about that girl Deecie. Do they think Corky killed her?"

"It looks that way."

"Why? That foolish old drunk. He was harmless. Wouldn't hurt a fly."

I wanted to tell her about my experience the night before, looking down the barrel of Corky's 9-mm, about scrambling away from the bullets he intended to kill me. About the bloodstained knife Corky had drawn across Deecie Style's neck. Instead I took a comb and tried to bring some order to my tangled mop of curls. I yanked and tugged and nearly combed myself bald.

"Why?" Edna repeated.

"Money," I said. "It looks like some of those Shamrock Society guys were involved in an armed-robbery ring. They got jobs working security at these bars and restaurants so they could figure out how to stick up the owners when they went to make ATM deposits. Corky was involved. We don't know for sure, but we think somebody else put him up to killing Deecie. She knew Corky because he worked at the liquor store with her sometimes. She probably thought the same thing we did, that he was a sweet old drunk. She was terrified of the cops, but not Corky. Good old Corky."

"Fooled us all," Edna said.

"Say, Ma," I said, remembering something. "Was it Baby or Sister who told you about the run-in we had over there at Deecie's apartment complex?"

"Neither one," she said.

"Then how did you find out about it? I sure didn't tell you."

"You had a call," Edna said. "While you were gone. I didn't think anything about it at the time. It was a man. He asked for you. When I said you were out, he laughed. Asked me if I knew where you were. That's when he told me what had happened. About your nearly getting yourself killed over there."

"What man?" I asked. "He didn't leave a name?"

She shook her head. "He hung up before I could ask him anything else."

"Could it have been Corky?" I asked.

She shrugged. "Maybe. It was just a man. I was so upset about your taking the girls over there, I didn't give it a lot of thought."

What if it had been Corky? I thought. So what if he'd been trying to warn me off. It didn't change things. He was still a killer.

I'd found the key in my jeans pocket, and I kept turning it over and over.

"What's that?" Edna wanted to know.

"Something Deecie gave me," I said. "Probably the thing that got her killed."

42

William wore a disposable blue paper hospital gown, Faheem had a pale yellow gown and a green plastic pacifier.

The room was quiet except for the creak of the rocking chair and the soft sucking noises made by Faheem, who was nestled against William's chest.

"This man who killed Deecie. He dead?" William asked.

"Yes. He killed himself last night."

"And you say Deecie knew the dude?"

"He worked as a security guard at the liquor store some nights. She probably thought he was a nice guy."

William shook his head. "Man, what kind of a man would do something like that? Kill a girl? Cut her throat?"

"Fuckin' evil man, that's what kind," Monique Bell said savagely. "White man like that, he think nothing about killing a little nigger girl. So what? One less nigger in this world, that's good news."

"Hush up," William ordered. "I don't want

Faheem hearing that talk. Don't be saying the f-word. And I don't want you saying the n-word in front of this boy either."

"He's heard it before and he'll hear it again," Monique said, unabashed.

"Not from me," William vowed.

"Shee-it," Monique said, disgusted.

"You asked about Corky Hanlon," I said. "I don't know what to tell you. He wasn't always like that. He was a sheriff's deputy. He had a wife, kids. He went to church and he coached baseball. He took the neighborhood kids fishing. Somewhere, though, he changed. He started drinking more. He . . . went . . . bad." It sounded lame, even to me.

"Bad is right," Monique muttered. She picked up the remote control from the table beside Faheem's crib and clicked on the television.

The noise filled the already cramped room, made the walls close in.

"Turn that mess off," William ordered. "I'm tryin' to get this boy settled down."

Monique rolled her eyes, stood up, and gathered her cigarettes and lighter. "I'm goin' outside for a smoke, if that's all right with you," she said, glaring at William.

When she was gone, Faheem seemed to relax, snuggling against William's chest. His eyelids fluttered a little, then closed.

"Is he getting better?" I asked. "I mean, I assumed since they put him in a room, he's feeling better."

William nodded. "Lot better. The doctor said maybe he can go home tomorrow."

"Home. Where?"

He winced. "They talking about foster care. Since Deecie's dead, and his real daddy gone, the social worker say that's the best thing."

"What's Monique have to say about that?"

"She raised h— Cain," he said, grinning sheepishly. "But she's got to work. And now she's got to move, too. The apartment manager told her this morning as soon as the cops get done, she got to get out. He's gonna put her stuff out on the curb, starting today."

"They can't do that," I said. "It's subsidized housing. They can't just kick her out like that. Not without cause."

"Tell that to Monique. She's going out looking for a place after she leaves here."

"How do you feel about putting Faheem in foster care?" I asked.

"At first, I was real mad," William admitted. "I mean, Faheem, he thinks I'm his daddy. He calls me daddy. But your friend, that Linda Nickells? She come over here last night to talk to me. She's a real nice lady. She called a lawyer she knows, and this lawyer says she'll help me try to get Faheem back.

My mama's got an extra room at her house, and she says she can watch Faheem while I'm at work. Soon as I can show I'm working steady and got a place for us to stay, the lawyer lady says she'll help me get the papers to adopt Faheem."

"And that's all right with Monique?"

"She don't like it, but she knows she can't keep Faheem. She's mad right now. Mad at that dude that killed Deecie, mad at me, mad at you, 'cause you didn't stop him. But she'll get over it."

"What about you? Are you mad at me, too?"

He had a right to be. I'd convinced Deecie I could keep her safe, then let her down in the worst possible way.

He rocked a while. "No," he said finally. "You couldn't help it. I couldn't help it either. Deecie, she made up her own mind what to do when she left this hospital. She just thought she could take care of herself and Faheem without anybody else. But she couldn't. That's all."

I'd stopped at a gift store near the hospital, brought along a present. It was a small, fluffy, yellow giraffe. I took it out of the gift bag, tiptoed over to the rocker, and laid it in William's lap. Faheem's eyelids fluttered open. His lips smiled around the pacifier. The chubby hands closed over the giraffe, then he nodded off to sleep again.

Monique was outside, leaning against the emergency room entrance, puffing on a cigarette.

"I hear they're trying to kick you out of your apartment," I said.

"Fuckers."

"Do you want to move?" If I were Monique Bell, Memorial Oaks would be the last place on earth I would want to live.

She shrugged. "Bus stop is right there on the corner. Grocery store a block away. I got friends. Got me a good apartment in the corner. Where I'm gonna go if I leave there?"

"Let's take a ride," I said.

Memorial Oaks, the apartment complex Monique Bell lived in, was federally subsidized Section 8 housing. I didn't know all the ins and outs of that program, but I was pretty sure the manager couldn't kick Monique out without just cause.

We found him in the hallway outside Monique's apartment. He was a huge blubberball of a white man, with the kind of high fleshy hips usually seen on women, not men. He was supervising two teenagers who were dragging all the furniture out of the apartment. A strip of yellow crime scene tape lay discarded by the front door.

"Hey!" Monique yelped. "Get your hands off my shit." She grabbed a kitchen chair away from one of the kids.

"Hi," I said. "What's happening here?"

"I don't know you," the manager said.

"Hey," he called to the kids, "come on, get moving. I'm not paying you clowns to goof off."

"I'm Callahan Garrity," I said. "I've been retained by Miss Monique Bell to make sure her rights are protected."

"She's got no rights," he said.

"Does she pay her rent?"

He looked at me. Annoyed, like you get at a mosquito. "What's it to you? The cops said I could clear the place out, that's what I'm doing."

"Unless she's several month in arrears in her rent, I don't believe you can just kick her out. And even if you were allowed to kick her out, you'd have to give her written notice and time to respond to that notice."

Bullshit, all of it total bullshit. But it sounded pretty good, even to me.

"If any of her belongings are damaged or stolen," I said loudly so the teens could hear me, "she could have legal recourse against you."

His face took on a mottled purple shade. "That carpet in there is ruined," he shouted.

"Blood all over the place. Door busted in. That's cause to throw Monique Bell on the street."

"Her niece was the victim of a vicious crime," I said, taking my cell phone out of my purse. "I think I'll call a friend of mine at the newspaper. It'd make a good human-interest story, don't you think? 'Grieving Family Evicted After Niece's Murder'? A photo of Monique standing forlornly by all her belongings. We'll make sure to get the crib the baby slept in. That always gets people, when a baby is made homeless."

I started punching numbers on the cell phone at random. "City desk? I'd like to speak to Elliott Diggs, please." Diggs was the newspaper's city police reporter.

"She'll have to pay to have that door replaced," the manager said, hedging. "And I'm not cleaning that carpet. That's not normal maintenance."

I put my hand over the phone. "What's that? What were you saying?"

He turned and walked away. "I said she can stay, goddammit."

I gave the teenagers twenty bucks to start dragging Monique's stuff back inside. While Monique started giving them orders, I walked ahead and went inside, pausing at the threshold to get a fix on the half-empty living room.

The murderer had trashed the place. A stereo and television set were smashed against a wall, sofa cushions slashed open, bookshelves upended, drapes yanked from the windows.

In the kitchen, pots and pans and dishes were thrown on the floor, packages of food strewn about, glasses and dishes smashed to bits.

There were two small bedrooms. The larger of the two was littered with clothes, shoes, and jewelry. Dresser drawers had been pulled out, and the mattress had been pulled off the box spring. A path had been cleared in the room where the landlord had started removing the furniture.

The bedroom where Deecie died smelled like a butcher shop. Most of the furniture had already been removed, revealing worn gold shag carpet that carried a deep red stain. In the adjoining bathroom, I saw the heat vent where Mackey said the detectives had found the missing moneybag. I took the key out of my pocket, tried it in all the doors in the apartment. Not even close.

"Leave that mattress out on the curb," I heard Monique screeching at one of the teenagers.

Time to go. I wasn't going to miss Memorial Oaks.

I scrunched up against the hall wall to let

the kids come by with a heavy chest of drawers. When I felt a tug at the hem of my jacket, I looked down.

The little girl gave me a shy smile. Her hair was done in neat little plaits, each one secured by a different-colored rubber band. She wore a purple sweater and pink pants and bright yellow sneakers.

"Hey, there," I said. It was the little girl I'd seen the first time I'd come to Monique's apartment.

She looked away, watching Monique follow the boys into her apartment.

"My name's Callahan," I told her. "You told me your name last time, but I can't remember it."

"It's Tanya," she said, digging the toe of her sneaker into the carpet. "My mama say Deecie dead. The amb'lance men came and took her away, and Mama say Deecie ain't coming back here no more."

"That's right," I said. I walked outside to check on my van, which I'd parked in a no-park slot at the curb. Tanya followed along behind me. It was still early. The ball players and drug dealers and kiddie prostitutes hadn't yet begun to congregate outside. I sat down on the curb, and Tanya plopped down beside me.

"My mama say a bad man cut Deecie and

made her bleed. She say if I don't mind her, the bad man might get me, too."

"No," I said firmly. "That bad man went away and he's never coming back here again."

"Okay," Tanya said, inserting her thumb in her mouth. She sucked it for a while, and picked at the shoelace of her sneaker.

"I got a secret from my mama," Tanya said.

"Is it a good secret or a bad secret?"

She fidgeted. "Just a secret. Deecie told it to me."

"Did she? Would you like to share it with me?"

"You got any candy?"

I thought about it. There was half a pack of breath mints in the ashtray in the van. I got up and got the breath mints, and handed them to Tanya. I felt a little like a child molester, the classic stranger giving candy to a kid.

"Ain't you got no chocolate candy?" she asked, clearly disappointed.

"Not today," I said.

"Oh." She popped a mint in her mouth and made loud sucking noises.

"You wanna see where my secret's at?" she asked.

"Sure."

I stood up and she took my hand in hers. We walked through the breezeway connecting the apartment buildings, around the back of the block.

The area had been a parking lot once, but the asphalt was cracked and broken, and rusted garbage cans, piles of tires, and two or three abandoned cars were all that was parked there now.

Tanya walked up to a dilapidated white Toyota station wagon. The hood was gone and so was everything under it. The rear tires had been removed, making the car appear to be sitting on its haunches, like a dog awaiting a treat.

The little girl reached in her pocket and brought out a key. I held my breath. Tanya wrinkled her forehead in concentration as she worked the key back and forth, finally getting the door lock to pop. With both hands she managed to wrench the driver's side door open. She gestured grandly at the grubby interior. "This is my clubhouse," she said. "You wanna come in my clubhouse?"

"Sure," I said. I walked around to the passenger side and opened the door. It smelled like mildew. The plastic seat coverings were cracked and peeling, but somebody had tried to cover them with faded pink bath towels.

On the floor of the car was a stack of plastic fast food cups, a shoe box full of crayons, and a naked black Barbie doll.

I got in. Tanya climbed up into the driver's side and knelt. She grasped the steering wheel and began spinning it to and fro, making happy little motor noises in the back of her throat.

"Are we going on a trip?" I asked.

She nodded.

"Where shall we go?" I asked.

Her dark eyes sparkled. "We goin' to Disney World. See Mickey Mouse and the Little Mermaid. And we gonna see Sleeping Beauty's castle, and have some ice cream."

"Let's go!" I said.

She made more motor noises, and we steered the car down the imaginary streets of Disney World, with Tanya pointing out all the hot spots, which seemed to include McDonald's, Burger King, and the ice cream store.

"You wanna see a movie now?" she asked, finally tiring of the game.

"Sure," I said. "Is it a good movie?"

"I don' know," she admitted. "It's Deecie's movie. That's the secret. But Deecie's dead. And my mama say she'll whip my behind if I don't quit playing in my clubhouse."

She clambered over the backseat of the car, reached under the seat, and brought out a black videotape cassette, which she handed to me. "Can we go watch Deecie's movie now?"

We walked hand in hand back to the front of the apartment building, where we were met by Austine Rudolph, the older woman who'd talked to me about Deecie the first time I'd gone to Memorial Oaks.

"Tanya," she scolded. "Where'd you get to, girl? I was worried to death 'bout you."

Tanya looked down at her shoe. "I just showed the lady my clubhouse. Deecie dead. She can't go there no more."

"I'm sorry we worried you," I told Mrs. Rudolph. "She just wanted me to see her secret place. That white Toyota out back. Was that Deecie's?"

"Faheem's daddy," Mrs. Rudolph said. "That was his car. He left it here when it quit running. Left Deecie and Faheem too. Good riddance."

Mrs. Rudolph took Tanya's hand. "Just don't be going off with strangers no more, you hear me? Bad things happening around here. We don't want nothing bad happening to you."

When I got home, the house was empty. I got a Diet Coke out of the refrigerator and went into the den, where I popped the videotape into the VCR.

The film quality was about what you'd expect: lousy, mostly out of focus, with grainy, ghostly images flitting in and out of what was vaguely recognizable as the Budget Bottle Shop.

A time counter at the bottom of the screen started at 11:00 hours. I fast forwarded until the time was showing 23:00. The video's plot wasn't much better than the quality.

There is the back of Deecie's head. Her neck is long and slender. For a moment, I thought about that neck, necklaced in blood. Then I blinked and forced the image away. Customers come in. They browse, select their bottles and cans, pay, and leave. Business is steady. Why not, it's a drinking man's holiday. St. Patrick's Day. When the counter shows 11:45, Bucky walks in the door. His tie is loosened, he's left the jacket in the car. He looks around, waves at Deecie. She waves back. Not a care in the world.

Bucky goes directly to the glass-doored beer cooler. He opens the door, stands there, looking. He closes the door, walks up to the counter, talks briefly to Deecie. They seem to be sharing a joke. The last joke. Now Deecie ducks down and when she stands up, she's holding the baby. Bucky gives Faheem a little chuck under the chin. Cute kid, he seems to be saying. More conversation. Now Bucky goes to the door leading to the stockroom, opens it and walks in.

I watched the time counter carefully. Three

minutes passed. At 11:49, Bucky throws open the door of the stockroom and strides quickly toward the door, a six-pack of beer in his right hand. But there's somebody else right behind him, coming out of the stockroom. It's a man. He walks rapidly toward Bucky, his face turned away from the camera. When he finally comes into the camera range, I can see that he wears a dark stocking mask and holds a small pistol in his outstretched hand. Bucky turns, drops the six-pack of beer, and reaches for the mask. He rips it halfway off, and I can see the expression of fear and shock on his face. The gunman pushes Bucky's hand away, points the pistol at Bucky's skull, and fires. Bucky crumples to the ground. The gunman stands still, looking down at him, hesitates, then stands over Bucky and fires another time, directly into Bucky's head. He stands up straight, looks directly at the camera, pulls the mask down, and approaches the counter. Deecie's back is still turned to the camera, but I can see she is holding the baby. The gunman stands in front of her, the pistol pointed at her chest. He hesitates, looks toward the stockroom door. Another figure emerges from the stockroom, shouting, pointing at Deecie. He wears a baseball cap with a bill that shades his face, but the build is familiar. He's wearing a dark blazer, a twin to the one Bucky wore earlier in the evening. He's got a potbelly, walrus mustache. The gunman drops the pistol, turns, and runs toward the stockroom. Both men disappear. Now only Deecie is visible. Deecie, seen crawling on the floor. Now standing, she walks over, looks down at Bucky's unmoving body. Waits a moment, then walks toward the stockroom. Two minutes later, she emerges, runs to the front door of the store and comes back. The tape abruptly turns to black.

I stop the film, rewind it, and watch it, twice more. The film quality is atrocious, but I can see enough. In slow motion, I can see Sean Ragan's frightened face as Bucky rips the mask away. The other man's face is not visible, but the figure is one I've seen before. Despite the middle-aged paunch, he stands erect, the way the nuns taught him to stand all those years in parochial school. He would have been their favorite altar boy, clever, nice manners. Smart. How proud the nuns were, when they heard he'd become a police officer, later a much-decorated detective. The nuns never would have recognized their Johnny Boylan now.

43

It was a day of blinking lights. First the VCR, then the answering machine. Two calls from clients who wanted to discuss scheduling a spring cleaning date, and a message from C.W.

"Callahan!" His usually laid-back voice had a new tone of urgency. "Uh, you could have been right about Lisa Dugan," he said. "Part right, anyway. I checked the call-out sheet for the night Bucky was shot. She was where she was supposed to be. But there's something funny about the sheets for the night Sean Ragan was killed. She was supposed to be off that night, but instead she showed up at the scene and helped canvass the area for suspects. Call me."

Dugan. What was it about that woman that made me all twitchy? I knew for certain now that she didn't have anything to do with Bucky's shooting. Still, I wasn't ready to let her off the hook. Not yet.

There also was a message from a voice identifying himself as Agent Halstead with the FBI, urgently requesting a meeting.

Agent Halstead wasn't in. I left a voice mail. I tried calling Lloyd Mackey. His secretary said he'd be gone all afternoon, but she graciously allowed me to leave a voice mail for him, too. I was starting to get lonely for the sound of another real live human being.

In the kitchen, I started to make myself a sandwich, till I glanced at the clock. Noon already. Sean Ragan's funeral was scheduled for one o'clock at Sacred Heart Church downtown. Damn. Wedged into the downtown hotel district, Sacred Heart was a beautiful old cathedral, with almost no parking. No question that I would go to the funeral. Certainly not for Sean Ragan, the murdering bastard. Not even for poor old Corky Hanlon, who'd probably be denied a proper Catholic burial of his own. I would go for Bucky.

I looked down at my clothes. I was wearing a black turtleneck tunic and black leggings. No time to change now. At least the color was appropriate.

Traffic in Midtown was heavy for a weekday. And as soon as I turned onto Peachtree Street I knew why. I was in trouble. A cop stood in the intersection ahead, directing traffic away from the church. I turned down a side street and found another cop directing traffic at the next intersection.

When it came time to turn, the cop motioned for me to turn right. I rolled my window down and stuck my head out the window. "I'm trying to get to Sean Ragan's funeral," I called. "Where's the best place to park?"

"Macon," he shouted back. Then he waved for me to move forward. I gave him a grateful nod and ignored the resentful honks from the line of cars in back of me.

Both sides of the streets leading to the cathedral were lined with police cruisers, parked nose to nose, with barely enough room for one car to creep through what was left of the center lane. I made it up one block and could see it was no use to try going forward. The streets ahead were a solid wall of more cruisers. I turned right onto International Boulevard and saw four television camera vans with their extended satellite antennas parked on the sidewalk that ran alongside the Marriott Marquis. I pulled up behind a blue van from the local ABC affiliate, found a piece of notebook paper, and scrawled on it "NBC NIGHTLY NEWS PRODUCER. NO TOW!"

I said a little prayer to the god of parking spaces, tucked the note under the windshield, locked the van, and set out for Sacred Heart on foot.

The streets were packed. I'd never seen so many cops in one place in all my life.

They were all in dress uniforms, dark blues, dark greens, blacks, browns, and grays. Most had black armbands fastened to their sleeves, and the black slash covering their badges. Twice I had to move off the sidewalk and into the street for a line of cops walking their K-9 unit dogs. They were big animals, German shepherds and Rottweilers, straining at the ends of their leashes. I looked down at the dog tags dangling from their collars; they were replicas of their handler's badges. Those too wore the black slash.

At the triangular point where Peachtree and Spring came together in front of the old red-brick church, the streets had been cleared of traffic, but the sidewalks were packed five deep with mourners.

Just as I glanced down at my watch, church bells began to toll. The sound came from up the street, not from Sacred Heart, but from the other big old downtown churches: St. Luke's Episcopal, Peachtree United Method-ist, North Avenue Presbyterian, and the Shrine of the Immaculate Conception. So many chimes, each in a different key.

I struggled to work my way toward the church doors, but as I got closer, I saw it was useless. A uniformed honor guard of Atlanta police officers stood at attention on both sides of the massive oak doors, forming a solid wall of blue reaching all the way to the curb in front of Sacred Heart.

As soon as the bells finished tolling, the motorcade began arriving.

The motorcycle units came first. Row after row of gleaming police Harley-Davidsons, their big engines throbbing as they slowly rolled down Peachtree. I quit counting after the first fifty hawgs rumbled by. Behind them I could see waves of uniformed patrolmen marching on foot. After the noise of the Harleys, the street was eerily quiet except for the steady measured beat of three hundred pairs of black mirror-polished Florsheims meeting the pavement in unison.

I heard the bagpipes and drummers before they marched into view, and began inching my way toward the curb to see for myself.

Sure enough, it was the Shamrocks. The bagpipers, got up in tartan kilts, short green velvet jackets, and green tams, marched six abreast down the street, playing a ragged but no less moving version of "Amazing Grace." I craned my neck to see if I recognized any of the pipers, accidentally jostling a woman in front of me. She shot me a look of annoyance. "Sorry," I muttered, inching forward.

I was at the curb as the pipers passed. Directly behind the bagpipers came three dozen men and women, all dressed in the same dark-green blazers and black slacks they'd sported the night before at Manuel's Tavern.

John Boylan marched past, and I spotted Lisa Dugan in the group too.

There was a break in the procession as the Shamrocks lined themselves along the curb, the bagpipers switching to a song I didn't recognize at first.

When the first gleaming black limousine pulled in front of the church, and one of the Shamrocks stepped forward to open the door and help Alexis Ragan out of the backseat, I recognized the song.

"Danny Boy." Normally, the song makes me choke up. This time, I wanted to hit somebody.

Alexis Ragan faltered for a moment, getting out of the car. John Boylan stepped forward, leaned down, and helped her out, offering an arm to steady her. Such a gallant gesture. Boylan was big on the gesture.

They stepped away from the car, which rolled forward, and the hearse moved up in line.

Two members of the APD honor guard marched to the rear of the hearse, and six of the Shamrocks, Kehoe among them, stepped up to shoulder the flag-draped casket onto their shoulders, before it was handed off to the honor guard.

Alexis Ragan glanced backward once at the casket, and stepped onto the curb, where she was joined by the mayor on one side and the chief on the other. Each took an arm, and the pregnant widow walked unsteadily up the steps to the church, teetering a bit on her black high heels.

Just then we heard a commotion overhead. Every face in the crowd turned skyward as six dark-blue helicopters came thudding past the spires of the church. When they were directly overhead, the helicopters maneuvered into a V-formation and hovered there, until the helicopter at the base of the V peeled off and banked away from the others, sharply upward, toward the heavens.

"Missing man formation," whispered an elderly man beside me as he held his ball cap over his chest.

He meant Sean Ragan, of course, but I was thinking of Bucky Deavers, as I watched the helicopter skim past the low gray cloud cover above Midtown Atlanta. There had been a window near his bed on the seventh floor of Grady Hospital, and I wondered if any light ever came in through that window. I wondered what sensations he might still possess. Was it possible he might see the blue state patrol helicopters, hear the chop of the rotating blades over the roar of the traffic on the Interstate rippling along beside the hospital?

A flash of motion at the street caught my eye. The Shamrocks had lined themselves up and were marching single file into the church, right behind the chief and the mayor and Alexis Ragan. But now a short, stout figure in a blue flowered dress darted into the middle of the line. She screamed something I couldn't quite make out, her voice shrill and obscene in the quiet solemnity of the moment. And then a shot rang out. John Boylan did a quick half-turn, his face registering not fear, but only surprise, before he crumpled to the pavement.

Marie Hanlon dropped the pistol, and the crowd surged forward and seemed to swallow her whole.

44

It took fifteen minutes for the cops to clear the streets enough to get an ambulance to Sacred Heart. I watched while they loaded Boylan into the ambulance, then started weaving my way back toward the van, dodging in and out among the confusion of traffic and rubber-neckers. By the time I got back to the Marriott I was panting for breath and my black turtleneck sweater was soaked with sweat.

After the funeral, I'd intended to take the liquor store videotape to Lloyd Mackey, lay it all out for him, a neat little package. Arrest these people. So much for plans. I switched on the radio. WGST, the all-news station, was full of the story. "Suburban Housewife Goes on Shooting Spree at Downtown Church" was the top-of-the-hour headline. Two o'clock. It had taken me that long to get back to the car. Traffic was impossible. While I weaved and backtracked through a maze created by closed-off and one-way streets, I tried to come up with a plan.

It took twenty minutes just to get to the intersection of Peachtree and Ponce de Leon. But by then, I had the germ of an idea.

The big F-10 pickup truck was parked in back of the Budget Bottle Shop, in the same spot Deecie Styles had described seeing it on the night of St. Patrick's Day. So he was there. And the alley door was propped open with a plastic milk crate.

Talk about the luck of the Irish. Hah. I thought of Bucky Deavers. And Sean Ragan. And Corky Hanlon. And John Boylan. All of them dead or near dead. The radio news report said Boylan had been shot in the back and was in critical condition when he arrived at Grady.

Near death. The thought somehow cheered me.

I parked the van at the back of the lot, behind a Dumpster, out of sight from the back door. I tucked the videotape in the pocket of my peacoat, and my fingertips brushed against the 9-mm. Next time, I promised myself, I would be the first to draw. Next time. I jogged over to the open door, closed my eyes for a moment, and opened them again to adjust to the darkness.

The forklift was in the same corner it had been in the last time. The same stacks of boxes and cartons were shoved against the walls of the stockroom. As I edged my way inside, I heard the low tone of a man's voice. A wedge of light spilled out from the top of the office wall partition.

I crept closer, squatted down behind a stack of cardboard cartons. Through the half-open office door I could see a pair of legs, propped up on the edge of the battleship-gray desk. Skinny legs, clad in dusty black trousers. A gap between trouser hem and sagging white sock tops showed a pair of pale hairy ankles.

I willed myself to relax, to breathe. Slow down. Listen.

Viatkos was angry.

"No, goddammit," he said. "I will not sit tight. There's an FBI agent sitting in a car parked in front of my house. Another guy's sitting in front of the store. The guy had the nerve to come in here and buy a Coke and a bag of nacho chips, not half an hour ago. He's still out there, been out there three days now. And Boylan — Christ! This is terrible. You people call yourselves cops?"

He listened, but wasn't appeased. "Christ! A thousand cops lined up downtown and some little old lady in tennis shoes steps up and puts a bullet in Johnny. Only in Atlanta!

"What?" He seemed surprised. Awestruck really.

"For real? No shit? It was Corky Hanlon's old lady who shot Johnny? Honest to God? They're sure it was her?"

He listened again. He sighed. "Jesus. What a colossal fuck-up. I should have known better. Dealing with a bunch of fuckin' bog-trotters. These people could screw up a one-car funeral."

I heard him shuffle some papers on his desk, heard the creak of the office chair when he leaned far back in it.

"No," Viatkos was saying. "Don't come here. I told you, the FBI's baby-sitting me. Not the house, either. Let me think. Yeah, okay. Sounds like a plan. Yeah. Half an hour."

Viatkos hung up the phone. The chair creaked again and I heard the sound of metal file drawers opening and closing. More papers being shuffled.

He stepped out of the office abruptly and I dived back behind the cartons to keep from being spotted. He opened the door leading to the store and leaned in.

"Louie?" he called. "I'm outta here for a while. Got some errands to do. The bank, a few more stops. The Budweiser truck should be here before four. You can sign for it. I'll be back later, you can go home, I'll finish up. You can handle things by yourself. Right? Good."

Viatkos closed the door again and walked briskly over to the office. No time to waste. I made a dash for the alley door, praying Viatkos would take his time gathering his things, enough time for me to get in the van and allow a discreet distance between us. So I could follow him. Follow where? And who was he meeting? Another of the Shamrocks? Lisa Dugan maybe? I hadn't forgotten what C.W. said about the funny business with the call-out sheets. Was it somebody who'd been a partner in the ATM holdup ring? Antjuan Wayne? Was that possible?

I burst through the back door and stumbled on the back step. Before I could catch myself, an arm reached out and grabbed me around the waist, squeezing me so tight in the middle that it knocked the breath out of me. Then I was spun around, and a cool, callused hand closed over my mouth. The scream died. I looked right into Lisa Dugan's eyes.

"Shut up," she hissed, clamping the hand down tighter across my mouth. "He'll hear you."

She half pulled, half dragged me in the direction of the Dumpster.

"What?" I tried.

"Shut up," she repeated. "You'll spoil everything."

When she was satisfied we were far enough

away from the back door, she let me go.

"What are you doing here?" I demanded.

"Same thing as you," she whispered. "I saw you earlier, standing outside the funeral at Sacred Heart. I saw the way you looked at Boylan. Before that woman shot him. God." She gave a little shiver. She was still wearing the green blazer.

"I tried to follow you. I've been in Atlanta over a year, but I still don't know those downtown streets very well. You lost me over on Poplar Street. It was pure luck, finding you here."

I stared at her, dumbfounded. Too much had happened.

"You still think I'm mixed up in this mess, don't you?" she asked.

"What am I supposed to think? You got all offended when I tried to tell you what was going on. That one of the Shamrocks shot Bucky. Face it, you're one of them."

"I'm not a killer. Not a thief," Lisa protested. "You say you know Bucky. Do you think he'd be involved with somebody like that?"

"I'm not sure what to think anymore," I said. "I thought I knew Corky Hanlon, too. He cut a girl's throat yesterday, then nearly blew me away last night. His wife was my Confirmation sponsor, did you know that?"

But Lisa wasn't paying attention now. She poked her head out from around the Dumpster to check on Viatkos.

"What was your plan?" she asked. "Were you just going to go in there and confront the guy? Bully a confession out of him?"

"No." I turned and motioned toward the van. "Look," I said. "He's coming out of there in a minute. I've gotta go."

"I heard," Lisa said. "I was right behind you in the storeroom."

"I'm going to follow him. See where he's going." I hesitated, looked into her calm hazel eyes. "I found the tape."

She looked blank.

"The videotape. From the store. The night Bucky was shot. It's why Deecie Styles was killed. Ragan shot Bucky. It's on the tape. He was wearing a mask, but Bucky managed to pull it partway off. And Boylan was right there, too. He was in on the whole thing."

"You saw this on the tape?"

I nodded.

"Where is it?"

"The original is hidden. I brought along a dupe. I was going to use it as a bargaining chip. With Viatkos. Maybe try to bluff him into thinking he was on the tape, too. He was there, I know that much. Deecie Styles saw his truck that night."

I walked over to the van, unlocked the door. I got in. Lisa Dugan came around and opened the passenger-side door.

"Viatkos is going to meet somebody. His partner, I think."

She got in. "I still don't understand any of this. Why did they shoot Bucky?"

"He must have blundered into some kind of meeting between Viatkos and Boylan and Ragan. My guess is that it had something to do with a botched robbery down in Hapeville, the night before. I think Corky Hanlon and Sean Ragan pulled the robbery. But something went wrong. The victim tried to pull a gun and one of them knocked him out. They took the gun. A little twenty-two. The same one Ragan used to shoot Bucky the next night."

"You're saying Sean Ragan wasn't killed in a burglary?"

"Not hardly. Pete Viatkos is running this game. I think he ordered Ragan's murder. Ragan was a relative rookie. He'd screwed up. Twice. He was a thief, yeah, but he really wasn't cut out to be a killer. Maybe he was having second thoughts about his new career. Whatever. Viatkos had him killed."

"By who?"

"Whom," I corrected her automatically. God, I hate it when I sound like my mother.

"Corky Hanlon maybe. Or maybe it was Antjuan Wayne. Wayne definitely knows what happened. I hear he's waiting for the feds to offer him a deal. Then he'll talk. Tell all he knows. But in the meantime, what worries me is, Pete Viatkos is still walking around. A free man."

I leaned over and reached down into my purse on the floor of the van. Glanced over at Lisa's pocketbook, which was beside mine. One of those satchel-type tote bags.

I got my cell phone and punched a single number. I'd programmed it for speed dial long ago, for when I needed to reach the homicide task force and Bucky in a hurry.

"Who are you calling?" Lisa asked, glancing toward the back door again.

"Major Mackey. When Viatkos leaves here, he's going to meet his partner. It sounded like he was gathering papers. Maybe even some of the cash from the robberies. If Mackey's people can get a jump on Viatkos, they'll have the proof they need to implicate him as the ringleader. And his partner, too."

"Who's that?" Lisa asked, glancing again at the door, and down at her wristwatch. "Antjuan Wayne?"

I switched the phone to my left hand. It was ringing. With my right hand I reached down in my coat pocket and brought out the Smith

& Wesson. She wasn't even looking my way. I put the barrel under the tip of her chin. Now she was paying attention.

"His partner? Why it's you, Lisa, dear," I said, putting the phone on my lap for a moment. I grabbed her pocketbook and flung it out the open window. "Do I need to pat you down? That blazer's a pretty tight fit, so I'm hoping there's no hidden pocket where you might hide any accessories. Like a firearm."

I heard a voice on the phone. "Hello? Who the hell is it?"

I picked up the phone. "Major Mackey? It's Callahan Garrity. Could you hold for a minute?"

I turned back to Lisa, kept the gun on her chin. "That was you Viatkos was talking to on the phone in there. You followed me here, all right. Then you called him on that cell phone I saw in your purse. You told him I'd gone inside after him, didn't you? What was the plan? To lure me to some dark alley and deal with me the same way you dealt with Ragan? Make it look like a robbery? Or maybe a carjacking?"

"Garrity, dammit, I'm hanging up."

"Please don't do that," I said, keeping the S&W pointed at Lisa Dugan. "I'm parked in the alley behind the Budget Bottle Shop. I've got Captain Lisa Dugan with me. If you send someone down here very quickly and very quietly, you may just apprehend Pete Viatkos with a good deal of cash, and maybe even some papers incriminating him in this ATM robbery scheme. Not to mention the murders of Sean Ragan and Deecie Styles."

"What has Lisa Dugan got to do with any of this?" Mackey asked. "Are you out of your mind? Put her on the phone."

"He's coming out," Lisa said suddenly, pointing toward the back door to the liquor store.

Sure enough, Pete Viatkos emerged from the store carrying a cheap-looking vinyl briefcase. He slung the case into the truck and got in.

"What's the deal, Lisa?" I asked.

She folded her arms across her chest.

"Captain Dugan was Pete Viatkos's silent partner in the security guard and armed-robbery business," I told Mackey. "You should take a look at her call-out sheets for the last few months. Funny thing. Nights she was supposedly working other cases, cold cases mostly, bad stuff happened. Like the night Sean Ragan was killed. She was there. And Ragan died."

"He shot Bucky," Lisa whispered. "For what? Bucky didn't know what was going on. I could have taken care of things. Explained

457

them. Bucky wouldn't have said anything. The sweetest man on earth. And he loved me. He really did. Antjuan was supposed to take care of Ragan, but he wussied out. Just like a man. So I did it myself."

"Viatkos's truck is just getting ready to pull out of the parking lot in the back," I told Mackey. "It's a white Ford F-10. Georgia tag." I laughed. " 'BOOZ-1.' Cute."

"Stay where you're at," Mackey said. "We've got a man parked out front of the store. He'll come around and pick up Viatkos."

"That's your guy?" I asked. "Not the FBI?"

"He's ours," Mackey said. "One minute."

I heard his voice, talking to someone else. A minute later he was back.

"We're on it."

A dark blue Crown Victoria sedan whipped around the corner from the front of the store and shot back toward the narrow street at the foot of the parking lot.

"I'm impressed," I said.

"See you in five minutes," Mackey said.

45

"This is strictly against departmental policy," Lloyd Mackey said, coming into the interview room. He closed the door behind him. Went to the plate-glass window at the front of the room, twisted the blinds open. On the other side of the one-way glass, Lisa Dugan was seated at a table with a black detective I'd never seen before. She was still wearing the green blazer and the little plaid kilt. There was a long run in one black stocking, and she kept running her fingers through her short hair, staring at the window, then looking away.

"Who's that?" I asked Mackey.

"Prentiss. Internal affairs. A real prick."

"This is a waste of time," Lisa was telling the detective. "I want to see my lawyer."

"He's on the way," Prentiss said. He picked up a file folder, skimmed through some papers inside.

"Say, Captain Dugan," he said. "This here paper says you recently put a down-payment on a house on Valley Road. In Buckhead.

459

Pretty nice neighborhood for a cop. Sale price six hundred thousand dollars. The chief of police, she don't live in a neighborhood that nice."

"I'm good at investments," Lisa said. She clasped her hands, stretched them out on the table. Bored.

"She told me Bucky was working all those extra jobs because they wanted to buy a house together," I told Mackey. "So her kid could go to a nice school."

"We're waiting on a court order, see what's in her safe deposit box," Mackey said. "Viatkos had eighty thousand dollars in cash when we picked him up. Of course, he claims it was receipts from the liquor store. That he was on the way to the bank to deposit."

"Your boyfriend know how good you were at investments?" Prentiss asked, looking up from the file. "Detective Deavers? He have anything to do with any of these ATM robberies you set up?"

"I don't know anything about any robberies," Dugan said. She was twisting the claddagh around and around. I would have liked to rip it off her hand.

"What about Detective Deavers? What did he know about the robberies?" Prentiss asked. "You and Pete Viatkos recruit him?"

"What?" I exclaimed, looking over at

Mackey. "You people are still trying to prove Bucky had something to do with this crap? This is unbelievable."

"Not me," Mackey said mildly. "This is Prentiss's show."

"You'll have to ask Detective Deavers about these so-called robberies," Lisa said wearily. "He's the one who introduced me to Detective Boylan."

"Shit," I said, pounding the table with my fist. "She's going to put it all on Bucky. While we were waiting for you to show up? She admitted that she killed Ragan. To avenge Bucky."

Mackey nodded. "We've already asked her about that. She denies it. Denies everything."

He got up and closed the blinds, and flipped a switch shutting off the microphone from Lisa Dugan's interview room.

"Let's go back to my office," he said. "It makes me feel slimy, being this close to that conniving bitch."

I followed him back down the carpeted hallway. We went into his outer office. "No calls," he told the secretary.

He closed the door between the connecting offices. The videotape I'd given him was in the middle of his desk. It was a very neat desk for the commander of Atlanta's homicide division. Especially considering how busy he'd been for the past few days. There was a television and a VCR on a stand in the corner of the office.

We watched the video all the way through. He made the occasional note on a yellow legal pad, his felt-tip pen making scratching noises. When the video was over, he put the pen down.

"Your proverbial smoking gun," he said, gesturing toward the TV. "Of course, it doesn't do us much good, does it? Ragan's dead. Deavers is a vegetable. Boylan, if he makes it, probably won't spend a day in prison."

"What's the word on the bastard?" I asked.

"I doubt he'll feel like parading again anytime soon. Unless it's in the wheelchair division. The bullet's lodged so close to his spine, the docs say it's too risky to remove. As soon as he's stable, he'll be moved over to the Shepherd Spinal Center, to start rehab."

"The man's a murderer," I started.

"Doesn't matter. He's covered under the city hospitalization plan. Believe me, I don't like it any better than you do. My premiums will probably get jacked up to pay for this shithead's medical treatment. You know what I think? Corky Hanlon coulda saved the city a hell of a lot of time and money if he'd taught his wife how to aim a gun."

"I've got a feeling that was the first time in her life Marie Hanlon ever fired a gun," I said. "Last time, too. So what happens now?"

"I hear some people are trying to raise Marie Hanlon's bond money," Mackey said. "You know anything about that?"

"People in her parish," I said, shrugging. "Former neighbors." They'd charged Marie with aggravated assault. Set bond at five hundred thousand dollars. Edna had started manning the phone the minute she'd gotten the news. I'd kicked in five hundred dollars myself. After all, Marie had been my Confirmation sponsor.

"What about the tape?" I asked. "What happens with it?"

"Out of my hands," Mackey said. "For once, I'll be happy to pass the buck on this thing."

"It doesn't look good for anybody, does it?" I asked. "You've only got Ragan and Boylan on tape. You know Viatkos and Dugan were running things. Who else?"

"Stay tuned," Mackey said. "It looks as if Antjuan Wayne is going to be the key to all this. He's singing like a bird to the feds right now. He's afraid if Boylan survives, he and Viatkos will try and pin everything on him. So Wayne's ready to name names. The feds won't tell me squat, but I think there'll be more arrests. They're especially interested in finding the gunman who wore the FBI Academy ring."

I blushed a little. "You know something? For a while there, I thought it might be you. You're an academy guy."

"But you ruled me out," Mackey said. He raised an eyebrow. "Or did you?"

"I brought the tape to you," I pointed out. "I could have handed it over to that FBI guy. Halstead. That counts for something."

"I guess," Mackey said. "Maybe if I'd listened to you earlier, we wouldn't have this high a body count. Christ. A damn burglary ring. Nobody comes out looking good on this thing."

"I'm the one who got Deecie killed," I said. "I saw his car in her neighborhood, you know, but I didn't recognize him. I still don't understand how he tracked her down there."

Mackey squirmed in his chair, fidgeted with the pen, taking the cap off, putting it back on again.

"What?"

"She got herself killed. Face it. She wasn't the total innocent you thought she was. She stole that money. But it wasn't enough. She got greedy. She decided to blackmail Viatkos. When she left her kid at that hospital yesterday, she called the liquor store, told Viatkos she'd sell him the videotape of the robbery. For ten thousand dollars."

"I don't believe you. If Viatkos told you that, he lied. How could you know something like that?"

"You weren't the only one who was suspicious of Viatkos. After the second cop who worked for him was shot, we put a wiretap on the phone at the Budget Bottle Shop. But he was careful. Up until that moment, we never heard him discussing anything useful. Not until yesterday, when Deecie Styles called, offering to sell him that tape."

"No," I said flatly. "You knew? Why didn't you do something? You must have known they'd kill her."

"It didn't go down the way they set it up," Mackey said, dull-eyed. "The exchange was supposed to take place later that night. At the store. We had the tap on the phone at the store, but we didn't know where the girl was calling from. We had no way to know he already had Corky Hanlon out looking for her. Hanlon found her before we could."

"And slit her throat." I got up and stood at the window. Mackey's office had a good view of Midtown. I wondered if it had once been an assistant buyer's office, when the building had been a Sears store. I could see out across the city. The dogwoods along Ponce de Leon were fully budded out. A homeless woman waddled down the street pushing a rusty shopping cart full of soda cans. She had a lime green bath towel wrapped around her head, turban style. Three long-legged men in nylon shorts and racing singlets cruised past her on their late-afternoon run. She tried to ram one of them with her cart, then stood there calling after them, shaking her fist at her fleeing enemies.

"Well," I said, putting Midtown behind me. "Looks like there's blame enough to go around. You, me, Deecie, Lisa. Even poor old Marie Hanlon. Everybody. Except Bucky. He didn't deserve this, Major Mackey. He really didn't."

"I know," Mackey said. "I'm sorry."

Epilogue

April followed March, but I didn't seem to notice. A chill gray haze draped itself over my soul and I couldn't seem to care. Right before Easter we went to Nashville, Mac and I, and found a bungalow for him to rent in a close-in neighborhood. It had hideous orange shag carpet and smoked glass mirrors, but there was a big fenced backyard for the dogs, so we took it. We found a new favorite restaurant there, made love on a box spring in the new bedroom, listened to the Dixie Chicks.

Edna came up too. She found a grocery store that sold Dukes Mayonnaise and Luzianne tea, and set about making a garden in the sideyard.

Edna loved Nashville. She pointed out the daffodils waving from the roadside ditches, the pennants of white, pink, fuchsia, and crimson azaleas beckoning from every yard along every street. Nashville dogwoods were whiter, more robust than Georgia dogwoods, she insisted.

Every other weekend, Mac came home to

us. We made a routine, but somehow failed to find a rhythm to life.

Not long after she was charged with everything from armed robbery to racketeering to the murder of Sean Ragan, I got a jailhouse phone call from Lisa Dugan. "Come see me," she begged.

"Why should I?"

She sighed. "We need to talk."

"I don't want to talk to you."

"Would you like to see Bucky? I'm the only one who can make that happen, you know."

I went.

Jailhouse blues weren't especially flattering for Lisa Dugan's coloring. The blond highlights were gone, the outdoorsy tan a thing of the past. Her skin was blotchy, her hair greasy. Her nails were ragged and bitten down to the cuticle. She sat across a glass partition from me, her arms folded across her chest.

"Here's the thing," she said. "Right now, my mother is living at the house, looking after Kyle. But if I don't get out of here soon, my ex-husband is going to get custody of my kid. I can't let that happen. My lawyers think they can get a judge to set bond, if certain people don't oppose it."

"Why would I want you out of jail?"

"Because you want to see Bucky. And you're not going to do that unless I sign off on it. You sign a petition to the court, saying you don't think I'm a threat to you or any other witnesses, and I'll put your name on Bucky's visitors' list. Is it a deal?"

I nodded, got up to leave.

"You don't get any of this, do you?" she called after me.

"No," I said, not bothering to turn around.

"My ex stopped paying child support eight months ago," Lisa said. "You try collecting money from a cop who lives out of state. It's impossible. You know how much money we make. It's nothing. I had to do something. Had to feed my kid, get him in a good, safe school."

I turned around. "Wonder what kind of school Alexis Ragan's kid will be able to go to? And how about Faheem Styles? His mama's dead. What kind of a school will Faheem get to go to?"

It was all big talk and Lisa Dugan knew it. I kept my part of the bargain and Lisa kept hers. After that, the only constant in my life was Bucky. Mondays and Thursdays, I went to see Bucky at the nursing home where he'd been transferred, after the hope ran out. I took the new Dixie Chicks CDs and some Shania Twain, and, of course, the old Buddy Holly stuff he loved. "Not Fade Away" had been our song when we were partners. I'd play music and read him the newspaper. I kept him up on all the machinations of the lawyers and defendants. Told him how Lisa had been suspended from the police department without pay and was out on bond pending her trial; how Pete Viatkos's lawyers were asking for a change of venue; how Antjuan Wayne would be the fed's star witness against both Dugan and Viatkos. I even filled him in on my efforts to make the city give the reward money to Deecie Styles's heir, Faheem. At one point, when I told him John Boylan had filed a civil lawsuit against the city and the Hanlon family was seeking three million dollars in damages, I could have sworn I saw the ghost of a smile creep across his waxen face.

And then one Thursday morning in early May, I arrived and a nurse's aide stopped me at the front desk to tell me Bucky was gone.

"He was having difficulty breathing last night, and around two this morning, he just slipped away," she said. She patted my hand. "It's for the best."

I kept it all together until June, when the unexpected gift of a flower shattered my carefully wrought calm.

Neva Jean walked into the house that day right after lunch. She was holding an empty Coke bottle, with a single gardenia blossom poked into it. She held it out proudly. "Your neighbor, Mr. Byerly, he sent this over to you. He says it's his first gardenia this year, and he wanted you to have it."

Gardenia? Had summer come? I stroked the creamy white petals, buried my nose in the overwhelming sweetness, and when I looked up again, I was crying.

Neva Jean patted my shoulder awkwardly and backed away a little. "It's okay, Callahan. You just go ahead and cry, hon."

I walked out of the house and down the street without a word. The sun was blazing hot, and somebody was mowing a lawn and somebody else was running a power saw somewhere. The soles of my feet burned against the concrete pavement, but I kept walking and crying and sniffing, a block at a time. Nobody looked at me funny, because of the neighborhood we live in.

When it felt like I'd cried myself dry, I put the gardenia, now limp and brown-tinged, back to my face, and watered it with yet some more tears.

Edna can't stand my blubbering. The rare times in my life she's caught me at it, she blames it on breeding. "Damn Irish. Just like your daddy. He'd cry if a traffic light turned red. Cried at birthdays, weddings, christenings. Hell, I caught him once bawling his eyes out at the breakfast table. When I asked him why, he said the picture on the oatmeal box reminded him of his grandmother, and she'd been dead almost forty years at that point."

When I looked up from my crying binge, I realized I'd walked all the way up Moreland Avenue and had cut over to North Highland. I was standing across the street from Manuel's. I hadn't been near the place since the night Corky Hanlon tried to kill me. I looked like who-shot-Lizzie, but I didn't care.

Bishop's eyebrows rose when he saw me slide into the booth nearest the door in the front room. He brought me a Jack and water and sat down opposite me.

"Haven't seen you in a while. Not since —" He stopped, taking notice of my red-rimmed eyes and the soggy gardenia.

"Hell of a thing," he said, swabbing at the tabletop.

I took a long sip of bourbon. It was cold and sweet, and I clenched my teeth to keep from swallowing the crushed ice chips, letting the smoky liquid trickle down the back of my throat. Good medicine.

"Did you hear?" Bishop asked. "Some of the regulars, they took up a collection. They're getting a plaque made, gonna put it on the back of this booth. Put his name on it, like that."

That made me smile. "He'd get a kick out

of that." With my fingertip, I traced all the letters carved into the beaten-up oak tabletop. Phone numbers, graffiti, political slogans. In the far right corner of the table there was a deeply carved heart, with initials that had been colored in with a blue marking pen. B.D. + L.D.

I tapped the heart. "Love is blind, huh?"

"Never saw him like that over another woman," Bishop said. "He was totally ga-ga over her. He was in here late one night, right before he got shot. She was working late that night. He told me then, "Bish, it's L-O-V-E. She's the one. My soulmate.""

His smile was sour. "Doesn't sound like the Deavers we all knew, does it?"

"Maybe we didn't know him like we thought we did," I said.

Bishop got up, tucked his bar towel in the back pocket of his saggy black jeans. "Hell. Who knows anybody?"